Joker Joker

The Deuces Wild Series
Book 2

IRISH WINTERS

WINDY DAYS
PRESS

Deuces Wild

You can find Irish Winters

On Facebook

https://www.facebook.com/IrishWintersAuthor
/

On Twitter

https://twitter.com/irishwinters1

For news on upcoming releases, sign up for Irish Winters' Newsletter by clicking HERE.
http://www.irishwinters.com/newsletter.html

For more information about all my books, click here to visit Irish Winters' website.
http://www.irishwinters.com

The Dead Man's Hand

Old West lawman, gambler, gunslinger and showman, James "Wild Bill" Hickok, was murdered on August 2, 1876, while playing five-card draw at Nuttal & Mann's Saloon in Deadwood, Dakota Territory. Jack McCall, a disgruntled gambler, approached Hickok from behind and shot him at point-blank range in the back of the head, killing him instantly. McCall was later hanged for the murder, but by then, America had lost one of its premier Wild West heroes.

Legend tells us "Wild Bill" held two pair at the moment of his death, black aces and eights—the *dead man's hand*. The identity of the fifth card has been the subject of conjecture for years. For the purpose of this series, I've chosen a deuce of hearts for that card-in-the-hole, in honor of a little boy named Devlin who loved to play the violin. In honor of a father's undying love for his son.

Some players think wild cards are amateurish and juvenile. Others believe the more wild cards in the game, the greater their chance of winning. I only know that one Deuce and a pair makes three of a kind, and that sounds a lot like a family to me. You be the judge.

Deuces Wild.

Chapter One

I want to dance. Just once.

Winslow stood with the toes of her furry UGGs over the edge of what could be forever. It might not be one of those happily-ever-after kinds of forevers, but it would be everlasting. With her arms spread wide, she embraced this singular moment of her life. Knowing what she was about to do gave her an unfamiliar sense of control, along with a twinge of regret. It gave her the exhilaration of freedom. For once, she was in total control. Everything that happened up on this water tower was up to her.

The chilly autumn wind rippled over the downy strands on her bare head. Capriciously, it tugged at her baggy T-shirt and sweat pants, inviting her to—*play.* Such a universe of possibilities in a tiny word, possibilities she would never know.

Standing here like this had become a ritual of sorts for Winslow. When her health permitted, she sneaked out of her room and climbed to the top of the nearly constructed water tower, what would be the highest of its kind in Silver Spring, Maryland, when finished. Her mother might call standing on this water tower crazy. Winslow called it heaven.

Up here, she could wrap her arms around herself and cry if she wanted to. She could stare at the moon and talk to herself without being overheard, criticized, or judged. In her wildest dreams, she could pretend she was a wife. Maybe a mother. A nurturer of chubby cheeked babies with unconditional adoration in their eyes. She could entertain the possibility of a long life full of all good things—even the arms of a strong, passionate lover around her at night. Warming her with his kisses. Wanting her.

As if.

Fighting tears, she tipped a defiant chin to the gray clouds scudding overhead. Of all things, she had a *date* tonight. Not a real date though. The dance her control freak mother had talked her into wasn't a real prom, either. It was a scam, another scheme that Joyce Parrish had dreamed up and bullied her only child, and the local high school, into. Yes, there'd be a band, and yes, the graduating class had eagerly put this phony dance together, but ah! The chances missed. The opportunities lost! What a treat it would have been to have actually gone to that school. To have real girlfriends, slumber parties, and, heaven forbid, a genuine boyfriend instead of a blind date.

The wind curled around her worn body like a friend, whispering enticement in her taxi-door ears. *In one second—if you're brave enough—everything will end. All of it. The pain. The vomiting. Do it.*

I want to. The updraft from below watered her eyes. With it came the smoky scent of burning leaves. Tonight, those autumn leaves were just like her. Already dead on the tree, they just needed to fall.

Stop pretending you're happy when you're not. Give up. All of it could be over...

She nodded. Yes. Her happily-ever-after was a lie. It needed to end.

So do it. Lean forward. Just let go.

She wanted to. If only she were brave enough. Strong enough. Not just strong, but truly, powerfully strong for once in her life, if she could...

Just. Do. It!

"No," she said to the wind, which was her despair talking. She wasn't that crazy.

With her heart in her throat, Winslow stepped back from the edge. "But I want to!" she hurled at the October sky, itself filled with a brilliant splash of color at the end of what would have been her last day. Reds, pinks and oranges swirled against the dark backdrop of purpling blues of a beckoning storm off the Atlantic, almost in celebration at her failure to fly.

How dare they! "Don't think because I didn't *this* time that I won't do it *next* time. I can and I will. Someday. You'll see!"

The wind chilled to a whip, stinging her wet cheeks with God's eternal answer. *No, Winslow. You won't.*

God was smart like that, and He was—right.

The truth held her back every time. She wasn't a coward. If anything, this final act would've proven she had backbone. But who would take care of Pepe when she was gone? Who'd protect him from her mother's temper? Her heels? Mom might be sad for a day or two, but she'd survive. On so many levels, her only child's death would be a relief.

How many times have I heard that?

For the love of a little dog no bigger than a shoebox, she stepped back from the ledge. Poor Pepe would be lost if she didn't return home. He'd be devastated.

"I'm sick of lying," she whispered to the Almighty Listener in the stars. "I know it's selfish, but I want someone, somewhere to..." *To what? Truly care for me? Truly love me? Worry about me more than he worries about himself? Want me to live so badly that he might even fight for me? Ha. That would be Pepe.*

Resignation welled up from the soles of her favorite boots. October whispered over her cheeks, promising a cold climb down even as it kissed her nose with a bite of the upcoming winter. She stilled the sorrow in her broken heart. The end would come soon enough.

Just not tonight.

Meat.

Junior Agent Tate Higgins knew how to hunt it, trap it, and put it on his table. Raised by his hunter/trapper father in the pristine wilds of deepest Alaska, he knew the ways of the moose and caribou, the deep, dark heart of the deadly brown bear, the grizzly. He knew its cousin, the ferocious Kodiak, second only in size to the polar bear. All three were deadly predators against which most men didn't stand a chance. Except Tate.

He'd hunted them all. Bears weren't much different than he was. They survived in a rugged land where survival was measured by stealth, understanding the heart of your prey, and, most importantly, killing what dared hunt you. The powerful 300 Winchester Magnum he usually packed on a hunt, upped his odds. So did his fifty-cal Desert Eagle. A smart hunter lived by one rule when hunting the mighty bear: *Always shoot to kill.*

A licensed big game guide in his younger days, he'd made a decent living before he'd up and joined the Corps. There, his hunting and survival skills earned him a spot-on reputation as a rifleman, what could've been a lifetime career as a scout sniper. He'd served his country and his fellow Marines well before he'd decided, at the war-hardened age of twenty-six, that a lifer's career wasn't for him. He didn't need promotions or glory. Just to be left the hell alone.

So why was he standing under the dim porch light of a one-level ranch-style home on Maple Drive in Silver Spring, Maryland, in a tuxedo? Better yet, why was a fluffy, polar bear plush draped over his arm like it belonged there?

Because I'm stupid, that's why. Plain and simple, he'd drawn the short straw. This prom night was the once-in-a-lifetime death wish of a young woman with cancer, and because his FBI boss, one annoying-as-hell Tucker Chase, catered to special requests like this. The ex-Navy SEAL wasn't known for his compassion. Why now?

It wasn't that Tate didn't like helping others. He did. He just didn't have the skill set to deal with women, period. Be they smart as a whip or a brick shy in the brain cell department, be they squat or super-model leggy, he wasn't *that* man.

He was a loner. Always had been. No one ever called him suave or handsome. If anything, he was the opposite, a dusty John Deere to the feminine persuasions' sleek Mercedes, a workhorse of a Bradley desert tank to their streamlined Cadillac. His were blue-collar skills, ruggedly so. Not white collar. Never dapper. Certainly not tuxedo worthy. Only now...

He worked one finger between his neck and the stiff collar of his penguin suit to draw a decent breath. Because he couldn't show up empty-handed on prom night, he'd brought Fluffy along for the ride. He had to bring a girly gift for his date, didn't he? It couldn't be flowers. They meant something. Stuffed animals said nothing more than: *'Glad to meetcha. Good to know ya. See ya later. Bye.'*

At least tonight wasn't one of those high-class, spoiled-daughter-of-a-rich-ambassador dates. No way. He wouldn't be caught dead traipsing around D.C. with a celebrity brat on his arm, one who simply wanted to be seen with her own personal bodyguard. This was work. Not a date.

Chapter Two

Yanking at his tie again, Tate stabbed the doorbell one more time. Was it broken or what? His nostrils flared as the breeze drifting over the neighbors' lawns brought with it the metallic tang of nitrogen, phosphorus and dew. People in the lower forty-eight sure spent a lot of money on fertilizing grass. What a waste.

To the right, an economy-sized vehicle sat in the driveway. A Chevy Spark. Denim blue. Hatchback. No doubt the mother's vehicle. What was her name again? Oh, yeah, Joyce Parrish. Single mom. One kid dying of cancer. Last chance at happiness. Check, check, and double check.

Finally. The sound of heels clicked up to the door. He cleared his dry throat. It wouldn't do to fumble this one-night stand by saying the wrong thing right off the bat. Tate took one last swipe over his head, making sure the gel his buddy, Ky, said would work, was actually working. Usually Tate hid his unruly mop under a hat, but noooooooo. Tonight he'd had to play nice like frickin' Fred Astaire.

The brass knob turned. He took another deep breath and smiled. *Showtime.*

And there she was, the mother of the debutante he'd come to escort. Short spikes of silver-tipped black hair bristled over Mama Bear's scalp. Five diamond studs glittered from the five holes in her right ear. More silver dangled from the left, giving her a lopsided look. Sharp gray eyes raked him down to his glistening-in-the-dark black patent leathers and back up, pausing at his zipper, then at his chest.

Okay, so I'm stout and wide. I'm not Sean Connery. Get over it.

Sweat trickled down his left temple, but Tate refused to wipe it away or shift his feet. That would only prove how uncomfortable he was. This woman exuded a boatload of female nerve, but he got it. She was the same as that grizzly sow, protecting her young, fending off stalkers and such. He met her eyes when they finally made it back to his face.

"So you're the boy Dreams-Come-True sent to take my baby to the prom..." A sweep of her tongue over plump, shiny lips followed that slow, deliberate drawl. Her nose wrinkled at the sight of the stuffed bear on his arm. "Cute. Cliché, but cute."

Tate let the toy slide down his arm to his thigh. He let the *'boy'* comment slide too. Extending his free hand, he determined to see this night through because that's what jarheads did. They finished what they started. "Tate Higgins, ma'am. At your service."

When her eyes lit up, he wanted to kick his dumb ass. Who said 'at your service' anymore? Who'd he think he was? James Bond? Ky wouldn't have said something so dumb. Certainly none of the smoother talkers back on Alex Stewart's TEAM, Zack Lennox or Gabe Cartwright.

A television shrieked in the background, nearly drowning out Mama Bear. "Joyce Parrish. It's very nice to meet you, Mr. Higgins."

"Nice to meet you, too, ma'am." His head commenced pounding in the upper left quadrant, the beginning of a number ten migraine. He'd expected Cinderella to be ready and on his arm now, so he could sweep her off her feet and Get. On. With. It.

Mama Bear winked slyly, nodding him inside with a shrug. "Come on in. I'll turn the TV down so we can talk." She pivoted, and he got an eyeful he didn't need. Mrs. Parrish was wearing stiletto heels with those shorter-than-short white shorts that left a portion of her deeply tanned backside exposed. A slinky purple knit-top slid seductively off one shoulder. Don't think he failed to notice the lack of a bra strap or a tan line on that bronzed skin he didn't want to see. "You might as well come in. She's going to be a while."

Wasn't that just like a woman. Make an appointment. Show up late.

As Tate lifted his big feet and followed Mama Bear, his nose flared at the odd mixture of odors inside the home. Medicines. Disinfectants. Alcohol, as in beer. And something else. Peaches and garlic and dog. *Weird.*

Right on cue, a brave little beast roared up the hall at Tate's right, yapping all the way. His claws skidded on the hardwood floor at the last minute when his butt got ahead of his nose.

"Pepe!" shrilled Mama Bear, umm, Joyce. Err, Mrs. Parrish. Tate determined he would not succumb to terms any friendlier than *Mrs.* The way she'd acted, she might take it the wrong way. He'd never admit to Ky or the guys, but women intimidated him more than any breed of bear or that gold little Chihuahua she'd just sent sailing back down the hall on his back. "Stop it, you bad dog. Stop it! You behave, do you hear me?"

Tate winced at the repercussions of being enthusiastic in this household. The furry little bundle of energy rolled tail-over-teakettles a couple times before his nails dug in and he righted himself. When he did, he tucked his tail under his butt, and settled into a defensive position at the edge of the hall, quivering from head to toe. Not once did he take his mean little eyes off Tate. No. He hunkered one shoulder into the wall, glancing from Mrs. Parrish and back to the intruder in his house, still growling. Quietly, doing his job.

"It's okay. That little rat's not going to hurt me." Tate tucked the stuffed bear under his arm and crouched, offering the back of his hand for the dog to smell. "I'm not here to hurt you."

Pepe growled, but didn't accept the offer. Didn't even wag his tail. Wasn't that a sight? A two-pound mutt who thought he was big enough to take on a guy the size of Tate? What'd he think he was, a dragon? Tate clucked his tongue, hoping to make peace. Animals he understood.

Damned if Mama Bear didn't lean over him, her palms on his shoulders, her knees in his back. *Uncomfortable.* She squeezed her fingers. "My, but you're a big boy, aren't you? Did you play football? Lift weights? You've got some really nice muscles."

The hairs on the nape of his neck snapped to attention at the way she'd dragged *muscles* into a breathy stretch of innuendo. Not what he'd expected in a mom. Tate flexed his shoulder blades and stood, wanting her hands off. "No, ma'am, I don't play ball." *And I'm not here to play with you.*

The bundle of nervous energy down the hall had taken a nervous stand, but he wasn't barking, just shaking like a leaf and tracking Tate's every move with those sharp, pointy eyes. When a door cracked open to his left, Pepe turned tail, and, quick as a mosquito on the tundra with his belly full of warm, red blood, he scurried out of sight. The door closed softly behind him. *Must be the girl's room.*

"Hurry up, Winslow!" Mrs. Parrish shrieked. "Your date's already here. What's taking you so long?"

The blast from that female bullhorn was enough to wake the dead. So much for form and etiquette. Maybe Tate had worried for nothing. If the daughter was anything like the mother, he could wrap this escapade up quick and neat, endure a dance or two, a cup of punch, and be home by ten.

The rest of the house was small, at least what he could see of it. Maybe twelve hundred square feet. Single level. The front door faced south, the kitchen windows faced north. Two points of egress, both aligned in a straight shot through the front room to the kitchen. A narrow hall to the east with three doors, two closed, one open. Probably a bathroom. Master bedroom. The girl's room. Nothing special.

"Can I get you something, Tate? Anything?" Mrs. Parrish assumed familiarity where there was none, using his given name like she owned it, her voice laced with syrup. "A beer? A gin and tonic?" She lifted her shoulders and succeeded in dropping the collar of that flimsy knit top farther down her bare arm, exposing more shoulder. More skin.

"No thanks. I'll wait." Tate studied the living room décor instead of his *hostess with the mostest*. IKEA perfect, down to the corner sectional couch, the birch slider tables at each end, and the over-sized paper lampshade on a clear glass bottle on the one table. A single factory printed picture of a European castle, Neuschwanstein in Germany if he remembered right, decorated the wall. His home wasn't furnished any fancier, and damn, he'd rather be there.

Dropping the plush toy to the rocking chair next to him, he lowered his frame to the edge of the couch. Automatically, he dropped his arms to his knees and interlocked his fingers. This place suffocated the life out of him. There were too many walls. Not enough windows. He hated not being able to sit where he could track both exits. Tate needed more air.

Damned if Mama Bear didn't lift the stuffed toy and cuddle it to her chest as she took over the rocker. Giggling girlishly, she dipped her chin into the top of the toy's silky fur head as if he'd brought it for her. That was an odd ruse for a woman her age, to act coy and to flirt with her daughter's date.

The grinning Halloween Jack-O-Lanterns at the tips of her manicured nails stabbed the polar bear like rakes. Everything about her was garishly out of place for a worried mom about to lose her only child to cancer. Maybe those nails were her reward for suffering? For watching her daughter wither away? Who knew.

A breathy sigh trembled out of her. "She's dying, you know. Pretty soon it'll be just little old me and that rat-faced dog she loves."

Tate loosened his fingers and let them hang. Looking down at his feet, he mentally cursed his current boss for putting him in this awkward position of having to make small talk. Tate would've given his right nut to still be working for his old boss, Alex

Stewart. He never would've pushed Tate into this—this—*date*.

"That's why I'm here. The prom." Duh. Mama Bear already knew that, but Tate didn't know what else to say. The venom in her voice when she'd sent that poor little guy flying down the hall, clashed with her current declaration of sadness. Besides, Tucker had made it clear. Tonight, Tate had to act the part of a clever Chippendale escort, and he had to do it with style and finesse. No grunting was allowed.

That was the problem with working for the FBI's newly established Psychic Unit. Why on earth Tate found himself working there baffled him. He'd been more than content working for Alex, the owner of the best covert surveillance team on the East Coast as far as Tate was concerned. He'd liked the guys and gals on The TEAM, every last one of them. Them, he understood. The assignments too. But the FBI?

Not so much. From the moment he'd moved into that concrete monstrosity at the corner of Pennsylvania Avenue and Ninth Street in D.C., he'd been the odd man out. A misfit. A squared-off chunk of dirty glacial ice stuck in a crystal martini glass with two cozy olives, a pickled onion, and a prick. Ky and his wife, Eden, being the olives; Isaiah Zaroyin, the onion; and his new boss, Tucker Chase, the prick. Un-frickin'-believable.

Director Chase could make a wild bear think twice about attacking, and in the middle of combat, that was an admirable trait. But for a boss in charge of national security? No way. Alex had more class in his pinkie than Chase had in his hefty, testosterone-stoked body. The men were polar opposites, a legend and a wannabe, and damn it, Tate didn't want to deal with the political drama that came along with setting up this latest federal entity. He wanted out in the field, preferably far away from D.C. At least, a lot farther than Silver Spring and Mama Bear Parrish.

But since the day Eden Winchester insisted Tate had psychic ability, there he was. The truth was that he wasn't psychic. Gullible was more like it, or he'd never have considered Chase's proposition to join the FBI. If anything, Tate had, what was it called, an affinity for reading animals? That was all.

It wasn't like he could read their minds or anything, and he certainly couldn't predict the future like Isaiah Zaroyin seemed able to do. But Tate did have to admit that he understood animals better than people. He liked working with Ky and Eden, so, yeah. Like a good troop, he'd dutifully accepted the reassignment to FBI-land. That was the day Chase got all teary-eyed when he'd nicknamed the psychic unit *Deuces Wild* after his kid. *Whatever.*

"Your boss pays you well for doing stuff like this?" Mrs. Parrish asked, her head cocked, her eyes wide and innocent looking. "You know, escorting sick kids to zoos and stuff?"

Tate stifled a grunt, the first of the evening. "He pays me enough."

She hugged that fluffy polar bear tighter, squeezing the fluff out of it. "Like how much?"

He looked her in the eye. "Enough."

"So what are you? Indian? Mexican? From South America?"

The nerve of this woman. "American," he answered. She didn't need to know his mother was Inuit, his father Caucasian. If ethnicity was a game changer, she should've stated her preferences on the waiver she'd signed.

"You want me to pluck your brows while you wait?"

He honestly had to look twice at that rude question—through said bushy eyebrows. "Excuse me?"

"No offense, but I'm an aesthetician, and I'm trained to know what people need to make them more aesthetically appealing. Those brows of yours are good enough for a caveman, but it's hard to see your sexy brown eyes and..." She fluttered her fingers at him before she sighed and focused on her nails. "Never mind. Just trying to make conversation, but let me know if you're interested before you leave, okay? I can give you a full treatment down at my spa, and trust me. I'll take good care of you."

I'll just bet you will. This woman was blatantly trolling for a man, but Tate was *not* that guy. He went back to looking at his shoes. Whoever the guy was who'd dreamed up patent leather for men was an ass.

Tate thought he looked like a spit-and-polished mannequin on display.

"How long do you think you'll be? Out tonight, I mean. 'Til midnight? Later?" Was that hope in her voice?

Tate shook his head. "No, ma'am. I'll have her home by ten." *Not a minute later.*

"Are you serious?" Her brows lifted like McDonald's golden arches when she glanced over his shoulder at the clock on the wall. "That's no *date*." Sarcasm whipped out of her. "That's not even enough time for a decent prom. Don't you know anything about girls?"

Apparently not. Tate swallowed hard. Most mothers wanted their young ladies in early, didn't they? They were overly protective and downright bossy, weren't they? He took another stab at it. "Eleven?"

The stuffed toy fell on its back to the carpet. "Oh, for Christ's sake, Agent Higgins, how about two a.m.? Can you count that high? Or three? Don't you know a prom is all about firsts, not curfews? It's about magic and dreams and..." She rolled her eyes and shook her head as if she were talking to an idiot. Which, in a way, she was. "Damn it. The later you keep her out, the more free time I'll have. I could cruise down to Land's End for a drink and be back before Winslow knows I'm gone. Come on, man up. Give the girl what she wants. It's her one and only prom."

He balked. Magic? Dreams? First whats? This was him, remember, the guy who didn't like people to begin with, and chatting up women he didn't know even less. Dinner and a dance or two was enough time wasted on a blind date in his book. Forget the dreams. He was not Prince Charming. *What the hell's keeping Cinderella-What's-Her-Name?*

"Come on, big guy." Joyce reverted to a coy shrug of her shoulder. "You'd do that for me, wouldn't you? Moms need a night out once in a while too. What would it hurt? No one has to know."

Interesting. This woman gave off all the signals of a feline on the prowl, not the worried, over-protective mother of a terminally ill child. But what did he know? "I'll see what I can do."

A dazzling smile broke over her face. "Oh, my boy, you are too good to me. I knew I could talk you into it. Thanks so much!"

Again with the *boy. Whatever.* He cocked his head toward the hall. Waiting.

"Just remember, if you take her to a nice restaurant, no red meat. Winslow can't handle anything that takes days for her poor stomach to digest, understood?"

Didn't that figure? Him, the big game hunter, going out with a vegetarian? This date kept getting better and better. Not. "Yes, ma'am."

"Now, where were we?" Joyce turned all cozy once more. "Oh, I know. We were talking money. So I take it you're into investments and bonds and securities, stuff like that. I saw your ride. A Corvette's pricey. You must be fairly well off. How can you afford the insurance? What else do you own? Cars, I mean."

"It's borrowed." Which was true. The Corvette belonged to Ky. He'd bought it for his wife, Eden, after the birth of their baby boy, Kyler Lee. It was one of those things married guys did when they were over-the-moon in love with their woman and their life was good. It hadn't always been that way for Ky. He deserved every bit of what he had now.

Mrs. Parrish crossed her ankles and tucked her high-heeled toes under the rocking chair. She tilted forward, her fingers clutching the arms of that chair and her tanned thighs on display. "Oh, that's nice. What's it cost?"

How would I know? "Enough."

"You're a sniper, aren't you? A SEAL?"

Navy SEALs were all the rage on TV and in the movies. Not with Tate. His boss was a SEAL, and possibly the most annoying man he'd ever met. Point made. "USMC," he offered, then explained, "Marine Corps," in case she wasn't military savvy.

Not that she cared as quickly as she switched tracks. "I need a smoke. Would you mind joining me on the patio, so we can keep chatting? I don't want to smell up my house. It's not good for Winslow's lungs. They've been compromised for years."

"I'll wait."

She rolled her eyes, smiling in that annoying, beguiling way she had. "Oh, come on. What would it hurt? We've got time. The people from Channel Thirteen won't be here for another half hour."

That brought his head up. The people from... *what the hell?*

Damn, she was sly. Still batting her eyes. Going for clever. "You didn't know? Oh, yessss!" Damned if her ass didn't wiggle along with her cleavage. *How do women do that?*

"This whole Dreams-Come-True prom-thing was my idea. I'll do anything to keep Winslow's story in the news, and this will put her center stage for a couple days, right where she belongs. Everyone watches Channel Thirteen. She'll be famous." All five trick-or-treat fingertips fanned her cleavage. "My baby's going to be on the eleven o'clock news! Tonight! And who knows? They might get a shot of me in the clip too. Wouldn't that be something?" She offered another butt wiggle, fluttering her eyelashes. "What do you think? How do I look?"

"Fine," he mumbled. *Just damned fine. Where's the girl?*

The fanning continued. So did the prattle. Tate looked down at his glossy dress shoes and started counting to ten. At five, he loosened his tie as much as he dared without taking it off. That might excite Mama Bear. He rolled his neck, wishing he was fishing. Or hunting. Or scaling some lofty, icy peak where Kodiak bears roamed and annoying women were afraid to go.

At ten, he started on twenty.

Chapter Three

Winslow hugged Pepe under her chin so he could look out her window with her to see the fancy car parked at her curb. "It's certainly bright enough," she told him. If that belonged to her blind date, the shiny red Corvette promised a fun ride to the dance she didn't want to attend.

Pepe offered a wiggle and one quick wet kiss to the end of her nose.

Winslow had rescued him from her mother's charming insensitivity the minute she'd come back from the tower and climbed in through her bedroom window. Already dressed in the black gossamer nightmare that her mother had dragged home from the thrift store, she was as ready as she was going to be. It was a good thing the prom had been scheduled late in October. This dress would turn a fairy princess—which Winslow was not—into a ghoul.

Setting Pepe on her unmade bed, she pushed her feet into her single forbidden luxury, her brown Valentina UGGs. *Ahh. Instant comfort.* A woman could get used to them. Second hand? Of course. Scuffed? Absolutely. But Winslow loved the warmth the Shearling cuffs offered. Her mom would complain when she saw them instead of the black, glittery heels, she'd bought, but Winslow's feet were always cold. She needed something to keep her warm. Besides, their sunbeam treads left pretty designs behind when she walked in the snow.

If it snowed...

If she lived long enough to see another winter. Maryland winters could be unpredictable, but a girl on her first date could hope for a little magic, if only from the weather.

She stuffed the strappy heels her mother would no doubt prefer she stumble around in, back into their box and under her bed. Winslow wanted this one night to be about her, not her mom. She wanted it for herself. *If Mom wants to go to the prom, she can wear those torturous shoes herself.*

Now for her hair, or lack of it. Just because the guy sitting out in the living room didn't need to be seen with an anorexic skeletal woman right out of *The Nightmare Before Christmas*, Winslow sat at her second-hand vanity behind her bedroom door and selected her wig off its styrofoam head. She had two wigs, both cheap, but better than nothing. While one was reddish brown and short, she liked the dark-brown, longer one best. It was closer to her natural color and it highlighted her eyes, for what that was worth, as sunken and darkly shadowed as they were. But guys were supposed to like long hair, and that was what tonight was all about, being liked. For a change...

Peering into the cracked mirror, she studied her reflection. This prom thing was such a mistake. She had nothing to offer any guy. Anyone could see that. No hair. Nearly invisible brows. No matter how hard she pinched her cheeks, they stayed sallow and pale because, well, they were sallow and pale. That was Winslow—sickly and dying.

Why had she ever gone along with this idea? Oh yeah, brain check. Because she hadn't known about it until good old Mom sprang it on her over a bowl of cold cereal yesterday when she'd finally been able to eat.

She growled at her failure to stand up to her mother yet again, but what did it matter? Life had given her lemons, not health or the strength to fight *Mommy Dearest*. With what little time she had left, Winslow meant to make as much lemonade as possible.

Black synthetic strands slithered over her bald dome as she secured the wig in place. Just once, she'd like her real hair to grow this long. A sigh escaped, or maybe it was a huff of annoyance. She hadn't had real hair in months. Her trusty bandana would've been more comfortable, but hey. Everything wasn't about her, was it? This night was about that guy in her living room. He deserved a decent looking date.

And just because that guy didn't need to feel like *Jack Skellington* at the prom with a ghostly woman on his arm, Winslow applied a thin line of Maybelline kohl to her eyelids. It almost made her look as if she had lashes like those models in the magazines. Her fingers shook so hard she had to re-do the first attempt at making a proper line, then dab off the excess kohl with a cotton swab. Darn. That climb up the water tower had worn her out. This might be a quick date.

Next she applied black mascara to what was left of her lashes and a dab of pink blush to her dry cheeks. She added clear lip-gloss to her mouth, not tint. No one needed too much fake color. There. The woman in the mirror almost looked normal. Wasn't that the worst? *Almost?* As in almost a woman? Almost pretty? Almost alive?

Pepe growled as a vehicle rumbled by, its brakes screeching.

"What's up?" she asked her most faithful companion, happy for the distraction. "Did you hear something outside, my brave Honey Munchkin? Let's see who's here."

Lifting Pepe back into her arms, Winslow tucked him under her chin and peered past the sheer drapes at her window. *Oh, my gosh! Mom wouldn't do that to me, would she?*

But oh, yes. *Mommy Dearest* most certainly had. Channel Thirteen's news van had just pulled up to the curb. All the doors opened. Cameramen jumped out. So did that pretty blonde reporter from the eleven o'clock news, Shawna Truborn, along with five other guys. Shawna fluffed her pretty blond hair and marched up the walk while her crew set to work unloading lights and equipment.

Winslow's stomach squeezed a whopping dose of acid up her throat, threatening a projectile surprise at this latest indignity. Just when she'd thought she could endure the prom... this happened.

No! Just no!

"Honestly, I don't know what's taking that daughter of mine so long." Mrs. Parrish stood at the hall, her back to Channel Thirteen's camera crew and tapping her fingernails to her lips. "Must be first prom jitters. You think?"

Miss Truborn smiled like the true professional she was, all white teeth and charm. She ran a quick hand down the trim thighs beneath her sleek tan skirt. "I'm sure she's nervous, but trust me, this will be over in a few minutes. Then you'll have the digital recording we promised and the memory of the night you've always wanted. Aren't you excited?"

Winslow's mother turned on a matching dazzling smile. "Oh, yes! This is the best surprise ever. How's my hair look?" She lifted a few silvery spikes for show.

"You look fine!" A makeup artist appeared out of nowhere, fluffing Joyce's hair and powdering her cheeks, and who the hell cared?

Tate grunted quietly to himself, not wanting to offend anyone in this circus, but irked at Mrs. Parrish's attention seeking, tonight of all nights. This prom seemed to be more about her, less about the girl. In his book, a cameo during the news didn't compare to, say, her daughter living longer.

Channel Thirteen's crew had already hooked up lights, meters, and reflectors in the living room. His scant supply of patience for annoying people was long gone, replaced by an edgy need to survive the night. He clenched his fists. Tucker Chase was going to hear about this fiasco.

Finally, the TV crew was ready for show time. Mrs. Parrish trotted down the hall and rapped on Winslow's door, glancing over her shoulder at the camera, her eyes bright. "Oh, darling..." She paused to make sure the cameraman followed her. "Wakey-wakey! It's time for your one and only prom. Don't be shy. Bring that adorable Pepe with you."

"You'll have to forgive her," she winked, stage-whispering to her new friends in show biz. "But Winslow's got the ugliest little dog in the world. Just wait 'til you see it. I was thinking it'd make a real sweet picture, though, don't you think? My poor little girl with her studly date and her ugly dog?"

Studly? Make that migraine a solid twelve.

Miss Truborn's head bobbed, the mic in her hand extended forward to catch the drama as it unfolded. Joyce cocked one ear to the closed door and rapped harder, her brows furrowed, but her voice sugary. "Winslow? Do you need help getting dressed? Can you hear me, Princess?" With one crank of the knob, she fingered opened the door while she fluffed her spiked locks yet again.

As a tiny tan bullet beelined past her high heels and headed straight for the front door, she ducked her head inside the room and shrieked, "My baby's been kidnapped! She's gone!"

Chapter Four

Like hell, she's gone. She was just in there a minute ago. Tate jumped to his feet, fully aware he towered over everyone else in the room, and that unfortunately, he'd caught Miss Truborn's attention. She shot him a ten thousand mega-watt smile, waved her cameraman to her side, and shoved her mic in Tate's face. "And you would be?"

"Busy," he growled before he turned to Joyce. Something was off. She didn't look as panicked as—coy. Pepe scratched furiously at the front door though. What was going on?

"Where's Winslow?" Miss TV-land asked the dumbest question ever. "She's supposed to be here. We air in five minutes."

Guess your personal interest story had other plans. Tate rolled his shoulder, ready to take charge.

With one hand splayed to the wall in the hallway, Joyce dropped her lashes and fanned her face. "I don't know. This isn't like my baby at all. Who would take her out of her room like this? Who would do such a thing to me? Why?"

Wrong question. Tate shouldered around the cameraman and the equipment, not ready to assume that Winslow had been abducted, not yet. Why jump to that conclusion?

Palming the girl's bedroom door open, he took a step back in time. Whereas the furniture in the front room appeared new, at least newer, Winslow's bedroom was nineteen eighties junkyard retro. Make that leftover. The repainted dresser didn't match the pressed and chipped wooden headboard. Stains blotched the ratty carpet. The sheer drapes at her window sported runs and frayed edges. A tiny lamp with a pink polka dot shade sat crooked on the floor near the head of the bed. The light was still on. No nightstand. No closet. Cardboard shoeboxes were stacked everywhere. Even they looked ragged.

When the sheer drape billowed just barely, Tate knew what had happened. Winslow had taken off. Maybe the girl didn't want to go to the prom. Wouldn't that figure?

By then, her frantic mother had sunk to the nearest living room chair, her hand fluttering up high on her chest while Channel Thirteen's finest gathered around. "Someone's taken my baby. She's been kidnapped. My... my heart! It's pounding in my chest like it's going to explode. I'm just a poor, single mother trying to do what's best for my only child. What will I do?"

Stop assuming the worst, for one. "Where does Winslow usually go when she takes off like this?" Tate asked point blank.

Mama Bear shook her head. "You don't understand. My baby doesn't take off. Ever! She wouldn't do that to me. She loves me and I... I..." She arched her head to the back of the chair, her eyes closed and her long, tan legs on display. "This will kill me."

Pepe whined at the door, a plea only Tate seemed to hear.

"There now," Miss On-The-Spot-Reporter soothed, her cameraman peering around her, still documenting the drama. "We'll help you find your little girl. Quick, Chuck, get her a glass of water before she passes out."

While Chuck hustled for the kitchen, Tate waited, his gut not buying what his eyes were seeing. Winslow had to have been the one who let Pepe into her room. If she'd run off, she couldn't have gotten far, not if she was as close to death as her mother said.

Pepe did a dust devil routine, spinning and whining. Tate left the hubbub, and in two long strides, he crouched at Winslow's little dragon's side. "You know where she is, don't you, boy?"

Pepe barked one shrill, short yap, his pink tongue flicking over his nose and his eyes wide.

"You mind if I let your dog out?" Tate asked no one in particular, because at that moment, the hysterical Mrs. Parrish had let out an anguished wail any drama coach would've been proud of. Chuck stood waiting with her glass of water while the cameraman rolled *sensational* footage. But that was the press for you, the more drama, the bigger the audience. The story didn't even have to be true.

Tate bet on Pepe. He cracked the front door and man, that little guy could run. It was all Tate could do to keep up in his tux and squeaky dress shoes. "Boots," he cussed under his breath. "I need my damned boots."

The stitch in his side told him he also needed to keep up with the disappearing backside of his new buddy. But just when Tate thought he'd lose sight of Pepe, the rascal looked over his shoulder and slowed. Pepe knew something. Tate took the hint and hurried.

Man and dog headed east on Maple toward Dameron Drive. The Anacostia Tributary Trail System stretched beyond Dameron to the north and south, then rolled alongside Sligo Creek amidst plenty of trees. *Damn. Winslow could be anywhere.*

Pepe never hesitated. After cutting a sharp right at Dameron and Maple, he kept to the sidewalk. At Sanford Road, he dodged traffic and hightailed it across Dameron, headed to Forest Grove Park. By then, Tate was sweating up a storm. His white shirt clung to his skin. He jerked the damned tie off and stuffed it into his jacket pocket. The night was dark and chilly. Downright clammy. He kept up with the dog, wondering what Pepe knew that he didn't.

And then he spotted the ghostly figure climbing the water tower northwest of his twenty. Had to be Winslow. What was she thinking?

Tate jogged faster. A twenty-story crane towered over the tower, sporting an American flag at the top of its vertical boom. The concrete walls of the squat, silo-shaped tower hadn't been painted yet. There was no roof Tate could see, but shit. The dark blur climbing steadily up the side of it was no fly.

"She's going to fall." Ky and Eden would never believe this—him talking to a dog.

Damned if Pepe didn't whine as if he agreed though.

"Why's she going up there this time of night? In a dress? Do you know?"

Pepe didn't answer, a good thing because Tate was seriously worried Eden might be right about his ability to communicate with animals. Chihuahuas anyway.

He all out ran the final half-mile, his heart in his throat at the thought of this woman tossed by the wind to her death. Falling. Screaming. Another woman had fallen some years ago. Tate never wanted to hear a scream like that again.

Finally at the base of the tower, his hands on his knees and his lungs screaming for oxygen, he paused long enough to suck in one good deep breath. "You gonna... be okay while I go up?" he asked Pepe.

Pepe planted his tush, wagged his tail, and looked up anxiously to where the girl had disappeared over the top edge. His eyes bugged out in the way of tiny, squeaker dogs that thought they were dragons.

Tate followed the dog's gaze. This tower was taller than the older one it replaced, the one standing thirty yards to the north, maybe taller by half as much again. And wider. The older tower could've easily fit inside this newer version. Why couldn't Winslow have climbed that one?

The maintenance ladder she'd used beckoned. Cussing, Tate kicked his shoes off and latched onto the first metal rung, a good foot over his head. Pepe's mistress had to have jumped to reach it, further proving how crazy she was. He'd read the file her mother had provided his boss when she'd applied for this prom. Winslow Parrish was a tiny thing, but she was damned strong for a dying woman, and she had a good head start.

Curling his fingers under the rung, Tate pumped both biceps to get his heavy body off the ground, and—shit. The metal ladder was narrow and ice cold. Stretching, he grabbed the next rung, his body dead weight until he reached that first rung. Up he went. Hand over hand, his body swaying from sheer physical exertion. At the fifth rung, he had all fours on the ladder and climbing became easier. Step after step. Cussing all the way. At least the rungs were flat, not torturously round. The balls of his feet didn't hurt with every foot upward.

The wind blew harder the higher he climbed though, whipping beneath his tux jacket, chilling his sweaty body. He didn't dare call out to the girl. He couldn't take the chance. There'd be no way to catch a body hurtling past him on its way down, not unless he was suddenly lucky. Not likely.

Do. Not. Jump.

You know that thing they tell you when you're climbing vertical, that thing about not looking down? Obey that rule. Fear ratcheted up Tate's spine with every step. His heart pounded and his grip turned slick with sweat. Not good.

At the halfway point, he paused, but stopping was just as bad. There he was with no harness, no safety ropes, no better sense, and too much time to think. It'd been a long time since he'd free climbed. It took every last nerve to not look down.

He swallowed hard and kept going. At the top of the tower, the ladder came to a standing platform before the rungs wrapped up and over the top edge. Maybe eight-feet long by four-feet wide, the platform's rails gave him a temporary sense of security. It also gave him extra handle grips to pull himself onto what he hoped was an actual roof, not just the top edge of hollow concrete walls. It was just possible the Parrish girl had only climbed this rig to throw herself over the other side to her death.

Finally, he peered across a completed domed roof. The pitch wasn't as steep as its predecessor's, the reason he hadn't seen it from ground level. But this son-of-a-bitchin' tower was high. Maybe one hundred and fifty feet straight up.

What was this lunatic woman thinking?

It took a full minute to get his nerve up. Carefully, he took those last few steps off the ladder and onto the roof where there was no more rail to hold onto. He'd seen another ladder lying on the ground below on his mad rush to get to Winslow. It'd sure be nice to have it up here now.

His socks snagged on the roof's non-skid, painted finish, small relief when the wind buffeted his broad chest, challenging him to walk like a man. His mouth had gone dry as desert sand during the climb up, but if Winslow could do this, as sick as she was, so could he. Tate widened his stance, swallowed hard, and he straightened to his full height.

Oblivious to him, the girl twirled at the center of the domed roof like an idiot, her arms spread wide, her chin tilted upward, and her black dress swirling around her. At least her clunky boots offered substantial traction on the wide domed dance floor.

Ethereal. That's what she was. Winslow Parrish was a ghost of a girl in a bit of black, lacy fluff the wind could easily carry over the edge and beyond. She was a being not of this world. One who very much looked like she wanted to leave Mother Earth. She hadn't seen him yet, not with her face pointed at the sky. Not the way she was twirling and spinning.

He saw them then. The tears shining high on her cheeks.

"What are you doing?" he asked, his voice ragged from the climb and the fear that he might've come up here for nothing, that she could still jump and he wouldn't be able to get to her fast enough. That he wouldn't be able to save her, either.

The wind stole his words, and Winslow kept spinning, those massive boots holding her down. Spinning and singing? It was the mournful tone in her voice, not the words that reached Tate. He recognized the notes of sorrow and loss. Of bottomless grief. Hell, he could write a song on grief if he ever wanted to sing.

The tragedy in this woman triggered something down deep in his soul, something he recognized. An odd warmth unfurled inside his ribcage. His fist lifted to his sternum where that old loss still—hurt.

Closing the distance, he clutched the hand flying by him, but ended up catching her wrist. Good enough. He grabbed hold, startling Winslow, but he held on tight, damn it. She wasn't going over the edge on his watch.

The girl turned and squealed, her eyes wide with shock. Taking a backward step, she cocked her arm and...

SURPRISE! She nailed his jaw so hard that Tate saw stars. Stamping those clunky boots, she twisted away from him, screaming, "Let go! Help somebody! I'm being attacked. Help!"

Enough! Tate jerked her into his chest with her back to his front, trapping her hands in his. "Settle down," he ordered, his head against the side of hers, his heart pounding at the scary height of this volatile confrontation. All she had to do was struggle some more, and they'd both tumble over the edge. "Winslow, it's me. Tate Higgins. I'm the guy who's taking you to the prom, remember?"

Her mouth snapped closed, but her chest heaved like she couldn't catch her breath. She peered sideways at him, her eyes wild and—breathtaking. Green maybe? They were too big for her face, and they were so damned sad. Crystal tears clung to her dark lashes. "You... you scared me."

No shit. His gut screamed to get her down off this damned tower. To protect her. "Yeah, well, you scared me too. What the f—, I mean, what are you doing up here?"

Her chest heaved under the black lace bodice, pushing against the insides of his arms. "I'm... I'm living as fast as I can, Mr. Higgins."

Chapter Five

Just great. My nose is dripping, and heaven only knows what my mascara's doing, probably running down both cheeks. I bet I look like Gene Simmons and... Wah! Just wah!

Winslow didn't pull free from Mr. Higgins's big hands. She didn't want to. His skin was rough, warm and strong over hers, and she fit inside his arms like a little kid. It was a different world in here, surrounded by warmth and gentleness like she was. She didn't want him to let go. Not yet. She was too busy catching her breath. No one had ever joined her on this high perch before, much less held onto her like he was. He wasn't so much gripping her, but hugging her into the curve of his rugged body. The contact was incredible. Warm. Intoxicating.

Her heart still pounded from fright, but she'd settled down like he'd asked. Not like she had a choice. This big man was Tate Higgins, the guy she was going to the prom with? Ahem, the guy she *would've* gone with before she found out about her mother's latest despicable surprise.

Never had she felt so—alive. Energy pulsed from the sheer size of his body to hers. Despite the clothes between them, she felt every part of him. Every muscle. And there was so much. He dwarfed her, his arms as thick as tree branches, big branches. She clung to his wrists, her arms curled over his arms, holding on. Maybe even hugging him back. A little.

If this was God's answer to her prayers, He'd sent the most fearsome, spine-tingling archangel in His army. Winslow swallowed hard, working her throat muscles to make that seemingly impossible physical function work. As if. Not with her tucked up snug against this formidable man like she was. Not with him smelling as good as he did, either. She'd expected some geeky guy with acne scars all over his oily prepubescent face for her prom date, not a god.

He was a dark-haired version of Thor, if all that thunder in her heart meant anything. *I mean, look at him.* With tousled dark-hair trimmed at the neckline, the man who now had a solid grip on her was too good to be true. The tux made him James Bond drool-worthy, but his stocking feet made him cute in an adorable, tough-guy way. His shirt collar was open, revealing a thickly corded neck. He'd climbed that freezing cold ladder in his socks? Who did that for someone they didn't know?

"What are you doing up here?" he asked again, his voice deep and rumbling in his still heaving chest. Tempted to lean back and press her ear to that thick, masculine wall, she twisted around in his arms to face him. Her fingers landed on his chest. It wasn't a difficult enough question, but she couldn't seem to make her mouth work. Warm and, wow, strong, his pectoral muscles shuddered under her fingertips as if she'd just shocked him.

She shuffled her boots, angling one between his feet, careful not to step on his toes. The man was taller than her by a foot maybe, and he was gorgeous and dark and, *oh my, big,* as in built-like-an-ox big. Strong, if those muscles bunching under that white cotton shirt and straining those tiny pearl buttons running down his abdomen meant anything. Sturdy. He hadn't hesitated since he'd latched onto her, just maintained a safe place for her to—what? Fall apart in? Struggle against him? No way could she do either, not with her brain on its very first sensual overload.

This first time date of hers had an overpowering presence about him. Phenomenally broad at the shoulders, but tapered at the hips, he was built like a masculine, upside-down triangle. Not wrestler big. More lithe, more poised, like a cougar. Thick brows lent a fierce strain to his face, but in a gentle, protective way that made her want to curl into his arms like a house cat instead of fighting him like a wildcat. Genuine concern glittered in those black-as-midnight eyes of his. Not once had he squeezed her fingers or her arms too hard, not even at first when he'd seemed angry.

Body heat sizzled off of him, enticing her to relax into the safety of his thick arms. Against his muscular thigh. This man was that lighthouse in the storm of her life, and she'd honestly never felt this—special— not once in all her twenty years.

He scowled down at her, but there was tenderness in his eyes, not censure. "Did you hear me, Winslow?" he asked gently, unknowingly drawing her attention to his mouth. "Talk to me. What you're doing is very dangerous. Why are you up here?"

Winslow's silly heart pounded for a better reason than fright. She couldn't make her gaze move from his, *Mmmmmm, his lips*. Plump and moist, and so not what she'd expected in a paid-for-hire date. Her tongue slid over her bottom lip, her imagination on freefall. One taste. One touch. Caramel maybe? Wintergreen? Candy cane? She wanted to find out.

Dimples bracketed those manly lips like sharply dented parentheses, but those eyes... Thick dark lashes edged darker pupils that had yet to look away from her. They were so black and deep and piercing her with his question, which, oh yeah, she had yet to answer.

"I was, umm, dancing, Mr. Higgins," she explained, knowing he'd never understand, afraid he'd think she was crazy, like he didn't already. "I come up here... to dance while I still can. It helps me feel alive." If that didn't make her sound like an escapee from the loony bin, nothing did.

"It's dangerous. You could fall." His words clamped around her as tightly as his arms. Two broad palms overlapped at her shoulder blades. "Listen, do you mind if I, if we—sit down?"

"Oh, yeah. Sure." She nodded. She got it. He was probably afraid of heights which made him more of a hero in her book, since he was here and afraid and all, but... he *was* here. Truly here. Gosh, no one she could remember, besides Pepe, had wanted to be up here with her.

Not releasing her hand, Mr. Higgins lowered his bulky frame to a crouch, his free hand searching behind him for balance before he finally sat, taking her with him. She went easily, knowing her skinny butt would freeze once it touched that cold metal roof, but not wanting to upset him. People did crazy things when they panicked. She would know.

Mr. Higgins did something unexpected then. He lifted her sideways onto his lap, then circled her inside both of those big arms again, and... her heart started thumping like crazy. She couldn't fall, but neither could she get away if he turned out to be some psycho-stalker with a thing for stupid girls on water towers.

But that couldn't be, not as carefully as he cradled her. No, her heart was pounding because not once in all her years had a man held her like this. Never. Ever. Her father was some nameless scoundrel her mother had trusted back when she was young and innocent. He'd never stayed around long enough to look at Winslow much less hold her. She didn't have a name or a memory of him, not like the memory of sitting with Mr. Higgins that she would treasure for the rest of her life.

"Don't worry." His lips were close enough to her ear that she caught the vibration in his tone. "I won't let you fall."

Sweeter words were never spoken. Thrilled to be where she was, Winslow took another pull of the warm pocket of air between them. He smelled a lot like—heaven.

"B-but w-what about you?" She had to ask because he was big enough that he scared her. He could take her over the edge with him if he meant to. Okay, no. He wouldn't have climbed all the way up here just to throw her off. "Who'll keep you from falling, Mr. Higgins?"

He grunted. "I'm no lightweight. Trust me, you're okay as long as you're with me."

No, I'm not. Not if you keep being nice to me. "If you say so."

She couldn't relax, not sitting on some strange guy's lap like she was. It didn't help that she liked the tingle of his hands on her. Struggling to catch her composure, Winslow looked to the clouds scudding overhead, blown by the wind coming in off the Atlantic. White against the dark sky, the city lights below illuminated the undersides of the clouds, turning them into ghostly apparitions in a hurry westward, their tattered shadows trailing thin and wispy behind them like tails. The wind tossed at her dress, and she shivered, more because of her intimate proximity to her *date* than because of the cold.

The tension in Mr. Higgins's body dissipated. His grip relaxed. "So tell me the truth. Why did you sneak out of your room to come dance up here all by yourself? Did you see me or something? Did I scare you?"

What a silly question. "Why would you say that?"

He shrugged, running his palm down her bicep and up again. "Because you're here, and I'm not stupid. I know I'm nothing to look at."

Warmth spread from his touch and darn it, her body melted into his caress. People just didn't do that to her, at least her mother never had, and who else was there?

"Don't worry. You can't hurt my feelings. I figured you took one look at your date and decided you were better off missing the prom."

Angling her shoulders around to face him better, Winslow met his eyes to see what she'd missed. There was no ugly monster there, only him—Mr. Higgins. How do you tell a guy he's the most glorious male you've ever laid eyes on? "I would never do that. You're... you're..." *To-die-for-handsome.* "You're seriously good-looking."

He scowled even as a soft smile tweaked the corners of his mouth. "It's the tux."

"No, it's not. It's you. You look good to, umm, me." Winslow wanted to smack her empty head for sounding so lame. "I mean," she swallowed hard, thinking fast. "I did need a way out tonight, but not from you, Mr. Higgins. It's my mom and those TV guys and..." She lifted the hem of her obscenely grotesque prom dress, a frilly mass of black lace and silk and stuff. "My mom means well, but she goes overboard sometimes, and I can't handle what she throws at me. This whole prom-date idea was bad enough, but calling the television station and dragging them into it... how humiliating."

Too late she realized what she'd said. "I mean, I didn't mean... This date isn't bad or humiliating because of you, Mr. Higgins. It's me. I just... I just..." There was no way out. She snapped her mouth shut before sounding any more like a blithering idiot.

He chuckled. "Don't worry about it. I get it. Blind dates suck. How about you call me Tate from now on instead of Mr. Higgins?"

That she could do. Winslow bobbed her head, glad he hadn't taken offense where none was meant. Her mother would have. Then there would have been drama. Name calling. The usual.

"The view up here is pretty cool now that we're sitting down." Mr. Higgins, ah, Tate looked south toward D.C., revealing the profile of a rugged man, not a boy, against the city lights. Chiseled. That was the word that fit him the best. Tate's facial features were sharp and edged as if he'd been chiseled out of stone and left in his unpolished state.

"That's why I come up here," she admitted, the pounding in her heart somewhat under control. "I can think up here better than anywhere else." *Like home.*

"I get it. You bolted because Channel Thirteen showed. I don't blame you. I'm not a big fan of the press, either." His gaze swiveled back to her. "You don't talk to your mother much." He made that a statement.

She ducked her head into her shoulders, biting her lip. "Maybe you didn't notice, but Mom isn't much for listening. She's got two ears. She just doesn't use them."

"She didn't tell you she'd lined up the television crew." With his arm still around her shoulders, he kept up a slow, warm massage up and down her arm, his long fingers unintentionally also stoking the sizzling ember that had flamed to life deep in her belly. It had been a long time since Winslow had the tiniest inkling of arousal to deal with, not as depleted as her energy level had been. But damn. Something was happening in her body that she didn't want to stop. Sparks in the pit of her stomach were throwing off fireworks or—something. Delicious warmth tingled upwards as flames descended to—there.

"No, but that's Mom," Winslow explained, her voice breathy and her pulse rate climbing. "She gets an idea in her head, and, poof! Out it comes." *You're beautiful, Tate. Can I touch you? Pet you? Keep you?*

"Like that dress you keep tearing at. She bought it for you, but you don't like it."

Man, am I that obvious? "Are you a mind reader, Tate?" She liked the way his name sounded on her lips. The way it tasted, kind of manly. Kind of good. Like she wanted to keep saying it.

"Hell, no. I mean, no ma'am. I'm not a mind reader, but I know body language. You weren't coming up here to kill yourself, were you?"

"No. That might have been my intention earlier, but..." She snapped her teeth together as if she could unsay those words. Her brain seemed intent on sabotaging her with the truth tonight, or maybe it was just this guy.

Tate didn't look shocked or angry at that answer, just released her long enough to shrug out of his jacket and drape it over her shoulders. "Here. You're cold."

She snuggled into it, relishing the body heat he'd left behind. Ah, the jacket smelled clean and pressed and like him. When he tipped her into his chest and under his chin, the words spilled out in a rush. "I'm sorry you got pulled into this mess. You don't have to stay if you don't want to. I'll understand. I can climb down, and I know my way home. I've done it before. I'll be okay."

Not precisely true, but he didn't need to know how close she was to dying, and he surely didn't need to hang around for her funeral. That would be too embarrassing. Not like she'd be around to be embarrassed, but still. It'd be nice if he wanted to stay because he liked her, not because he thought she was crazy enough to jump. *Hmmm. Which I was. Earlier. Before the TV surprise.*

It didn't make sense, but earlier, she had wanted to fall to her death. She'd even railed against God. Months and years of being sick, of having to deal with her mother's immature antics, had gotten to her. Winslow was tired of the continual drama and the fight. She'd been ready to let cancer win. To give up. But then she'd resolved to go on for—oh, yeah. For Pepe. If anything, he was more like a guardian angel than a dog.

Tate placed one big hand on her bicep, anchoring her. "I'm staying. So's Pepe."

Tears of repentance welled up faster than an April shower. "He's... he's down there?" She hated that her voice ended in a timid squeak. Talk about being a bad date and a lousy dog owner. She had to be the worst of both.

"Yeah, he's down there." Tate nodded, his short dark hair catching the glow of city-shine. The masculine power of his oh-so-close proximity toyed with her senses. He'd shaved, but a dark shadow still cupped his chin and jaw, and honestly, no man should have lips like his. Her index finger lifted, tempted to trace that perfect Cupid bow and pinch the pillowy cushion of his lower lip, the notched upper. Her tongue skated over her bottom lip, imagining how his mouth would feel if he—*kissed me.*

"Yeah. That dog of yours thinks he's a dragon. He came after me at the house, but he was just being protective. You should be proud of him. He led me to you."

Winslow forced her lashes down, focusing on her fingernails instead of Tate's handsome face. "He's my best friend." More like her only friend. How pathetic did that make her?

When Tate didn't ask another question, which was kind of him, Winslow revealed her darkest secret. "I'm, umm, older than I look."

"Oh?" He cocked his head and waited.

She drew in a deep breath, afraid to out her mother, but needing someone to know the truth. "I just found out I was prom bait yesterday. I'm twenty, not seventeen like she told everyone."

"You're too old for the Dreams-Come-True program." Tate had a different way of asking. The more he didn't ask direct questions, the more she felt compelled to explain.

"They only help kids eighteen and younger, but Mom..." How to define Joyce Parrish? Bossy? A little bit under-handed? Loving in her unpredictable, domineering way? A little scary sometimes? Winslow ended with, "It's complicated."

Chapter Six

Tate held back a grunt. *Complicated, my ass.* Joyce Parrish committed fraud against a charitable organization with this scam. Big time. Not only that, she'd robbed some defenseless, deserving little kid of Dreams-Come-True resources. Not that Tate minded now that he had Winslow in his arms. She wasn't much bigger than a teenager, and she did have cancer. But there was no gray area to this argument, just a very definite line between right and wrong.

Then again, he'd never had a kid, much less had to deal with the prolonged illness and possible death of said kid. He might have done the same thing if his daughter wanted to go to a prom if he were in Joyce Parrish's shoes.

Desperate circumstances often called for desperate measures. Maybe Dreams-Come-True was Joyce's way of ensuring Winslow had at least one good memory to fall back on at the end. Poor kid. She should've gotten stuck with debonair Mark Houston or dapper Maverick Carson. At least, everyone said they were debonair and dapper. Handsome. Descriptors that didn't apply to Tate.

But still…

Winslow was no little kid. Thin and wispy, yes, but she was a pleasant surprise, beautiful with a hint of melancholy that hung off her shoulders like that wraith-like dress. But how far did her complicity go in this prom scheme? That was the question. Sure, she claimed it was her mother's idea. Who wouldn't divert blame when cornered? Had he and his boss had been drawn into a mother/daughter web of deceit?

Like a guilty accomplice, Winslow fidgeted with the wrinkles in her skirt, balling them in her fist only to smooth them out again. "Honestly, I didn't know what Mom was up to until she brought this dress home. She brought high heels too, and, ugh, they match. Can you believe it? They're covered in the same black lace as this dress, but I can't stand up straight in them. My ankles aren't strong enough. Mom says I'm too weak."

Tate nodded to keep her talking.

"And how did the television people know to come tonight, right before I was ready to leave? I almost waltzed right out of my room. I would've run smack into them. Who called them?"

So she didn't know about the Channel Thirteen either. *Interesting.*

"Mom tries to take good care of me and it's hard on her and..." Real affection for her mother colored her words and Tate got that. He did. Kids loved their mothers. "...and I don't know what I'd do without her."

He let her vent. This was no little girl. If anything, Winslow was all woman, uneducated in the ways of the world maybe, but feminine. Gullible, but soft. Pliable. Maybe too gullible.

He tried not to notice, but her hipbones were delicate against his belly, and the way she leaned into him, trusting him, caught him by surprise. Women didn't usually trust him like this—they never came close enough. Yet here Winslow was, her weight next to nothing on his thighs, her body warm and trembling inside his jacket. Yes, it was rented, and it was a small thing he'd done, but wrapping it around her had spiked an unfamiliar heatwave in his body. He needed to proceed carefully.

She reminded him of the female mule deer he'd come across once during a blinding blizzard in southwestern Canada. Lost in the fast moving winter storm, that doe had stood belly deep in heavy snow, her sides heaving and her eyes wide, with no refuge and no way to turn. Something deep inside his stoic, no nonsense hunter's soul had called to him to do what was merciful, instead of putting her down and out of her misery like he should have. The avid hunter turned into an animal rights activist that day.

Careful not to frighten the doe any more than she already was, he'd stomped a snowshoe trail from where she'd been trapped into a nearby stand of pines that offered the closest refuge. He'd left her to make up her mind, follow the trail and be safe—at least safer—or stand there and die. Wolves still roamed Canada. She would've been an easy kill. He'd hunkered down in his nearby hunting cabin, no more than a plywood lean-to with a wood burning stove and a few cans of dried food, MREs and such. By the morning, the storm had blown itself out, and the skittish doe was gone.

Funny. His gut kept telling him to keep an arm around Winslow. Like that doe, she needed shelter from the storm, only it wasn't storming. The wind had died down, yet the sensation to protect her had grown stronger.

Tate played it cool, taking in every nuance in her actions, every wavering vibrato to her voice. He meant to impart trust. As she shifted against him, it was difficult not to notice her lack of understanding of the ways of men. She didn't seem to realize the effect of her body on his. To her, they were probably just a boy and a girl sitting together on a water tower. She didn't squirm or grind against him. She didn't offer any lingering sultry looks. There was no guile to Winslow, only a profound sense of bewilderment at her predicament, as if she, like that doe, didn't know who or what to trust. As if she might still bolt.

She'd been picking at her dress, but now her fingers splayed innocently on his thigh, a sweet touch of feminine power she didn't seem to know she possessed. He tugged her hand into his, putting an end to any sexual misunderstandings. Winslow was nothing like her mom. Her nails were short. No garish black polish. No pumpkin decals. Pulling both of her hands to his mouth, he breathed heat into the slender, icy digits.

Her shoulders lifted, and along with that shy response, a smile curled her lips. She weighed next to nothing, one of those candle-in-the-wind types of women. Thin. Short. Willowy. Long black hair draped down her back, accentuating her lack of curves, but that smile. Once she'd unleashed even the barest hint of it, he hadn't wanted to do anything but sit there with her in his arms. Yes, he'd embarrassed her by dragging her onto his lap, but he needed her safe and warm. Her shivering alone could have gotten her blown away in the wind.

He worried about her faithful little soldier on guard duty below though. Trustworthy Pepe would be cold. Yes, Joyce needed to know her daughter was safe and sound, but Tate's gut told him Pepe needed to see his mistress too. Maybe more.

"Are you ready to face the music?" he asked.

Her thin brows slanted. "No. Please. Can we sit here a while longer? I'll be quiet."

That wasn't the problem.

"Go ahead and talk. I like listening to you." Most people annoyed him, but Winslow was different. Tate adjusted his position, fighting the urgent call his body was sending, the one that had sprung to attention the moment this waif of a woman landed on his lap. Grabbing onto her wasn't one of his smarter moves, but the worry that she'd sprint away from him necessitated it. Then. Now he was in a big bind.

"Does your mother know you come up here?"

"Uh-huh. She knows I go for long walks, but she doesn't know how many times I've climbed this tower. No one does." Winslow ducked her head into her shoulders, shivering. "Dying's taking too long."

That came out of the blue. Tate hadn't planned on getting this close and personal with his charge tonight. This was supposed to be one of those easy ops, a two-to-three-hour chore that required nothing more than civility and a corsage. Okay, so the corsage had morphed into a teddy bear, but the distressing vibes shuddering off this woman couldn't be ignored. Neither could her blasé talk of death. He let his palm slide up her arm to the nape of her neck, massaging the rigid bumps of her spine. It'd been a long time since he'd earnestly tried to comfort a woman.

"What kind of cancer are you dying from?" he asked as gently as he could.

"The worst kind, I guess."

Not the answer he'd expected. "You guess? Don't you know? Haven't you been diagnosed? What kind does your doctor say you have?"

Another shrug. "I've been to so many. Mom says they can't decide. What difference does it make? In a month or two, I'll be gone." She said that like it didn't bother her.

But it bothered him. "You make your death sound like a foregone conclusion, like everything's hopeless." Tate cocked his head to peer into her face. "Nothing's hopeless, Winslow. Even at the worst of times, there is still hope."

Yeah, he got why she'd say that. He had no business preaching to the choir, but her willingness to quit fighting was not his way. A warrior never gave up or gave in, not even when faced with the inevitable.

Her lashes fell. "It is for me," breathed out of her on a sigh. "Death's been coming for years. Sometimes I wish it would hurry up and get here and be done with." A strangled chuckle grumbled out of her. "The suspense is killing me. Literally."

With a swipe of her fingers, she dashed the glimmer in her eyes away and that made him mad. "That's not funny, Winslow. Never give up. You fight that cancer and you keep fighting it until you win." *Damn it.*

"It's not that easy. The medicines I have to take are awful and... some days everything's too hard." A single tear slid out of the corner of her eye. "Trust me, you don't know how hard keeping a smile on your face is until you're so sick that everything hurts, even a smile."

What was a guy supposed to say to that? Tate backed off his know-it-all, keep on-keeping-on USMC drill. Of all people, Winslow would know when it was time to let go. He got it then. That was why she was on this tower. From here, a person could almost believe they were looking at eternity. The world looked bigger. Brighter.

"This is all you've got, isn't it? This one sanctuary. This is where you can be yourself." *For as long as you've got left...*

He of all people knew the peace that solitude brought to a weary warrior. He and Winslow weren't so different, only their battles were. He couldn't bear the thought of her giving up though. Not yet, not as full of life as she seemed. She didn't look that bad, and she'd achieved quite the feat just by climbing this tower. The ladder alone took more strength than he'd expected, and he was physically sound, built for work like that.

One nod and a sniff, and she whispered. "I come up here when things get hard down there. Sometimes I'm too weak to make the climb, but every chance I get, I try. I've never been to a real dance, Mr. Higgins, but once. Just once..." She lifted the back of her hand, running one elegant finger under her dripping nose. "I thought Mom might be right about this prom. I know it's not right to cheat and lie, but I'd like to be young and carefree and on top of the world. I'd like to dance."

Well, shit. If there was one thing Tate abhorred, it was dancing. He couldn't do it. Didn't try. Never had. Ever. A man raised in the deep Alaskan wilderness had no business thinking he could soft-shoe-it to the beat of any band. He wasn't dapper and he wasn't smooth. Far from it. If anything, he was a clumsy bear in sheep's clothing, built like a box, and packed with muscle from the ground up. Bottom line, there wasn't enough whiskey on the face of the whole planet to get him out on a dance floor. Until she lifted those tear-studded lashes and shrugged like that dream of hers was another thing she'd given up on.

Aw, hell. This wouldn't be pretty. He'd have to focus on where he put his big feet so he didn't step on her boots. He'd have to be extra smart with how he did this, extra careful so neither of them fell, but if dancing was Winslow's last wish...

If it meant that much to her...

He went for broke. Dipping his nose to the curl of her ear, he asked, "May I have this dance?"

She did a quick double take. "With me?"

Yeah, he was just as surprised as she was. "Do you see anyone else up here?" He put on his best cavalier smirk, worried she'd say no after he'd worked up his nerve to ask. Mimicking the false bravado he'd seen his buddy Ky use on his wife Eden when he wasn't necessarily telling the entire truth about a tough op, Tate smacked the domed rooftop beside him for effect. "It's just you and me up here on top of the world, kiddo." Where all this debonair bullshit came from, he didn't have a clue. He just wanted Winslow to smile again. At him.

She was so damned pretty when she did, and that was the key, wasn't it? She hadn't given up hope, not if she'd been honest when she'd said, *'every chance I get, I try.'* That didn't sound like a quitter to him. No, she was just battle weary, and that he understood.

"Okay," she said, her tone soft and hoarse. Her hands went to her biceps, clutching them as if she were cold. "If you're sure. I mean, if you're not afraid you'll fall."

Clever girl. Whether she knew what she'd just done or not, that'd be the day Tate acknowledged fear to this brave woman. He braced one palm to the tower roof and pushed off, lifting Winslow with him. Easing her out from under his arm just enough to secure the tips of her fingers in one hand, he bowed like some courtly gent he'd seen in a movie long ago. "I may have two left feet, but we're going to rock this tower."

She ducked her head into her shoulders, that awful skirt of hers aloft in the wind behind her. If only his tux jacket fit better, she wouldn't look so frail. So sickly. As it was, the padded shoulders of the tux dwarfed Winslow, making her look more like a little girl than a woman.

With a quick step forward, Tate clasped her left hand in his right, put his left palm on her waist, and— ever so carefully—he performed one very slow revolution on top of the nearly constructed Silver

Spring water tower. Not the old short tower where it would've been safer. Not on your life. There he was under a chilly October sky, dancing up high in the sky with a woman who finally had stars in her eyes. Smiling stars.

Chapter Seven

Her eyes watered, but not from the wind.

This man. This once-in-a-lifetime, gentle man was dancing with her. Really dancing—as in close-up, holding her in his arms dancing like she'd only seen on television. But more, he held her carefully, almost reverently, like she was someone else, someone special. Like she might break. Like maybe she was a beautiful woman or maybe an actress. Anyone but—her.

It was a bittersweet revelation. He seemed so sure of himself. So gentle. His masculine scent billowed around her, filling her nose with yet another treasure she'd have to give up too soon. That's what hurt. This dream wasn't real. Not truly. When this Dreams-Come-True dance ended, Tate wouldn't hang around, not with her demise imminent.

This incredible moment would be over too soon, and she'd climb back down to earth and resume her tragic story. She'd feed and water Pepe until the very end, and she'd snuggle him in bed like she did every other night. She'd cry and tell him her prayers and her dreams, and he'd whine and lick her face. Her knight in shining armor would go back to his job in the real world, and she... and she... would die.

Reality check. Would Tate want to be there at the end with her? Would he show up to hold her hand like he was holding it now while she puked her guts up and faded away? Would anybody? *No. Of course not.* She didn't even want to be there.

Winslow couldn't stop her tears. Overwhelmed at the wishful rush of feminine feelings bubbling up in her tender virgin heart, she drew in a long deep breath, struggling for control. An odd geyser in that weakened organ of hers had spouted a definite plume, a heated geyser of *'I-want-to-live!'* She couldn't afford to let it loose. The strength of all that unexpressed angst for a life unlived might blow her and Mr. Higgins, umm, Tate, off the tower.

Tate. What a perfect name for a knight in shining armor. Short. To the point. Darn. What was she thinking? He didn't care about her. He couldn't. He didn't know her well enough, and he was just doing his job, a temporary, one-night job at that.

But for this one magic moment, for the first time in her life, Winslow felt—alive. Better than that, she felt wanted, maybe even pretty. She dared a quick glance up at him. No cleft in his chin. Just a strong, square jaw and the column of a muscular neck she wanted to trail her fingertips over, maybe trace a line from his Adam's apple to his ear just to feel what a man's shaved skin felt like. She'd never been this close to a man. Doctors didn't count. Neither did her mother's various boyfriends.

Tate's sideburns were trimmed short, close to that delicious looking ear. Winslow wanted to whisper in it. Tickle it—just to see him smile.

The spicy tang of aftershave drifting between his warm body and hers turned her insides to mush. Despite the dim light on the tower, she could see that he was darkly tanned, maybe olive-skinned. Tall. Dark. Handsome. A dream come true if ever there was one.

She ran a quick hand over her hair, making sure the wig hadn't shifted. He didn't need to know she was bald, or that she'd never done anything so brave or so brash as what she was doing right then. This was a fairytale ending she'd carry to her grave. All he had to do was keep up this charade a few minutes longer.

Winslow lost herself in the moment. She focused on the warmth seeping into her heart instead of all the what-ifs. None of them mattered. Who cared about the prom? She didn't.

As big as he was, Tate was light on his feet. He'd set an easy, slow rhythm for her, with all of her vast dancing experience, to follow. The longer they swayed back and forth together, the braver he got. He had to be listening to some song in his head, the way he'd relaxed and edged out of the tight circle he'd started in. Still holding her close, her temple rested on his chin, her heart in her throat, and his nose in her hair.

A deep baritone melody vibrated from his throat, one she didn't recognize. The title of the song didn't matter. Winslow closed her eyes and melted into the hard wall of his chest, the steel band of his arms. This was her one special night, and she clung to it. The rest of the world could wait.

Carefully, he lifted his arm over her head and spun her in a lazy circle, without letting go of her fingertips. He tipped her backward, catching her in the crook of his left arm, and time stopped. Winslow froze, her gaze riveted to the dark stranger bent over her, holding her as if she weighed nothing. Eyes as black as midnight poured a heady dose of mystery and male intensity down at her, and, ah! She couldn't make her lungs work. He'd drawn so close, his breath warm and sweet on her chin. Her sad, silly heart skipped a beat.

"May I?" he asked, a quaver in his whisper.

"May you what?" she dared ask. To hope. Lying there at his mercy, in a place so solitary no one could hear her laugh or cry, he could've done whatever he wanted to her. With her.

The sad truth sneaked up on her. He had everything to give her, but what did she have to give him? Nothing. It seemed impossible that he might want to kiss her anyway.

He searched her face, his lips pursed. "I'd very much like to kiss you, Winslow, if you'd let me, but if you'd rather not—"

"Yes," came quickly to her lips. *Please, yes.*

He paused, there at the edge of the most beautiful dream a woman could ask for. Slowly, he closed the distance. Not hesitantly as if he regretted asking, but ever so slowly as if he savored every last second. His lashes shuttered, but she couldn't dare miss the beautiful glow that shifted over his face. She kept watching as he pressed his mouth to hers and...

Her eyes closed as she gave into the magic of the moment. *He's kissing me.*

Tate was a luscious, secret world unto himself. Soft warm lips covered hers as the strong hand at her back pressed her upward and into her first kiss. The slightest rasp of his chin abraded her chin, and, *please don't let me wake up and this be just a dream.*

Tentatively, Winslow eased her fingers to the back of his neck, holding onto him with every prayer and wish she'd ever offered. *Please, let this be real. Let him be real.*

His tongue teased her tighter-than-tightly sealed lips, and... Oh, my, she did something terribly brave. Winslow parted her lips just enough to let his tongue enter her mouth. Tate groaned a most delicious sound in the still, cold night as the tip of his tongue swept over hers. The gruff rasp of that groan roared through her body like electricity. It tingled down to her toes.

She matched her tongue to his, amazed at the taste of him and the fire creeping through her veins. Instinctively, her body arched into the cradle of his, offering what, she didn't know, but wanting what he seemed to want from her. To be closer. Intimately closer.

Winslow braved a peek at the man who held her so reverently. The clouds had parted in the midnight sky above them. His eyes were still closed, but the stars shone in the sky beyond him, and the look on his face? Sheer adoration.

Forgotten strength coursed through her veins. This was her night, damn it, and she wanted every last burning second of it. She wanted him. Right there. Right then.

With full intent, she shifted one hand from his neck to his collarbone and then to his chest. She'd intended to walk her fingers down his stomach, but— she got caught up in sensations she couldn't resist. That powerful chest needed more exploration, definitely more touching. Corded muscles bunched at her fingertips like the sensitive withers of a giant draft horse. Her fingers skated over a flat, manly nipple that she would like to pinch. Just once.

He caught her wandering fingers in one hand, not warning her off, but flattening them to his sternum. Holding her close. Encouraging her. A warrior's heart thundered at the center of her palm, melting her.

She'd never been held so dearly by anyone. Ever. Not even her mother. *Especially not Mom.*

Every intimate feminine muscle clenched at the temptation of his body heat and his touch. Winslow didn't feel weak anymore, but daring. Brave. Maybe even audacious for once in her timid life.

She took over the kiss, growling with need, nipping at his bottom lip, her body on fire with the naughtiest, most exhilarating, downright wicked thoughts. If this was the prelude to sex, it was better than chocolate. If this was foreplay... *If this was love...*

Ah, no. She blocked that errant notion before it took root. Loving a man was beyond the realm of possibility, and she couldn't give into it. She'd accepted that hard fact when she'd turned sixteen. There was nothing sweet to it then and there wasn't now. Cancer victims didn't have that kind of luck.

"What am I going to do with you?" he muttered hotly into her open mouth, his eyes still closed as his tongue ran a lazy lap over her lips.

"Keep doing what you're doing?" She phrased that as a hopeful question and another wish as she kissed him again. *Please, don't stop.*

Tate ended her first sexual encounter with another wet kiss that left her spellbound and breathless. Pulling her upright, he kept his palm in the middle of her back while he pressed her to his chest. Oh, good. The thunder beneath his ribs matched the noisy beat of her heart. This man was shaken as much as she was by their close encounter. That helped.

He buried his nose in her hair, and for once, she didn't worry if her wig slid off her head. This kiss meant he cared for her, didn't it? He'd understand every secret she had yet to tell him, wouldn't he?

As surely as if the wind had pushed her, she knew it then. She—Winslow Parrish—a pariah in her own home—was falling in love. A tight knot blossomed in that hollow space in her heart. Tate was right. Maybe there was still hope.

Tate didn't speak. He couldn't. He'd just breached agent/client protocol in a big way, and he knew he'd do it again given the opportunity. Something about Winslow had brought his feral nature to the surface in a big, and yes, a hard way. His soul yearned to fix what was wrong with her, to fight that cancer with every last breath. To make her want to fight death as hard and as long as she could. That was how people were supposed to face the Grim Reaper. They were supposed to spit in the old man's eye, not lie down and give up like it seemed she'd been doing.

But his body? As wrong as it was, the need to kiss her had come out of nowhere, a storm he hadn't been able to resist. When her lovely peaches-and-cream fragrance wafted up between them, he was lost. Okay, so it came with a hint of garlic, so what? Between those other fragrances, nearly lost in them, was the alluring, feminine scent of Winslow, an addiction he had no intention of curbing.

He pressed another kiss to the top of her forehead. She was tiny. So helpless. She needed someone to help her fight that damned cancer growing inside of her. Someone stalwart and tough. Someone who meant what he said and said what he meant.

But she was strong in her own way too. He sensed an uncanny juxtaposition within her, a paradox he didn't dare believe. How could a woman so full of life be dying?

"I want you to promise me something." His voice was hoarse with the ache in his body. Maybe, in his soul.

Her head bobbed against his chin. "Okay. What?"

The innocence and trust in this woman humbled him. Just like that exhausted deer had done, Winslow seemed willing to follow his lead. That simple act of faith threw his life into sharp perspective. Was he up for a fight with cancer? Why not? It made more sense than most of the other battles he'd been in. "I don't want you to come up here unless I'm with you, okay? Promise."

"I promise." She sounded timid. Was this in any way the right thing for a man like him to ask of a woman like her? Or was he the biggest ass on the planet for taking advantage of her weakened condition, now, when she was dying?

The answer came swiftly. *Just do it.*

He swallowed hard. *So be it.* "It's time I took you home. Your mother will be worried."

"Okay," came the same timid whisper, this time with a tremor that rattled her body.

Tate lowered his face, tilting Winslow's chin upward with two fingers. Was she afraid of her mom? He smoothed the silky strands of hair out of her eyes and off her face, drinking in this last stolen moment. Deliberately, he tipped his lips to hers and sealed the promise. "I'll come back tomorrow if it's okay with you. If you feel the need, we'll climb up here then, deal?"

A smile danced through her eyes. "I'd like that."

How did he get so lucky? For the first time, Tate thanked his ornery boss for the assignment. Maybe Tucker knew something he didn't. It was possible. Tate took Winslow's head between his palms, tilting her forehead to better see into her eyes. "What color are your eyes? I think green. Pretty green. Am I right?"

She nodded, but lowered her lashes. "And yours are dark brown. Like chocolate fudge."

He pressed his lips to the end of her nose for one quick peck. "Unless I'm angry. Then they're black as coal."

Lifting her face to meet his gaze, an angel-soft palm skated over his cheek. "You don't ever have to be angry again."

Chapter Eight

Back on the ground, Tate snagged Winslow's fingers and pulled her into his side. He'd already put his shoes back on and snuggled Pepe inside the jacket with her, but he wanted her close.

Pepe was the man, er, dog of the hour. Like a good trooper, the little guy hadn't deserted his post, but he did run circles, yelp, and bounce like an insane jackrabbit when Winslow touched down. The tux jacket fit her better with him buttoned up inside of it.

Damn, she glowed. She looked happy, not sickly or weak. Or scared. To look at her now, Tate never would've suspected she was dying. Endorphins would do that to a person, only it had to be more than just the physical connection they'd shared. Tate couldn't explain it. He swiped a hand over his face, hoping he wasn't glowing too.

What he'd intended as a quick kiss had morphed into something else. One moment, he was fulfilling the last wish for some girl he didn't know, spinning her in a slow dance just to make her happy. The next, well... *hell.* The next he'd fallen head-over-heels for an incredible woman, and he was in deep trouble. Coming on to a client was not how a trusted agent acted.

But Tate never expected that a high could feel this good, this empowering. Normally, he was the quiet man in the room, the recalcitrant shadow in the farthest corner, and the first to bust out of Tucker's boring sit-rep meetings.

He avoided people because they annoyed him. Civilians seemed caught up in narcissistic trivia he had no stomach for. Cell phones. Gossip. Selfies. Celebrities. Who did what to who. What did any of that have to do with what was going on in the real world? He knew the hard side of life where good men and women died in the line of duty. Civilians didn't have a clue.

But now the night felt bigger. More open. The sky seemed wider. Higher. The few stars breaking through the last of the clouds sparkled brighter. Even the chilly autumn air felt brisk instead of chilly, lifting his spirits and reminding him of his home in far off Alaska. He had to look down to check his feet to see if they were touching solid ground.

His inner radar kept pinging on Winslow, relaying back every subtle nuance in her gestures, her steps, the way she breathed. Inhaled. Exhaled. Sighed. Everything. At the moment she was kissing bug-eyed Pepe's round little head and talking nonsense to the dog. Calling him Sweet Thing and Honey Munchkin. Girly stuff like that.

"Mom will be mad at me for skipping out on the prom," she murmured as they walked silently north to hook westward onto Maple. "She went all out for me and look how I repaid her."

He squeezed Winslow's fingers. "She'll get over it. I'll tell her you were with me, that it's no big deal." Who was he kidding? It was a damned big deal.

Winslow stopped short of the concrete walk to her door. "Oh, oh. The porch light's not on. She locked me out. I was afraid of that."

"Your mom locks you out?" How childish. The more Tate learned about Joyce, the more he knew she'd never make mother of the year, but Winslow was right. The car was gone.

"It's okay. I know what to do when she does this to me." Winslow headed for the east side of the house. At the first window, she stepped onto a concrete block standing on its end in the weedy flowerbed. "Here. Boost me up."

"No, ma'am." Tate put a quick stop to that. No woman was going into a dark house alone while he was there. He clamped a hand on her wrist, dragging her and Pepe back to the ground. "You don't have a key to your own home?"

Winslow offered a feminine grunt of disdain. "Are you kidding? Mom took that away from me a long time ago."

Yep. Joyce wasn't even a finalist. "Let me do it," he insisted, his foot already on the block. It teetered beneath his weight, but the barely-cracked window slid up without a sound, ending the argument. "Let me guess. WD-40?"

Winslow shrugged her shoulders. "I'm not entirely without wiles." There was that smile he was falling in love with. A little bit mischievous. A little bit naughty. One hundred percent womanly.

His heart did a funny flip until a car rolled by, its headlights grazing over the apparent B&E in progress. Tate got down to business. Hefting himself onto the windowsill, he stuck one foot between the sheer drapes, careful not to break anything on his way to Winslow's bedroom floor. This window might serve as an escape hatch for her, but he was bigger and wider. It was a tight squeeze. Finally inside, he turned and told her, "Go around to the front. I'll let you in."

One hand fell to her hip. "Why can't you just pull me up? I'm not heavy. Neither is Pepe."

"Because this is your *bedroom*. The last thing I need is to impugn your virtue, now move it. Double-time. Front door. I'll let you in."

Her eyes had stars in them again. "Aww, you say the sweetest things."

Me? Tate Higgins? That was a first. He nearly looked behind him to see if she meant someone else.

For two cents, he would've scooped her up and through the window right then and there, but no. They weren't teenagers, and he wouldn't give any of her neighbors something to talk about. "Will you stop standing there and do as you're told?"

Ducking her shoulders, she cuddled Pepe and nodded. "We'll meet you around front."

Tate made it down the hall just as Winslow and Pepe hit the front steps. Opening the door with a flourish, he waved her inside.

"Are you leaving?" she asked, flicking the living room light on upon entry.

"Do you want me to?"

"No, I just thought we could talk or something. It's not very late, and if I know Mom, she won't be back until late."

Tate's eyes narrowed, wondering at the conflicting impressions Winslow's mother portrayed. Mama Bear. Cat on the prowl. *Liar...*

He gave her the benefit of the doubt. "She's probably out looking for you. I'll stay here until she gets back." Tate lifted Pepe out of Winslow's arms and set the rascal on the floor. The little guy dropped to his butt and lifted one rear leg to scratch his ear.

"Welcome to my humble home," Winslow offered, her voice timid as she slid out of those man-sized furry boots, but kept snuggled in his jacket. "Do you like popcorn? I can make some while we wait."

No man in his right mind turned down an offer like that. "Sure. I'll help." Tate joined her at the gas stove in the kitchen, noting the austerity of the place. There was no phone on the wall. No toaster or blender on the counter. Pretty much not much of anything. He'd grown up without many modern conveniences, but the wilds of Alaska were known for that. Modern suburbia was not.

Winslow meant popping popcorn the old fashioned way, with oil and a frying pan with a lid and a whole lot of shaking going on. He settled his hip to the kitchen counter, his arms folded over his chest while Pepe slurped water from the dog dish by the back door. "Do you have a house phone in case your mom calls?"

"That would be the day." Winslow glanced sideways at him as she kept the fry pan moving. "She doesn't call home, but no. We had a phone at our last house, but not here."

"Why not?" He inhaled the delicious aroma in the air as popcorn started popping. *Mmmmmm. Nothing better.*

"I don't know. I guess because we move a lot, and Mom hasn't gotten it hooked up yet." Another shrug. "Do you want salt and butter? I do."

He couldn't resist the pixie smile on her face. "Yes, please. Why'd you move?"

"I don't know. You'll have to ask Mom."

This was a downright odd situation, an intelligent twenty-year old woman content to live at home with her domineering mother, the same woman who'd pitched a fuss over her missing daughter, then locked her out of the house. Tate suspected Joyce was down at Land's End drowning her sorrows instead of looking for the *kidnapped* child she'd declared she was *so* worried about. The spectacle he'd witnessed earlier bugged him.

Winslow seemed fairly energetic, and, as much as he hated to admit it, that bugged him too. If she was as close to dying as he'd been led to believe, how had she climbed that tower, not once, but twice in the same day? She wasn't even breathing hard. She seemed—normal. A little pale maybe, and thin, but, yeah. Normal.

"Yoo-hoo, Tate. I need a tall person." She arched her brows at the cabinet over the stove. "There's a popcorn bowl up there. Would you mind reaching it for me?"

Such a simple request, but the intimate gesture caught Tate by surprise when he lifted an arm over Winslow to grab that bowl. He towered above her, like a giant with an elfin princess. It made a guy feel better than he was. Prouder. At least bigger. At some intrinsic level he couldn't fathom, he felt more like an alpha male with Winslow instead of a beta.

Until he caught sight of the shoebox overflowing with prescription meds alongside the popcorn bowl. What the hell? Small plastic bottles. Some white. Some green. Some brown. Boxes. Zip-lock bags. All with prescription labels and containing pills and tablets. He set the large bowl on the counter near the stove, but he couldn't let that stash go without making a comment. "You sure take a lot of pills."

Winslow turned off the burner and transferred the popped corn to the bowl. "Nah-ah, those are Mom's. Mine are behind you."

He twisted around. *Holy shit.* She meant the giant pill holder beside the portable plastic file box? The box lid was raised with an index card taped inside that listed what looked like a twenty-four hour schedule. "You have to take all these?"

"Don't look so shocked." Winslow slapped the lid shut with her fingertips. "It's a lot of meds, but these nasty things have kept me alive for years. I don't have to like them. I just have to take them."

"All of them? Every day?" There had to be close to fifty prescription bottles in that box. He'd never seen a pillbox with five seven-day rows before. Count 'em. Five.

She jiggled the aromatic bowl of steaming kernels under his nose. "Let's eat."

The nervous light in her pale green eyes stopped his prying. Her meds were none of his business. What did a guy like him know about cancer patients and their treatments anyway? *Absolutely nothing.*

Tate took a deep breath and followed his nose to the front room behind Winslow. She had no womanly figure, and that get-up she had on was no help, not the way it hung off her hips like a rag. But she did have a nice sway to said hips, and the glow off the lamplight caught her glossy black hair. It swung as she walked, but even that poked at him. Cancer patients didn't usually have hair.

He froze. *Damn, I'm dumb. Look at her. Really look at her. In the light.* Yes, there was a definite sparkle in her eyes, and he suspected he'd put it there, but now it was plain to see how anorexically thin Winslow's body was beneath that swishy skirt. She had no meat on her bones. No fat. Her eyes seemed too large for her face because they were ringed with dark shadows. Her pale complexion seemed paler now that he could see her clearly. Her brows were thin, nearly transparent. Even her fingers were slender and bony.

She set the bowl of popcorn on the coffee table and curled in the corner of the sofa with a sigh. Tate lowered his bulk beside her. Damn, she was small. "You're tired."

Stifling a yawn, she nodded. "I think I overdid it today."

He didn't play the sneaky game of yawn and stretch. Tate just wrapped one arm around her shoulder and tipped Winslow into his side. "You're cold. Let me warm you up."

"Thanks. I tend to get chilled at night." She curled into him, shivering, and instantly, he wanted more than just this one trumped-up night with Winslow. There was something about her that took him back to the days before *it* happened, when life was good and the sun still shone every morning. His fingers commenced a slow massage on her bicep, as if they couldn't touch her enough.

As frail as she seemed, a unique energy radiated off Winslow. It glowed in her tired eyes like a tiny ember that needed enough air to burst into flames. He'd recognized it up on the water tower, under the stars. It was the same expression he'd seen on too many faces in dirty, far off villages where war had raged too long and too hard. Where people, mothers and fathers and children, just wanted to be left alone to live their lives in peace and quiet.

Winslow was like those people. She was desperate to live, while he, one of America's so-called finest, one of the proud and the brave—Oorah!—had been building walls to keep people out. Cursing away the very thing she was fighting to hang onto.

Humbling. Damned humbling.

It was easy to imagine a better way forward with her head resting on the side of his chest like it was. A man could almost believe in himself again. What was it the talking heads of the world said, that it only takes one woman to change a man? The right woman?

"If this isn't enough popcorn, I've got some leftover bacon from breakfast. It's crispy, but I could reheat it. I know guys like meat."

"Wait. You're not a vegetarian?" First the kidnapping scam, then the locked door, now an outright lie about her daughter being a vegetarian? What was Joyce thinking?

"Hmmm, not hardly," Winslow murmured. "It's one of the few things I can eat that stays down. If you ask me, bacon should be in a food group all by itself. Right?"

Yes, and I think Joyce should stop lying to me.

The popcorn could wait. Winslow made a very small and fragile armful. It was the little things he noticed now that they were inside. Her gentle hand on his stomach, so light he barely felt it. The way her hair smelled of peaches. That hint of garlic in the air. The solid muscle to her bicep. She probably got that from climbing the water tower.

Like any dog, Pepe made himself comfortable alongside Tate's other hip—right before he climbed onto Tate's lap. Holding Winslow and her little buddy almost made him feel at home.

"So tell me about yourself. What's it like escorting women everywhere?" she asked, her voice quiet. She had to be exhausted.

Tate shrugged, one corner of his mouth curved into a half smile. "Don't know. This was my first. How'd I do?"

Her head came up, her eyes bright with questions. "This isn't your job? But the tux and the car and—"

"The Corvette belongs to my buddy, and the tux is rented. I work for the FBI."

"And..."

He settled for the FBI mission statement. "I protect the American people and I defend the

Constitution of the United States." *Truth. Justice. The American dream. But I'm not Superman.*

"What does that mean?"

Tate cleared his throat, re-evaluating what that mission statement meant now that he had an armful of Winslow. The Bureau's pomp and ego used to bug him, but now...

"Basically, FBI agents are involved in preventing terrorist attacks, cyber-based computer attacks, espionage, and corruption. Things like that." There was no sense delving into the Deuces Wild thing and his uncanny gift with animals. "We protect people's civil rights. We combat organized crime."

"And you dance," she said coyly.

That merited a snort. "Not hardly. That was another first." It was time to change the subject. "My life is boring. Tell me about you."

Her gaze wandered down the hall to her bedroom, and he wished he'd never asked. She drummed her fingers on her knee. "Let's see. Where should I begin? Hmmm. You already know I'm twenty, and I like high places. I read a lot. I love my dog and my mom. Umm, never mind. I've got a better question. What's your dream job? I mean, if you couldn't work for the FBI, what would you rather be doing?"

She'd just dodged the question, and Tate let her. "That's easy. I'd be back home in Alaska, fishing. Maybe hunting." He stopped short of saying *'anywhere else but here'* because that didn't feel precisely accurate any longer. Here seemed a pretty damned comfortable place to be, stuck between a sweet woman and a two-pound dragon whose paws twitched in his puppy dreams.

The popcorn sat forgotten on the coffee table. Winslow yawned, and that was the last thing Tate remembered.

Chapter Nine

A cold draft stirred over Winslow, right before she heard a hiccup and a snide, "Well, isn't this cozy?"

Winslow snapped wide-awake. She'd fallen asleep on the couch snuggled in Tate's arm, and damn. Mom was home. At least they were both sitting upright instead of lying together. That wouldn't have been good.

She rubbed a quick hand over her eyes, as warm, and, yes, as cozy as she'd ever been. "Hi Mom," she said guiltily. "I, umm, guess we fell asleep while we were waiting for you."

"You're in late," Tate grunted at her mother, but he didn't jerk his arm away from Winslow as she'd half-expected. Pepe didn't move either. He stayed on Tate's lap, one eye on Joyce.

"Yeah well, you know what? This is my house, and I can come and go as I damned well please, flyboy."

Mom's gray eyes flashed like steel grinding sparks. "What are you still doing here, Agent Higgins? Oh, never mind. I can see perfectly well what you're doing. You're pawing my daughter. It's time you left."

Tate didn't budge at her flippant demand, but neither did he remove his fingers from where they curled protectively around Winslow's shoulder. "I'm not pawing your daughter, ma'am. I'm holding her, that's all. As I told you before I left, I went out to look for her because you claimed she'd been abducted. Where have you been?"

Despite his warm hands, Winslow shivered. He had a lot of nerve to confront her mother. "It's okay, I—"

"It's not okay, missy." Mom's tone cracked like a whip of midnight lightning. "This guy has no business questioning me in my house. He has no right—"

"I have every right," Tate replied evenly. "You're the one who thought your daughter was kidnapped, or at least that was the conclusion you jumped to when your television friends were here. Is that where you've been, searching high and low for Winslow? Filing a missing person's report down at the local precinct? Did you think to take a picture of her with you when you filed?"

Oooo, sarcasm too. Either Tate was brave or stupid.

Mom's face turned a nasty shade of red as if she'd been caught in a lie—or when she was about to invent one. Her eyes narrowed like they did before she went nuclear. She pointed at the still open door. "Get out. Now. Do you hear me? Go home or wherever it is you guys crawl into after you've defiled someone's daughter, you—you—"

"Mom!" Winslow hadn't meant to raise her voice. "Tate brought me home and it was cold and I made popcorn. That's all. We were sitting here waiting for you and we fell asleep. Nothing else happened." She pointed at the popcorn bowl. "Look. We haven't even eaten it, we were so tired."

"I'm supposed to believe that?"

"Believe it or not, Winslow's well over legal age," Tate said, his voice low and steady. "It's none of your business."

Winslow swallowed hard. Okay, that was not how to handle her mother. She tipped forward onto the balls of her feet just as a breath of alcohol drifted across the room. Crap, not again. Mom had been out drinking with her buddy, Ike, as in Ike Pitt the biker, the loser, the 'I-need-a-place-to-crash, you-got-any-spare-change?' freeloader.

A cringe crawled up her spine at the thought of her mom being with the guy. Every time he'd been to the house, he'd smelled of body odor, cigarette smoke, and booze. Ike creeped Winslow out the way he looked her over when her mom wasn't looking. *Eww. Just ewww. Mom, what do you see in him?*

"Maybe you should go," Winslow suggested to Tate even as she stared her mother down. "You've been drinking, haven't you, Mom?"

A wrinkled nose was her only answer. Yeah. Mom wouldn't admit anything because she didn't think she owed anyone the truth, not even her only child.

Tate leaned forward with Winslow to the edge of the couch, upsetting Pepe from his nice warm perch. "I'll go if you tell me to."

"Then go. Please." She turned to him, her hand on his thigh and her heart wanting him to stay. "It's okay. She'll be fine once I get her to bed."

"You'll put *her* to bed?" Man, he had some handsome brows, but right now, he looked on the verge of starting something she couldn't finish.

Winslow nodded. "Yeah. We take care of each other."

Those sexy brows dipped low, shading his eyes. "It's not her I'm worried about. I've got no way to get a hold of you once I leave. Here." He shifted in his seat, blocking her mother's view as he dragged his cell phone up from his pants pocket and pressed it into Winslow's palm. "Keep this out of sight. My number's on the *if-lost-contact* label on the side. Call me if you need anything, promise?"

She certainly seemed to be making a lot of promises to this guy. "I will," she gave him what she could. "But I'll be okay, Tate. Honest, I don't know why you'd think I wouldn't."

Something flitted through those smoldering browns that went nearly black. His sudden intensity took her breath. This wasn't how she wanted her first date to end, not with him leaving angry and her mother about to let loose with one of her screaming, drunken tirades. Without thinking, Winslow leaned into him. Wanting more time with him. Needing another kiss. Another life wouldn't be so bad either. "Goodbye Tate," she whispered.

He shook his head, his brows so low she could barely see his pupils. "Not goodbye, just later, Winslow. I'll call tomorrow. Don't lose that phone."

She bobbed her head. "I won't. I promise."

"Will you just leave?" Her mother waved her hand at the still open front door, fluttering her fingers for him to step on it.

Winslow couldn't believe how nasty she was being to Tate. She'd been plenty rude before, just not with strangers. Especially not with men. This was a new low.

Tate put his palms to his knees and lifted to his feet with deliberate slowness. His bones cracked when he flexed his shoulders, then arched to stretch his spine. It was as if he'd just issued Winslow an enticing invitation to join him. She wanted to run her fingers up his back and cup her palms to his hips and do a whole lot more to that gorgeous male body.

Pepe stayed close to Tate. The little guy had found a new friend the way he looked up at him and blinked. Her dog looked as smitten as she felt. But it was time for Tate to go. She gulped down a lifetime of insecurities. He probably had work tomorrow, and well, no matter what he'd said, this might be the last time she saw him.

She didn't see it coming. Ignoring her mother's foot tapping, he grabbed Winslow's free hand and pulled her up against his chest. "I had fun tonight. Thanks for dancing with me."

Ah, the dancing. Yes. A shiver raced up the back of her neck at the memory. She intertwined her fingers with his. "Thanks for asking. Tonight..." There was no word for the connection she felt with this charming man, so she shrugged and said, "It was perfect."

"It was, wasn't it. I don't usually dance, but tonight was... nice." He nodded toward the floor. "Pepe did all the hard work though. He led me to you. He deserves a dog treat before bed."

Good old Mom huffed loudly at the now opened front door, but it was all Winslow could do to let Tate's hand go. She ducked out of his jacket and handed it over. He'd given her a once-in-a-lifetime gift tonight. A sweet smile tugged at the corner of his mouth, just before he dipped down low and captured her lips with his. That goodbye kiss stole her breath. Once more, the old world she knew dropped away and the wet warmth of his mouth became everything. His hands were firm and warm on her biceps. His tongue danced softly over her sealed lips, inviting her to join him in another sizzling tango.

Winslow didn't dare, not with her mom watching. A sigh of resignation breathed out of her as she let one hand wander to the nape of Tate's neck and pulled him into her for just—one—more second. One more taste. The scent of him spiraled up around her cheeks and into her nose, filling her with the call of the wild outdoors and the wind. Always the wind. That would forever be how she remembered Tate. In the wind and the dark and all those stars.

Her mother coughed. Rudely and loudly. Annoyingly so.

Really Mom? She had no right to be so—so—motherly.

Winslow swallowed hard as Tate eased back from her, still smiling and the brown twinkle back in his handsome eyes. His lashes were thick and curled like black butterfly wings at rest. She hadn't noticed that until now. There was so much she didn't yet know about him, and she wanted it all. Every last detail. Everything. When was he born? Where did he live? Who were his parents? Any brothers? Sisters? Dogs? Cats?

So much of life was slipping through her fingertips that she could barely stand to let him go. She filled her lungs with that woodsy scent and dropped her hands, her heart up high in her throat. Choking her. Reminding her that there was a harder goodbye in her immediate future.

Again with the intrusive cough from the doorway, and Winslow brushed the back of her hand over her eyes. Yeah, she was a crier, but she knew her mother. Tears brought ridicule. The worst was yet to come.

Tate slung his jacket over one shoulder before he cupped Winslow's damp cheek. "Tomorrow," he whispered. "Trust me. I'll be back."

She turned into his palm, wishing he'd stay. "I'll be here."

Tate was barely out the door when her mother slammed it shut and growled, "We need to talk."

He stood at the top step of Winslow's porch, his ear cocked to the uproar in the house behind him.

"You let a man into my home while I'm gone?" Joyce bellowed, her door no more than closed.

He couldn't detect any comeback.

"Go to your room!"

She talked to her adult daughter like that? Tate gritted his teeth imagining his old man taking that tone. There would've been a war.

"Did you hear me?" Joyce reverted to shrieking, but Tate had yet to hear one whimper of justification from Winslow. Was she taking this verbal assault lying down? Was she that timid she wouldn't stand up for herself?

"You know what, I'm tired and I don't care," Joyce yelled, the extra loud emphasis on *tired* hard to miss. "I'm sick of putting your needs before mine all the goddamned time! That's all I ever do, and now, you've humiliated me in front of the world. The world! Do you hear me?"

Maybe Winslow had gone to her room so Joyce had to shout to be heard? Tate canted his head. It was more likely Winslow hadn't resorted to fighting at her mother's level. Whether she knew it or not, speaking calmly might be what incited her mother.

"Well, I'll tell you what you did. Channel Thirteen aired the coverage they shot of me tonight on the eleven o'clock news just like they said they would. Oh, yes they did, and you made me a laughing stock in front of all my friends, you ungrateful shit!"

As it should have been. He allowed a tiny smile. No one forced Joyce into contacting the news. Hadn't she gotten what she'd hoped for, a digital recording of the night *she'd* always wanted?

The sharp clatter of high heels on linoleum punctuated the one-sided war of words. "Yes, you did! You missed your one and only prom! Who do you think I did this for? Me?"

Precisely. Yes, Winslow missed being sensationalized and exploited to further the media's and her mother's agenda. *Pretty good night if you ask me.*

When Pepe let out a shrill yelp, Tate winced. That poor little guy had probably gotten his butt handed to him for straying too close to Mama Bear. A door slammed from inside the house, and Tate stepped away. He hadn't intended to be a snoop. It just happened when a guy was slow on the uptake, only Tate wasn't that slow. He now knew more than he wanted about Winslow's mother, and most of it, he didn't like.

Ky's Corvette was still at the curb where he'd parked it. Joyce's sedan was back in the driveway. The sky was clear, and after that catnap with Winslow, Tate was energized. He rolled his shoulders and flexed his fists. The night felt young. Now what? He had half a mind to text Winslow with the extra phone he'd left in Ky's ride, but first...

He needed to check out Land's End.

Chapter Ten

Winslow held her breath, waiting for the nasty hurricane in her house to settle down. When her mother slammed her bedroom door in her usual huff, Winslow gave her a few minutes before she dared knock quietly. "Mom? Can I come in?"

"Go away." Just like every other time. It took some coaxing for her mom to calm down once she'd gotten herself spun up. Tonight's display had been particularly unfortunate. Her mom could be the kindest person on earth. Too bad Tate hadn't caught that side of her. He needed to come over for dinner one night and get to know the real Joyce Parrish.

On second thought...

Winslow rapped once more, still as soft, still as determined. Exhaustion tugged at the frayed corners of her weary mind. It had been a tremendously long day, but she couldn't go to sleep until she and her mom were on good terms. That was her rule. "I'm coming in."

"Stay out!" Mom might've screamed, but Winslow knew she didn't mean it. This meltdown was just her way of dealing with the stress of the awful burden she'd been given—her dying child.

Winslow entered quietly so as not to start another tantrum. Her mom had taken up her usual position, sitting on the far side of her double bed, facing the wall, her shoulders heaving with her distress. Rounding the end of the bed, Winslow sat beside her, fighting for the strength to turn her mother's temper around. There were many days she wasn't sure who the child was in the house.

Sweet Pepe peeked in at the door, but she motioned him away with a flick of her fingers. He didn't need his little butt kicked again, the poor boy. That was her mother's worst sin. She treated Pepe like garbage, which kept Winslow on the look-out for her best bud. Pepe was the one worry she hadn't solved yet. He'd need a home when all was said and—done.

Winslow gulped. She barely owned anything, so her few personal items could go to the trash. If her mother discovered her journals, well, wasn't she in for a surprise? Winslow had poured her heart and all of her lost dreams into those college-ruled, ten-by-seven, composition tablets. All of it. The bad days. The good days. She'd kept them hidden from her mom because, well, a lot of those entries had to do with the whirlwind called Joyce Parrish and the destruction she left in her wake.

Winslow knew to her soul that her mom would bounce back after the funeral. But Pepe? Who would love him after she died? What would her mother do with him? Yeah. Pepe's future was her greatest worry.

Life had been hard on her mother, it was no wonder she fought everyone. Born the youngest daughter of a strict Southern Baptist preacher in Georgia, she'd run away from home and her eight siblings when she'd gotten pregnant at fifteen. Poor Joyce ended up in Arizona, hence the name of her precious baby girl, so called after the memorable line from Glenn Frey and 'The Eagles', hit of the 70's, "Standin' on the corner in Winslow, Arizona." *Yada, yada, yada...*

Winslow hated the song, but she understood. At that time in her mother's life, nothing had come easy. Impressionable and trusting, Joyce fully believed the handsome stranger she'd fallen in love with. After he'd proved himself to be otherwise a liar, and left her pregnant to fend for herself in the middle of nowhere, she'd made her way back to the East Coast all by herself and struggled to find work. She couldn't go home because her daddy declared he couldn't stand the sight of her after the shame she'd brought the family. He'd disowned her. Joyce hadn't heard from him since.

From then on, day in and day out, through winter snows and summer drought, (or so the story went),

Joyce had slaved, worked tables, counters, and such to put herself through beauty school while tending to her child—as hard as it was to juggle all those jobs. But when Winslow turned three, life pulled the rug out from under poor Joyce once more. Her child came down with a terrible sickness that ended up being cancer. Oh yes. It seemed Winslow's illegitimate birth wasn't a blessing as much as an endurance test.

"There, there," Winslow soothed, stroking her mother's hand and wishing she could be a better daughter. If only she had more time. "Why do you get yourself worked up like this, Mom? Why don't you trust me after all we've been through together?"

Her mother only half-glanced at her, just enough for Winslow to see her eyes brimmed to overflowing. She lifted a hand to her lips. "But that's the thing, I do trust you. It's him. Mr. Higgins is the problem. I don't trust men, you know that. He'll use you up and spit you out just because you're sweet and innocent like I used to be, and you don't know better. He'll break your heart, believe you me. It's a big world out there. I'm just trying to protect you from learning every lesson the hard way like I did. You don't know what men are like."

But Winslow did know. She'd certainly heard how awful the lot of them were often enough. All except Ike. For whatever reason, he'd slithered under her mom's dirt-bag meter.

"Tate's different."

Her mother grabbed her wrist and pulled her into her face, so close Winslow could smell the booze on her breath. "No, he isn't. I saw him looking at you like you were a piece of meat. He's a sneaky one, that one. All he wants is his hands in your panties."

Embarrassment flamed Winslow's cheeks at the picture her mother had just planted in her mind. *Tate's hand in my panties. Hmmm.* Her tummy clenched at the deliciousness of that slim possibility.

She drew in a slow breath, weary from the drama. Her mother had a knack for wearing her down quicker than the cancer did. Resting a calming hand on her mother's arms, she said, "Please don't say that. It sounds... dirty." *And kind of hot.* "Tate was every bit the gentleman while you were gone. You would've been proud of him."

Her mother wasn't a bad person, and she didn't normally talk like that, she was just what she called, high strung. Temperamental. She'd always considered herself one of those sleek thoroughbreds at Kentucky Downs, those prancing, temperamental horses destined for fame and glory, the ones that had to be pampered and handled with kid gloves. Only she'd been blessed with a sickly child who was taking years to die, and so she'd failed being the petulant filly at the gate before she'd ever set one foot on the racetrack. At every turn, life had been unfair to poor Joyce, and Winslow understood how her mother felt. She truly did. Death was an ill-tempered and capricious master that cared for no one. Waiting so long for it to arrive made her death sentence worse. She wished, for her mother's sake, that the cancer would kill her faster, so her mom could get on with her life. Maybe then she'd be happier.

"I don't want to talk to you right now." She sniffed and scraped Winslow's hand off her arm. "Go play with your boyfriend."

"Mom, he's not my boyfriend. Honest. Tate's just a..." Winslow shrugged one shoulder. He did seem like a boyfriend, but what did she know about such things? "He's a friend." *A really good friend and a dynamite kisser.*

"Tate, huh? You call him by his first name already, do you? You two sure looked cozy."

"I suppose we did, but Mom. He came looking for me tonight, and he found me. That's all. Then he walked me home—"

"Where were you? On that damned water tower?"

That took Winslow aback. How much did her mother know? "The water tower?"

Her mother nodded her chin at her with a huff. "You're not as sick as you pretend. You're stronger than I am some days, you just put on a good act."

Winslow's eyes widened. "I'm what? Faking cancer?" *Now I've heard everything.*

Her mother growled. "No, you're not faking, it's just that... I'm just... oh, damn. I'm just mad because he found you when I couldn't. I looked and looked though, and when I was nearly about to give up..." She let her words hang.

"You went to Land's End," Winslow finished for her. "I know." All bad days ended at Land's End. Most good days too. That was the culmination point in their perpetual circle, the one they'd been locked in as mother and daughter for as long as Winslow could remember. A good stiff drink—or two—was her mom's way out of difficult decisions. What kind of daughter would Winslow have been if she failed to understand that one fatal weakness? Hers was cancer. Her mother's was a drink now and then. What was the difference?

"Never mind. I'll go fix your medicine."

Winslow made a face. "No thanks. Not this late. It'll make me sicker on an empty stomach."

"But you can't miss a dose. That's what the doctor said."

"Which one this time?" She had so many.

"Bly."

Winslow couldn't help but grunt. What an awful moniker for a healer. Dr. Bly sounded like a murdering pirate on the high seas. "I forget. Is he the one who practices out of his home or the guy who looks like an eighth grader?"

"The one who practices from his residence." Her mom lifted one shoulder. "Don't you think he's cute?"

"No, Mom. He's not cute." *He's old.* "I guess you're right though. I'll have to take the medicine whether I like it or not. Could you put ice in it when you blend it this time? I can hardly gag it down when it's lukewarm."

"Why sure." That seemed to do the trick. Her mom reverted to the gentle woman she could be. Running her fingers through several strands from Winslow's black wig, she cocked her head into her daughter's and crooned, "Hush little baby, close your eyes. Mama's going to make you a big surprise."

Odd. That song used to help Winslow fall to sleep when she was younger, but tonight it sounded—off.

Tate hung out at the bar at Land's End, a darkly lit POS stuck mid-block between a used car dealership and a vacant lot full of weeds and trash. The name fit though. Land's End was the epitome of a dive, a real ass end if ever there was one.

He was not one of the drinking crowd. Never had a use for noisy drunks or people who frequented bars, but this was Mrs. Parrish's stomping-grounds, so there he was. The pistol he'd left in Ky's Corvette while on his 'date' was now holstered under his left arm, available and ready should trouble come calling, but concealed beneath a light jacket.

From the street, purple lights in squiggly neon announced this dive's foremost reputation as a strip joint. No surprise there, not with the two-legged crud bellied up to the bar with him. It wasn't so much a place to drink as a runway for the three trolls stalking under the spotlight in too much make-up, six-inch heels, and not much else. The strobe lights, mounted in a groove that ran down the center of the bar beneath them, blinked a harsh rhythm that accentuated their gyrations but cranked up the headache in Tate's skull.

Just as he'd kicked back his stool to leave, Janice, the perky blonde waitress with too much black eyeliner smudged on her eyelids, peered around his broad bicep. "Can I get you another drink, honey? Whatchu having? Another Corona?"

He hadn't noticed her husky smoker's voice when she'd hit him up for his first order. "I'm looking for Joyce. You seen her?"

Down came the brows as the shutters closed tight. "You a cop? A lawyer? Her ex?"

Joyce had an ex-husband? Interesting trivia.

Tate tipped back the last of his Corona and let the barmaid wait. That'd be the day he looked like an ex. At the last swallow, he swiped the back of his hand over his mouth and added a bite to his bark. "I was her damned daughter's prom date tonight. Just wanted Joyce to know I took Winslow home, safe and sound like I promised. Tucked her in myself."

That did the trick. Janice knuckle bumped Tate's bicep and all but gushed. "Well, look at you. What a gentleman. But no, Joyce and Ike left an hour ago. I won't see her until tomorrow night 'less something comes up."

"She didn't mention no Ike to me. What's he to her?"

Janice leaned her shoulder into his bicep, her fingers to her lips as if shielding her answer from prying eyes. "Pitt's the biggest loser on the street, but hey. Maybe he's got something in his pants she wants, you know what I mean?"

Tate let the innuendo slide, not interested in matching her lowbrow humor. "She comes here often?"

A vigorous head bob made all those blonde bangs bounce over Janice's over-tweezed brows. "Hell, she works here, and Ike's my best regular. He's here every afternoon and all Friday until closing time. You wanna enter the competition?"

Tate wasn't that kind of quick on the uptake. "For what?"

Hip bump, and damn, Janice could swing 'em. She about knocked Tate off his stool with that left hipster hook of hers. The woman would've been a looker if she'd hike that bustier up about three inches higher. Right then, she was giving Tate an eyeful of more than just her creamy flesh. He focused on the empty longneck in his hand. Women who threw themselves at men annoyed him, not that he had much experience. But a cat in heat was the same in any species.

"Why, the competition to be my best customer, what else?" she shouted over the opening blare of the band in the corner, a sad looking trio of lead and bass guitarists and one stoner who had a difficult time gripping his sticks. "I wouldn't mind getting to know you, big guy."

Big guy as in big stupid guy if you think I'm falling for that line. Tate laid a twenty flat to the bar and sealed it with the wet kiss of the bottom of his empty bottle. "Thanks. I'll do that." *As in never.*

He tipped two fingers to his forehead in a quick salute and left Land's End and Miss Janice's come-ons behind. Out on the sidewalk where the air was fresh, he dragged his cell out of his pocket and sent Winslow a quick text: *"U up?"*

When no reply came back, he hit remote unlock, and the Corvette blinked at him from the curb. Once in the driver's seat, he started her up and texted Winslow to call him. It'd be good to hear her sleepy voice while he pictured her snuggled with Pepe in her bed. But his other phone didn't answer. Winslow was probably asleep, which was just as good. She had to be exhausted, if only from all the fresh air she'd gotten.

Tate gunned the engine, slammed the shifter to drive, and peeled onto the street. As prone as he was to silence, he hated it now. Something was off in that little home on Maple Avenue.

Winslow swallowed hard, needing the retching in her stomach to cease. A woman could only take so many dry heaves, and she'd been heaving for hours. Her ribs and back ached. Her stomach. The worst medicine in the world was that brown gunk her mother mixed in the blender with bananas and rice water every day. If Winslow never saw another banana in her life, it'd be too soon.

Not like that mattered. She didn't have many days left. Still...

She'd like to live out what was left of them in semi-comfort. Not this.

Her mouth watered with the upcoming spew. Her throat twitched. Winslow swallowed hard, battling for control over her body's reflexes. Early morning. Every day. She heaved until she had no strength left to hang onto the toilet. Some days, her body's reaction to the chemo drugs gave her no choice but to lie down and accept the comfort of the tile floor. Cold sweats raked the back of her neck and sweat dripped down her spine. Death surely couldn't hurt worse than this.

Not certain if her stomach was finished torturing her, she crept up the counter to the sink and flipped the faucet handle to cold. Just one sip. That was all she dared take. If it stayed down, she might be done. If not...

Too shaky to hold the plastic glass that she kept by the sink for early mornings, she dragged her knees off the floor and hunkered her hips against the counter. That way, if she cocked her head, all she had to do was tip her mouth under the faucet. The cold trickle hit her lips in a splash that dribbled down her chin, but it was *oh, so, so good.* She sucked up another small swallow, but stopped at just the two. There was no sense downing what would only come back up if she drank too much too soon.

Nothing felt or tasted so good as that first drink of cold water after—*that.*

She let her weary body slide to the floor in a crumpled heap and turned her back to the cabinet, her sweaty hands in her lap, and a new day begun. Life sucked rocks. It truly did. Every day. It was hard to remember how happy she'd been up there on that tower last night, but she was, *was* being the key word. The word she'd been fated to live by. *Was...*

If only death would step on it and end this misery.

"Are you still in there?" her mother yelled from the hall.

You'd think the women would speak softly. Didn't she know vomiting induced awful headaches? She should. She'd had enough hangovers.

Winslow growled a pathetically breathy, "Yes," the best she could give after what her poor body had just been through. Where else would she be? It was morning, right? Wasn't this where she ended up every darned day at this time? *Why do you have to ask?*

But instead of voicing her frustrations to the woman who truly was doing all she could to help, Winslow lifted a shaky hand and erased the evidence of her body's harsh betrayal from her lips. She only wished she could hide the sour fragrance of *Eau de Vomit* in the air as easily.

When her mother didn't call out again, Winslow rasped louder, her voice thick with fear that any exertion might start the whole throwing-up-shebang all over again. "You can come in now."

Knock. Knock. Knock. Apparently her mother hadn't heard a thing she'd said, or she wasn't listening. *For heaven's sake, put your cell phone down and pay attention. I'm sick. I can't keep answering silly questions.*

At last the door opened wide, shoving Winslow's stocking feet out of the way. Mom stomped in, her hands on her hips, the cell phone still in her fingers. "Why didn't you answer me? Didn't you hear me call? I need to use the bathroom too, you know. You can't sit in here on your butt and tie it up all day."

Sitting on my butt? Yeah, that's me all right, just sitting around with nothing better to do than vomit my guts up. Winslow stabbed the heels of her hands into both eye sockets. She couldn't deal with her mother's drama. Not yet. Joyce made being violently ill sound like Trivial Pursuit.

Rolling to one hip, Winslow grabbed the edge of the counter with one hand, the toilet seat with the other. It took time and concentration to get on her feet as unsteady as her legs were, but she made it. Bile lifted up the back of her throat, but she forced it down like a trooper. A whimpering trooper. *Please. No more. Let me be done.*

Her mom was already leaning over the sink, primping in the mirror, spiking the tips of her already spiked hair. "Don't you just love this new cut? My girlfriend Janice styled it for me. She used a new kind of mousse. What do you think?"

I think I don't care. "Looks good, Mom. Real good," she murmured, but thought, '*Since I'm nearly spit-and-polish hairless. Thanks for nothing.*'

Afraid if she moved too quickly she'd hurl on her mother's shoes, Winslow made her way to her bedroom at the end of the hall, the single safe place in the house where Pepe, if he knew what was good for him, had better be hiding out. One good kick from her mother's pointy heels could hurt him. He might get rambunctious, but he needed to keep out of sight for a while.

Her mother slammed the bathroom door behind her, on the phone, still as self-absorbed and as clueless as ever. Winslow had come to terms with her mom's seeming lack of concern years ago. Nothing Joyce said could hurt her feelings anymore simply because that was what happened to people after they'd suffered through their loved one's long-term illness. They developed tough skins and callous points of view when they realized they were just as helpless. They pulled in their tender feelings and they built walls to protect themselves from the inevitable. If anyone understood walls, Winslow did.

Only now, in one short night, Tate had breached the wall she'd built. He'd climbed the castle tower of her heart (so to speak), and he'd even fought a dragon to get to her. Ha! Pepe a dragon? Hardly. But it fit the knight-in-shining armor dream she seemed caught up in.

The drunken stagger to her room took longer than usual. Winslow kept both eyes squeezed tight to block the gazillion megawatts of sunlight peeking through her sheer drapes. The wonky way her brain reeled after a bout of vomiting offered no clue as to that precise word. She used to know such things since she'd devoured any reading material she could get her hands on. Books were intimate friends that allowed escape from bitter reality.

This latest episode of nausea was the worst yet. When she'd first started this particularly nasty regiment of chemotherapy, she'd been sick, but nothing like this morning's bout. Her body felt burned to the core. She collapsed to her stomach, hoping to quell the nervous flutter that foretold more retching. At times like this, she knew she could never be an atheist. Prayer was her only refuge. *God, please no more. Make it stop. I promise, I'll be good.*

A sweet dog's nose snuffled at her sweaty neck before Pepe caressed her cheek with puppy kisses. Tugging him into her arm, Winslow stuffed her nose in the short fur on his hard little head. "I'm going to miss you in heaven, my baby Honey Munchkin. I love you so much," she told him from the depths of her dying heart. A tear trickled out of her eye. Just one.

That was all the moisture her body had left to spare.

Chapter Eleven

"What do you mean I can't see her?" Tate asked as politely as he could, his arms crossed over his chest, his feet spread at the barely cracked Parrish front door. Once more he'd left his pistol stowed in his vehicle out of respect. Aggravated, he couldn't get a decent look at Mrs. Parrish through that narrow view she maintained, much less a glimpse of Winslow or her dog. What now?

"You heard me," Joyce snapped. "Beat it before I call the cops, boy."

Where does she get off calling me boy? "The police? Seriously?" He rolled his neck, tired of arguing with this obstinate game player. It wasn't as if he'd come to steal Winslow away like that imaginary kidnapper last night. "All I want to do is see her, ma'am. I told her I'd be back today. Please let her know I'm here."

Joyce scraped those Halloween fingernails over her forehead like he was giving her a headache. Without offering further explanation, she closed the door another inch. "Thanks to you, she's been up sick all night, so no. You can't see her, and she wouldn't want you to see her the way she looks anyway. You have no idea what we've been through with this cancer or what you put her through yesterday. Get off my porch or so help me—"

That did it. "What I put her through? The prom was your idea Mrs. Parrish, not mine. I'm the one who found her after you called the television station and turned the night into a circus, remember?"

"Is that what she told you?"

Another poisonous glare flew down the hall, and damn. He shut his big mouth before he caused Winslow more problems. Her mom had a short, unpredictable fuse. "Listen. Please. I don't want to cause trouble, but I made her a promise last night, and I'm a man of my word."

He went for broke and lifted the red crystal vase filled with bright red Columbines from beside the front door where he'd hidden them. Flowers like these grew wild near his place in Alaska. The original plan was to surprise Winslow and take her for a ride. Get some fresh air. Maybe tell her what life was like for a kid growing up in the outlying reaches of the Yukon. Maybe get her to open up too, but now... "Here. I brought these for you."

Joyce blinked at the bouquet, then opened the door and did a quick grab-and-slam. There he stood with his mouth open, wondering what happened. She certainly moved fast when she wanted to.

Gulping down what was left of his pride along with his plans for the day, Tate was halfway to the sidewalk when Joyce called out behind him, "Five minutes. I'll give you five minutes. No more."

The door was now wide open. She stood with one hand on her hip, the other on the jamb, and the flowers nowhere in sight. Tate hightailed it back to the porch where he could see straight through to the kitchen and back door. He searched for one peek of Winslow, but no. The flowers sat in the center of the kitchen table though. How damned nice of him.

"Thank you, ma'am," he said politely, needing to stay on Joyce's good side.

That same musty whiff of antiseptic, garlic, and dog assailed his nostrils when she closed the door behind him. "Go on. You've already been in her room. You know where she is."

He felt the need to make it very clear that nothing improper took place the night before. "You need to understand that I've only been in your daughter's room twice and both times very briefly. Once when she first went missing. I checked for evidence of foul play, remember?" *While you faked being overwrought.* "Second, when we came back and found the front door locked." He didn't remind Joyce who'd locked Winslow out or who'd jumped to the conclusion she'd been kidnapped in the first place. That still bugged him. "I couldn't leave her, could I?"

He could almost hear the clank of hackles lifting off Mama Bear's back. "Are you saying I locked my own kid out of her house? Is that what she told you?"

Touchy, touchy. He raised both palms to placate Joyce. "No, ma'am, I'm just stating the facts as I saw them. The door was locked. I had to get Winslow in out of the cold, so I climbed through her window to unlock the front door. We waited for you to get home. End of story."

Her nostrils flared like no matter what he said, she wasn't going to believe him.

See, this crap right here was precisely why he'd spent most of his adult life avoiding people. Verbal communication, at its best, was a poor method of, well, communicating. People always jumped to conclusions. They looked for the worst in each other. They over-reacted or said what they thought you wanted to hear, or they outright lied to your face. A man had to be pretty damned astute to understand, much less process, what another guy meant instead of just what they said.

And then there were women... Talking with them was another language entirely. Using words to express what was on your mind sucked boulders, and no, the-more-words-the-merrier rule didn't apply with men or women. Who needed this bullshit merry-go-round?

"Four minutes," Joyce said slyly.

He flexed the growing aggravation off his shoulders with another, "Thank you, ma'am," then ducked down the hall.

The repugnant odor of sickness grew heavier with every step. Winslow's door wasn't closed, but there he stopped, one foot in the hall and the sweetest sight of her in her room. Dressed in shorts and a T-shirt, she'd crashed face down on her bed, her pillow clutched under her chin. A tall stack of books climbed up the corner between a messy closet and the window. The prom dress she disliked last night was now hung on a wire hangar in the door-less closet. Her crazy, furry boots stood at the bottom of her bed like sentinels waiting to run off on another risky adventure. The blankets were half on Winslow, leaving one leg extended, one delicate foot bare.

Pepe's tail started waggling the second he spotted Tate, but Winslow didn't budge. The scent of garlic and dog were stronger in her room. She must've been real sick.

Tate went swiftly to her side. A pink bandana covered her head, and it hit him. How could he have missed a detail so obvious? All that silky black hair was a disguise, a wig. He should've known, but he'd been distracted. Make that enamored. The tangled mass of hair she'd worn last night now rested on a Styrofoam head in her closet, alongside another of wavy reddish-brown.

Damn. Losing her hair must've been tough on Winslow. A guy wouldn't have minded as much, but women loved to fuss over their styles and gels and colors and such. Damn this cancer. It had stolen everything from Winslow, her self-esteem along with her health. Poor thing.

With one knee to the floor, he leaned in close and rested one palm gently to her forehead. If she woke, fine. He just needed to touch her, to be there with her for however much time Joyce allowed. His thumb swept over the bright flush on Winslow's cheek.

"I told you I'd come back," he whispered. "Check out your mom's flowers when you wake up, and you'll know I was here like I promised."

Her breath smelled strongly of garlic as if she'd eaten Italian for breakfast, maybe something with the herb in it, maybe to soothe her stomach? He remembered that much from his mom's homeopathic remedies. Crazy, beautiful Winslow was one sick lady.

When Pepe burrowed into the blanket nearest her and grumbled under his doggie breath, Tate knew damned well Joyce was standing behind him and watching. She couldn't give him one second of privacy.

He risked a glance over his shoulder. Sure enough. Joyce glowered from the open door. A thousand questions begged answers, and he would've preferred a rapid-fire situation report like he'd get from his men in the field, but he couldn't risk irritating this prickly mama bear.

"Is she sick often?" he asked quietly.

"Yeah, every morning when the sun comes up." Joyce lifted one hand to study her nails. "She gets a cramp and runs to the toilet and pukes her guts up for a couple hours. Then she crawls back to bed for half the day. Makes it real hard to get ready for work."

He pivoted on his knee to speak eye-to-eye. "What kind of cancer does she have, Joyce? How long are we talking, months? Years?" he asked softly.

Her shoulder shrug said nothing, but the unlit cigarette poking between the two fingers at her thigh did. She wanted a smoke break.

"This has to be hard on you," he offered sincerely. "I'm sorry."

"Yeah, well..." She looked over his head to the window. Tap, tap, tap went the filter end of that nicotine bullet on her thigh. "It'll all be over soon."

That was so not the sentiment he expected to hear from a loving mother. No tears. No hint of sorrow. Just cold facts delivered with a hard, black underscore. But that was cancer for you, and she'd been living this scenario for years, not him. What'd he know? Only that he wanted more time with Winslow. Another dance. Definitely a real date. "I'll stay with Winslow while you take a break. Me and Pepe will keep her company if you'd like."

Joyce flicked a pink Bic lighter up and lit the cancer stick, inhaling a long drag before she turned her head and aimed her second-hand-fumes down the hall. "That dog..." She turned and left with a grumbled, "Whatever. I'll be back."

Tate had the feeling she had more to say about Pepe, so he waited until he heard the back door open and close before he ruffled the stubby fur on the loyal guy's head. "You need to keep your nose out of her way, you hear? Mama Bear might eat you for breakfast."

Like a puppy, Pepe rolled to his back, all wiggles and grins.

Winslow stirred. "Mom?"

Tate leaned in close. "No, beautiful. Just me and your pet dragon."

Dreamy, tired eyes peered at him. "Oh, hi, ummm..." She stretched, upsetting Pepe, not that it bothered him. He just tucked his paws up under him as he resituated his bungalow in the blankets, content to stay beside his mistress.

Winslow's eyes widened. She swallowed noisily. Her brows pinched. "Tate? You're... here?"

He nodded. "I told you I'd be back."

"B-but..." One hand flew to the top of her head and the telling pink bandana. "You're... really, darn it, you're here. In my room." She didn't say that like it was a good thing, more like she meant to say, *oh shit*.

He smoothed a hand over her trembling fingers on her head. "There's no place else I'd rather be." Which was true. He felt better seeing her for himself, and knowing the truth about her lack of hair didn't hurt either of them. She was embarrassed. He got that, but she could get over that.

"Oh, God." She buried her face in her pillow. "Now you know. I'm hideous. My... my hair..."

"Will grow back," he finished tenderly. But didn't he put his size-eleven foot in his big mouth with that thoughtless stab at kindness? No, her hair wouldn't grow back. She was dying. She wouldn't have that kind of time. *Get with the program, Higgins.* "I'm so damned sorry, Winslow," he breathed, his chin to her arm. "I didn't mean to hurt you."

She sniffled, but turned her too big eyes to him. "It fell out months ago. I'm..." Monster tears welled up. "I'm not the person you thought you saw last night. I'm like that ugly dress. I'm... I'm bald."

He wanted to pull her into his arms and kiss her and tell her he didn't come there because of her hair, damn it. "Yes, you are, Winslow, but that gives me a reason to buy you a proper USMC beanie to wear." His heart swelled in his throat. He'd just met this gentle woman. He didn't want to have to say goodbye so soon.

She twisted out of her sheets and blanket to sit cross-legged on her bed. Swooping Pepe into her arms, she tucked him against her chest and planted a kiss on that dome between his ears. Swiping her fingers over her face, she asked, "You came to see me?"

Tate settled a hand on her knee. "Yes, ma'am, I did. It's sunny today. I hoped we could go for a ride or something, but you look like you need more rest."

She swallowed hard, rubbing her chin over Pepe's head. The silly guy had his eyes closed and a smile on his furry face. "It gets worse every day."

He believed her. The darker circles under her eyes declared it. "Are you thirsty? Hungry? Can I get you a glass of juice or something?"

Her head ducked into her shoulders drawing his attention to the hollows at her neck and collarbones. She was so thin. "I'm never going to know what champagne tastes like, am I?"

He hadn't seen that coming. "You want champagne instead of juice? I can do that." *If it makes you smile, I can do anything.*

"No, Tate." She reached one slender hand to his cheek, her palm sweaty. "I just want to live."

He wanted that for her too. He wanted her to dance on that water tower again. With him. But that wasn't what lay ahead for either of them, was it?

He summoned his inner *Iron Man* to the losing battle, needing the cocky guy's bullshit attitude to get through the death barreling down the road at them like an out of control eighteen-wheeler on black ice. Tate offered Winslow what he could, a breath of denial to soften reality. "If you're feeling better tomorrow, I'll come back and we'll go to a pub I know. It's not far. I'll order us a bottle of the best champagne in the house, and we'll toast to that little dragon at your side. How would that be? I hear champagne's supposed to tickle your nose."

Those sad green eyes widened under her pale thinning arch of brows. "You've never tasted it, either?"

"No," croaked out of him, a pathetic ache in that small word. He had a future full of champagne if he wanted it, but it wouldn't mean anything without Winslow at his side to enjoy those bubbles.

She looked to be on her deathbed, and he didn't want to let her go. He couldn't. She'd done something to him the second he'd spied her dancing on that tower with her arms opened wide to the sky. Why her? Why did she have to die? Why not some degenerate in prison who deserved the death penalty? Why not anyone not—her? "I've never done a lot of things." *But I want to now. With you.*

Tate gulped down a bitter dose of self-recrimination. Damn. He shouldn't have lingered on the water tower with her last night like he had. He shouldn't have kept her out in the cold. It was thoughtless and foolish, and yes, she hadn't wanted to go home, but he should've been smarter. Her condition today was his fault. He knew better. Yes, he'd given her his jacket, and he'd put her on his lap to keep her off the cold metal, but she was still dying right before his eyes.

"I'd like that," breathed out of her on a sigh. "It'd be nice to eat out once in my life. I could buy."

Another off-the-charts revelation. She'd never been to a restaurant? He didn't particularly like them, but he wanted to be the man who held her chair while she sat to dine at one of the finest D.C. had to offer. Maybe Old Ebbitt's or Hamilton's. "Why don't you let me worry about that? You just dress warm tomorrow morning and plan on enjoying yourself. I'll bring the Corvette." *Ky won't mind.*

"You seem to be taking care of me a lot since you and Pepe found me."

His heart caught in his throat. Could he tell her how much more he wanted to care for her? How much he liked her? Was that even the right word? It couldn't be love already, but something unique and wonderful had bubbled up from his stoic soul. Did he dare explore his feelings for this gentle spirit, the one fading before his eyes, any further?

Tate settled for, "There's nothing else I'd rather do."

Chapter Twelve

Tate stood with his back to Winslow facing the hall, his fists clenched and his shoulders heaving. Her mother wasn't happy, like that was a shocker. He hadn't said anything in his defense, and Winslow didn't dare. She had no comfort to give him, but this time, her mother was right. Winslow desperately needed rest, the penance she deserved for her foolish antics the day before.

Pepe snuggled under the blankets with her, but her heart broke for Tate. He didn't deserve the nightmare she was caught up in, and it hurt to see how broken up he was. Her mother was making it worse, chewing him out, when it was obvious his heart was breaking.

Winslow wanted him back at her side where she could get her hands on him, where she could lie and tell him everything would be okay even though they both knew it wouldn't. Where she could kiss him. It seemed unreal how much she'd grown to care for him in less than a day. They'd only just met. They didn't know each other, and yet—they did. Her spirit had recognized his the moment he'd reached for her on that tower. They were two old spirits lost in the stars, now found.

It felt like one of those nick-of-time stories, only it wasn't, was it? More like *'too little, too late.'* She winced at the awful truth. She needed more minutes and hours. More days!

"I told you five minutes, but did you listen? No, and now look at her," her mother hissed, pointing at Winslow who actually felt better since Tate arrived. "I take a simple smoke break and she looks like death-warmed-over when I get back. What'd you do to her now?"

Death-warmed-over? Great, Mom. Boost my spirits why don'tcha?

"I'm sorry." His voice cracked, and Winslow was desperate to intervene. He had nothing to be sorry about. They hadn't had time to do anything. Geez!

"It's okay, Mom. We were just talking."

But Mom was on a roll. "You stay out of this. It's time you left, Agent Higgins. I'm calling your boss as soon as his office opens Monday. Rest assured. He'll hear about this and heads will roll." She always went for the dramatic. Who'd she think she was, Marie Antoinette?

Tate dipped two fingers into his shirt pocket and brought forth a business card. "Be my guest. His name's Director Tucker Chase. Here's his number."

She snapped it out of his fingers without reading it, her eyes flashing. "Get. Out."

Tate's gaze collided with Winslow's. "After I say goodbye."

"Oh, no, you don't. I said—"

"Mom! What is wrong with you? It's just goodbye. Leave him alone."

Joyce shot Winslow the nastiest glare. "Fine, but I'm not leaving. Make it quick. You're on my time now." Her toes began tapping.

Winslow swallowed hard. *Why did she have to make everything so difficult?*

Tate turned those broad shoulders of his and came back to the bed. This time he sat at the edge as he ran a quick hand over Pepe's head peeking out from the blankets. He was like that, considerate of the tiniest guy in the room, and Winslow could tell Pepe liked him for it. Heck, she liked him for it.

"I will come visit you," he said with conviction. "Don't go anywhere."

She wanted to smile and laugh and be coy and say, *'Ha. Where would someone like me go, to the Bahamas?'* Only no part of this conversation was lighthearted or funny, and what he'd meant to say was, *"Please don't die on me while I'm gone."* She could read the despair in his eyes, but she couldn't promise him that, could she?

Yesterday's slice of seemingly good health was a generous gift from the universe, a fluke that might never happen again. Death was her constant companion. Not the stars. Not luck. And now, not Tate. This life was just a dream, and a short, bleak one at that.

A sob choked out of her before she could call it back. She blinked, her eyes misted with regret. This could very well be the last time she saw Tate and the thought of him leaving was killing her.

He blinked hard, those tender lips of his pressed thin and tight, his eyes black. That was Tate. Angry once more. It seemed a natural part of him, as if he dwelled in a perpetual shadow. As if it ruled him.

"I've fallen in love with you, Tate," she whispered, meaning it with all her heart.

He shook his head. "Don't say that. You don't even know me. It's too soon."

She cupped his jaw, relishing the scrape of his shaven skin in her palm, loving the brisk scent of him. She'd never look at another pine tree the same. Like there was time to see another pine tree. Yeah. This was the hardest thing she'd ever done: *Find the one guy who looked at her with more than pity. Lose him a day later.* "I know enough. You fought a dragon for me. You're my Prince Charming."

He blinked furiously, to no avail. Prince Charming rescued his princess, something Tate wouldn't be able to do. Not with cancer to fight instead of a dragon or an evil stepmother. A single diamond tear rolled down the side of his nose before he brushed it manfully away. "Champagne," he said, his voice tight. "I owe you your first sip of champagne, and I intend to deliver."

She nodded. "Yes. Champagne. Maybe chocolate covered strawberries too."

That broke the tension, but then he stood, and he was leaving, and her frightened heart clamored up high in her chest. "Don't go!" blurted of her mouth. Winslow sobbed. Just once. Saying goodbye was so hard. Too hard. "Please, Tate. Don't go. Don't leave me. Mom, make him stay. I don't want him to go yet. I..." *I love him and I need him and if he leaves I'm afraid I'll die today.*

Her mother didn't offer any kind words, but he sat back down at her side again, the tenderest light on his face as the mattress squeaked beneath him. He brushed her tears away with his thumb, his body blocking her mother's view. "Hey, you, listen up," he murmured confidentially. "I told you I'd be back, Winslow, and I will. I don't make promises I don't intend to keep. You rest now, and trust me to do what's best for you, okay?"

She felt like a little girl being tucked in bed for the night and promised a treat if she'd be good and go to sleep. The man had mad skills. It worked. She gave him all she truly had to give, her heart and her soul and every lost wish on a star. "I do love you, Tate. Believe it or not, I know I do, and I promise I'll be here. I will." *I won't die. I'll wait for you.*

He leaned in closer. "I believe you, Winslow, and..." He closed the deal with a warm, wet kiss that darn near incinerated her. She lifted her fingers to the nape of his neck and held on tight, holding her one light in the darkness while the rest of her world fell apart. If cancer was bad, letting go of this man was worse. A thousand times worse. This was goodbye.

Of course, good old Mom made one of those rude, grating grunts that echoed through time and eternity like fingernails on a dry chalkboard. Tate swept his tongue over Winslow's lips one last time before he eased back and let her go.

She tried to be brave. He patted Pepe's butt and stood, his back straight and his shoulders squared. He made a handsome sight facing her mother like he was, like he could take on her and the world. He stuck one hand out to Joyce like a gentleman. "Thank you for letting me visit your daughter, Mrs. Parrish. I'll see you tomorrow."

Mom had the nerve to wrinkle her nose at him like he was beneath her instead of shaking his hand like a lady. She jerked her head toward the front door. "We'll see about that."

With his gut screaming to run back to Winslow, Tate forced his feet to the ride he loved, his Jeep, a restored 1948 Willey's four banger with a better than decent layer of Clear Coat over the gloss black paint job. Four bald eagle decals posted each corner like sentinels, and an American flag graced the entire back window, its colors unfurled. Read 'em and weep, my fellow Americans. This man was a Marine come hell or high water or war, but at that precise moment, he couldn't have cared less about his ride or his allegiance. Something rare and damned painful was happening. His son-of-a-bitchin' heart was breaking over a woman he'd just met.

It made no sense. How had he gotten in so deep with Winslow? Why her? Why now? It hadn't yet been twenty-four-hours, and the callused heart he'd brought to the game had all but cracked like an egg on the edge of a sizzling hot griddle.

He placed both palms on that glossy hood, fighting for composure. Ky's garage queen, the Corvette, was back in its stall on a patch of USMC navy-blue carpet Ky had actually spent good money on. But Tate had bigger problems this Saturday morning. Not only was he leaving Winslow behind, which was killing him, but he had a mission at the crack of dawn Monday that would take him to the southern tip of California. That left him the rest of today and Sunday—if he could get back into that house to see her.

He glared over his shoulder at the Parrish home. How could he go? But how could he stay? He slammed his ass into his ride, his gut screaming to march back in there and steal Winslow away for that flute of champagne. Instead, he tucked his dark glasses on and turned the ignition, his heart torn between helping Winslow deal with her last days on earth and his job. At least Winslow had his phone. She might be sleeping already, but he couldn't wait.

Tate sent her a quick text, just three happy faces. That was all. Women liked emojis, didn't they? He hoped she did.

No answer.

His fingertips commenced a nervous drum roll on his thigh. *Damn. Damn. Damn.* This would've been a good day for a ride. Last night's storm had blown through, the sun was high and the weather was warm. She would've enjoyed the change of scenery, especially the autumn colors splashed along the Potomac, turning it into a river of golds and bronzes, yellows and reds.

But now...

He sent a thumbs-up emoji to let her know all was good, that he was thinking about her. She hadn't seemed too savvy with all the digital toys on the market, but surely she'd get the drift when she received the notification and read the screen. He just wanted to assure her all was well. Sometimes that single gesture after an emotional breakdown made the world right.

Not today.

Still no answer. He didn't dare sit outside the Parrish home too long, but he couldn't make himself leave, either. He stalled until he had no choice. He had a rented tux on his back seat to return. Setting his volume high in case Winslow texted, Tate glanced in his rearview before he gave up and pulled into traffic. He could make it to the wedding rental shop and back before noon. No problem. If only his gut believed that line.

Heading southward, he turned the radio to his favorite sports station. The Chicago Cubs were playing the Cleveland Indians. Top of the seventh. The score was three to six. *Go Cubs.*

But he couldn't concentrate. Joyce's power trip had taken a scary turn. She'd gone from flirty and downright suggestive yesterday evening to nasty this morning, and he had yet to understand what he'd done that triggered it. The woman should've been relieved last night when her daughter was safely home, yet that was when the accusations started. Was she jealous of Winslow?

Maybe, but that didn't explain her refusal to let him visit today. No, Joyce was already angry when he'd shown up, but again, he couldn't put his finger on any concrete explanation. He hated to think it, but could Joyce be cracking from the strain of being Winslow's sole care provider? It happened. Family members were often emotionally and physically drained by the time cancer took its toll.

Still...

Something in that house didn't add up.

His cell chimed a text alert. Winslow. About time. Tate eased his Jeep into the nearest parking lot and killed the engine before he read what she'd written.

No emojis, just complete sentences. Okay, noted. Drop the cutesy crap. She preferred real conversation, but—

He dropped his sunglasses to the tip of his nose to read. This was no reply to his text, it was a call for help. A digital scream. *I can't find Pepe. Anywhere!*

Tate dialed his old phone. A sobbing Winslow answered. "She took him, Tate. I know she did. She's gone and she hates my dog and she took him and—"

"Who? Your mother?" He needed to be sure.

"Ah-huh. I heard the car and by the time I got to the front door, Pepe was gone, and I'll never see him again, and he's... he's..."

Tate closed his eyes, the image of Winslow sobbing tore at his heart. "I'll find him. Trust me. I'll find him."

"B-but how? W-what if she... k-kills him?" Winslow melted, crying so hard he couldn't get a word in.

"She wouldn't do that." *Would she?* Still Winslow wept, and he wished he were back with her. He tried again. "Come on, your mom knows you love him. She probably just..." What? Took the little guy for a haircut? A spin in her car? A walk? Not hardly.

Tate sucked down the dread bubbling up in his soul. If Joyce didn't return home with that little dog, she'd break Winslow's heart. There was only one thing he could do. The tux could wait.

"Hang on," he declared. "I'll be right there."

Chapter Thirteen

By the time she heard Tate pull up to the curb, Winslow could barely breathe. Her baby was gone and her mom hadn't returned yet. Winslow already knew it wouldn't make any difference when she did, not whether she cried or begged or swore or railed, either. Pepe wouldn't be coming home.

Mom had done the same thing with a stray cat that Winslow had gotten attached to. *Not fair!* The second she gave her heart away, her mother spoiled everything. Winslow sank to her knees, desperately tired of fighting the world. *Why's Mom doing this?*

Tate stormed through the front door she'd left open for him. "Where is she?" he asked, his eyes as black as sin. "Do you know? When did she leave?"

"Right after you. Tate... I didn't even get to tell him goodbye, and he'll be scared, and... and..." She covered her mouth and choked, the thought of her sweet boy in some dark, unfriendly place, scared and shivering, was more than she could bear.

Tate put his arms around her, one hand on her stupid bandana as he tucked her under his chin. "Shh. We'll figure this out together." He swallowed so hard she could hear his throat muscles working.

"How?" She wanted to believe, but this was the last straw. The one bright spot in her life was lost to her, stolen at the worst possible time. She buried her nose in Tate's shirt, lost and scared and so damned mad. "I hate my mom. I really do."

Tate didn't argue. He didn't patronize or offer useless words either, just pressed his chin to the top of her head and let her cry. At last, she gulped back the deluge and took a deep breath. "Why is she doing this to me? I don't understand her any more. It's like she's mad at me all the time."

Winslow lifted her chin and met Tate's gaze. His eyes were beyond black. More like molten obsidian. A fire had been lit in those smoky depths. "She wouldn't be doing this just to get back at you, would she? To prove a point?"

"No, Mom's not like that. She's... she's..." *Only she was precisely like that.* "She used to be kind, Tate. She used to be nice." *She used to be a lot of things.*

The sound of a car in the driveway ended Winslow's rationalizations. "Mom's home. Let me go." She couldn't be seen in his arms, not after the trouble she'd caused last night or this morning. Winslow stood on her own two feet, shaky but as fierce as she could manage. The minute the front door opened, she asked, "Where's my dog? Where'd you take Pepe?"

Mom looked at her with that innocent 'Who me?' expression, the one she used every time Winslow caught her in a lie. "Why, Princess, I—"

"Don't Princess me, Mom. Where's my dog? Where's Pepe?"

Tate stood at her side, his hand cupping her shoulder. Lending her strength.

Her mother's eyes swept over him, taking it all in, right before they arrowed back to Winslow. "Don't talk to me like that just because *he's* here." She directed her pointy chin at Tate. "I told you to get lost, flyboy."

"Mom," Winslow raised her voice. "This isn't about Tate. Where's Pepe? What'd you do to him?"

She knew what was coming the moment her mother cocked her head in that coy way she had when she wanted her way. "Winslow, I did what's best for you. I took him to the pound. I know this is hard to understand, but he's too much work for you, baby, and look at you. You're worn out and you're sick every day now. It's time to let go. Stop trying so hard to be something you're never going to be. You can't hold onto him forever, can you? Besides, it will break my heart to see him trotting around here after you're gone, you know it will."

Winslow ground her teeth, she was so mad. "You had no right!"

And the gloves came off. Joyce tossed her head and every one of those studs in her ear flashed. "I have every right. Who pays the bills around here? Who feeds that measly mutt while you're lying on the bathroom floor throwing up every morning? Who cleans up after him and you every single goddamned day? I'll tell you who, I do! Just me! So don't think for one second that you can tell me what I can and can't do!"

"But Mom, I've always taken good care of Pep..."

"But Mom nothing!" By now her mother was eye to eye with Winslow, and Winslow knew the war was lost. She should've spoken softer. She should have coaxed and wheedled, not confronted. Most of all, she never should have yelled at Joyce in front of Tate. She'd embarrassed her mom in front of a stranger, *not good*.

Winslow bowed her head to hide her tears and her defeat. Once more, she'd lost. She wasn't strong enough to fight her mom. Never would be. "It would've been nice if you'd at least told me what you were doing," she said, her soul beaten to a pulp. This fight wasn't just about Pepe. It was about Tate and cancer and her mom's father and all the wrongs ever committed against Joyce Parrish since the dawn of time. "I just wanted to tell him g-goodbye."

"You've only been gone an hour, Joyce," Tate growled, his fingers digging into Winslow's shoulder, reminding her he was still there. But he shouldn't have been. That was the problem, him watching the fight.

Winslow turned to tell him not to engage, that it was useless, but he wasn't looking at her. His chin was set in a hard angle and sparks flashed from his eyes to her mother. She had to stop him before he said anything else. "It's okay, Tate, I—"

"Shut up, Winslow. It's not okay and you damned well know it. No parent treats their kid like this."

Winslow cringed. She wasn't up to a prolonged battle on two fronts, not the way her broken heart felt. All she could see was her poor Pepe sitting behind the rusty bars of a concrete cell somewhere, quivering, alone, and scared of the other dogs because they were all bigger and meaner than him, and... and... *He won't last a day.* A sob choked out of her. She wiped a hand over her eyes. *My poor Honey Munchkin. This is all my fault. I never should've loved you. What good did it do you?*

Tate took a step around her, standing between her and her mom, his hand on Winslow's forearm.

"What's it to you, Agent Higgins?" Joyce asked, her anger replaced with a haughty tone. "You're nobody, just some guy I hired to take her on a date. You couldn't even handle that, could you?"

"What's it to you?" he shot back at her. "And where have you been? I've only been gone an hour and you left the minute after I did. That gave you a half-hour to drive somewhere and a half hour to get back. Cut that by the twenty minutes it took you to do whatever you did to the dog, and you didn't go very far from home, did you? Wherever you dropped Pepe has to be close."

He raised his index finger to the ceiling. "The pounds are closed weekends, so that was your first lie. Today. The Potomac's too far and the traffic's too busy to get there and back in an hour, so the river's out. If you dropped him in Sligo Creek, someone had to have seen you. There are too many homes and families up and down that riverbank for something so cruel as drowning an animal to go unnoticed. Some kid might've rescued him and called animal services by now, for all you know. Whatever you did to him, I will find out." Tate took a step into her comfort zone. "And if you've hurt him..."

Winslow couldn't breathe. There wasn't enough air in the whole house. Her heart stalled. He'd just called her mother out. The room tilted and her heart stopped beating, but wow. This man was a magnificent beast all unto himself. Protective of a Chihuahua. Standing tall and brave. Fierce. She'd never had anyone fight for her and Pepe the way Tate just did.

Her mother sniffed. "You don't scare me, Agent Higgins, so back off. I only have my daughter's best interests at heart, but you..." Her nose wrinkled again. "You're just *some guy*." She smirked at Winslow as if she had nothing to worry about. Slapping the front door shut, she strolled down the hall. At her bedroom door, she turned around. "I'm calling the police, Higgins. Want to bet who wins this fight, big shot?"

Her shoulders sagging in defeat, Winslow watched her go. "She'll do it, you know. She'll call the police and—"

Tate whirled on her. "Bullshit! What the hell's wrong with you? Can't you see she's manipulating you? Shit, Winslow..." His eyes were black, his brows slanted over a dark, scary countenance. He stabbed a finger at her. "You love that little dog, I know you do, but the minute your mom shits all over you, you lay down and take it. What the fuck is wrong with you? Stand up for yourself! Fight for what you believe in. Stop kissing her ass!"

Winslow couldn't do anything but stare, her defenses melted under the heat of his blast. The fight went out of her. She sank to her knees. "But I... I..." *I what? I am too weak? I am dying? I'm afraid of my mom? Well, yeah. I need her. She's all I've got.*

Tate jerked her off the floor and into his arms, his hot breath in her neck as he settled on the couch with her. "I'm sorry. God, I'm sorry. You're sick and you didn't deserve that."

Breathing hard, she rested a hand to his heaving chest. She didn't know what to say. He was right, in a way. She was sick, but she'd honestly never thought about standing up to her mother because, well, she *was* weak and dying, and her mother was the only one there to care for her. What he said made sense. Her mother was out of control and cruel and... Darn.

Winslow had never strayed outside of her mother's influence except for those few getaways to the tower. She didn't know where or how to begin standing up for herself. She wasn't that kind of a daughter, and Joyce certainly wasn't that kind of mother.

Tate tipped back into the couch to look at Winslow. "Will you be okay until I get back?"

She nodded, her nose dripping, but so what? Tate had seen her at her worst. "Where are you going?"

"To find Pepe." He cupped her jaw between his thumb and forefinger. "You still have my spare phone, right?"

"I do."

"Keep it with you, even if you have to tuck it inside your bra or under your belt to keep it hidden from your mother." He glanced down the hall. "Don't let her know you have it, and don't go anywhere without it, do you hear?"

"Yes, but how will you find him? Where will you look?" She sucked back the hopelessness of the day. "He could be anywhere."

Tate's lips pressed into a thin line. "I honestly don't know, but I've got friends. They'll help me."

"I should come with you."

He tipped his forehead to hers, his hands soft and gentle on her cheeks. "I wish you could, but you're sick, Winslow. Stay here and try to get some rest. Wait for my call. I *will* bring Pepe home to you."

He sounded so sure. She let her fingers run up his chest, wishing he were already back and Pepe was safe. "Thank you, Tate."

He pulled her under his chin, and for that one moment, Winslow believed.

Damn Joyce Parrish! Anger ran straight down his leg to the Jeep's accelerator as Tate sped down Maple to Dameron. What kind of mom dumped the family pet when her daughter most needed the comfort of her furry friend? Why couldn't she wait until Winslow's time was done? Why now?

He wrenched the wheel, wishing it was Joyce's self-righteous neck in his grip instead. The problem with rage was it consumed every last brain byte, and he didn't have the luxury of wasting time with the lack of self control. Not with Winslow's life so close to ending, maybe Pepe's now too. He hadn't meant to let his temper get the best of him, but damn it to hell! Joyce was a bitch for what she'd done.

Tate ran a quick hand over his head from front to back, needing the rush of blood under his scalp to clear his mind. He could count on Ky Winchester to help. Eden too. Maybe some of the guys from The TEAM. Maybe not. Where does a man start searching for a two-pound dog in a twenty-mile radius? Joyce couldn't have gone much farther than that.

He sucked in another deep breath to get his mind back to zero. He had to think. This was Joyce Parrish he was talking about. Sneaky. Mean spirited. But not the brightest. What would a woman like her do with a dog she wanted to make disappear? The city pound was closed weekends, and he'd bet any no-kill shelters were closed too. That left what? Pet shops? The rivers? The freeway? A bridge? He wouldn't put it past Joyce to stuff the little guy in a bag and drown him. She was the type, but could she be that cruel to her daughter?

Tate knew damned well Joyce was that cruel. He wasn't so sure she'd do her own dirty work though, not as pristine as her jeans and T-shirt were when she'd waltzed through her front door.

Sligo Creek seemed the closest bet, but he didn't bank on it. With his cell in his hand, he parked south of Maple on Dameron, scrambled out of the Jeep and took off jogging east, watching and listening for the yap of the fierce little dragon that loved Winslow.

Tate had one person he knew he could always call. He thumb-dialed his buddy's number as he ran. Ky answered with, "What's up?"

"I need a peek at every home security or traffic cam within a ten mile radius of 212 Maple Avenue in Silver Spring, and I need it now. Can you do it?"

"I'm right in the middle of something, but, yeah. Eden will understand if I don't hang this chandelier today. Hang on."

Tate cocked his head at the sound of a dog barking nearby. False alarm. Pepe's shrill voice couldn't compare to the baritone woof of that Rottie straining at the end of his fifty-foot leash. No way.

He listened as Ky thumped his phone and called Eden to 'hurry quick.' She was the golden goose in the FBI's latest, greatest unit. A true psychic. Nothing like Tate. But they were talking about Joyce, the woman who'd claimed she worked as a beautician while she actually chased tips at a sleazy strip joint. Where did her buddy Ike Pitt live? Or her girlfriend, Janice? What were the odds…?

Tate could've sworn he heard Pepe whine, only he didn't. But maybe he did have an affinity for animals, with this particular two-pound dragon anyway. Tate opted for a quick, look-see at Land's End over dredging Sligo Creek or waiting on Ky and Eden. He hung up on his buddy and stuffed his cell back in his pocket. Ky'd understand, and if he didn't, he'd call back.

The Jeep got Tate to Land's End in less than ten minutes, right inside the window of Joyce's quick errand. He went in armed, his leather jacket concealing his firepower.

Janice looked up in surprise from the table she was serving. "Hey, big guy. You miss me?"

He slowed his momentum, scanning the empty dark dance floor for trouble. "Looking for Joyce. You seen her this morning?"

Janice rolled her eyes toward the back room. "You just missed her, why? Does this have to do with Winnie again?"

"Winslow's sick." That wasn't exactly a lie. "She needs her mom." *And her dog, damn it.*

Of all things, some tattooed slime ball with a six-inch purple Mohawk sticking up off his bald head, peeked out of that backroom, and wouldn't you know. Ike Pitt had a pet carrier in his right hand, one of those cloth carriers that looked like a big purse, ahem, a *man bag*. Pepe had damned well better be in that bag.

The little guy must've sensed Tate. His excited yelp cinched the deal. Tate left Janice cold and headed for Ike, counting the ways to dropkick that POS.

Ike finally looked up and caught sight of him. He stopped dead in his tracks, bug-eyed, his mouth hanging open. Like a chicken-shit bastard, he yelled, "Fire!" and dodged out the door behind him while the few patrons in the bar jumped to their feet and headed for the front door.

Tate palmed his pistol as he pushed off his feet, ready to crack any heads that got in his way. Ike was fast. Tate was faster. Smarter. Ike made the exit in record time, but Tate was in good shape. He easily closed the distance between him and the ass-end of Ike once they were in the alley.

Risking a panicked glance over his shoulder, Ike caught sight of Tate's weapon. With a shrill, "Don't shoot!" he tossed the man bag at the open dumpster on his way past, missing it, but hitting the brick wall behind it. Damn him. Tate opted to rescue Winslow's baby and let Ike run. He'd barely holstered his piece and tugged the strap of that man purse, when...

BOOM! His body trapezed end-over-end to the pavement.

Winslow's stomach lurched, and down she went to her hands and knees, facing linoleum once more. The kitchen spun and she seriously considered lying flat on her stomach to make the nauseous joyride stop. But wow. This attack came on fast. "Mom," she called out before the walls caved in. They ducked and bobbed like they could do exactly that.

No answer.

Just great. When I need you the most, you're pouting.

Her gut twisted in agony. "M-mom," Winslow tried again, the floor dipping up and down, side to side, making her seasick. Only this wasn't a boat. This was the end.

Chapter Fourteen

Some asshole just shot me! Where the hell is he?

With his pistol in hand, Tate gritted his teeth and dragged his ass off the pavement, keeping an eye out for the chicken-shit who'd shot him in the back. Or who'd tried. Tate planted his back flat to the wall beside the dumpster, sweat dripping in his eyes and his heart pounding. He slapped a palm over his bloody bicep to slow the flow. Whoever'd just taken that shot hadn't hung around to make sure he was dead. Their mistake.

Couldn't have been Ike. He'd been running in the opposite direction, and he hadn't looked back once he'd dumped the man bag. Could've been Janice. If so, she was a pretty fair shooter. She'd hit Tate's arm high, nearly at his shoulder. Nothing serious, but the bloody flesh wound burned like a bitch.

Adrenaline jackhammered his legs to the pavement while Tate dragged his blowout kit up and out of his pocket with his good hand, his weapon still ready in the other. His head pounded with the impact of meeting asphalt after that hit. It hurt worse than his arm.

Blood dripped off his elbow, and his vision went wonky, but he hung tight. Shaky, but tight. He peeled the sterile wrap off a pressure bandage with his teeth, then he tore his shirt sleeve and slapped the bandage to his upper arm before he passed out. This was nothing new, but no Marine faints in the line of duty. They might die, but they didn't pass out.

Most of the time.

Shaking like a frickin' wuss, he blinked, his focus fluctuating like someone was playing with the on/off switch in his head. A smart Marine never left home without his trauma kit, a lesson drilled into new recruits during basic training, but damn. Either no one had heard that gunshot or he was in no man's land. No one was coming to his aid.

He shook his head to clear the buzz, his senses on high alert. Poor Pepe. He hadn't made a peep since he'd hit that wall. The man purse, now on its side, wasn't moving. *This will kill Winslow.*

Tate kept his head low as he crab-walked sideways to where he hoped that little soldier waited. Winslow didn't need another POS nightmare to deal with. Righting the padded dog carrier, he breathed a gutful of relief. Pepe was shaken, not stirred. Not dead.

But he wasn't his jovial self either. *Shit. He's hurt.*

"Hey guy," was all Tate had to say to get a tail wag and an urgent whine. He took no chances. Pepe was hurt, but Tate needed to make sure they both lived through the day. With his gun leading the way, Tate pushed to his feet. He tugged the man bag's strap over his head and hoofed it out of the alley with Pepe snug at his side.

Safe in his rig out front of Land's End, Tate set his weapon on the console and called Ky while he scooped Pepe onto his lap. The poor little guy jitterbugged like an addict needing a fix until Tate tucked him under his chin and drove one-handed from the bar. Not easy when a guy was dealing with his own dose of rage.

"I'm in trouble," Tate ground out when Ky picked up. "Need you at 212 Maple Ave. Possible endangered adult, Winslow Parrish. Watch out for her mother."

"On it," Ky responded. "You hurt?"

Tate hung up instead of wasting time explaining. He needed to be in two places, but Pepe needed a vet. The next call went to Harley Mortimer, another one of Stewart's finest and possibly the best K-9 handler on the East Coast.

Harley picked up on the first ring. "Whazzup, Tate?"

He hated to crush that lazy, Saturday morning drawl Harley had going. "I need a good vet in Silver Spring. Quick. You know one?"

The drawl evaporated. "Why? Who's hurt? What kind of dog?"

"A Chihuahua." Tate gritted his teeth. Pepe's whining had turned pathetically sad. If that bastard Ike had seriously injured this little kid...

"I'm just across the river. Meet me in Georgetown in fifteen, at..."

Tate only half heard the address. Winslow's dog had just gone limp. "I need you here now!" He stuck his phone into the crook of his neck while he pulled over. "I can't lose this dog!"

"On my way," and Harley was gone.

Tate shoved his Jeep into park, determined this fierce little dragon wouldn't die. Pushing his seat back, he stretched Pepe on his lap between his thighs. There was no bleeding. No broken bones. No bumps on his head, and honest to God, Tate hadn't a clue what else to look for. Hunched over Pepe, he stared at the dog's chest, watching it lift with each breath. Each shallow breath. Until it stopped.

No! With blurry eyes, Tate lifted that tiny soldier's face to his mouth and did what any brother would do for another. He blocked Pepe's nose holes and pressed his mouth to the dog's mouth. Crap. That didn't work. Pepe's mouth was too long.

Tate wiped his lips and tried once more. Circling Pepe's snout with his thumb and index finger this time, he sealed the dog's lips and carefully administered mouth to mouth. That went better.

With each gentle puff, he checked quickly to see if Pepe's chest moved.

Nothing. Start over. This was a fragile little animal. If that fall hadn't hurt his brain, oxygen deprivation would. Anxiety clawed up Tate's spine. One too-big puff of air could kill Pepe. The clock was ticking.

Another round of *'breathe and pray'*, but this time the air hissed out of Pepe's lips. The seal wasn't tight enough. With every failed attempt, Winslow's sad eyes stared back at Tate from the rearview mirror.

Live, Pepe. Damn it, live!

Tires screeched at the rear of the Jeep, and all at once, Harley was in the passenger seat, stuffing his lanky frame nearly onto Tate's lap. "Let me take him," he ordered, one hand under Pepe's head, his arm bracing the rest of the dog's floppy body.

His wife, Judy, had a mat rolled out on the sidewalk outside Tate's ride. Tate joined the Mortimers on his knees, ready to do whatever they needed, pathetic uselessness choking his gut. "I didn't know you were a vet." *Please be the kind who works miracles.*

"VA," Harley shot back at him as he laid the little guy on his back, his long slender fingers moving expertly over Pepe's ribcage. The dog's tongue lolled from between his slack jaws, not a good sign.

"Veterinarian assistant," Judy interpreted. "He's back in night school." Dressed in black business slacks and a crisp white button-down blouse, she looked as if she'd been somewhere important. Tate didn't ask where. He didn't care.

Harley seemed to have forgotten he had company. Hunched over Pepe with his nose nearly on the dog's stomach, he placed Pepe on his side and lifted one furry arm at a ninety-degree angle. Harley cocked his head, listening for what Tate didn't know. Maybe a heartbeat? A breath?

"Sometimes..." Harley let that word hang as his fingertips began a slow massage high on Pepe's ribs close to the little guy's armpit. Harley pressed in rapid compress-release bursts. It took less than a minute of canine life-saving know-how until Pepe's legs stiffened like short fence posts. He sneezed and snorted and sneezed again and...

"Sometimes, a little guy just needs a big guy's helping hand, don't you?" Harley murmured.

Tate wiped his eyes before Harley could see what a mess he was. But this was Pepe, Winslow's one and only bright light. She needed this little trooper in her life for what was still to come.

When Harley lifted his head and Tate got a good look at the twinkle in those hazel eyes—

Best day ever.

"You saved him," he said lamely, blinking like crazy.

"No, you saved him," Harley corrected. "I couldn't have found you if you hadn't left your phone on so I could track you."

I did? Tate couldn't remember where his phone had gone flying.

"You want to tell me what happened?"

Tate placed a hand on Pepe's hard little head while they both recuperated. "His name's Pepe. He's my client's dog. Winslow Parrish. Her mother, Joyce..." He dragged a shaky hand through his hair and started over. "My client's Winslow Parrish. I was supposed to escort her to her first prom last night. You know the deal. It was a Dreams-Come-True prom thing, only she's got a seriously whacked-out mother, Joyce. The prom was a farce. Winslow took off last night, then her mother dumped her dog this morning, and I... I left Winslow to find him. I promised I'd bring him back alive."

"That whacked-out mom wouldn't be why you're sporting a bloody shirt?" Judy spiked a brow at his bicep.

Oh, that. There was no sense going all John Cena with Judy. She was a top-notch ER nurse who'd seen enough alpha males in her career to know better than to accept the standard, 'I'm good,' for an answer.

"Step into my office," she said as she pushed up from the sidewalk and nodded toward the fire-engine-red Jeep on Tate's rear bumper. "I keep a first aid kit in the back seat. Let me take a look at that."

"No," Tate answered. "Ky's on his way to Winslow's house and I need to meet him." *And I'm as good as I'll ever be.*

Judy winked. "If you say so."

Harley wrapped the shivering dog inside a plush towel Tate hadn't noticed until then. "I'll take this little critter home with me for observation. Pepe, you said?"

Tate curled his fingers under the dog's chin to steady the shivering little dragon. He didn't look so fierce at the moment, more like he'd had his ass whipped. "Yeah. Pepe. How you doing, tough guy?"

Pepe closed his eyes and the shivering ceased. His tongue darted out, nailing Tate's thumb with a quick puppy-kiss before he wriggled to get out of Harley's grip.

"No, you stay right where you are. Harley's the man." If that didn't make Tate look as whipped as Pepe, nothing did. He chanced a furtive glance at the man known as the East Coast Dog Whisperer. "He's all Winslow's got, Harley. Anything happens to Pepe, it'll break her heart. Take good care of him."

"Don't worry," Harley assured. "Me and Judy will keep him at our place until you're off duty. Go get your girl."

Tate gave Pepe one last pat on that hard little head, but he had to set the record straight. "She's not my girl."

Judy locked her arm through Harley's with another one of her sly winks. "If you say so."

The world was on fire, but Winslow couldn't scream. The line sticking in her throat strangled her with every lurching, frantic breath and swallow. Helpless to yank it out or breathe around it, she struggled to reach it, but no matter how hard she tried, her arms and legs wouldn't move. She'd been restrained, and she couldn't catch a decent breath. Useless tears drenched the sides of her face until finally, someone— thank God!—leaned over the top of her with an anxious, "Damn it. You're awake."

No shit.

Hurriedly, that kind woman eased the tube up and out of Winslow's spastic lungs and raw esophagus. Between choking and gagging, she was free, but the nightmare of what she'd just endured still suffocated. Her wrists were freed next, allowing her to curl in misery onto her side, gasping for air and trying to understand where she was and what had happened. Her throat burned at the violation of what she now knew was a ventilator, a machine that breathed for her—when she was unconscious.

How close to death was she that she'd needed mechanical help doing something so basic? "Where...?" Even that one word hurt, cracking the last of her courage to dust.

The woman, a stout, salt-and-pepper matronly type in pink scrubs with little yellow chicks scattered over the fabric, finished releasing the restraints at Winslow's ankles. That was when Winslow noticed the catheter tube running over the side of the bed. It was true then. She was dying. How humiliating to be reduced to this level of dependency.

"I'm sorry, honey. I came as fast as I could when I heard the alarm go off, but these old legs aren't as spry as they used to be." The woman reached above Winslow's headboard and immediately the raucous beeping quieted. Winslow hadn't noticed the ventilator's alarm over the screaming panic in her head.

"You're at Dr. Bly's private clinic, sweet thing. You'd crashed when you arrived, so he had to intubate you. That's why the restraints. Most people panic when they come to, just like you did, but don't worry. It's over and you won't need a respirator now that you're breathing on your own. Take it easy. I'll be right back."

Winslow reached for the woman before she made it out the door. "My phone," she croaked, her hand outstretched, needing her lifeline to Tate. She'd come to in a hospital gown, nothing more. Not even her bra where she'd hidden the cellphone. "I need—" she swallowed hard "—my phone."

Miss Salt-and-Pepper marched back to her side and firmly gripped Winslow's sweaty hand before she tucked it under the blanket. "I swear, you kids these days are all the same. You don't need your phone, young lady. You need to rest, now go to sleep. Besides, your mother has it."

She couldn't have hurt Winslow worse. If Mommy Dearest had Tate's phone, all hope was lost.

Chapter Fifteen

Despite the delay with finding Pepe, Tate made it back to the Parrish home before Ky, but Joyce's damned car was gone. Parking hurriedly, one front wheel on the curb, he marched to the front porch and pounded for good measure, then illegally entered. Joyce could sue him for B&E, but he needed to see Winslow right damned now!

Didn't that make him a fool? He should've known. The house was empty. He checked the few rooms, and *man, the difference between Joyce's room and Winslow's was telling.* Joyce lived like a diva, while her daughter lived more like a transient who'd moved in with a few cardboard boxes. Not only was the house empty of people, the closet in Joyce's bedroom had been cleaned out. Her stylish dresser drawers stood open and empty, while all of Winslow's things were still in their places. Even her wigs.

By that time, Ky had roared up in his Corvette and hit the ground running. "What's up?" he asked, when he met Tate coming out of the house. Dressed in jeans, with his sleeves rolled up, that was Ky for you: Ready to pitch in and help at a moment's notice.

"She's gone. That mother of hers took her and—" Tate punched the air with his fist. "Son-of-a-bitch, I should've known. It was a distraction. She dumped Pepe to get me out of here, so she could move Winslow."

"You're bleeding," Ky pointed out.

Tate bowed his head, his chest heaving. He wasn't bleeding. He was dying inside. If Joyce moved Winslow this fast this time...

If she had no problem getting rid of Pepe like she did...

Why hadn't she taken Winslow's clothes and wigs with her? Were they leaving town or...

The scary answers to that multiple-choice quiz wouldn't quit.

He shot a look at Ky, but saw past his best buddy's grim face to the army of green trash receptacles lining Maple. *What the hell?* The ninety-six gallon residential trash bins were all parked at the edge of their appointed driveways like good little soldiers waiting for pick-up, their lids down and their rear wheels in the gutter. Except for the one at the side of the Parrish driveway. A white fluffy arm dangled at the lip of that green monster. *It can't be. No way.*

Tate rolled off the porch for a look-see, his heart thumping in his chest like a damned snare drum in the USMC marching band. Joyce wouldn't do something like that, would she? He lifted the lid and... *Son-of-a-bitch.*

The stuffed polar bear he'd brought for Winslow's phony prom now lay on top of yesterday's garbage. He'd forgotten the silly thing with last evening's drama, but there it was, its belly eviscerated and foam-rubber stuffing scattered over the rest of the trash. But worse, the bear's head was tucked face up in the stomach cavity where all that stuffing used to be. Its black plastic eyes were missing.

"Holy shit," Ky muttered. "What happened?"

Tate couldn't answer. The damned thing had been staged, not just tossed out. Joyce wanted him to find it. Sure, the bear had been a last minute thought and a kid's toy at that. It meant nothing and Winslow had never seen it, but the vicious damage inflicted on that simple, funny looking toy had to have taken time and forethought and—*malice.*

Tate forced his throat muscles to swallow. What kind of person stooped to this level? Ike? Janice? Joyce? All of them? Were they working together? To what end? If not all three of them, what point was Joyce trying to make? Simply that she was all-powerful where Winslow was concerned? That he was powerless to do anything to help her daughter? That Joyce could and would do as she pleased?

Point taken. At the moment, that was precisely what Tate was—powerless. Winslow was in danger, but he had no concrete evidence other than this toy in the garbage and the fact that Winslow's things were left behind. Just an unsettling suspicion that Joyce intentionally meant to hurt her child. But mutilated bear could be explained away. His suspicions and a quarter wouldn't buy him a cup of coffee. He could hear his boss: *Evidence, Tate. The FBI is all about real evidence. Not your gut.*

Bullshit. Sometimes it is all about a man's gut. His instincts.

Tate leveled a shrewd eye at the Parrish picture window. The blinds were closed, but his gut squirmed like it used to before the word had come down on overseas ops to hustle, gear up, that he and his squad were headed into combat. Joyce knew damned well what she'd done when she'd left the bear here. Like this.

Message received loud and clear, you bitch, he growled to himself. *But if you hurt Winslow, I'll tear you apart like you did this toy.* The prom nightmare just kept getting scarier.

"Isn't that the present you bought Winslow?" Ky asked, his eyes shadowed beneath his brows.

Tate nodded, his heart pounding. He heard his mouth say, "I don't know where she is."

"Understood, but why is that a problem if she's with her mom? That's the safest place for her."

"No, it isn't." Tate explained what he suspected while Ky absorbed every last detail, nodding in his usual calm way, his eyes scrolling from Tate to the mutilated toy in the garbage. When the story ended, Ky looked Tate in the eye and told him true. "You've got nothing but circumstantial evidence, and you know what Tucker thinks of that. Not that I care. I'm here and I'm willing. State your game plan and I'll back you up all the way. Eden will too. She's just waiting on our babysitter. How can we help?"

That was Ky to his cotton socks. The man was as solid a friend as they came and twice as loyal. But what was there to be done? Tate shook his rising paranoia for Winslow off, thankful for brothers and sisters who never let him down. "Easy. She's got my phone. We track her GPS."

The growl of a rowdy performance engine roaring up Maple brought Tate up short. A flaming red Dodge Challenger headed his way. *Son-of-a-bitch*. Tucker Chase was officially in the house.

Chapter Sixteen

"This is an unsanctioned operation, Higgins," Tucker stated unequivocally, one hand on his hip, the other flat to the hood of his pricey muscle car. As usual, he looked pretty damned sure of himself. He'd come dressed for a day off in that black button-up shirt tucked into black jeans with his Aviators shoved high into his dark hair. Isaiah Zaroyin came with him, and right now, they stood on opposite sides of the Challenger like two oddly matched bookends straight off the cover of GQ.

Both of the tall, dark variety, Isaiah was the loyal Robin to Tucker's passionate Bat. Known for his rock 'em, sock 'em style, the ex-Navy SEAL now directed the Bureau's innovative psychic unit with barely a hint of finesse. Isaiah, his right-hand man, was the intellectual of the pair, prone to quiet introspection prior to deliberate decision making instead of leading with his fist or his chin. He didn't swear, drink, or womanize, and Tate was fairly certain Isaiah didn't eat meat, either. He was the purist. The idealist.

Yeah. Total opposites. And there stood Tate with nothing but his gut and an almighty gift of *affinity for animals*? BFD.

If Eden had accompanied Ky, the whole fam-damn-ily would've been there, but she wasn't, and Tate was thrilled that, for the moment, he had one less psychic digging around in his head. The story of his life. He'd always sensed Tucker, Isaiah, and sometimes, Eden, tiptoeing around his psyche when they thought they knew better, which was exactly why he blocked them. Maybe that inner sense that he was being infiltrated at a very intimate level was one of those psychic talents he didn't want to have, but had.

At least Ky had the sense not to pry into Tate's mind, but that was a good buddy for you. Respect, man. It all came down to respect.

Tate knew he wasn't a deep thinker, nor did he have Tucker, Isaiah, or Eden's level of education, sophistication, or looks. He got that. If this was a game of Deuces Wild like Tucker had nicknamed his team, then he, Tate Higgins, was the freakin' joker in the deck. He was the odd man out, the throw away card.

All these kids were citified, while he was the unsocialized beast that refused to be tamed, a ragged wolf that preferred the clarion call of the mountains over the collar and chains of human society. Who was he kidding? He was no wolf. Truth be known, he wasn't much different than the bulky bears he'd hunted high on the bony back of the Aleutian Range. Prone to solitude. Uncivilized. And damned proud of it.

"Understood," Tate replied, not backing down, "but like it or not, I'm going after her." If Alex Stewart had been standing there instead of Tucker, Tate would've added a respectful *Boss* to that declaration, but he didn't. Tucker was just *a boss*, not *the Boss*.

Tucker ran his fingers through the inky black curls at his forehead, exasperation sparking in his eyes. That he, one of the biggest jerks on the federal payroll, now ruled his own FBI team, irked Tate no end. Tucker was no rule keeper. If anything, he was the blatant rebel in the Bureau, the gunslinger who should have been kept on a tight leash instead of given a badge. So why the slow roll? Oh, yeah. Now he was *important. Who gives a shit?*

Tucker shrugged a shoulder in Isaiah's direction, his eye still on Tate. "Can you get a read on the Parrishs?"

Like his evil twin, Isaiah met Tate's gaze head on instead of looking at his boss. "I'm not picking up anything, but Eden could if she were here, provided one of us can get back inside that house and retrieve something from either mother or daughter. Eden works best when she can make physical contact with an item the victim handled. You know that."

"I can get inside," Tate offered. There was still that side window.

"With a warrant?" Tucker qualified, that cocky gleam in his eye.

The urge to hit something—an ex-Navy SEAL would do—curled Tate's fingers. Tucker was a great one to worry about warrants, considering how his previous MO as an agent had always been to shoot first, apologize later.

"Exigent circumstances," Tate bit out. *Deal with it.*

Tucker's brow spiked, the bastard. "You'd risk your career for an endangered kid you just met?"

That did it. "She's not a kid, she's... she's a..." Even Tate heard that unquantifiable ring of doubt to his tone. What precisely was Winslow, just some woman in a bad spot? His girlfriend? He couldn't name his feelings. They were what they were. Winslow needed help out of a bad situation, and he cared. Tucker was wasting precious time she didn't have.

"You think she's endangered, don't you?" Tucker asked, his tone softened, those dark eyes of his taking Tate apart atom by atom.

"She's sick to the point of dying and her mother's acting erratic." Tate knew that would go farther with his boss than calling Joyce a liar right off the bat. "Mrs. Parrish might be suffering a nervous breakdown. She got rid of Winslow's dog this morning, and she took a knife to the thing I brought Winslow last night. I know Joyce is under a lot of stress with what's going on with Winslow, but she's got a shitload of prescription meds in her kitchen too."

Okay, probably shouldn't have added that insider information to the mix, but the more Tate talked, the weaker his argument sounded, even to himself. A missing dog, a worried mother, and a ruined toy bear did not a murderer make. The fact that Joyce had only packed her clothes wasn't a clincher, either. There could be a reasonable explanation for everything. All he had to go on was that knot in his gut that kept urging him to run.

Tucker's lip lifted. "You're kidding me. Joyce Parrish knifed a stuffed bear?"

How many times do I have to say it? "Yes. She gave Winslow's dog to her boyfriend this morning without telling her, and she hacked up the bear." Was this just mother/daughter drama he should've kept his nose out of? Was his gut wrong? Was it enough?

"Why do you think I wanted you on my team?" Tucker asked, changing directions.

Tate rolled his neck, pissed that he'd let his guard down and not willing to answer that loaded question.

Tucker crossed his arms over his beefy chest, deliberately appraising Tate, his eyes scanning him up and down but always zeroing back on his eyes. "She means something to you." He made that a statement.

Not answering that, either.

A light clicked on deep in Tucker's dark blues. He cocked his head and his eyes narrowed as if he finally understood something. "The first time I met Melissa, I knew. So help me, Tate. We're going to find Winslow and we won't stop until we do."

Not exactly what Tate expected, but okay. Better than nothing.

Turning on his other agents, Tucker snapped his fingers. "Isaiah, I want that warrant within the hour. Tate's right. We've got a clear case of exigent circumstances and a possible endangered woman. Until we know otherwise, we'll proceed under the premise that Winslow Parrish is in danger. We err on the side of her safety, not her mother's. You know the judge I mean. Make it happen. When that warrant gets here, Tate, you'll enter that house, and you'll find me something that belongs to the mother or the daughter. Ky, get your wife here, and..."

How bizarre. Understanding and decisive action from the over-the-top alpha dog when Tate least expected it. That shift in the universe didn't make Tucker a drinking buddy by a long shot, but it allowed Tate to release the breath he hadn't realized he'd been holding.

He'd worked with Tucker before on a couple TEAM ops. The man was a flaming A, and not as in Type-A personality, either. He'd mellowed since he'd gotten married, but he still tended to lead with that big chin of his. Begrudgingly, Tate had to admit Tucker wasn't so different than Alex Stewart. Both men continually went above and beyond the call of duty to God and country, and their abrupt management style annoyed anyone who got in their way. With that stellar trait in common, Tate was willing to trust Tucker. A little more.

He took another deep breath when Isaiah took off in Tucker's Challenger for the warrant. It took Eden less than half an hour to show, and by then, Tate was wound tight with pre-combat jitters all over again. When Isaiah rolled back on the scene with warrant in hand within minutes of Eden's arrival, Tate made quick work of retrieving a single item of Winslow's from her closet, that silky black wig.

They had all day to execute the search and seizure warrant. After a quick round of hello-how-you-doings, Ky's gorgeous blonde wife took a seat on Tate's Jeep fender, sifting the strands of black hair through her fingers. Sitting there in soft blue jeans and a bulky cream-colored sweater, she looked the least like an FBI agent.

But Eden Winchester was so much more than just a pretty woman. She had a knack for psychically targeting people under extreme duress, which was how she'd connected with Ky. Tate now knew it was Ky who'd set their initial encounter in motion the night he'd cried out for relief from a torture cell in far off Afghanistan. Lo and behold, Eden's genius brain waves picked up Ky's psychic plea to die, and look at them now. Happily married with a three-month old son, Kyler Lee, so named after another TEAM agent,

Lee Hart, the man who'd physically rescued Ky. But it was Eden who'd gotten to Ky first, and who'd helped him hang on mentally until Lee showed up in person.

Her psychic talent worked better if she had a personal item of the victim's—damn, Tate hated putting Winslow in that category. According to Eden, personal possessions retained a shadow, for lack of a better descriptor, of whoever handled them the most. That shadow enabled Eden to trace the victim, and, in most cases, to project a psychic suggestion to the victim.

Tate didn't know how it worked and he didn't want to. He was the muscle and the gut; they were the *'Brainiacs'*. But he also knew that once he let Eden in, she would be able to read his deepest memories, what made him tick. His despair. His emotions. Without trying, she could lay his heart bare. She'd know what happened those many years ago that still felt like yesterday. Yes, she'd keep his confidence, but damn. She'd still know, wouldn't she?

Tate stood his ground and let her do her thing. He needed her psychic magic more than his pride, especially since Tucker and Isaiah had gotten uncharacteristically mute except for an occasional brow lift between buddies. Yeah. They were chatting up a psychic storm in front of everyone, yet behind everyone's backs at the same time. *Damn them.*

Eden pursed her lips. "Why didn't you track her through the GPS in her phone?"

"Because it's not pinging," he answered. "We tried. Someone's removed the battery." *Or broke it.* Which meant Joyce might be smarter than he'd thought.

Ky had taken the spot on the fender next to Eden. She curled her index finger for Tate to come closer. "Are you sure her mother's at fault?" she asked, her voice lowered, "because honestly, all I'm picking up from Winslow is concern for her mom, not fear for herself."

"I'm not sure of anything," Tate admitted point blank, "but that's how Winslow rolls. She's kind and sweet, but she defends her mom every single time, no matter what Joyce does to her. And trust me, Joyce Parrish is not a nice person. She's lied to her daughter about where she works, and she's cruel to Winslow's dog, at least she was before she dumped him. The problem with Winslow is she's been under her mother's thumb her whole life. She doesn't have any friends and they've moved around a lot. She's been sick most of that time, so I can't blame her. Her mom's point of view is all she knows."

Blonde hair dripped over Eden's shoulder. "So you think Winslow is caught in a toxic codependent relationship?"

Whatever that meant. Tate gritted his teeth, frustrated he didn't have the masters in psychology that Eden did. "From what I've seen in the last twenty-four-hours, I think Joyce is... I don't know, jealous of her daughter. It's as if she needs Winslow to be sick." He ran a hand over his scalp, growing more frustrated trying to explain the mother/daughter relationship he'd witnessed. People were a mystery he didn't care enough to unravel, and words were not his friends. Talking with Winslow was easy in comparison to explaining his observations to Eden.

"It's like the prom thing, Eden. Joyce didn't set that up because Winslow wanted to go dancing. She didn't know about it until the day before when her mom showed up with a dress and shoes."

"But Winslow wanted to go to the prom after she met you, right? You did dance with her." Eden said that like it was a good thing. She was doing it. Reading him. Revealing him.

Tate swallowed hard before he responded. "She wants to live so, yeah. I asked her to dance on the water tower. Just once and—"

"Water tower?" Eden asked, her fingers still tangled in the silky strands of that wig.

Tate chin nodded eastward. "Three blocks that way. The new Silver Spring water tower."

A smile curved Eden's lips. "That had to be some dance."

He didn't have to look at Ky to know his buddy's brows had both just arced like the golden arches. *So I danced. Get over it.* "Joyce pitched a fit when Winslow took off last night," he offered by way of distraction. "She told the television crew that someone kidnapped her daughter."

"The media was here?" Eden asked. "Let me guess. Channel Thirteen. That stands to reason. They partner with the Dreams-Come-True people."

Ky cocked his head. "Why'd her mom jump to that conclusion? How long was Winslow missing?"

Tate shrugged. "Maybe five, ten minutes." *Did mothers really envy their own kids?*

Eden's eyes narrowed. "Tell me more about Joyce."

Tate growled. He'd already told Ky most of his suspicions, but retelling them brought everything into sharper focus. "Joyce lies," he stated emphatically. "I've caught her several times. Winslow thinks she works at some spa as a beautician." Tate knew that wasn't the right word, but it escaped him at the moment. "But she doesn't. Joyce barhops at a strip joint called Land's End. She runs with some loser named Ike Pitt and another barhop, Janice. I don't know her last name, but I'm pretty sure one of them tried to kill me when I was there earlier."

"And like a bonehead, he won't let me treat the bullet hole in his arm," Ky intruded.

Tate shot him a dark look that meant shut the hell up. He'd patched the hole in his bicep. It wasn't dripping. Case closed. But the more he lined up the mental pool table in his mind, the clearer the shots. "Up there on that tower last night, Winslow belted me a good one when I first came up behind her. I was afraid she was going to jump, so I grabbed her. Yeah, she's thin, and you can tell by looking at her she's running on empty, but she seemed healthy—at least healthier—last night."

He rubbed his jaw remembering. "And get this. The ladder's a good hundred steps from bottom to top, and that first step up is a good six-feet off the ground. She had to run and jump to reach the bottom rung, and it was cold and windy last night. That had to be a tough climb for a dying woman to make twice in one day." What he wouldn't give to have her back in his arms. He'd keep her warm.

"So you think she's strong and capable," Ky added. "Not sick? Are you sure she's not faking it?"

"Absolutely. You should've seen her this morning. She seemed healthy last night, but today…" Tate bowed his head. The difference between Winslow's health from last evening to this morning was cataclysmically different, but why? What happened between then and now? Was Winslow sick because she'd overdone it or because of all her meds?

Tate tapped a finger to his bottom lip, remembering. Joyce had also insisted Winslow was a vegetarian, but she wasn't. Another lie. All he needed now was the eight ball in the corner pocket to run the table, but it—that final clue—was missing.

"I hate to tell you, but all I'm getting from Winslow at the moment is the sense that she's given up." Eden's brows angled to a delicate V, her gaze on Tate. "She doesn't want to hurt the people she loves any more, and she's thinking about you, Tate. She wishes she could tell you that she… she loves you."

God, kick me when I'm down. Tate jabbed his fingers into his pockets and stalked right up to Eden's knees. "She only thinks she loves me because she's naïve and in a bad spot. Where is she?"

Eden shook her head. "No, Tate. She wanted to spend the night with you, didn't she?"

He admitted nothing. "We hit it off. Where is she?"

"She's pretty sure you love her, but she also thinks you're afraid to say it because she's dying. That you're afraid you'll get hurt if you get too close to her."

Hurt didn't come close to how he'd feel if she died. He didn't know when it happened, but he cared about Winslow more than he'd planned to. Her death would destroy him. Yeah. He wasn't much different than Pepe in the craving, loving, I'll-do-anything-for-Winslow department.

"She's a very sick woman, Tate, but she came to life last night when you asked her to dance, didn't she? That single act of kindness meant the world to her. She's convinced that was the first time in her life that anyone truly cared whether she lived or died."

Rrrriiiiiippppppppppp. There went his heart, torn to pieces and the bits tossed to the wind. Now the whole world knew how seriously stupid he was, him, a tough Marine falling in love with a tiny little woman after—hell, less than a day. Because that was precisely what had happened, but did he have the balls to tell Winslow how he felt when he'd had the chance? No, damn it. Like that other woman years ago, he'd let this one down too.

To make matters worse, Tucker had come up behind Tate and now he'd heard everything. What could Tate say or do? Nod like he'd gone mute? He growled instead. "Where the hell is...?"

Tucker cut him off. "Yeah, Eden, where are we going? Don't keep this man waiting."

"I'm not sure, Boss," Eden replied steadily, her eyes still on Tate. "I'm picking up a mishmash of strange patterns from her. It's as if she's coherent one moment, the next she's struggling with something, her guilt most of all. Honestly, I think she believes it'd be better for everyone if she died."

Eden's gift: The ability to hone in on a victim despite the miles between that person and her, and now, to make Tate feel like crap. She was doing a bang up job. One more sucker punch like that last one and he'd go ballistic.

"Where is she?" Tate asked One. Last. Time. *Just tell me.*

Ky chimed in. "I'm catching a drift of antiseptic and bleach. Men's cologne, so there's a male in close proximity to Winslow. A tinge of blood like she bit her lip. She might be in a hospital or a clinic."

Tate whirled on his brother. "You can?"

Ky's nose wrinkled. "Yes, I can psychically pick up on smells and odors at a distance. Tastes. Stuff like that. Sometimes it corroborates what Eden's honing in on. Don't go psycho on me."

But Eden hadn't honed in on anything but feelings so far. As if she sensed Tate's desperation, she lifted a handful of Winslow's silky black hair to her nose and closed her eyes. One minute passed. Two. Tate held his breath. Eden he trusted.

Without opening her eyes, Eden said, "Ky's right. She's in a medical facility but not a hospital. She's due north of our location, but she's invisible to the eye. She's hidden in plain sight. Most people would walk by the place and not realize what it is. I see a sign in the lower left pane of the front window. But I can't make it out."

Chapter Seventeen

"There, there," Joyce said, patting Winslow's arm. "It will all be over soon."

Winslow believed it. Her lungs burned with what felt like crippling acid instead of air sacs. Her heart faltered, skipping to an irregular beat then running too fast, here at the end of time. "Mom," she rasped, struggling to reach her mother's arm. "I'm sorry."

Joyce shrugged out of reach. "I know, but it's done. I tried my best, now just lay there and be still."

But Winslow had more to say. "I wish I'd been born... different. You know. Stronger. Healthier."

"Stop talking," Joyce murmured. "If this doesn't work, we'll head out to the West Coast. You'd like a road trip, wouldn't you?"

That made no sense. "A road trip? Now?" *If what doesn't work?* "Why are we going on a road trip?" In a way, that was kind of sweet, taking a road trip to—

die. Maybe she could die on a mountaintop at day's end, watching the sunset like they did in the movies. Or on a beach with the wind in her nose and the screech of seagulls overhead while the waves lapped over her lifeless body. Anything would be better than lying in this hospital bed and waiting.

"Because Oregon, California, and Washington have assisted suicide laws," Joyce said sweetly. "If we can't make it that far, there's always Colorado." She spoke out of the corner of her mouth to some blurry figure at her side. "You can get a license there, can't you? Oh, Vermont too? You're right, closer is better."

"W-what?" Winslow shook her head, fighting to make sense of this crazy conversation. Was someone else in the room? If so, she couldn't see them through her daze. "Assisted suicide? Mom, no. You can't do that. Do you hear me?" Suicide was never the answer.

"I hear you, but it's time to finish what I started in Arizona all those years ago. You know. It's time to move on. To begin anew. A time to be born, a time to die, and all that jazz."

Winslow struggled to swallow, sure she was hearing things. "Why are you giving up? Because I'm sick? D-dying? Please Mom, don't do this. You have to go on after I'm... after I'm..." It was so hard to say the words. *Dead. Buried. Gone.* "You can make a new life for yourself after... it. I know you can. You're a survivor. Things will be easier for you without..." *Me.*

This crazy argument was breaking what was left of Winslow's heart. First she'd lost Pepe, then Tate. Now her mom was planning to kill herself? If there were an easier way to die, she'd gladly do it and spare everyone she loved this misery.

Joyce leaned into Winslow's face as if she needed to be sure Winslow saw and heard every last word. "Oh, I'm not giving up, Winslow darling. You are."

"Will you stop pacing? I've already set things in motion," Tucker reassured Tate.

Eden hadn't yet pinned down an address, but Tate was tired of waiting. "What's that mean?"

"That I've got a six-man team canvassing the neighborhood, knocking on doors, and already looking for Winslow. There's an APB on the wire for Joyce Parrish's vehicle. We'll find her."

"It's a blue hatchback," Tate added.

"Understood, and I've got a crew checking every security cam this side of the Potomac." Tucker's gaze scrolled to Ky's wife, still sitting on the hood of the Jeep. "You're certain Winslow's north of our location?"

Eden nodded. "She was. I can't get a clear picture now. Like I said, her brain patterns are all over the place."

Tate cursed under his breath. Joyce could be in West Virginia by now for all he knew. He clapped Ky on the shoulder and headed for his Jeep. "Time to move, Eden. I'm going hunting."

Instead of arguing, Tucker nodded. "Isaiah, go with him. Take the neighborhood due north. Ky and Eden, canvass the neighborhood northwest of Maple. Keep in touch."

"What if she comes back?" Tate asked, his cell buzzing at his hip holster. "Shouldn't someone stay here?"

Just then everything went sideways. Everyone's cell phones chirped or buzzed with incoming alerts.

"Higgins," he answered, his gaze riveted on Tucker as all agents answered the same callout from the FBI switchboard. "Be advised. Maryland PD is in pursuit of a vehicle matching your description. Subject is traveling eastbound on Woodrow Wilson Bridge at a high rate of speed."

"Copy that," Tate echoed his teammates. This nightmare could be over with once that Maryland police officer caught up with Joyce. But the WWB was south of their location, not north. What was wrong with Eden's gift? Had Joyce outsmarted her? Was she on the run?

Tucker glared at him. "You're not going near that bridge."

Like hell I'm not. Tate no more than squared his shoulders than his phone buzzed an update. "Be advised the vehicle is in the water. Maryland Highway Patrol and Coast Guard are on the scene. No FBI assistance requested at this time."

In the water? As in the river?

"Move it, Eden," Tate ordered as he scrambled into his Jeep. Lead foot to the pedal. Screeching tires. He couldn't get away from Maple fast enough. Over the Potomac. Dodging busy Saturday traffic to get through Alexandria, Virginia, to the WWB. By the time he hit the George Washington Memorial Highway, he was halfway there and going out of his mind. He checked his rearview for that red Challenger. Sure enough. The Grim Reaper was riding shotgun and the Devil was on his ass.

Faster!

The Woodrow Wilson Bridge was a phenomenal engineering feat, a drawbridge that spanned the Potomac between Alexandria, Virginia, and Maryland. But for a small car like the Spark to have gotten over those guardrails, the driver had to have been traveling damned fast.

It couldn't have been Joyce. Just frickin' could not. Eden had placed her north of Maple, not south. WWB was in the opposite direction. All Tate could think was getting to Winslow as fast as he could. Before she drowned. God, maybe she was the one who'd been driving. Maybe this was her way of ending herself.

Gridlock. Damn it! He two-fisted the steering wheel, a cocktail of fear, desperation and anger in his veins, driving him as he glared at the lanes of deadlocked traffic ahead.

Of course, gridlock. The eastbound lanes leading onto the bridge were closed because of the accident.

Pulling off the highway, Tate grabbed the first available open parking space in a strip mall and took off running. If Tucker meant to follow, he'd better be in good shape.

Tate cleared the distance in record time. Finally at the scene and his lungs on fire, he caught his first view of the bedlam. Emergency vehicles blocked all traffic lanes. Fire engines, EMTs, police cruisers from both sides of the river blocked the bridge. The Coast Guard had divers in the water, and Tate's heart sank. No one told him to stand back once he'd flashed his FBI badge, but there was no way to help Winslow now, other than taking a seventy-foot plunge that would rob manpower from the search for her and divert it to his sorry ass.

What could he do but stare over the guardrail at the point of the breach and pray like he'd prayed all those years ago? *Dear Baby Jesus, let her live. Take me. I'm ready and I'm willing, but please. Let her live.*

"Survivors?" he barked at the nearest officer on the scene, fearing the worst.

"None so far," the man replied evenly.

"Witnesses?" Someone had to have seen what happened and who'd been driving that vehicle.

The officer looked up from his tablet long enough to point at the Toyota Camry parked across the concrete divider in the westbound lanes. "Mr. Hamilton over there saw the driver make a hard right from the passing lane. From all we know—"

"Was a woman behind the wheel? Short, dark hair? Thin?" *With narrow mean eyes and a nasty temper?*

"How'd you know?"

Sucker punch. *Murder/suicide?*

Tate couldn't answer, not with his heart splattered to the pavement at his boots. Why would Joyce do this? How could she kill herself and her daughter? Why hadn't he seen her breakdown coming, if that's what this was, sooner? How many times had he heard of cases like this, where loved ones took drastic measures to end their suffering spouse or child's life, rather than watching them die? *I should've known this could happen.*

The whole damned universe narrowed into a spinning vortex that arrowed down on him, pressing him under karma's wicked boot heel. Tate gripped the guardrail, needing something to hold onto before he passed out or threw up. How dumb was he that he'd missed all the signs? Why hadn't he taken action sooner or done something—anything!—to save Winslow from her mother?

He bowed his head and closed his eyes to make the nausea climbing up his throat back off. But he couldn't catch a breath. This was just like—then. He could still see *her* pretty dark eyes. They always twinkled as if she knew a secret. Soft and brown like his used to be, only at the end, hers were filled with the terror of that one misstep. That one mistake he could never correct.

It could've happened to anyone and not been fatal. Yet her fingertips had stretched for his and curled like claws, trying to grab hold of him, but clenching only air. His strong, capable and totally useless hands, as hard as he'd tried, had remained too far away to latch onto and save—her. The backward fall. Shit, the bloody touchdown. The gut-busting wail he'd sent heavenward to a God who seemed to pick and choose whom to save and whom to let—die.

Tate could still see the grotesque mask of terror that even in her hopeless situation, she'd tried to soften with her one last scream of, "I love you, Tate!" Her last words. His eternal damnation. Love, it turned out, didn't mean jack in the high, craggy peaks of the Alaskan wilds.

"You could've saved her," he breathed, his throat ragged with the regret and the futility of having saved so many others when he couldn't save the women he'd loved. Either of them. "Do you have to take everyone?" he asked the Lord.

A heavy mitt landed on his shoulder. "Tate," was all Tucker had to say to open the floodgates.

Damn. Tate didn't have the strength to shove his boss's hand away. He'd been ambushed again, but he couldn't let his boss see him, not like this. He kept his head bowed and breathed through his mouth, blinking before one tear fell, needing oxygen and a way out of this nightmare called his life.

The busy world of law enforcement and first responders swirled around him in the far right traffic lane, but eventually, the fire engines rolled on to other calls where other people could be saved. Shortly after they left, the EMTs packed up and followed their lead. There was nothing left for any of them to do here.

Three of the six police cruisers on scene turned off their flashing red and blues, and rolled eastward. One lane reopened with two officers directing the heavy traffic. Then another lane opened. Engines revved. Horns honked. People resumed their busy lives while Tate's stood still.

He'd only known Winslow less than twenty-fours hours. How'd he get so deep into her when he'd been celibate by choice most of his adult life? Why her? Why now? Why this one young woman when so many others had passed by without him giving them a second glance? When he thought he'd never be whole enough to take another risk?

The Lord giveth and the Lord taketh away. How well he knew.

It'd be good to hear what news the divers relayed to the police and the Coast Guard. What they'd seen. Who they'd found, if anyone. Not that it mattered. The car was fathoms below the choppy surface, maybe sitting on the bottom by now. You couldn't see the roof from the bridge. The Coast Guard's life-saving drill had changed to body recovery.

No one submerged in the chilly Potomac could survive this long, especially if their health was already compromised. It wasn't humanly possible. Tate knew the odds. Chevy Sparks turned too quickly into Chevy Anchors. They had no capacity to maintain a large enough air bubble like you saw in those murder mysteries on television. That crap wasn't real. But death was. Death and guilt and drowning, and that hollowed out cavern where his heart used to be—those things were real.

Tucker didn't have the brains he was born with, just stuck to Tate like glue, his hand firm and solid on Tate's shoulder. It almost felt—warm. But Tate was no dummy. Tucker only stayed on his six because he was afraid Tate might jump next. Funny. Part of him wanted to, but his grief-sickened mind kept thinking of that fierce little survivor back at the Mortimer ranch, the one still waiting for Winslow to come for him. *Yeah. Pepe. The dragon.*

In a way that damned dog was saving his life. He didn't have anyone now, and Tate couldn't bear the thought of that homeless, throwaway dog in anyone's arms but his. If this was the end, Pepe was all that was left of Winslow. They needed each other.

"You ought to head back to Maple," Tucker mumbled. "You know. See what else Ky and Isaiah found in the house. Maybe—"

"No." Tate forced a swallow. He didn't need busywork, and nothing on Maple would bring Winslow back to life. Fighting the crush of despair, he locked onto the icy depths of the river and refused to give Joyce the upper hand, even in death.

He wouldn't leave until he saw Winslow's limp lifeless body. Yeah, he knew he was stupid to stand there and wait. Any minute now, Tucker would pull rank on him and send him home, but Tate had nothing left, and no reason to want to live in a world without Winslow.

Like that kid all alone on that mountain in Alaska, he did the only thing he could. He hoped against hope.

Chapter Eighteen

Tucker proved to be a stalwart companion. Hadn't offered one patronizing piece of advice the entire afternoon. Just showed up at the railing and stood there like a brother instead of a boss. But at the end of the day, it didn't matter. No car. No Winslow. No sense standing around once the fog rolled in and the Coast Guard divers called it quits.

The CG commander doused the spotlights, then gathered his men out of the river and turned his ship toward home. He'd left a marker buoy to resume the search early Sunday morning, weather permitting, but for tonight, his work was done.

Across the river, National Harbor was lit up in all its early Christmas shopping glory, but Tate's heart was locked up tight. He forced his fingers to let loose of the metal guardrail that held him up, but getting his boots to step away from the scene below was something else again. His eyes held fast to the bobbing whitecaps. Expecting. Still hoping. Still praying. Any minute now, Winslow might bob to the surface. She might gasp for help and he meant to dive in and be that breath of life for her.

"Where are you going?" Tucker asked as if Tate had waved goodbye or something when he'd done no such thing.

"Nowhere," he bit out. He didn't mean to come across like an ass, but he was *that* close to falling apart, and if he stepped away from the rail—for even a second—it meant he admitted Winslow was gone. That she'd drowned. That Joyce won. The thought of Winslow's lifeless tiny body in the icy water stole Tate's breath.

"You need something to eat, Tate. Come on. I'll walk back to your car with you. We'll go somewhere for a cup of coffee." Tucker made the mistake of cupping Tate's elbow.

Tate jerked free of the compassion offered. He didn't need it or the sympathetic undertone in his boss's voice. "I'm staying."

Tucker was right. Tate knew it, but how did a man give up and walk away from the woman he had no business loving? Like the drizzly rain now falling, his tears blurred his view of the river. The whole damned world turned fucking tragic.

His phone rang. He swallowed a gutful of despair and choked out, "Higgins," instead of *'What the hell do you want?'*

"Tate? That you?" The tone in Harley's three words sounded suspiciously compassionate, like Tucker's.

"Yeah. What?" He didn't need sympathy. He needed to be left alone.

"Were you going to stop by and visit this dog tonight? Pepe?"

Tate brushed the back of his hand over his eyes. "Yeah," he croaked. *Soon. Really soon.*

"When?"

Why did when matter? Once he stepped away from Winslow's watery grave, he'd just admit he'd lost her. That he'd given up hope. What mattered the time of day?

He coughed hard and loud, his lungs close to shutting down. He needed to breathe, didn't he? Why? Explain the need for pulmonary function to a man who'd just lost the woman he loved. Yes, loved. *I shouldn't have told her it was too soon. I should've said thank you. I should've told her I love her too.*

"Because I've got a dog on my hands that won't settle down no matter what I try, and trust me, I know dogs. I've tried everything."

Tate nodded more to himself than in answer. Why was Harley calling a man who'd never owned a dog in his life? He had no advice to offer. Like Winslow, he didn't really know Pepe, either. Right then, he didn't know anything.

"Is he hungry?" he asked the obvious. *Then feed him.*

"Hey man, are you okay?" Harley sounded genuinely concerned. Maybe he didn't know where Tate was or that he was standing on the Woodrow Wilson Bridge, feeling like his world was ending. Maybe Tucker hadn't leaked the news.

"Yeah. I'm good," Tate lied. *I'm fuckin' wonderful.*

"If you say so..." Suspicion filled the interlude. "Anyway, this little guy hasn't stopped barking since we got home. He won't let my boys play with him, and he bolts the door every chance he gets. He wants out, but I don't dare let him in case he runs off. I'm thinking he's looking for his owner. Was her name Winslow?"

"Yeah. Winslow," Tate ground out, that sweet name harder to speak now that he knew he'd be leaving her behind in the next few seconds. Maybe minutes. "I'll be right there."

"You got my address?"

"Yeah. On my way." Didn't it figure? When it rained, it poured.

Tate stuffed his phone back in his pants pocket and turned his head to the left where Tucker couldn't see. The traffic was steady and noisy at his six. A good blanket of fog had rolled in, covering everything in the river but that pulsing yellow beacon on the Coast Guard buoy. The sky let loose with a steady rain. Damn, this was hard.

He swallowed his angst and blinked against the wind, life's bitter lesson learned once more. *Don't fall in love. It isn't worth the pain.*

Only he knew better. Loving someone was worth everything. Even standing here with his heart in his throat, he'd do it all again for those few hours he'd been privileged to spend with Winslow. He was dumb like that.

"Shitty day," Tucker said simply when Tate turned his back on the guardrail and headed west. Once he made up his mind, he set a brisk pace to his Jeep, needing the solitude it would offer.

Tucker hadn't parked much farther from the Jeep. He went one way without so much as a good-bye. Tate went the other, headed to the Mortimer dog kennels, needing to be left alone.

The road to Harley's was bleak and busy. By the time Tate rolled up to the cedar log home Harley had built for Judy, the rain had stopped, but he was bone-tired. He hadn't eaten all day and his gut—no, make that his heart—hurt.

Harley had two boys, twins nicknamed Little Alex and Georgie, the one after Alex Stewart, the other after some guy Tate couldn't remember, maybe Harley's old man. One of them came scrambling out the front door, and wouldn't you know, Pepe raced behind him, yapping his head off.

Tate shoved his Jeep door open, intending to jump out and intercept the four-legged mutt before he got away, but damned if that hound dog didn't head straight for him. With one mad dash, Pepe was inside the Jeep and on the floorboards by Tate's boot. Another leap put him on Tate's lap where the crazy dog set to licking and kissing Tate's chin. God, that little dog felt good, warm and wiggling and full of everything Winslow had lost.

Tate lost it, right then and there. Every last piece of self-restraint. He buried his face in Pepe's neck, fighting the tsunami of grief lifting up in his heart. This bundle of joy had no idea he was kissing the man who'd let his mistress down. This dog was dumb and blind and—precisely what Tate needed.

He heard Harley at his open door, but he wasn't man enough to look his friend in the eye. "I heard," Harley said as he reached a hand to Tate's back. "I'm sorry."

"Yeah," was all Tate could manage. Damn, it had been a long time since he'd felt so shattered. He hated losing control like this. Hated. It.

"The offer's still good, buddy. Judy will be happy to treat that bullet hole in your arm, no questions asked."

Tate nodded, his chin bumping Pepe's hard, excited head. A golden ray of light spilled out the wide front doors of the Mortimer home like sunshine. Another little guy the same size as the one with Harley, stood at the doorway with Judy, and damn. Didn't the sight of a happy family gnaw at Tate's heart like a dog with a bone.

He had no one to go home to. His loft in Occoquan, North Virginia, was just another apartment. This time of day it'd be dark and empty, cold because he kept the thermostat set on low the days he worked late. He just didn't want to be there. Not like this.

He choked back the lump in his throat. "Nah. I'm good."

"No, you're not, Tate," Harley said firmly, his fingers digging into Tate's shoulder. "Times like this are when you need to be with someone. Come on in. You need a beer."

A big red danger light broke through the muck in Tate's head. Harley was a recovering alcoholic. If he was offering beer it had to be… "Root beer?"

Harley's brows knitted together in sheer kindness, a hard gift to accept on a day like this. "Of course. Judy would kick my ass if I fell off the wagon and left her to tend these two hellions."

"Aw, Daddy. You swored," Mini-Harley mumbled.

"Yeah, well, don't you go telling your mom on me now." Harley placed a wide palm over the kid's head and ruffled every last hair. "It's guy talk, son. That's all. See if you can lure Pepe away from Tate and let's go inside, Georgie. Come on, Tate. It'll do you good. If we're lucky, Judy will feed us."

"I heard that," the lady in question piped up from the porch. "I'm waiting, Tate, and yes. We're having homemade pizza tonight. Please stay and eat with us."

Pizza and root beer. Almost sounded tempting. But no. Tate couldn't choke down anything. "Another time. It's been a long day and I've got to buy dog food and… stuff."

"Damn. Almost forgot." Harley turned on his heel and headed back inside, leaving one of the twins with Tate. Georgie was it?

Maybe around five-years-old, the little guy climbed into the Jeep and onto Tate's lap with Pepe. He made himself at home, playing with the steering wheel and the shifter like he was driving. Being a kid. Damned if the little guy didn't smell like he'd just had a bath. Judy was a good mom, just like... *her*.

Tate closed his eyes, his battered heart so damned raw that his chest hurt when he breathed. He needed to leave before he turned into a blubbering mess, but just then, a soft little-boy hand patted his cheek. Once. Twice. Then it settled against his neck as Georgie twisted his little boy body around to look at the man behind him. "Daddy says puppies are like guardian angels only they don't got wings," he whispered.

Tate nodded, not needing any more of the milk of human kindness.

"He said they wake us up and keep us safe from the boogey man and other monsters."

"They do, huh." Tate had to say something.

The kid nodded. "Yeah, they do, and we should never be 'fraid of the dark, 'cuz if we got a dog in the house, we're safe and protected *all the time*," he said, bobbing his head at those last three words.

The kid made sense. Harley's dogs were German Shepherd or Malinois, not the Chihuahua type. In their world, Pepe was nothing but a snack-sized hors d'oeuvre. A cupid angel maybe. Nothing as fierce as those flaming archangel types Harley trained.

"You have bad dreams?" Tate asked to keep the conversation off him.

The boy nodded. "Ah-huh, and I keep a nightlight on 'cuz it gets dark at night, but sometimes Awex bees mean to me and he turns it off."

Awex, meaning Little Alex, Georgie's twin.

"But Daddy lets Rooster sleep with me now, and I ain't ascared of nuthin'."

"Who's Rooster?"

"My very own puppy, and I have to brush him and feed him and pick up his poop in the yard every single day before Daddy gets home 'cuz I'm a good dog owner. I'm wesponsible." He said that with his chin stuck forward.

"You mean responsible."

Georgie's head bobbed. "Ah-huh! I one of the good guys 'cuz I is wesponsible."

Cute kid. "Do you think Pepe's big enough to keep a guy like me safe tonight?" Tate doubted it. Not with the kind of nightmare he had coming at him.

But the little guy nodded even as he patted said guardian angel on his head, making Pepe blink with every pat. "Ah-huh, and he might steal your covers too, but it's okay. Dogs is man's best friends, you know."

Tate swallowed hard. He knew that about dogs, just hadn't taken advantage of it the way Harley had. The man raised several dozen security dogs every year, making some available for local law enforcement. Others, trained as service dogs for veterans with PTSD, went to deserving men and women returning from the wars. Word was Harley donated those dogs out of the goodness of his heart. He'd suffered with PTSD once. He knew the difference a good service dog made in a ragged man's life.

And there sat Tate with the tiniest service dog ever, shivering up against his chest and doing what dogs did best. Just being there when the whole world fell apart. Maybe Georgie was onto something.

In a minute, Harley came back with a five-pound bag of dog food and Tate was good to go. He eased the kid to the ground. "Thanks, Georgie. How about Pepe and me come back for a visit someday? Would you and Rooster like that?"

The kid's smile looked just like his dad's, a little crooked, but just as wide. "And we'll play fetch and hide-and-seek and Legos?"

"You bet." What else could Tate say?

Harley put a hand to Tate's shoulder. "You need anything, you call me. Judy and the boys would love to have you and Pepe stay with us. We've got the room."

Tate put the Jeep in reverse. "Tell Judy thanks, but no. Another time."

He might take Harley up on his offer, but then again...

He might not.

Chapter Nineteen

It took less than an hour to get home from Harley and Judy's. By then, Tate was spent, his heart broken and the pieces of it crushed to dust. Most guys would resort to alcohol or violence at this point. Not Tate. He scooped Pepe into his arms and headed up the side steps to his loft. Drinking hadn't brought anyone in his life back. Why start now?

The rustic complex was small. It had been built around an old grain mill and housed maybe ten residents at the most. He rented the entire top level, more of an attic with a wide open set of brick-walled rooms, high wooden beams, an east facing set of floor-to-ceiling windows, and a view that couldn't be beat. Except tonight.

At the top step, Tate keyed in his access code and opened his door. The day outside had turned gloomy and dark, matching his mood. He shut the door and locked it out. Moving through the place, he kept hold of Pepe. "Take it easy, boy. You're with me now."

Working for Alex Stewart with Ky and the guys had been the highlight of his life after the war. He'd belonged with those men and women. He fit in. Despite his reluctance to befriend many of them apart from Ky, he'd understood them. They talked the same language and they'd lived through the same crap. But now...

Life on the Deuces Wild Team was an endurance test, a trial by one fire after another. A gauntlet he couldn't escape. He wasn't psychic and he didn't belong. There seemed no limit to the beating the universe exacted from him.

Tate scrubbed his fist over his sternum. The hollow spot below the bone ached. That pain never went away, but today, it felt like a sucking black hole had opened beneath his ribs.

In his kitchen, Tate flipped on the light over his stove and set up a food and water station for Pepe alongside the butcher-block counter. He doffed his clothes on his way through his darkened living room to his bedroom, needing a shower and to be far from the world. A tiled fortress would have to do for now. If only it held sorrow at bay.

Cranking the water to hot, he ripped the bloody bandage off his bicep. Stepping into the shower, he lathered up, head, shoulders, knees, and toes. Rinse one. He lathered up again. Same drill. The tears started on the third reiteration, somewhere between shoulders and knees. Tate put his forearm to the tile beneath the scalding water and leaned his head to his arm.

He wasn't a soft man. Never had been. Didn't know how to start. But this damned day had resurrected every last ghost from his past, tenderizing him to his limits. Until today, there'd only been one that mattered, and he relived her last moments on earth in brilliant three-dimension Technicolor. Now there were two.

Losing Winslow amplified the other loss. The guilt. He'd been what, twelve when the first happened? What was he now, twenty-six? Twenty-seven? Going on ninety? He'd lost track. Birthdays ceased counting the day she fell.

Weary and battle sore, Tate ended the shower, redressed his wound, and pulled on a clean pair of black workout pants and a charcoal-gray T-shirt. Back in the kitchen, he turned off the light, searching for Pepe. "Where are you, boy?"

A quiet whine and a scratch sounded at the door. Tate rounded the corner to his living room, the big empty room with windows. "What are you doing in here? Come on. I'm beat. Let's hit the sack."

Pepe jitterbugged, cast his eyes to the doorknob, then back at Tate. Guess the dog needed to go outside, as in right damned now. Tate didn't have a leash. Did he dare take the chance?

Scooping Pepe up, he told the dog as he retraced his steps down to the parking lot and entered the chain-link fenced in dog run, "If you take off on me, you'll be lost. You don't want that, do you? I sure don't." *Like it or not, I need you, little guy. You're all I have left of Winslow.*

Great. He was talking to a dog, out loud and in his head. Tate scrubbed his face and yawned. So damned tired. He shut the gate before he let Pepe loose. The little guy didn't need to do his business. No sir. He'd no sooner hit the ground than he ran to the farthest side of the play area, scratched at the chain link, and yapped like he wanted out. Not happening.

"I brought you here to pee, little guy. Get it done or we're going back inside." *Maybe I will have a drink.*

Yap, yap, yap. More fence scratching. No leg action and no peeing.

Tate made short work of the distance between him and the dog. Scooping Pepe up, he'd just cleared the gate when the little guy wiggled out of his arms and took off for the road. "No!" he yelled, running after the dog. "Come back. You'll get hit by a car!"

The dog kept going. Tate could barely keep up. He yelled at the disappearing Chihuahua's backside with every pounding step. "Pepe, stop! Come back." *Damn it, not you too!*

When that failed to work, he bellowed, "Winslow!"

Damed if that little guy didn't stop in his tracks and spin in a couple of tight ADHD-type circles. Still posed to run, Pepe stopped, his ears perked up.

Tate's heart sprang to life, a snare drum trapped in his chest. Did Pepe know something he didn't? Like last night when the dog led him to the water tower. If he'd found Winslow then…

Tate crouched to one knee, his hand extended, his palm up and his fingers curled to entice the dog forward. "That's what you were trying to tell Harley, isn't it? You're not hungry; you know where Winslow is. She's not in the river, is she?"

Pepe offered one short sharp yelp, his nose still tending toward the road, as if to say, *"I don't know what you're talking about but come on! We gotta hurry!"*

Tate swatted his thigh. "Then come here, boy. Let's go get Winslow together."

Pepe glanced at the open road, then came running with a, "Yap! Yap! Yap!"

Damned if Tate didn't hear: *Yes! Yes! Yes!*

Holy hell. I am psychic. With dogs.

That was how he and Pepe ended up back on Maple. Pepe was the missing eight ball, now in play at the final hour. Tate didn't need an address to locate Winslow and he didn't need GPS. He had Winslow's best friend. At least, her 'second' best friend.

It made sense on a morbid level. Not the road trip, but her mother orchestrating an assisted suicide for her cancer-ridden child. All the pain would end.

Winslow would be at peace. Joyce would finally, after seventeen *arduous years of torture and self-sacrifice*, be free to build a real life. She could marry that loser Ike if she wanted to. Winslow cringed at the thought, but if that was what her mom wanted...

Or Joyce could leave town. Obviously, she wouldn't have to worry about feeding a dog she didn't like. There was nothing to hold her in Silver Spring except her job at the spa. Yes. Assisted suicide certainly put a nice big, black bow on Winslow's cancer, once and for all. Except Tate said he'd find Pepe, and Winslow believed him. He was kind and caring, and he liked her Honey Munchkin and...

A sob croaked out of her. *I don't want to die yet. I'm not ready. Tate's not here yet, and I don't even know if he knows where I am and... Please. I don't want to die.*

Tate had made her cancer sound like a challenge last night, instead of the death sentence Winslow thought it was. He was the only person who'd brought real comfort into a dark and dreary world where a girl needed to climb a water tower just to get an uplifting perspective on a life that really, really sucked.

And those stars in the sky when he'd kissed her. The fire that roared to life when she'd kissed him back. With her eyes closed, Winslow let her tongue slip over her bottom lip and got lost in the memory. It certainly couldn't hurt to dwell on Tate, not here at the end of time. It wasn't like she was going anywhere.

I'll pray harder, she promised her Heavenly Father. *I'll go to church. I'll be kinder to my mother. I'll try harder. I promise...*

Another sob eked out. There was no way she could pray harder. Already, she sensed how close the Lord was to her when she'd lain on the bathroom floor that morning, so ill she'd wanted to die. He was there when she awakened, day after day, to lethargy and exhaustion that robbed the joy out of snuggling with Pepe. If anyone knew what she was going through, *He did.*

There was no sense in bargaining what she didn't have to offer.

Lifting one heavy arm, she touched a finger to her lips, savoring the memory of Tate's lips on hers. He'd smelled so good, so manly, of cedar and wind and— life. But the taste of his mouth was what she missed now. Breath-mint and spice. The prickly brush of his close-shaven chin. The scent of his warm breath in her face. The gentlemanly way he'd asked permission before he'd kissed her. The curl of heat in the pit of her belly, when he'd pressed his lips to hers. It seemed, for a moment there, to bring her body back from the edge of the grave she'd been standing at for years. Then he'd slipped his tongue between her lips and he'd kissed her.

My first kiss. She clenched her legs together as the same sensual response flared even now in that dark hopeless hospital room where people like her were stuck until they—died.

Aaaannndddddddd... *Bullshit!* burst through the daze in her downward spiraling brain. It was Tate's word, and a good word. It was a strong word. The ragged image of him in all his angry glory when he'd challenged her mother sprang to throbbing vivid life. *What the fuck is wrong with you, Winslow? Stand up for yourself. Fight for what you believe in. Shit, stop kissing her ass!*

"B-b-but you're supposed to be nice to me. I'm... I'm dying here."

Bullshit!

My heavens. This shadow of Tate, or memory, or whatever it was, didn't seem to have many words in its thesaurus.

"You think this is living?" Okay, now she was getting downright maudlin, arguing with herself and imagining talking to Tate. It had to be the drugs the nurse had put in her IV.

Winslow traced her tongue over her bottom lip, surprised at the taunting memory her brain had summoned in this her final hour. The taste of him and that single dynamic word—*bullshit*—changed everything.

Almost. She was still flat on her back with an IV drip silently feeding nutrients—or something—into her depleted system. She was still headed for Oregon. Wasn't that where they were going on their one and only mother/daughter road trip? Winslow couldn't remember. Funny how they'd never gone anywhere before, but now they were. The faster-than-fast, packup-and-leave-town trips every other year didn't count. Those mad dashes from one place to another had only been to evade bill collectors or nosy neighbors, and they weren't fun.

What changed? Why assisted suicide now when Winslow's death seemed so imminent? Was Joyce desperate to be done with this awful burden-of-a-child she'd been stuck with? Had she come into some extra money that made this trip feasible?

Bullshit!

Winslow allowed a small smile. She could almost see Tate spitting that word at her. His brows would clash together. His pupils would turn black and fierce. "Okay, okay, I get it. You're mad because you don't understand my mother, and that's okay bec—"

Bullshit!

Winslow stopped making excuses to the annoying shadow in her head. It seemed intent on having the last word, so she let it win. *I have got to be on drugs.*

The question remained though. Why hadn't her mother ever taken her on a road trip before, just for the fun of it? If she could do it now, if she could finally afford to facilitate the end of her daughter's life with a cross country road trip, surely she could've done something to enhance that same life, you know, to liven things up in a pleasant, fun, mother/daughter kind of way?

Winslow might not have gone to school like normal people, but she'd seen happy parents with their happy children. Everything in the world wasn't unfair. Life wasn't one cheat after another though it might seem that way to the single parent of a dying child.

For that matter, why no movie nights or picnics or walks in parks? Those things didn't cost much. Why no holiday celebrations that didn't include booze? Ever? It was almost as if Joyce had kept Winslow out of sight and in the shadows. Or down…

Was she ashamed of her daughter? Winslow tried that conclusion on for size. No. Joyce wasn't ashamed of her daughter or she wouldn't have set up the whole television debacle over the Dreams-Come-True prom thing. And yet, Winslow knew to her soul that her mother loved the spotlight. Who could blame her? Winslow couldn't. Her mom deserved a little attention now and then.

But so do I…

She cocked her head, expecting another wicked blast from her favorite memory, but there was none, so she followed the train of thought Tate's shadow had set loose from the station. *Fight for what you believe in.*

He made it sound easy, but honestly, Winslow had never fought for a thing in her life, not with her energy tied up in her battle with cancer. Her mother was a strong and vicious adversary. Case in point: Pepe. Joyce meant to win her battles, and she wasn't above kicking a person when they were down. Or smacking a helpless little dog that only wanted to snuggle in Winslow's bed.

Now that the assisted suicide engine was also on the track and picking up steam, Winslow didn't want to die. It was one thing to stand at the top of a water tower and think about it, but quite another to have someone else planning it on your behalf.

Oh yeah, Vermont. That was the other state that allowed assisted suicide. It was a lot closer than Oregon, California, or Washington. Too close for comfort.

I have to get out of here. Winslow opened her eyes and lifted up to her elbows. Exit door straight ahead, just beyond her feet. IV to the left. A closet or maybe a bathroom door at her right. No overhead light fixture. Just the ambient glow from an outside light showing through the blinds on the window to her left.

A little thing called curiosity wiggled to life way down deep in the basement of Winslow's trusting, only child's heart. Assisted suicide, huh? That was to be her first real foray into the world, to let some guy she'd never met before help her die? Not a pleasant trip to the ocean so she could run headlong into the surf? Not a night out on the town, whatever that entailed? But assisted suicide, huh? *Nothing says motherly love like—that.*

Winslow glanced at her IV line. Whatever drug was in that light golden fluid, it seemed to be helping. She could think, and she actually felt like standing on her own two feet.

Tugging the blanket off her legs, she swung both feet over the edge of the mattress. *I feel—good.* Her toes wiggled. They'd look good with toenail polish, bright turquoise maybe.

"Bullshit." She kept her voice low, but that word tasted good on her tongue. It had a certain zing to it. A touch of defiance. She wanted to go to Florida, not Vermont. No! To borrow Tate's salty vernacular, what the fuck was her mother thinking getting rid of Pepe? Who died and made her God?

Anger rippled proud and strong up Winslow's backbone, leaving a surge of self-righteousness in its wake. Sweet little Pepe had never done anything to merit Joyce's temper. Okay, so maybe once or twice he'd had an accident as a puppy, but Winslow was the one who'd cleaned up after him, fed and cuddled him.

"Bullshit," she said as she eased cautiously off the mattress. She was tired of hearing how hard things had always been for her poor, poor mother. *Newsflash, Mommy Dearest. Trade places with me for a while, why don'tcha? Let cancer eat up your life, steal your energy, and, oh yeah, all of your hair. You think having a baby out of wedlock was the end of the world? Get over it already. I've been a good kid.*

Sheesh. Where had all this self-actualization come from? Winslow giggled. From Tate. Who else?

Careful so as not to tug the line to her catheter, she settled both feet to the cool linoleum floor and stood. How hard could it be to remove an IV line and a catheter? She intended to find out.

The IV line was easy. She simply peeled the tape off the back of her hand, pulled out the needle, and just like that, she bled a little, but she was free. Winslow draped the plastic line over the tree and left it there. Now for the tricky part. Tipping her butt to the bed, she pulled her hospital gown up and tucked it under her chin to keep it clear in case this little foray into medical land didn't quite work out. But seriously? This was her body. Not the nurse's. Not the doctor's. And come to think of it, not her mother's. *Another newsflash—I can do this.*

Winslow grasped the plastic tubing that ended somewhere up inside her very private parts and... out it came, as easily as one, two—*ow, that pinched a little*—three. She figured quickly how to keep the business end of that plastic tube high above the bag attached to the side of her bed, but seriously? Once she tied the plastic tubing into a knot, the problem was solved.

She headed to the door to her right that had to be a bathroom with a sink to wash her hands, maybe take a shower. Along the way, she spied a brown paper bag stuffed with some of her clothes. Good enough. *I'm already packed and I'm on my way.*

With shaky fingers, she sank to her knees and selected her light purple T-shirt with *BOSTON* splashed in bright violet, caps across the front, and an old pair of washed-too-many-times Rider jeans, the hems ragged and stringy. More digging in the bag revealed several clean pairs of cotton panties and a bra, not that she had much to put in it. But that was what distinguished girls from women: They dressed appropriately, and if there was one thing Winslow was sure of since she'd met Tate, she was all woman.

Sucking in a deep breath of freedom, Winslow squared her shoulders against the inevitable battle. She had places to go that didn't include a road trip to death, *thank you very much, Mom.*

The ceiling-to-floor tiled bathroom housed a simple sink attached to the wall inside the door and a full tub/shower combination at the far wall, all in that lovely institutional shade of mint green, the kind that screams *they're-coming-to-take-me-away, ha-ha.* A silver commode hung between the tub and the sink, which was good since the alignment of those facilities gave Winslow handholds on her way to the shower. A floor drain marred the floor, but it made sense in a creepy way. The janitor probably hosed the place down between patients.

At the shower, she turned the shower spray to warm and stripped. The sight of the hospital gown floating to the floor brought her special word to the tip of her tongue. "Bullshit," she told that item of clothing with a certain sense of relish. "You've taken too much this time, Mom. I'm out of here."

With her sassy attitude in place, Winslow lifted one shaky foot after the other and climbed into the tub. She made quick use of the hotel-sized bar of Dial soap resting in the wire rack beneath the showerhead. Shampoo would've been nice once upon a time, but she didn't waste time crying over spilled milk—or lost locks. Hair didn't make the woman. Fortitude did. She slicked a layer of suds over her bare head, rinsed, and called it good.

Bowed beneath the shower spray with her palms splayed to the wall, she watched the suds slide over her scrawny body to her toes before they escaped down the drain. Each one of those tiny, foamy bubbles carried a piece of her old self away. She wasn't a spineless, sickly woman anymore. She was Winslow Arizona Parrish, and damned proud of it. She might be shaky, but she felt good for a change. And squeaky clean.

Tate might never know what his angry outburst did for her, but she found herself relying on it now. "Bullshit. Bullshit. Bullshit," she whispered, one more time for good measure, only louder. "Bullshit!"

How delightful! When at last she sank to the edge of the tub to towel off, her hands trembled, but that was a good thing, wasn't it? She was on her way, still a little weak, but growing stronger every minute. She could feel it.

Back in the room, she dressed as quickly as she could. Once she'd stood up to her mother, where would she go? The phone Tate had charged her to keep was long gone. She had no money. Still rattled at her tenuous situation, she looked for her shoes. Flip-flops would've been nice. Or slippers. *Just great. Nothing.*

Oh, well. Winslow drew in a deep breath. Swallowing decisively, she walked to the door half expecting it would be locked, but it opened easily into a hall with more closed doors. There was no guard, which she'd half expected, probably because no one expected her to live.

Ha. I'll show them.

Stiffening her chin, she gulped down her fear of the unknown and took slow, stealthy steps on her way to freedom. Tonight was the night. An exit sign marked the way out. Winslow peered through the door's security window. Night had fallen. Her mother's car sat alone in the rear parking lot looking sad in the rain. Winslow turned the knob and—

"Where do you think you're going?"

Crap. Mom. Winslow shot a desperate glance over her shoulder. "For a walk," she declared as evenly as she could muster. There was no need to fight. Not yet. "I need some fresh air."

"Get back into bed this minute." Typical Mom snark.

"When I'm done with my walk." Winslow pushed the door outward, fighting the urge to bolt when the moist cool air poured inside. Reasonable people shouldn't be afraid of their mothers. "I feel good today, umm tonight, and I'm just going for a little walk in the rain. Want to come with me? It'd be fun to laugh and talk and—"

"Get back in bed!"

Something snapped inside Winslow. "Bullshit!" she volleyed back. "I feel good and I'm going for a walk. Either come with me or—"

Joyce cleared the distance in seconds, her chin up and her eyes flashing. With one vicious punch, she knocked Winslow to the floor. "You're not going anywhere."

Winslow rolled to her shoulder, lifting her hands and arms to ward off the attack, but she wasn't quick enough. The last thing she saw was the silver needle coming at her.

Chapter Twenty

"What are you doing?" Tucker asked when Tate launched out of his Jeep.

Wouldn't you know? Not only had Tucker not taken his own advice and gone home for the night, neither had Isaiah, Ky, or Eden.

"You won't believe what we've found," Ky muttered as he swiped a hand over his sweaty forehead. "Your girlfriend kept journals. We've got enough evidence to charge her mother with neglect and abuse."

Good to know. Tate would've loved to have stayed and chatted, but he didn't have time. "Later," he said as he set Pepe's feet to the Parrish front lawn. Lo and behold, the little guy whizzed like a trooper—right before he headed east as fast as his four little paws could go.

"Follow that dog," Tucker barked.

Tate had to look twice. That was what he'd meant to say. He knew he'd had an in with the four-legged sleuth disappearing down the street, but was it in any way possible that he also had a psychic link with his boss? *Impossible.*

Dogs outgunned humans when it came to their sense of smell. After what Tate had witnessed in the wilderness with wildlife, and during combat with military working dogs, he couldn't dispute the uncanny devotion of this tiny canine to his mistress.

Pepe found Winslow before and he would do it again. Two sets of boots pounded the concrete at Tate's six. He didn't waste time looking. Had to be Ky and Eden. A burly engine growled alongside. Had to be Tucker's Challenger. Where was Isaiah?

"Don't lose that dog," Tucker yelled from his open window.

No shit. Tate kept his eyes glued to Winslow's four-legged guardian angel instead of answering. He didn't know where Isaiah went, and he didn't care. At the corner, Pepe angled left. Tate followed his lead. The little guy glanced over his shoulder as if he needed to be sure Tate followed.

Keep going, buddy, Tate urged his canine mastermind. *Faster. Find her.*

Another block. Then another. Tucker rolled alongside. Pepe was panting plenty by then, but still going. Not slowing. The damned little guy was the Energizer Rabbit all over again. He racked up close to two miles, through puddles and mud, and still Tate followed, his T-shirt and pants drenched with sweat and his hamstrings on fire, but not losing sight of that dog.

Another block north and he lost Ky and Eden. One hurried backward glance told him they'd stopped together. Eden was off to the side of the sidewalk, rubbing her foot. Sprained ankle maybe. Tucker pulled to the curb where the Winchesters had stopped. He waved Tate to keep going. Like there was a choice?

But where was Pepe taking him? To the left again, apparently. All righty then. Tate cut across the brightly lit intersection. He dodged the slow-moving sedan in the right turn lane with its blinker on, jumped the two-foot high hedge at the corner, and headed west. By then Pepe was nowhere in sight.

Wiping the sweat out of his eyes with one quick swipe, Tate slowed his pace, squinting as he walked onto what seemed an ordinary residential street. Old fashioned streetlights designed to look like gas lamps cast a yellowish glow over modern mom-and-pop style homes. Kids' bikes lay where they'd been ditched on driveways, lawns, and walkways. Lights glowed from a few picture windows. Tate just couldn't see the hospital that Eden thought she'd seen.

But Pepe had led him there, and that was good enough. Tate slowed his pace, sure the dog wouldn't have taken off and left him. But what if he had? Pepe hadn't slowed down one bit on this mad dash. Maybe he was chasing tail? Tate shook his head at the idiotic notion. No. Pepe was true blue. To the core. He was on Winslow's scent, not some puppy-dog quickie.

The street was quiet in an abandoned kind of way, as if the earlier rain kept everyone indoors. The silence should've eased the angst creeping up Tate's spine, but it served up another surge of acid in his gut instead. It reminded Tate of a horror movie where the axe murderer looked like the guy next door, only he had ten shallow graves in his backyard. It was that kind of silent, the eerie kind that pricked your last nerve until you could hear the splat of each individual raindrop when it hit the sidewalk.

"Aarf!" Pepe wagged alongside some kid's pink Barbie Jeep at the end of the driveway two doors down.

Tate cut through the adjoining yard to catch up. The house Pepe had stopped at looked different. Tidier. No kid-paraphernalia littered the postage-stamp lot. All windows were dark and shuttered. A printed sign sat in the front window between the glass and the blinds, but Tate couldn't make out what it said. Bars covered the few basement windows that he could see, but it was the antiseptic odor on the air that cinched the deal. This had to be the place.

He infiltrated the property with the stealth of a scout sniper, his weapon drawn and his six senses on high alert. Yes, six. He counted his gut as perhaps his most reliable sense.

He'd no more than rounded the rear corner of the house, when he spied Joyce's Chevy. Pepe changed tactics then. Instead of leading, he nudged Tate's leg with his nose as if to say, "I found her, now it's up to you. Go inside and get her."

Tate dropped to one knee on the driveway behind the sedan, one hand on Pepe's head. "Are you sure Winslow's inside?"

Pepe spun one circle, danced and whined.

"I sure hope you're right, because tonight I'm breaking and entering based on the word of a dog." *How frickin' bizarre.*

Another whine. Tate gave Pepe one last pat before he crept to the first window at the back of the house. The damnedest thing happened next. Pepe took off like a shot back to the front of the place, yapping his head off. Tate's heart nearly dropped to the asphalt at the racket that little guy set up, but before he could call the crazy mutt back, the front porch lights flashed on. Some guy yelled from inside the house, "Hey, Joyce. This your dog?"

Pepe was going for distraction. *What a dog!*

Winslow startled awake with a bale of lint in her mouth and her usual splitting headache. Her neck hurt like she'd strained it to the point of breaking it, and for a moment, the ceiling bobbed and weaved overhead in the dark. But the nausea wasn't what woke her. It was Pepe. Barking. He sounded frantic. *Great. He probably has to pee, and Mom's ignoring*

him, hoping he'll wake me. Good thinking, Mom. It worked.

Why'd she have to be so mean to the little guy?

Flopping to her back, Winslow leveled one arm over her eyes to block the dimmest ray of light screaming through the window, blinding her. Daily migraines sucked, but this one was so much worse. She could barely flutter her lashes. One of those light blocking curtains would sure come in handy. Yeah. Splitting migraine. Darned near incapacitating. Not fun.

"I'm coming," she groaned at her faithful companion. Somehow, that crack in her voice must not have inspired confidence. Pepe launched another round of frantic yapping. What was wrong with him? He sounded like Munchkin-gone-crazy.

Winslow lifted to her elbows, then sat upright only to bow her head to her knees, fighting the deepest lethargy to get her butt in gear. Mom would smack him if she had to let him out, so Winslow needed to hurry. She shook off the dizziness in her head and pushed to her feet, her legs shaking like crazy. Only...

Where am I? This isn't my room.

Exhausted, she dropped back to the—*hospital bed? How could you do this to me, Mom?*

Slowly, like gooey, sticky molasses in the dead of winter, her failed escape attempt came back to her. Her pick-me-up shower. The clean clothes. The hypo.

Worse—the evil glint in her mother's eyes when she'd plunged that needle into Winslow's neck.

Blinking back tears, she took stock of her situation. She was back in that POS hospital gown, but without the catheter or IV drip. The room was colder. Cupping her biceps didn't slow the shiver that raced up the back of her neck. She wasn't supposed to be here and everything was so hard!

Bullshit!

Wow. Wherever that came from, it actually— helped.

The shrill yapping of her brave little dog brought her head up once more just as she heard him scratching at her window. That couldn't be right. With one eye closed, she rotated her pounding head to the right. How on earth had Pepe climbed up to that window? How could he be in two places at once?

Her stomach threatened swift retaliation, but wait. Could it be Tate making that noise?

The possibility of that miracle staggered Winslow. She lurched a drunken, wobbling path to the window. It took an enormous effort, but at last she succeeded in capturing those pesky strings to lift the blinds. She pulled as hard as she could and...

Wow, his eyes were scary big and black. That black T-shirt he had on looked tight and hot-damned nice stretched across his magnificent chest. "Tate? What... what are you doing here?"

He gestured with his fingers to hurry, open up, but she was beyond weak. It took painstaking effort to work the simple lock at the top of the lower pane. "I'm trying," she mumbled through the glass, which, now that she was up close to it, looked all sorts of wavy like that old-fashioned glass the pioneers used in their one room log cabins on the prairie and...

Where was I? She leaned her forehead to see through that funny looking glass. *Oh. Tate. He's waiting for me... Outside... Hmmm. I wonder why?*

The moment she barely lifted the pane, he stuck all eight fingers through the opening and pushed the window open.

"Whew," she exclaimed breathlessly, dizzy once more.

He tilted to the side. *Oh wait. That's me.* Winslow put one elbow to the ledge and her chin on her hand to stop listing. *God, he's handsome.*

"Give me your hands, Winslow. Both of them. You need to come with me. Right now."

"But I'm... umm, Pepe's... W-w-where exactly are we going?" She'd never felt so discombobulated before in her life. Was any of this real? Worse, was this what happened to people's brains when they died? Was that what this out-of-body experience meant, that she was on her way—out of her body? The next thing you know, there'd be a tunnel of light, and she'd see ghosts, and...

"We dancing?" she asked for no good reason other than she was fairly certain Tate and she had done this exact same thing before.

He extended one muscular and very wet arm through the window. The man's shirt was drenched, delineating the thickness of his chest and the girth of his biceps. Water dripped from his hair, running down his face. "I'll explain later. Come on. Hurry." He latched one arm onto her waist and pulled her hip onto the window ledge.

"I can't dance out this window." Her brain wasn't making sense. Neither was her mouth.

His lips thinned to a slant. "Hang onto me, Winslow. I'll lift you."

"I'll fall."

"No, you won't. I'll catch you."

He didn't make sense, either. How could he catch her if she wasn't falling? Now, if he meant to take her dancing, then she'd fall. Lifting one heavy foot, she tucked her knee up high enough to put that bare foot on the sill. "Okay. I'm ready," she breathed.

Shadows danced at her peripheral. She leaned forward, but made the mistake of turning back to call Pepe. She knew he wasn't there, but the movement upset her head and stomach and...

Whoosh! The room spun around her like a top. She fell out the window and... *oomph!* into Tate's arms and against his very warm, wet chest. She turned to lick his neck, but damn. Sunlight was a killer, only it wasn't the sun blinding her, not unless somebody'd hung it on a lamp post in a shiny wet parking lot full of puddles of stabbing reflected pain. She covered her eyes with both hands at the lightning strike to her retinas. "Turn it off, Tate. Please, turn it off."

Pepe kept barking, but he wasn't bouncing around like his usual self, and she couldn't see him, and that meant... *Damn. I don't know what anything means anymore.*

Winslow let her heavy head loll onto Tate's chest where she knew she was safe, her eyes closed tight and her mind weak from all this mental exertion. Pepe not being with Tate meant something bad, but she couldn't figure precisely what.

Tate dropped smoothly to the ground from whatever mountain he'd been standing on, his hand cupping the back of her head like she was a baby or something. Even that small jump created a shockwave in her skull. She groaned, not so much from pain, but... okay. From pain. But why'd her body feel like it was burning from the inside out? Why was Tate stealing her? What on earth did her mother mean by suicide? *My suicide?*

"I'm gonna die," Winslow cried. "Su... su... suicide. I hafta kill myself only—"

He growled like a wolf. "You're not going to die, Winslow."

The funniest word bubbled up through the fog in her head. *Bullshit.* Wasn't that odd? Nothing made sense. Just Tate. Just Pepe. They'd come for her and they could have her.

"I wanna go dancing," she whined into the warm recess of his neck. He smelled so good.

"Shhh," he whispered, his arms around her like the steel bands around a very skinny barrel. "I've got you now."

"Hmmm. That's nice." Winslow burrowed into that safe warm place, drawing in the rugged scent of pine trees, rain, and clean, manly sweat. Lifting one trembling hand, she wanted to kiss him, but her hand fell limply to his shoulder, then slid pathetically down his chest. She didn't have the strength to thank him for saving her from... *whatever*. The last thing she remembered before everything went black?

Tate's piercing whistle.

Chapter Twenty-One

Thank God for Tucker and that smoking hot SRT Hellcat parked in the shadow of a large, leafy tree, its 6.2 liter hemi-V8 purring in the rainy, dark of a successful night. Winslow was in nothing but a frickin' hospital gown, and with her acting as loopy as she was, Tate didn't dare ask her to grab a blanket before she fell out that window.

Joyce shrieked from inside the house, "Winslow! She's gone! Call the cops!"

Time to roll. With Winslow tucked under his chin, Tate cussed himself for not planning better. Talk about going off half-cocked. He didn't even have a blanket.

Tate whistled for Pepe again, no longer worried about being noticed. Joyce wouldn't pull that coy, 'Oh, no, my baby's been kidnapped,' routine this time.

She needed cameras rolling for that. This time would be different. Tate had no doubt she was armed.

Winslow's anxious Chihuahua beat feet to the car and cleared the open passenger door a scant second ahead of Tate. Tucker motioned Tate to hurry just as the front porch light flashed off, then on. There she was, Mama Bear Parrish, screaming her guts out. "You bring her back this instant! I'll call the police! I know it's you, Tate Higgins! Do you hear me?"

"Call 'em!" Tate shot back at her. He made sure she got a good look at who had her twenty-year old daughter this time. Let her call the police. Hell, let her call the President. Tate was certain Ky and Eden had gathered enough evidence to put Mama Bear in prison.

With the next shower of rain in his face, he angled Winslow inside Tucker's muscle car. He'd no sooner set her sideways on his lap, when Tucker tossed a plush blanket over Winslow. Thank God. His boss had thought of everything. Tate wrapped Winslow up nice and snug.

Mama Bear kept screaming for her 'Poor, sweet baby!' but did she step one foot into the drizzle? Did she make any effort to chase after Tate when she knew damned well he had her daughter? Not on your life.

"You ready, Tate?" Tucker asked, a funny light glimmering beneath those thick, black lashes he was peering out from. The guy made everything seem like a game, as if he got off on the adrenaline.

"Holy Cross Hospital. Step on it, Boss." The telling word popped off his tongue like he'd meant to put Tucker Chase in the same category as Alex Stewart. *WTF?*

The double-barrel horses beneath the hood launched the Challenger up and off the wet pavement like Seabiscuit punching out of the gates at Pimlico. Nothing better. Tate cupped Winslow's head into his neck and hung on as the G-forces shoved him back into his seat.

Her breathing was so shallow that he had to cock his head nearly to her lips to hear her inhale and exhale. Her body shook, but not from the cold or the rain. She'd already been trembling plenty at the window and talking out of her head. Something was damned wrong with her.

It wasn't until Ky's hand clapped onto his shoulder that Tate realized he and Eden were stuffed behind him in the cramped backseat. "Oh, hi. How's your ankle, Eden?"

"She rolled it. Weak ankles. Who knew?" Ky teased.

Tate didn't get the joke. All he could see was Winslow's pale face when she'd tumbled out of that window, her strength gone, the rain streaming down her neck, and no bandana in sight. The few tufts of downy gray fuzz on her head were plastered to her scalp. She'd be so embarrassed to know Tucker, Ky, and Eden had seen her like this. He smoothed the blanket over her head and tucked her in like a nun.

"Hurry," he breathed, his big, wide palms pressing Winslow into the cradle of his body, needing her to accept all the heat he could offer. Her vertebrae were noticeably distinct under that blanket. *Please don't die,* he begged silently. *Not you too.*

He should've known better. There was no such thing as a solitary man thinking desperate thoughts in a car full of psychics. He'd no more than finished his prayer when Eden's fingers stroked the back of his neck. *"Trust Winslow, Tate,"* she pushed into his mind. *"She's just beginning to understand that she has personal power. Trust her. She wants to go dancing again—with you."*

He choked as that tender kindness rendered all of his psychic blocks useless. *"I love her,"* he told Eden mentally, his heart stuck in his throat. *"I know I shouldn't, but I do. I can't lose her too."*

"You won't," Isaiah chimed in from wherever he was. It sure wasn't from inside Tucker's car. *"Take a deep breath and know that we've all been where you are right now. You're not alone in this, Tate. We've got you covered."*

Tate nodded, ashamed that his emotions had gotten away from him. Damned if Tucker's big, wide hand didn't slap his knee next. He didn't say anything. He didn't have to. Tate got the message. He wasn't alone.

But he had been that day on the mountain. He'd been alone and scared out of his mind at what he'd done, and by the time he'd made it down, it was too late to save—*her*. This time had to end differently. Winslow was still alive, and they were on their way to a hospital, and he had four other agents who—

"Friends," Isaiah cut in psychically. *"Get used to it, Tate. I know you can hear me, so stop pretending you can't. You've got more friends than you want to admit."*

He swallowed hard. *"Yeah, I hear you,"* he sent back. Okay, friends then. He had four friends ready to go to the mat for him. Tate bowed his lips to the top of Winslow's bare head, wishing he'd brought that USMC cap with him. She was shaking so hard.

As if he had to prove something, Tucker stepped on the gas and made it to the emergency entrance in minutes. Tate lost control of the situation then. Somehow—maybe he could teleport—Isaiah was already there with a team of medical personnel and a gurney under the overhanging roof. They lifted Winslow quickly from Tate's arms. In a second, she was covered with heated blankets and on her way inside. He ran to keep up.

Isaiah clapped a hand to his shoulder at the ER entrance. "Just so you know, your Jeep's parked outside when you're ready to go."

Tate slapped his pants pocket. Oh, yeah. He'd left his keys in the Jeep when he'd run after Pepe. So that was where Isaiah had been. "Thanks."

"No problem."

The orderly or doctor or whoever that guy up ahead with the gurney was, took a sharp right along with his team of two women. Tate and Isaiah followed him down another hallway and into an open bay with smaller rooms around the peripheral. Winslow's gurney went into the third exam room to his left.

"What'd she shoot up with this time?" the guy who looked like he was in charge barked as he pressed a stethoscope to Winslow's chest. Nametag: Dr. Keegan, M.D. "She on heroin? Meth? Grab me the Narcan."

This time? Tate's fists clenched. They thought she was a drug addict. "No, it's not that. She's on some kind of cancer meds, and—"

Isaiah cleared his throat as he set a large Yeti cooler that Tate hadn't noticed he'd been carrying, on the narrow counter by the sink. "Dr. Keegan, I'm FBI Special Agent Isaiah Zaroyin, and this is Special Agent Tate Higgins. This woman is Winslow Parrish, and she's in FBI protective custody."

He shifted his feet as he flashed his badge. "You're right. She is on some kind of drugs, but she isn't an addict. I've brought all the medications from her house and any combination of these may or may not be in her system. These are evidence, sir, and they may not leave my sight. Chain of evidence, you understand. If you want, I'll gladly sit with one of your people while they log these pharmaceuticals into your database. We believe Miss Parrish has been under the care of an unscrupulous relative whom we are attempting to apprehend at the moment."

"I know where she is," Tate bit out. *The bitch.* If not for Winslow needing emergency transport, he'd have stayed at that house and arrested Joyce—the hard way.

Isaiah acknowledged him with one quick nod, his fingers tapping the plastic handle on the case. "You're not dealing with an addict, Dr. Keegan. You're dealing with a woman who's been methodically poisoned for years, and all the proof you need is in this cooler."

Tate's heart stopped. He turned on Isaiah. "How do you know all this?"

Isaiah leveled a look at Tate—*that look*—the one that made him feel like Isaiah could see straight into his soul. He probably could. "I wanted to tell you before, but there wasn't time. When you went after the nine-one-one on the bridge, I had the FBI lab run what was left in a hypo we found on the kitchen floor at Winslow's house. Someone's been playing doctor with several low dose prescriptions and this..." His fingers drummed the case, "is every last bit of drug-related paraphernalia and every last prescription bottle I could find."

Tate's eyes dropped to the giant-sized cooler. *Holy shit.*

Isaiah nodded as if he agreed or as if he'd—heard.

"Linda, go with him," Dr. Keegan ordered one of his nurses. "I want to know every last drug we're dealing with in ten minutes! STAT!"

While Isaiah ran out of the exam room with the taller of the two female nurses, Tate focused on

Winslow. By then, she was in the hands of capable nurses and doctors, all with grim faces. Machines were being moved next her bed. The hospital gown she'd come to the hospital in was being removed, so Tate ducked out to let them do their job, and to give her the privacy she deserved. He took a seat outside her cubicle, but was quickly directed to a private room where, damn. Everyone was already there waiting for him. Ky. Eden. Tucker too.

"Where's Pepe?" he asked, stalling to get his emotions in check.

"One of the K-9 handlers from the local police department has him for now, but Harley's on his way in. He'll keep him as long as you need."

While Ky clapped a hand to Tate's back, Eden grabbed his sleeve and tugged him down to her level. She hugged him. All he could do was let her while he buried his face in her shoulder and lost it.

"She's going to be okay," Eden murmured, her mouth to his ear. "You have to believe that, Tate. This isn't like that other time. You're not stuck on a mountain with no help in sight. There's a reason Joyce didn't poison Winslow outright. Think about this with me, Tate. Come on. Let's sit down. There's a lot you don't know."

It took him a minute to let go of Ky's sweet wife. He'd worked the op with Ky that saved Eden's life and the lives of a few hundred other FBI agents not long ago, but with her delicate body enfolding him like she cared... like he wasn't the guilty bastard he knew he was... almost like his mother used to hold him... yeah. It took a long couple of minutes to blink the weakness out of his eyes and face his—*friends.*

"You lost your mother when you were a kid, didn't you?" Damn that Tucker Chase. He tossed a towel at Tate the same time he ripped the scab off a damned deep wound.

Tate looked at his arrogant jerk of a boss through lowered brows. *The ass.* "What's it to you?" he growled, his fist clenched at being outed in front of everyone. It was just possible Ky hadn't known.

Tucker raised both hands to placate. "It's the same reason I know where you live. I've trusted the Bureau before, and found out the hard way that decision wasn't smart. Everything went bad because I didn't know that the guy at my six had betrayed us. This is my team now, so yeah. I know what happened up on that ridge when you were a kid. Your mother fell to her death, and you think you're responsible. It's called survivor's guilt."

"I am responsible." Tate dragged the towel over his neck and chest. Shit, why'd Tucker think he had to do this now?

"And I say you're not. How old were you when it happened?"

Tate wanted to knock his boss's fat head off and every last tooth out of his big mouth. "You're all so smart, you tell me." He whirled on Ky and Eden. They were just as bad as Tucker, butting in where they had no business.

The damnedest light glimmered in Tucker's face. "You were twelve, Tate," his said softly, his bluff and bluster gone. "You were the same age as my kid was when I finally got him away from his mother and back into my life. You were a little boy. God, you were just *twelve*..." He let the word hang, and as it hung there, the room filled with the stone-cold memory of the day a twelve-year-old boy stopped believing in magic and miracles and fairytales. When that kid became a hard man at Death's mercy.

Tate hooked the towel around his neck and glared at his arrogant boss. Even at twelve, he'd been sturdy and strong, built for nothing but a lifetime of toil and labor. It served him well that day. Alone, he'd dragged his mother out of that canyon in the tarp he'd always carried with him for emergencies. Only he'd never expected the first time he'd use it would be for—her.

He swallowed hard remembering the many times he'd fallen to his hands and scraped his knees because his legs gave out on the lonely trip home. The stinging sleet that fell over him and his mom, covering them both in a shroud of ice before he got her home. The tears at every lousy step. The bleakness in his dad's sharp-as-razor eyes when he'd seen his son, when he knew and screamed, "What have you done?!"

Jesus Christ, what could a kid say to regain his father's love after a crime like that? *Not a damned thing.*

Eden hadn't let go of his wrist yet. Neither had the memory let go of his heart. His chest heaved with the burden he'd packed since that day. That was why he disliked people. They hadn't lived through what he had. They could all afford to be happy and carefree and gossip and joke. He couldn't. Life ceased to be even remotely good the day he'd let his mother—*my Mom for Christ's sake!*—die. *I couldn't reach her. She fell. And every time I close my eyes, she keeps falling...*

"I know," Eden sent to him, *"and I'm so sorry, Tate."*

Tears brimmed at his lashes, threatening yet another breach he couldn't allow. This was no sitcom they were discussing. This was the deepest, rawest hole in his heart, and by hell, it was off-limits. Tate summoned his one and only psychic skill, and he slammed the door in their faces. "Back off," he growled, enforcing his number one rule. *I don't need people.*

"You never had a grip on her, did you?" Tucker again, damn him.

Shifting his boots and widening his stance, Tate stared him down, daring the man to say one more word.

Cue the silence.

Now everyone knew what kind of a man he was. And yeah, he understood why his father had screamed at him like he did that day. Hell, Tate had screamed right back at him. "I did it! I killed her!"

Because it was him up there on that mountainside. Just him! Not his dad. Not some plucky hero come to save the day like happened in the movies. It was just some kid who'd let his mom die.

His dad knew better, and so did he. They'd both ended up crying and holding each other until the night grew too dark and the storm too fierce to stay outside with her. Tate swallowed hard, damned near choking on the sharp lump forever caught in his throat.

But they couldn't leave her outside, not with bears roaming free and wild. Wolverines. Foxes. Eagles. They'd brought her into the cabin so no animals could get at her. The next day, they'd wrapped her in her favorite blanket and dragged her back up the mountain she'd loved. They buried her in her favorite place in the sun, high above the spot where she'd fallen. It took a while because of the storm and the ice, but, yeah. They got it done, he and his dad and a lot of tears.

Life was never the same after that. When she died, she took the sun and the stars with her, the scent of the sea on the wind and Tate's reason to live. He still woke up screaming some nights, lost in those last few seconds of her life. Always reaching for her, but always coming up empty-handed.

After that day, he grew restless and wary, antsy that something just as unforeseen could steal his father too. Little did he know his dad was already gone. When the morning came for Tate to enlist,

Shane was nowhere to be found. Tate ended up alone at his mother's grave to tell her where he was going and why, but he couldn't locate his father then, nor any day since. The man who'd raised him and loved him and taught him all he knew about the Alaskan wildlife just up and left him behind.

"Her name was Rain," Tate said quietly, giving his team something if they'd just shut up and leave him alone. "Rain Higgins." *And she loved the wilderness and fly-fishing and living off the land and... me. She loved me.*

"You lost your father around the same time." Isaiah came out of nowhere with those words. He stuck a Starbucks in Tate's hand. A venti. With a sleeve.

Random acts of kindness like that will get you every time.

Tate blew out a long sigh. As much as he didn't want to, he said, "My dad. Shane. He walked into the trees early one morning. Never came back." *I don't know where to look any more...*

It was then he noticed that heavy hand on his shoulder belonged to Tucker, not Ky. Eden and Ky now stood at one side, Tucker on the other. Eden's eyes were plenty red and teary. Ky's face was grim. Isaiah's across the way was—thoughtful, as if he was trying to decide something.

Yeah well, me too. Like if I should quit this chicken shit outfit and go look for my dad. Like if I should shut the hell up. Tate looked down at that

Starbucks in his hands, sick of being the center of attention.

"My kid, Deuce…" Tucker cleared his throat. "He, umm, Deuce lost a good buddy back in Vietnam. My ex took him there, and, anyway, Deuce met this skinny little orphan. Luke. It was tough the way he got killed, and Deuce still has nightmares. He wakes up screaming some nights, and I… and I…" Tucker coughed. "I feel so damned useless. Me. A SEAL and an FBI director. None of that means anything when I can't fix what happened to my kid, and, damn it. A father should be able to fix anything for his kid. It's like a knife in my heart that I can't. If I had a time machine, I'd go back and do things differently, but I… I can't. Life doesn't give us second chances. Evil exists and bad things happen, and that's just the way it is. I'm sorry. I'm sorry for your loss."

That was unexpectedly—weird. It almost sounded as if Tucker had a heart for a second. Tate stood there and took it until his boss caught him in a big-guy bear hug, spilling his coffee in the process. "I'm sorry," the cocky son-of-a-bitch growled against his cheek. "I'm damned sorry about your mom, Tate. I know you miss her every day."

Like that helped? Finally hearing someone acknowledge that she'd lived, and that he'd loved her with all his heart? Knowing all of that was gone? Tate blew out a deep breath and pushed Tucker away. He didn't hug men and enough was enough.

Ky and Eden patted him down with hands full of napkins and they mopped the coffee off the floor. Isaiah disappeared for a minute, then returned with another Starbucks, and it was time to change the subject.

"Tell me what you know about Winslow and her mother," Tate ordered.

Chapter Twenty-Two

When you're dying, you're supposed to see a bright shining light that pulls you toward it, and that light is supposed to be warm, and you're supposed to feel good, aren't you?

Winslow didn't. She'd been poked and prodded from every possible angle by the time she pried her bleary eyes open. But then she had to shut them again. The rows of overhead lights in this new nightmare were too bright. They turned the insides of her eyelids a vivid pinkish red even with her eyes closed. *Turn them off. Someone, please.*

She groaned and angled her head to the side, her lips parched. "Lights," she meant to say to no one in particular, but her dry mouth made it sound more like "blah."

A shadow blocked the brilliant glow enough that she took a chance and cracked one eyelid to see the crinkled straw sticking out of a plastic bottle headed her way. She took a long draw on that water bottle, thankful for small miracles. When she'd soaked the gritty sandpaper in her throat enough that it stopped hurting, she whispered, "Could you please turn the lights off?"

"I'm sorry, but no. I can't," someone replied.

Winslow couldn't decipher the gender of that voice. It was too fuzzy. Too far away. And fading fast. She closed her eyes and gave in to darkness.

"What's Joyce Parrish's real name then?" Tate couldn't believe what Isaiah had just told everyone. His clothes were dry by then, the towel tossed to a vacant chair.

"Hattie Beauregard," Isaiah replied without missing a beat. He'd rejoined the team, his cooler of evidence now safely locked in Tucker's car. "She was born in southern Georgia to James Beauregard and his second wife, Augusta. His first wife, Beulah Rae, died under suspicious circumstances when their bedroom caught fire. Augusta brought three boys with her into the marriage, the sons of her previous husband, Duke Forrest, who by the way, died in a hunting accident. Between Beauregard and Augusta, they had nine children that lived, five that didn't."

"Let me guess," Tucker drawled. "They died under suspicious circumstances."

Isaiah gave the barest nod. "Let's just say that Jerry Springer would have a heyday if this family ever made it to his stage. Two of Beauregard's boys are in prison for armed robbery, another for murder. One of the girls is serving time for ditching her newborn daughter in a garbage can. Another's in jail for poisoning dogs and cats in her neighborhood. You might've seen that one on the news. It was local."

He took a breath. "Besides the name Joyce Parrish, Hattie's got a string of aliases from state to state, not just in Georgia, plus charges from forgery to petty theft. She's done jail time twice, nothing serious. I've tracked the newspaper stories about her as far north as Montana, and all the way to New York. She hasn't strayed out of the country yet, but I wouldn't put it past her now that she knows we're onto her."

"When'd you have time to do this?" Tate asked, hoping this wasn't another sign of Isaiah's superior psychic abilities.

"Easy," Isaiah shot back at him. "I know some guys in the Bureau. You ought to try it, Tate. The FBI can be helpful."

"Pretty gutsy, don't you think? To demand an FBI escort for her daughter's phony last wish?" Ky added.

"And look at this." Eden slid an old newspaper clipping across the coffee table they'd gathered around while still sequestered in the waiting room. "Isaiah's friends at the Bureau also found this in

Hattie's place. Apparently, she likes to keep mementoes."

Tate lifted the clipping to his nose. The yellowed article had been mounted on black cardstock. It was a black and white picture of a younger Joyce Parrish and her daughter in front of a Salvation Army Christmas Tree with the headline: *"Devoted Mother of Dying Daughter Demands Personal Visit From Macy's Santa."*

While Tate scrutinized Joyce's nervy face, Eden slid several other clippings to his side of the table. All mounted on black cardstock, every last clipping disclosed a photo of Joyce with a brash headline about some noble deed she'd done for her daughter or something she'd demanded be done for Winslow.

The shot of her at a Baptist Church spring bazaar to raise money for cancer awareness spotlighted Winslow sitting in a wheelchair, her legs covered with a blanket. Tate peered closer. Damn, Winslow looked like she was maybe ten-years-old in that shot, but she was so skinny and her eyes were sunken. How long had this been going on?

There were more. From the Louisiana State Housing office to a Social Security office in Idaho, all showed Joyce making a public statement of how hard life was for a poor single mother with a cancer-stricken daughter. One audacious headline read *"Don't You Guys Get it?"*

At every state Joyce stopped in, she'd used her daughter's illness to draw attention to her plight. In one shot, she looked like quite the harried single mother. Her hair was longer then, disheveled, and Winslow was maybe three or four, hanging onto her mother's neck and staring at the camera with those too-big-for-her-face eyes. She was a scrawny kid even then.

In a more recent shot, Hattie had turned into Joyce with short spikes of silver-tipped black hair and that same predatory sneer. Winslow was older and walking, at least on her feet. But the camera caught her looking away while Joyce glared into the lens. The caption? *"Caretakers Are People Too!"*

"So she's a scam artist and she's used her daughter to do what? Get rich?" Tate asked.

Tucker shook his head. "See Tate, that's why I want you on my team. I like you. You're a straight shooter, one of those what-you-see-is-what-you-get kind of guys. You're not devious like Parrish, so you can't relate to her. The scary thing is that she's not after the money or the state housing she's been living in for years."

"Then what does she want?" Tate asked, baffled. *Just spit it out.*

Tucker leaned forward, his elbows to his knees. "Have you ever heard of Munchausen Syndrome?"

"The mental illness? Sure. I've heard of it." *I think.*

Whereas Tucker had leaned into the fight, Eden leaned back and crossed her ankles. "Munchausen Syndrome is a mental illness where a person deliberately exaggerates symptoms of an illness they may or may not have. Often, they hurt themselves on purpose, maybe alter their urine to produce specific test results, or they contaminate their blood by…" She shrugged, "…eating certain toxic plants, maybe taking drugs. They shop from doctor to doctor and clinic to clinic to get the diagnosis and/or drugs they want. Some are only into non-traditional or non-FDA approved drugs because they're easier to get. Some just want the hard-core narcotics. Others just want the attention."

"I get it. They're hypochondriacs." That term he understood.

"No, Tate. This is different. Hypochondriacs suffer from anxiety. They worry obsessively about their health or about a specific condition they may or may not have. They're constantly examining themselves for the slightest deviation from what they consider to be normal. But they don't treat themselves, Tate. People with Munchausen Syndrome actively treat and hurt themselves in pursuit of the medical treatment they think they need. They undergo unnecessary surgeries. They seek out medications, and often, they attempt suicide."

"Why?" He had to ask.

Tucker tapped his index finger to his head. "It's a mental defect, Tate. They want attention."

"Not necessarily, Boss," Ky interceded. "Munchausen Syndrome is more along the lines of an obsessive-compulsive disorder where these people can't control their impulses. It's a real mental condition."

"Which brings me to Munchausen Syndrome by Proxy," Eden said. "MSBP."

Tate rolled his neck at this field trip into psychobabble land. Dr. Keegan. That was who he needed to hear from, the sooner the better.

Eden kept going. "I believe Joyce Parrish is suffering with MSBP. It can lead directly to child or elderly abuse."

That perked his ears up.

"It's different from Munchausen Syndrome in that the caretaker, more often than not the mother of a disabled child, makes up symptoms or childhood illnesses for her healthy child where there are none. I've read cases where mothers have inflicted physical harm on their child to get the medical treatment they wanted. They've wrapped their kids in plastic to raise their temps, they've over-medicated them, and worse." Eden shook her head. "I can't imagine how any mother could hurt an infant so vulnerable as my Kyler. It boggles my mind. He's so cute."

Ky snorted. "He's a fat little pig, is what he is."

"Kyler's a baby beast," Tucker interjected.

"That's because he's built like his father. All muscle," Eden added. Tate couldn't miss the genuine affection in Eden and Ky's banter, the way his face softened at the mention of his son or wife. The way Tucker watched them like he was Kyler's proud grandfather.

Tate shook it off and refocused on the problem at hand. He'd given Joyce the benefit of the doubt, thinking she might've reached the end of her compassion after dealing with Winslow's cancer for so long. He'd even empathized with her. "You think that explains why Joyce, umm, Hattie, poisoned Winslow?" he asked, his elbows on his knees and his steepled fingers to his lips. Eden's hypothetical didn't quite sit right.

"I think it's possible, yes. Think about it. You mentioned Winslow felt fine Friday night, good enough to take a swing at you when you startled her, and good enough to climb that water tower ladder twice in one day. But come Saturday morning, she was violently ill. Why was that?"

That was just this morning. "I don't know, but today when I was at the house, I thought I might be watching her die. So you think what? That Joyce gave her something to perk her up Friday to get her through the prom date, then something else to make her sick this morning?"

Eden skipped a beat before she nodded. "It's possible. We now know that Joyce, or Hattie, came from a large, strict family where it's possible she was abused. If she was, she's carried that twisted role of parenting into her adulthood. In her mind, she's in control now, so she's quick to exercise that control in the only way she can—on Winslow."

Tate pushed back from the table, not buying that excuse. "She doesn't act like she's been bullied or hurt." She was an evil, conniving bitch. That was the only Joyce/Hattie he'd seen.

Yes, he'd tried to make her fit the compassionate mold because she *had* cared for her critically ill child into that child's adult years. It made logical sense that the only caretaker would be worn out, discouraged, and sick of her station in life. Who wouldn't be bitter by then? Caretakers were the invisible victims tasked to endure a thankless job, often with no relief in sight and no acknowledgement that they suffered too.

But that assessment didn't gel. The Joyce he'd seen was a mean-spirited woman who'd gone out of her way to kick a two-pound dog, then emotionally abused her child worse than the dog. No. Something uglier than MSBP was at work here.

Eden nodded, her lips pursed. "You know as well as I do that battered children tend to cover for their parents out of an innate sense of loyalty. Kids are like that. They love unconditionally. Isn't that what Winslow's been doing?"

"That's because she's kind and pure and—" He couldn't go on, not with her maybe dying a few doors away. What was taking that doctor so long?

"You're right, but she's been in an abusive situation for years, whether she recognized it or not. From everything I can pick up from Winslow's mind, she's not like her mother, but she has problems, Tate. It's called learned helplessness. Unless they've got a strong personality, sick people are vulnerable to coercion, real and implied. They're too sick and too weak to understand how to defend themselves. They end up just going with the flow."

"You're talking torture," Tate hissed.

"Yes, but let's get back to Hattie. If what I believe happened to her during her childhood, her belief system is warped. In her mind, she sees herself as disgusting, foul, stupid, and ugly. Given that patterning, how can she see anyone else differently?"

Tate stared at Eden, waiting for her to answer the rhetorical question.

She leaned toward him. "It's simple, Tate. She can't. No woman who sees herself as unlovable could. Her perspective is warped. Her normal is a scary world where everyone else is as disgusting as she believes she is. They have to be, otherwise she's the one who's wrong, and I'm sorry, but this kind of person isn't able to accept blame, criticism, or defeat. She craves the power that attention provides like a drug, so she can't afford to be wrong. Worse, there's almost no way to treat someone with MSBP because they'll never admit they need help in the first place. Why would they when they're the only one in their world who's right?

Tate brushed a hand over his head, unconvinced. There was no gray to morality in his mind. People made decisions. They needed to be held accountable for what they did and who they hurt. The end.

The corners of Eden's mouth curled as if she'd read his mind. "We know now that Joyce Parrish is an accomplished liar and a con artist, especially if she persuaded medical professionals to prescribe the quantity of drugs we found at her house."

"She could've gotten them on the streets for all we know," Tucker muttered.

"It's like this," Ky added. "Hattie can't accept love because she can't comprehend how someone like her is worthy of it. If anyone told her they loved her, which I'm willing to bet Winslow did as a child, that person lost her respect the instant they revealed what she believes is their fatal flaw."

"The minute Winslow told her mother that she loved her," Tate translated, "she became a target?"

Eden nodded. "Possibly. Or something as insignificant as Winslow telling her mom that she looked good. It's hard to know precisely what sets people with MSBP off."

Tate didn't care. "She tried to kill Winslow." *You can't whitewash that.*

"You bet," Tucker agreed, "and it's our job to apprehend her and hold her accountable to the fullest extent of the law."

"Which brings me to another point," Eden said. "Why didn't we arrest Hattie this evening when we had the chance? We should have. We had all the evidence we needed."

"Because we had to get Winslow to a doctor," Tate declared.

"And because Hattie expected Tate to come through Bly's front door," Isaiah said. He'd been quiet through most of the discussion. "In fact, she was prepared for it. She couldn't wait."

"Dr. who?" Tucker asked.

"Dr. Bly. That's where Tate found Winslow. He's one of the guys who's been treating her."

"You know that for sure?" Tucker asked. "Because I've got to tell you, I've been kicking myself for not calling in backup—"

"If you had, they would've been blown to bits, Boss. That house is wired to blow."

Tucker's brows arched. "With what?"

"According to the guys there now..."

That got Tucker out of his chair. "You called more of your *friends*—who by the way are FBI agents—without telling me?"

Isaiah shrugged. "Isn't that what you pay me for, to take care of business while you're breaking speed limits to get Winslow to safety?"

"Yeah, well..." Tucker's hand skated over his head, raking at his scalp. "So what'd our guys find?"

"The same thing McVeigh used, fertilizer and fuel."

Tucker bumped the heel of his hand to his forehead. "Shit, that bitch is as crazy as he was. She could've turned that whole neighborhood into a smoking hole. All those people!"

Exactly. Tate glanced at his boss, for the first time thankful he worked with psychics who could see through doors, walls, and lies. And him. Maybe this crazy Deuces Wild team would work after all.

Chapter Twenty-Three

Dr. Keegan finally cracked the door and signaled Tucker to join him in the hall, but Tucker had the good sense to wave Keegan in, and Tate was damned glad he did. Now was not the time to keep anything concerning Winslow from him.

Keegan took a seat at the coffee table, his wrists to his knees. "Miss Parrish is breathing on her own now, and—"

"When wasn't she?" Tate growled.

Keegan spared him a tired, impatient scowl from beneath deeply furrowed brows. "She had a reaction to one of the chelating agents we gave her to sequester the arsenic away from her blood proteins. That's all I meant when I said she wasn't breathing. She took a bad turn, but she's better now. That woman's suffering from arsenic poisoning on top of whatever else is in her system."

Keegan didn't seem worried about HIPAA restraints. Maybe because they were FBI? "We've given her three units of blood, induced vomiting, and began a bowel cleanse to intercept and clear what poisons we can, but she's very sick. The quicker we find out precisely what we're dealing with, the sooner she'll feel better. Understood?"

"Thanks," Tate offered like a lame ass. He deserved that blatant chastisement. But arsenic? He hadn't seen that in Joyce's house of horrors. "Are you sure it was arsenic?"

The doctor's right brow spiked in that superior way the profession had when talking to non-medical personnel. "Positive. At first, I thought maybe DMSO. It also smells like garlic. That garlicky scent is a classic indicator, plus her teeth show signs of prolonged vomiting, another indicator."

"What's DMSO?" Ky asked.

"Dimethyl sulfoxide. Some alternative medicine types used it to treat cancer in the past, hell, maybe they still are, but I didn't see that on the list of everything you guys brought in."

"She was ill this morning," Tate offered.

"Well, she's damned sick now." Keegan drummed his fingertips on the tabletop. "I ruled out DMSO, but I'm sure it's arsenic. That explains her hair loss too. Her stomach pains. Hell, it explains most of her symptoms." He leveled a stern eye to Isaiah. "The meds in those prescription bottles you shared don't match the labels. Where'd you get them?"

Isaiah stiffened in his chair. "You're kidding me? Every last one of them came out of the Parrish home."

Keegan's gaze dropped to his shoes as he shook his head. "Never mind. It's not your fault. We see this all the time. People think they can disguise their illicit drugs in leftover prescription bottles. They forge new labels. They lie. They cheat. They trade prescription meds for something stronger, or just for something else they want. You guys want to tell me what's going on with Miss Parrish?"

Tucker cleared his throat. "We suspect she's been poisoned over a long period, maybe most of her life. We're investigating, but—"

That earned Tucker one pissed off ER doctor. "Who the fuck did that to her?"

Tate was beginning to like this guy.

"At the moment, her mother's our only person of interest," Tucker answered honestly, "but we're too early in the investigation to know for sure."

"Nail her ass, will you?" Keegan's smacked the coffee table, then pointed to the ER cubicle he'd just come from. "Do you have any idea what that poor girl's been through? What she's going through right now?"

Tate nodded. "Yes, sir, I do. I'm the one who found her and—"

"God bless you, sir," Keegan bit out. The man seemed as emotionally involved with Winslow as Tate. "We see too much of this kind of abuse these days. Babies. Children. The elderly. Jesus Christ, what's this world coming to?"

And there you have it. Tate couldn't explain the world because he didn't understand it, either. Hence, he stayed clear of most people, but Dr. Keegan had definitely gone up a notch in his playbook. "Thanks for taking good care of Winslow, but what about her cancer?"

Keegan's smooth forehead shifted into rows of wrinkles as he leaned forward, damned near into Tate's face. "What fucking cancer?"

"Doc," he bit out. "She's dying of cancer. That's why we think her mother's been poisoning her, to kill her so she doesn't have to take care of her anymore. That's why Winslow's lost her hair. Couldn't you guys—?"

"Sorry, Tate. I might have interrupted you when you were checking her in," Isaiah said. "Dr. Keegan might not have heard what you were telling him."

"What kind of cancer?" Keegan barked. It was easy to see by the twitch under his left eye that he was riled all over again.

"She never said what kind," Tate admitted. "Her mother didn't say, either." *Or wouldn't.* "All Winslow told me was it didn't matter, that she'd be dead soon anyway."

Keegan exploded off his chair. In a passionate display of emotion, he slapped his hand to his forehead before he faced Tate. "You guys are the FBI, aren't you? Right? Isn't that what you told me when you brought her in?"

Tate nodded.

"Then do something! Arrest her damned mother! Do it today! Tell me what you need to press charges on her, and I'll do everything I can to make sure she doesn't hurt another person like she's hurt her daughter. To knowingly inflict a cancer patient with multiple poisons like this is unconscionable."

Precisely what Tate needed to hear. "We can't find her at the moment, but trust me. We'll get her."

Keegan sat back down. "Good. See that you do. In the meantime, I'll order more blood work, but to answer your question, no. I didn't detect any obvious signs of cancer during my preliminary exam. Let me get back to you on that."

Tate had to know. "Can I see her now?"

Keegan shook his head. "I'd rather you didn't. Like I said, what we're putting her through right now isn't fun, and once she feels better, she'll be in dialysis. A day would be best, but at least give her until late morning if you don't mind."

I mind, but... "Okay," Tate answered. This guy he could respect, but he wouldn't leave Winslow here alone by herself. Not after all she'd been through.

Keegan settled down. "Besides, you look like you could use some sleep yourself."

Tate let him think that. Sleep was one of those things he'd learned to live without.

"You're coming home with us," Eden spoke up.

Tate shook his head. "No, I'm good."

"Ha," she shot back at him. "If I had a nickel for every time Ky told me that, I'd be on my way to Jamaica with a Pina Colada in my hand by now. You men. You're all the same."

Of course, Tucker had to put his two cents worth into the mix. "It's either Eden and Ky's place or mine, Agent Higgins. You decide."

Oh, no, the dreaded *Agent Higgins* card. Scary. *Not.* Tate darn near smiled at his boss's sorry attempt to pull rank. He'd worked for Alex Stewart, remember? He'd been intimidated by the best. It didn't work then, either.

"I've got my Jeep," he said because he had to say something. "Thanks, but I'll be fine."

This time when Tate stuck his hand out, Keegan latched onto his wrist as if they'd served and fought together. "Twenty-Sixth Infantry, Second Brigade Combat Team. Iraq," he said.

Tate answered with an automatic, "First Battalion, Sixth Marines, Twenty Fourth MEU. Afghanistan."

And a new friendship was sealed.

"I'll be looking for you in the morning," Keegan declared to Tate with an edge in his voice. "Bright and early."

"I'll be here," Tate vowed. *Because I'm not leaving tonight.*

That earned him another hard glint from Keegan's sharp eyes, but he didn't challenge what he probably knew was a lie. "Goodnight then."

When the good doctor closed the door behind him, Tucker arched his back and stretched his hands over his head. "Guys, it's been a long day. Beat it. Isaiah, have your *friends* secured the Parrish home or do I need to go back there?"

"I'm headed back now, but yes. A couple agents are still on site."

"Good. First thing in the morning then."

Ky and Eden trailed behind Tucker. Isaiah stayed long enough to toss his Starbucks' empties in the trash before he headed out. Tate left with Isaiah because he needed to know where his Jeep was parked. Besides. He had something in there for Winslow.

"You're parked over there," Isaiah chin nodded to the row at his left, tossing Tate's Jeep keys to him.

"Thanks," Tate said as he caught the key fob in the air.

Isaiah stopped where he stood. "Hang in there, brother. We *are* going to get Joyce or Hattie or whatever she's calling herself now."

That brought Tate up short. "You think she's already changed her name? Her appearance?" *Of course.*

"Count on it."

"But do you know for sure? Can you get into her head?" *Like you get into mine?*

Isaiah shook his head, his eyes gone black. "That's why I needed you on the team, Tate. I can't get into Hattie's head. She's blocking me, just like you do."

"I block you?" *Seriously? It works?* Tate walked back to Isaiah, thrilled for the confirmation of a skill he hadn't been certain of until now. "It was you who wanted me on this team, not Eden?"

"Eden advocated for you, but I pushed Tucker into it, not like it was hard to do. You have an innate psychic power unlike the rest of us. Don't ask me how it works, but you decide who you let into your head, and when. I've got to tell you, it's darn frustrating. I can read Tucker easy, Ky and Eden, too, but you? No can do."

Didn't that lift a weight off Tate's shoulders? All along he'd felt like the odd man out. "So what can you do about it? Reading Joyce, I mean?" *Not me.*

"Nothing. It's simply the way it is. Some people's minds are easy to decipher; some aren't. I can't get much of a read from Tucker's wife, Melissa, either. Her brain must be wired like yours."

"But..." Tate grasped for something to say. Anything. "How can I help?"

"For starters, you can let me run a couple tests on you first thing in the morning. Let me do a couple mental exercises with you when you're fresh."

"What kind?" *Not all the psychological profiling bullshit again. No more EEGs. Hell no.*

A grin split Isaiah's cheeks. "Relax. I'm not going to torture you. What I have in mind we can do sitting at a table in the hospital cafeteria. No big deal."

Tate stared Isaiah down. The man was guileless; hardly what he'd expected in the son of a mad scientist. "Okay," Tate said, agreeing to be a test rat for the first time in his life.

Isaiah nodded his goodbye, and with that, Tate strolled to his Jeep, flashed on the headlights, and waved as Tucker drove past with the rest of the Deuces Wild team rammed in his Challenger. Once they were out of sight, Tate locked up his Jeep and headed back to the ER admitting desk for her room number.

Guess Dr. Keegan must've spread the word about Winslow's protective FBI custody order. All Tate had to do was flash his badge and Nurse Haley was eager to help. Tate caught the nearest elevator and *Operation Guard Winslow* began in earnest.

On the third floor, he cleared the elevator and turned left, needing to see how she was doing with his own eyes. At the open door to her room, he cocked his ear, not wanting to disturb what might be happening on the other side of the curtain.

Silence.

Stealthily, he cleared the curtain, and slosh went his heart to the floor. Winslow was as pale as a ghost, her skin nearly translucent. Flat on her back, her arms had been folded over her chest, her hands clasped together. All she needed was a lily and she'd be ready for a casket.

He went to her and lifted her hand to his lips. His heart swelled with tenderness for this woman. Her fingers were warm, but so tiny. He'd never noticed before how delicate they were. How clean and pure.

"Hey," he said quietly, just in case she needed a friend.

Winslow peeled her eyes open as Tate tipped his forehead to hers, his simmering brown eyes soft with unshed tears. "Where am I?"

"At a real hospital," he whispered. "With real doctors and nurses. You need dialysis, Winslow. Do you know that that is?"

She nodded. *God, do I have kidney cancer?* That was supposed to be a painful, quick death, but please, not now when she'd finally met a man who seemed to see her. A whimper got away from lips. "Why?" she cried, blinking hard. "Has the cancer... has it gone to my kidneys?"

He traced her quivering bottom lip with the pad of his thumb, his fingers gently squeezing her chin. "No, Winslow. You tested positive for arsenic poisoning, along with a few other prescription meds and barbiturates that had no business being in your system."

"Me?" she squeaked, her voice pathetically timid. "There were drugs in me? Illicit drugs? And arsenic?"

He nodded, his eyes incredibly tender.

"B-but..." She couldn't imagine how those things got inside of her, unless... *No. Mom wouldn't do that to me.* "Who gave that stuff to me?" she asked, hating that fear had reduced her voice to a thin whine.

Tate lifted her hand to his lips, his eyes black with foreboding. "I think you and I both know who's behind this. Didn't you say your mother made you drink a smoothie every morning?"

"Yes, rice water and some healthy stuff. Bananas!" She latched onto that healthy fruit to prove her mother's innocence. "But Mom wouldn't drug or poison me. I know she wouldn't. She's... she's..."

"She's crazy is what she is." Tate turned Winslow's hand over and placed a gentle kiss to her knuckles, not taking his gaze from her. "The FBI lab tested what was left in your smoothie glass and a hypo they found in your mother's bedroom. There were traces of arsenic in your drink, and the results aren't back on the hypo."

"That can't be true. My mom's a gardener, Tate. That's it. That's why she keeps arsenic around. I think it's in the fertilizer she uses. Maybe she just didn't wash her hands when she fixed my drink. She came in from working in her flowerbeds, and she was in a hurry and she must've forgot. She wouldn't hurt me. I know she wouldn't."

Tate didn't argue, just kissed her knuckles one by one, his mouth soft and sweet on her skin. His tongue trailed a line to the back of Winslow's hand where he ended with a kiss.

She couldn't think under that sensual assault. How could he suspect her mother of such a terrible thing? The need to protect her mother lifted proud and fierce and—false. Winslow took a deep breath as the truth she'd suspected for some time settled into place like the last fallen domino in a long line. *Mom tried to kill me.* Tate—*I can't believe I'm saying this*—was right, and she knew it. Winslow gulped down the bile creeping up her throat at that bitter acknowledgement. This was hard. Yes, her mom was a prima donna and prone to dramatics, and she could be a little bit mean. Well, make that a lot mean, but...

Wow-wow-wow-wow-wow-wow-wow. All those days of feeling crappy and throwing up until Winslow thought her head would explode. All. Those. Years.

"My mom tried to kill me," she murmured more to herself than to Tate, her heart shredded at the worst betrayal any child should have to endure. He kept hold of her fingers even as a sob choked out of her. "She... she...." And the dam broke. "Where's my dog? I want my dog. I want Pepe."

Tate smoothed a big, manly hand down her bicep. "Don't worry. I found him and he's having a sleepover at a friend's house, so take it easy. Go back to sleep. Everything's going to be okay."

But it wasn't, was it? Tate didn't know the worst part yet. "She... she wanted to take me on a road trip." *She was going to kill me.*

His nostrils flared as his brows narrowed to one fierce V.

"To Oregon, I think." That was the only state Winslow could recall. "Assisted suicide's legal there."

"What?" snapped out of Tate like a lightning strike.

It broke Winslow's heart to confess what she now knew to be true. Her mother wasn't just mean. She was evil. "I thought it was a good idea at first, you know, to save everyone the trouble of taking care of me, watching me waste away, and..." She choked on that word—*die.*

"You're no trouble," he growled. "No trouble at all. Stay with me. I'll take care of you, damn it. You'll be surprised how easy it is."

Tears brimmed, blurring his handsome face. She needed to hear that. "Thanks, but—"

He nipped the knuckle he'd just kissed. "No buts. You don't tell someone you love 'em in one breath, then hurt them the next. People—mothers—just don't do that."

Winslow clutched his hand to her chest as an exquisite pain sliced her heart. Did he just tell her he loved her? "B-but then I started to feel better. I think there was something good in the IV Dr. Bly gave me, and I decided, umm..." She lowered her voice to a whisper. "I decided... bullshit." Saying that word out loud heated her cheeks. Winslow fastened her gaze to the blanket, so Tate wouldn't see it embarrassed her to cuss.

"Bullshit, huh?" he whispered back at her, his lips on her knuckles again. "Say it again."

She cleared her throat, but couldn't meet his eyes. "Bullshit?" she said a little louder only it came out like a question.

"You can do better." He pressed his index finger to the bottom of her chin and made her look up. So much tenderness rained down on her, it was impossible to look away. "I like that word on your tongue, Winslow. Say it again, only this time like you mean it."

"Bull—shit," she declared with a shoulder shrug and a titch of attitude. His word gave her a sense of resolve, as if she hadn't been sick and defeated most of her life. As if she could fight back. "I decided I wasn't going to die, Tate. What my mom wanted me to do was... it was bullshit."

The first genuine smile she'd seen on his rugged face blew her away. Even his eyes sparkled. "That's my girl. Did you use that word on your mom?"

Best. Day. Ever. He couldn't have said anything sweeter. "I wanted to, but..." She shook her head, still sorting through what was real and what seemed like a dream. "I'm not sure I got the chance. But you like it?"

He winked and that sweet light in his eyes turned Tate into the handsomest man she'd ever met. "Yeah, I do, especially the way you say it. It's over, Winslow. You need to take care of yourself from now on and let me worry about her."

"No, I can't. Not now, I—"

"Yes, you can," he breathed, the tip of his nose touching hers. "I have something to mark this brand-new day. Consider it a birthday present."

An olive drab beanie with bright gold USMC stitched on one side dangled off the fingertips of his other hand. He shook it out and tugged it over her head and made certain it was snug, pinching the edges of it around her face until it covered her ears. "I figured your head might get cold. Hope you don't mind. It's mine, but it looks a better on you."

She couldn't help ducking her shoulders as the warmth from that cap shifted down her bare neck. Winslow touched her fingers to the gift, her silly eyes glimmering at the kindness from a man who'd recently been a total stranger. The beanie wasn't fancy, but he'd remembered. He knew how she felt about people seeing her bare head, and that counted.

"Thank you," she squeaked, blinking hard and trying not to act like a sap.

"Listen to your doctor and get better. You're safe now."

She nodded, but lifted her right hand and circled the nape of his neck to pull him in closer. "Kiss me again?"

"Oh, yes, ma'am." He obliged, his lips soft and warm and that delicious windblown scent of pine the best thing ever. She closed her eyes and risked licking his lips, needing the minty taste of him back in her mouth, which tasted oddly like *Listerine* now that she thought about it.

When he cupped her head, his big hands holding her with care, the tenderness in his kiss broke her heart wide open. Winslow tugged his face into the crook of her neck so he couldn't see her cry. Like she stood a chance of hiding her puffy eyes and runny nose.

He scooped his arms around her and hunched over her, rocking her like a little girl while she clung to him. "Hey. Don't cry. I'm not leaving you. I promise."

She sniffed. "I'm not worried about you leaving, but I can tell, Tate. No one's loved you in a very long time, have they?"

A sardonic something tweaked one corner of his mouth even as a shadow filtered over his face, kind of like the shadow an airplane makes when it's flying high above a field of golden wheat, bright one moment, dark the next, then bright once more. "Don't tell me you're psychic too."

He said that so seriously, she nearly laughed. "I don't think so. Are you?"

"I most definitely am not."

What an odd conversation. The tension eased out of Winslow's body like air hissing from a deflating balloon. Over all, this hospital room was a nice change from her mother's house where the temperature was always set to sixty. Her toes were warm, her fingers too. For the first time in ages, her stomach felt relatively calm, and she could take deep breaths that filled her belly without making her choke or cough. She almost felt—good.

But there was something Tate wasn't telling her. She could read it in his eyes. "Where's Mom?"

"To be honest, I don't know. She was screaming plenty when I got you out of Dr. Bly's clinic, but where she went from there is anyone's guess."

"You didn't arrest her?" Winslow shivered at that alarming news. *Mommy Dearest* always seemed to get away and she always got even.

"Not yet, but don't worry. We will. Did you know Bly lost his medical license for prescription fraud two years ago?"

Winslow cocked her head. "He's not a real doctor?"

"Oh, he's real all right, and he's about to be arrested as an accomplice for attempted murder."

Somehow, that didn't surprise Winslow. "What about all the other doctors I've been to? Were they frauds, too?"

Tate shrugged one shoulder. "We won't know until you give us their names, will we?"

Unbelievable. Her mom had dragged her from doctor to doctor. Were any of them licensed? "I'll have to see if I can remember all of them. There were so many."

"Do me a favor," Tate mumbled, his voice deliciously deep and rumbly as he kicked out of his boots. "My back aches from standing here. Stop thinking so hard and scoot over so I can join you."

It took a minute of rearranging lines and wires, but Tate fit just fine after he lowered the side rail and settled on his side next to Winslow. He eased one arm under her head and tugged her under his chin. His shirt was damp around the edges.

"You're cold," she told him.

"Not anymore," he whispered.

The weariness of all the revelations of the day pushed Winslow toward sleep. She was warm, and with his solid shoulder and arm for a pillow, her lashes fell. She let her fingers wander under his shirt to his skin. Just because.

He'd kept her from floating away in the wind that night on the tower, that night in the stars. A sizzling energy tingled up from her fingertips to her arms at the pleasant touch of an all-male belly. It was precisely what the doctor ordered.

Chapter Twenty-Four

Tate couldn't—didn't—wouldn't—think of sleeping. Not with Winslow's delicate frame hugged up against him like it was. She'd been bathed somewhere along the line, probably after all that purging Dr. Keegan had put her through.

Honeysuckle. Her skin smelled like the wild honeysuckle that grew everywhere during short Alaskan summers. He pulled the scent of it and her into his lungs, his heart not pounding quite so hard now that he knew she would live. For now she slept soundly, whimpering ever so often for no reason—other than she had survived one helluva life and the liar who'd made it so. But that life was over now.

Tate hadn't the heart to tell Winslow who her mother was or that her last name wasn't Parrish. She'd had enough to deal with, but Joyce or Hattie or—whatever her latest name was—was still out there.

He couldn't blame Tucker for failing to call it in. They'd all been spun up to reach Winslow in time.

He stared at the ceiling, fully expecting some zealous nurse to barge in and tell him to, "Get out of here!" or ask, "What do you think you're doing?"

Until that happened, he pressed his lips to Winslow's forehead. Did he love her? He probably shouldn't, not as inexperienced as she was with the world of men, but God knew he did. Was it smart? Maybe not. Was it real? Absolutely. From that first meeting, tenderness for Winslow had stormed Tate like a squall over a boat lost in the Bering Sea. The fierce love that he felt for her happened fast, but it was sure and true and, by hell, he'd die to protect her.

Yet he hadn't told her how he felt, and he knew why. It was too soon, and even now, he was acting like a predator, snuggling in bed with her as sick as she was. Winslow was in no condition to comprehend what adult love entailed, nor the challenges ahead of her. As sheltered from the world as she'd been, the better thing now would be for him to back off, and for her to go to school and live a little. She didn't need his needs screwing with her mind after all her mother had put her through.

If he were smart, Tate wouldn't tell Winslow he loved her, either. He'd step back into the shadows and watch from afar while she learned to drive and went to college, while she tested her wings and found a good job, maybe got her own apartment. He'd let her make friends and be happy and realize what independence was about, and most importantly, how strong she was. All those important things she should've been experiencing instead of planning to die.

Damn, he hadn't seen any of this coming from that one inconvenient blind date. Yet here she was, cuddled in his arms. Warm. Trusting. Breathing steadily into his neck like a lover.

The simple escort job he'd cussed Tucker for had become Tate's chance to be more than just a warrior. Not that he'd grab onto that chance. He shouldn't. This was Winslow's time to shine, not his.

Tate bowed his forehead to hers, and despite sharing a bed with her at the moment, he vowed to back off and let her live a good long life. It didn't have to be with him, though he wished it could. Winslow needed to heal and grow into the woman she was meant to be, with or without him. She just needed to finally be free of the cancer and live.

He pulled the blanket up to her chin and overlapped the bottom edge of the beanie to be sure she was extra warm, that no draft would chill the back of her bare neck. Winslow had an elegant neck, a creamy white column that lent a regal tilt to her head when she walked, one she didn't seem to realize she had.

She must've gotten that trait from her unknown father, because Hattie didn't have it. Her neck jutted forward like a turkey buzzard's, but Winslow's was almost—proud. Regal. Even up there on the tower last night and as thin as she was, she reminded Tate of an English princess in a lavish wedding ceremony he'd seen once on TV. A real princess, not a Disney one. That was Winslow. His princess.

He smoothed a hand over her shoulder to her elbow. She fit against him like an oyster in its shell, and wasn't that the best comparison? He was the barrier between her softness and the cruel, hard world, like a shell destined to protect her pure heart and perfect soul.

They weren't exactly spooning, but this was a better position. This way he couldn't poke her with that hound dog in his pants. He couldn't scare her with the man he was. He'd been careful to keep the blanket between them to ensure no nurse or doctor checking on Winslow would think anything improper was going on. Winslow was still so much a little girl. She needed time to grow up, and he intended to make sure she got it.

This sweet woman asleep in his arms had brought him back to life in more ways than one. Sure, his body was rocking for her, but he could control that urge, and he did. She'd touched a part of him he'd locked up in the cellar of his heart where it hadn't seen the light of day since he'd lost his mother. Seemed he had a heart and soul after all.

Tate scraped his teeth over his bottom lip. He found it peculiar that this fragile woman had gotten through his defenses, but she had.

He pressed a kiss to the knitted beanie, smelling her scent on it as well as his. They didn't really know each other, and yet they did. Tate closed his eyes and let loose a sigh. Yes, he was a very stupid man, but for this one brief moment, or until the nurses made him leave, he held on to his whole world.

Winslow stretched her back and arched her body all the way down to her toes. She tugged her beanie back on tight. There was nothing sillier than her big Dopey ears sticking out from under a nice warm hat. Since she'd lost her hair, they'd resembled taxicab doors flapping in the wind.

The musky scent of pine and man flesh lifted into her flared nostrils and... *Oh. Tate.*

She ran her nose along the warm pectoral muscle she was pressed against, thrilled he was sleeping as sound as he was, letting her get away with this tiny stolen intimacy.

The scent of him brought back memories of the crazy chain of events from last night. Him catching her when she fell, although how she'd fallen out of that window was still a little fuzzy. Pepe barking like a demon. Her mom and that insane talk they'd had about assisted suicide. There was a shower mixed up somewhere in there too.

The rest were intangible feelings she couldn't quite grasp with all five senses. Not yet. But tumbling out of that window and into Tate's arms? That moment stood out from the rest. He'd caught her just like he'd said he would. He'd saved her.

Her body ached, but strangely, it felt better too. It wasn't many days that she woke up not needing to make a mad dash to the toilet, so this was a nice change.

But Tate... Ah. She risked waking him as she let her fingers flutter over his impressively muscled chest. The solid slabs of pectorals. The valley between them. The heat of his skin beneath his shirt, and, *oh my,* the steady thump, thump, thump of his heart under her palm.

Winslow flattened her hand to absorb every last throbbing beat. She was in tantalizing territory where the faint scent of clean male sweat teased her feminine nature like a hook teased a trout. All she needed was for him to open his eyes, and she'd be caught.

Feeling giddy at her outrageous boldness, she dipped her fingers along that ridge between his pecs and ran them lightly down to his abdomen. Still dressed except for his boots, the man was relaxed, his belly expanding with every breath. Heat flared in parts of her body where it hadn't flared before. Talk about needing a moment to enjoy the thrill of manhandling.

She forced her naughty fingers from strolling lower beneath the blanket to his belt and jeans. Was this how true love felt? Exciting and trembling and hungry and overheated and daring all at once? She hoped so.

Her heart thudded at the illicit contact, but could she stop? *Uh-uh.* Da-yum, he smelled good. She closed her eyes and rubbed her cheek over his ribs, just a little as she purred like a cat. She wished he'd wake up, but at the same time, she was glad he didn't. This quiet moment of exploration belonged to her, and she wanted to luxuriate in the sensual magic of his sleeping body for as long as she could.

The man was dead to the world, but dark and handsome. Drool-worthy. Absolutely. His skin tone was somewhere between golden tan and bronzed, and he had the cutest eyelashes, curled like ebony butterfly wings resting high on his cheekbones. Dark stubble shadowed his angular jaw. Trimmed sideburns ended at his ear lobes. A straight nose extended from thick dark brows, pinched together as if he were angry about something even in his sleep.

Imagine that. Tate angry. That was the one emotion he seemed immersed in, and she wondered who'd hurt him so badly that he dreamed about it? How dare they?

For the first time, she noticed the tiny vertical lines between his brows, three tiny creases, as if he'd frowned one too many times and his face got stuck that way. No laugh lines at the corners of his eyes though. Lying there in his arm and examining him, it was easy to see the little boy beneath the surface. The angry little boy...

She could've lain there and watched him forever. His hair had been nicely spiked the first time she'd met him, but now it looked even sexier, all rumpled like it was. Darned if her overheated brain didn't jump tracks and trigger the need to know what his bare chest looked like. Was it clear of chest hair, thick with it, or barely dusted? That'd be good to know.

The tip of her index finger ached to trace a line from that masculine nose down to his lips and from there over the scruff on his chin to...

Uh, uh, uh. Her whole body clenched at the temptation, nearly waking him. He grunted and wrinkled his nose, spoiling the delicious thought of where she wanted her fingers to end up. How did a man feel—down there? She'd never felt so naughty before, nor so tempted.

Winslow had no idea where all these lust-filled ideas were coming from, but wow. She liked them. They got her heart pumping in the most delicious way.

Drawing in another deep breath, she put her lust on hold for the day that she felt well enough to do more than just get herself excited and stimulated and—wet. A wicked smile cracked her face as she snuggled against the man in her bed, molding her breasts and stomach to the finely carved edge of his ribs and hip. Okay, so it would've been tons better if she'd been at home in her bed, only...

No, it wouldn't have been better. Not at all. Just the thought of all the wasted days and nights and life in *that bed* deflated her wayward ambition. *Assisted suicide. Wow. What was Mom thinking?*

Her dying would've made her mom quite the heroic martyr, come to think of it. Once more, Joyce Parrish would've been that *poor, poor single mother* standing facing the cruel world alone, her only child forced to take matters into her own tiny hands and—die.

Winslow bit her lip envisioning the drama of the day after that supposed voluntary suicide. She knew better now. This was another one of her mother's scams, another trick to get people to feel sorry for her. If Winslow had a dime for every gas station and grocery store she'd been dragged into, so her mother could drop off donations jars, begging for loose change for her poor baby, well, she'd be one rich woman by now.

How could any mother suggest suicide for her daughter? If that depressing thought wasn't a buzz kill to Winslow's virginal—but awakening—libido, nothing was.

So many things made sense now. The late night, get-out-of-town-in-a-hurry departures. The continual rounds of new doctors and holistic therapists. The 'alternative medicine' people. Joyce had hauled Winslow to an Indian shaman one time in New Mexico. Had she ever intended her daughter to live or was her whole life nothing but a smokescreen for—what? Ego? Vanity? Some twisted version of motherly love?

What Tate had said felt right—Joyce Parrish was crazy. Winslow didn't want to admit it, but finally free from her mother's clutches, finally able to breathe without feeling dizzy and nauseous, she faced the facts. Her mother *had* tried to kill her, not once, but apparently many times over the years. What Joyce did was indefensible and downright criminal. What if she'd succeeded? Joyce Parrish would be a murderer. A lying, deceitful, child-killer. But worse, no one would've been the wiser.

Another shiver skittered up Winslow's spine at what she'd very nearly *not* survived. What would her mother and that fake doctor have done with her body if they'd killed her? Would they have hacked her up into manageable pieces and stuffed her in a garbage can? Would there have been a burial? Would anyone have come? *Would anyone have cared?*

Oh, no, no, no. Winslow couldn't dwell on what could've been. The possibilities were too frightening. She draped her arm over Tate's strong, warm chest and, one last time, she rubbed her cheek into his shirt to dry her tears. If he hadn't come into her life when he did, this could've ended so badly.

The steady sound of him breathing lulled her toward sleep. She thought back to that moment on the water tower when she'd told God she was sick of lying and pretending to keep peace with her mother. All she'd wanted then was for one person—one someone—to see her, as in truly, finally see her for the person she was.

Winslow swallowed her tears instead of drenching Tate's shirt more than she already had. It seemed God had sent her exactly who she needed.

Chapter Twenty-Five

He woke in a dream, a very warm, sensual dream with a woman's gentle fingers where no woman's fingers had been before. Rubbing his right nipple.

Tate looked to his left and absorbed the pleasant view of Winslow snuggled under his arm, her left arm extended across his chest and her fingers tucked between two buttons of his shirt. Even sound asleep, her index finger and thumb were busy pinching that flat protuberance on his right pec.

A smile slid over her lips. What was she dreaming about? Her dog? Probably...

He set his chin to the top of her head, content to let her play. There might come a day when he'd turn that play into something more, but for now, he needed to check in with his boss. Tucking her in nice and tight, Tate lifted her fingers to his lips and planted one warm, moist kiss before he pulled away from his sleeping princess. She moaned, but burrowed into her pillow.

Pulling the blanket up to her chin brought a deep sense of male satisfaction. It was a small thing, but somehow it felt like so much more. Wasn't he surprised when he rounded the curtain and spotted Isaiah's long legs spread next to Winslow's door in the hall. "What are you doing here?"

Isaiah arched his back and stretched, both arms high above his head. "Guarding our client," came out in a mumbly growl.

"Why?"

"Because Winslow's in protective custody, and you looked..." Isaiah lifted a hand to his mouth and coughed. "...a little preoccupied."

Heat swarmed up Tate's neck to his cheeks. He shook it off. "Does Tucker know you're here?"

"It was his idea. He knew you wouldn't leave Miss Parrish." Isaiah dipped his head once at a police officer sitting across the hall on a fold-up chair, then scrambled to his feet. "The next shift just arrived. Want to hit *The Skillet* for ham and eggs? We could do the mental test there."

The Skillet was a local greasy spoon, Mom-and-Pop kind of place where a guy could get a good cup of coffee and platter-sized pancakes with a hefty side of bacon. But that would mean leaving Winslow, and no offense, just because that blue shirt showed up to guard Winslow didn't mean squat. "No thanks. It can wait until you get back."

Isaiah lifted to his feet. "Knew you'd say that. Sit tight. I'll bring you something."

Tate watched him go. The guy was taller than him by a few inches, and Isaiah was what women called debonair. There wasn't a rugged thing about him. He dressed sharp, always crisp and cool, and he was one of those perpetually levelheaded guys. A civilian, he'd never served, unless that one trip to Vietnam with Tucker Chase to get Deuce Chase away from his maniacal mother could be termed service. It seemed more like a sentence to Tate.

But Isaiah was what experts called a level ten psychic. He wielded uncanny mental influence over some individuals, but not all. The psychic world was one of mankind's final frontiers where there were more unknowns than knowns, where people who believed they were psychic were openly ridiculed as heretics like Galileo was back in the 1600's, when all the *smart people* were positive the world was flat.

The distinction that he might be a pioneer into the new frontier called psychic universe didn't impress Tate. Palming his cell, he thumb-dialed Ky.

Eden answered. "Hi Tate, how's Winslow?"

"Sleeping. Have we picked up Joyce Parrish yet?"

"You mean Hattie Beauregard?"

"Whatever. Is she in custody?" *Please say yes.*

"Not that I've heard. Tucker's got all the police departments in the tri-state area on the lookout for her, but get this. Ky and I have been looking into the names of the physicians on those prescription bottles we found in her kitchen. Just like Keegan said, more than half are bogus, and a good percentage don't match the label."

"She's been giving her daughter whatever she could get her hands on?"

"I'm not sure. There are some antibiotics in the mix, but most of these pills are for pain or anxiety. Lots of Oxycodone, some diuretics, a couple beta blockers."

"Any chemo-type drugs?"

"Everything but." Eden huffed through the phone. "I'm beginning to wonder—"

"If Winslow ever had cancer." Tate raked his fingers over the bristles on his chin. Just how depraved was Hattie to lie to her kid about something so awful? "Can't Keegan run a blood test for that?"

"I think he'll need to run more than one test to determine cancer or not. The body produces blood serum markers, Tate, certain proteins in response to cancer cells. Sometimes a cancerous tumor produces its own substance. Doctors look for that marker to screen certain cancers. It might take a while before he knows what's actually going on." It sounded as if Eden shuffled the phone from one ear to her other, probably because she was holding Kyler. "But the sensation I get when I handle those bottles is scary, Tate. I don't think Hattie cared what she gave Winslow. I think she wanted certain reactions, like nausea, drowsiness, or pain."

"She deliberately dosed her daughter to make her sick?" *The bitch.*

"Exactly. She needed to control her, so she's been giving Winslow a toxic cocktail for who knows how long."

"That's why she was so ill yesterday morning," Tate bit out. "I'll bet Joyce, I mean Hattie, punished her for missing the prom and for making her look bad. Think about it. She had the TV primed and ready to make her a star, but when Winslow didn't show, she looked stupid."

"Maybe..." Eden let that hang before she blind-sided him with, "Winslow's a very lucky woman."

"How do you figure?"

"Because she's got you in her corner."

Tate swallowed hard. *Oh, that.* It would do him well to remember that Eden knew everything. He nodded though she couldn't see him standing there, his arm to the wall and his forehead to his forearm. "Thanks," was all he could say. Winslow most definitely had him. Maybe in the shadows, but he'd be there for her no matter where she went or what she decided to do with the rest of her life.

"Did we ever find out who the woman was who went into the river?" In all the chaos, he'd nearly forgotten that another family out there was missing their mom or sister.

"Ah, yes, about that. I checked with the highway patrol. Mrs. Alder. Sixty-one-years-old. She'd been drinking and lost control of her vehicle when it hydroplaned. They pulled her body out this morning. It's quite sad because her husband died last week, and she was probably drunk because she was grieving. No one else was in the vehicle with her."

As guilty as he felt for that poor woman, Tate was relieved the Coast Guard hadn't fished Winslow out of the river. "So where's the boss?"

"He's meeting Isaiah at some place called *The Skillet*, but I know he's headed your way after."

"Good. I need to talk to him. Later."

"Before you go..." The sound of a happy baby cooing told Tate that Kyler was on her lap. "There's something else, Tate."

"Okay." He waited.

"Ky's taking your place Monday."

"He's going to California? Who decided this?"

"It was a mutual decision. Tucker wants you here until this business with Winslow is settled. And oh yes, the local police apprehended Dr. Bly on the interstate headed north. He's down at the local precinct."

"Was Joyce..." *Grrrr*. "...Hattie with him?"

"No, but trust me. Everyone's looking for her."

Interesting. "There's something else you need to know, Eden. Hattie was taking Winslow to Oregon for physician assisted suicide."

Tate jerked the phone from his ear when Eden shrieked. "Oh, my gosh! That woman! She'd better pray I'm not the one who catches her." And somehow, Tate knew she was hugging Kyler close, because Eden was a good mother. She'd be doing something like that.

"What kind of a woman plans to kill her child?" she hissed. "I can't imagine what Winslow's gone through. Does she know?"

"She's the one who told me."

The sound of stiletto heels clattering up the hallway brought Tate's head around. Damned if Channel Thirteen's Shawna Truborn wasn't headed his way, a cameraman on her six and a sexy sway to her hips. "Listen. I've got to go," he told Eden. "I'm at the hospital if you need me."

She signed off with a quick, "I figured that. Bye, Tate."

Miss Truborn's eyes lit up. "Agent Higgins! What are you doing here?"

Tate shoved his phone in his back pocket and crossed his arms over his chest. This exuberant, nosy woman wasn't getting past him to Winslow. "I think the better question is what are you doing here?"

X-rays. MRIs. EKG and EEGs. Blood work and enough other pokes and prods to make a grown woman cry. By lunchtime, Winslow was sick to her stomach and would soon be on her way to dialysis. She'd be lucky to be out of there in four hours.

A doctor visited after she woke up to find that Tate had left, but the doctor was all business and so serious. About forty-years-old with short brown hair and a receding hairline, he wore light gray scrubs and wire-rimmed glasses that he peered over when he talked to her. He'd brought a clipboard with him. "I'm Dr. Keegan. I was the physician on call last night when you came into the ER. I'd like to continue as your physician if you're okay with that."

She'd never been asked if she was okay with anything before, but he seemed nice. "Umm, sure." *I guess.* What could it hurt?

He nodded one curt nod and handed the clipboard over. "Good. I hoped you'd say that. I know this is after-the-fact since I've already treated you, but it's typical hospital protocol since you couldn't sign for yourself last night. Sign on the bottom line of the first sheet that you agree to let me treat you."

She accepted the board with trembling fingers. This was a first, her giving permission for medical treatment. Her mother usually took over right about now.

But the papers were filled with too many terms she didn't understand. Insurance. Primary physician. Mediation? She didn't want to waste this guy's time. He seemed so much more important than she was. Pressing her lips together, she had to admit, "I don't know what this is telling me, umm..." Where was Tate when she needed him?

Dr. Keegan jumped to his feet and came to her side. The spicy drift of men's cologne and clean, pressed cotton came with him. "I can help. Which part don't you understand?"

"This right here. Insurance? What's that?" Winslow peered up at him and inhaled. He smelled good.

The man was older than Tate, slender. His fingernails were trimmed and clean, nothing like Ike's. Several dark hairs graced the top of his index finger as he traced the section she meant. He wasn't hurried, but seemed genuinely interested. The kind glint in his eye calmed her nerves. "Ah, insurance. You have been out of circulation for a while, haven't you?"

"I guess." *Like forever.*

"Where to begin." He sat in the chair he'd dragged to her bedside. "Insurance can be quite complicated, but basically, it's what pays the bills around here. If you have a good health plan, you won't need to worry about anything but your deductible. But if you have no insurance, that's another story." After a few more cursory explanations filled with more words she didn't get, he paused. "Would you like one of our patient advocates to pay you a visit? She or he can explain your health care options better than I can. They're quite good at maneuvering through all this legal terminology."

"Yes, thank you. I'd appreciate that." But she did sign the page that authorized him to be her doctor before she handed the clipboard back. Writing her signature on the dotted line felt strangely empowering.

He tucked it under his crossed arms, but stayed seated. "So talk to me, Winslow. Tell me what happened yesterday. Why did you get so sick?"

And just like that, the room chilled as if her mother were there watching over her shoulder, ready to jump on her for saying the wrong thing. Winslow tugged the blanket up to her chin. "I don't remember," she lied.

He nodded, his eyes sharp. "Don't worry. It's understandable. You came into the ER with a high level of arsenic in your system, a few other drugs too. Do you get headaches often? Migraines?"

She nodded. "And I throw up a lot, nearly every morning."

"Body aches? Toothaches? Do your bones hurt before you open your eyes in the morning? Do you have night sweats? Dry skin?" Her symptoms rolled off his tongue like he knew her inside and out. By the time she'd admitted to everything on his long list of physical ailments, his brows narrowed. "So tell me. How have you lived through this nightmare? What did you do to keep your spirits up when you were sick for so long?"

"I have a little dog, umm, his name is Pepe and he sleeps with me."

A crooked smile breached Dr. Keegan's mouth. "What kind is he?"

"A Chihuahua. He's tan and he shakes a lot, but Tate calls him a dragon."

Dr. Keegan cocked his head. "Tate Higgins? Did you know him before yesterday?"

"No, I just met him Friday. He was supposed to be my prom date and…" Winslow fidgeted with the edge of her blanket. "It's a long story."

He smiled encouragingly. "I've got time."

Where to begin? "It was a Dreams-Come-True thing, a prom, only it wasn't real, and I didn't know about it until my mom had it all set up and—" How embarrassing to have to admit this to a handsome man who looked like he cared.

"Have you ever had a convulsion that you can remember?"

Winslow had to bite her lip at that question. "No, but yesterday afternoon I couldn't think straight. I was dizzy and confused, and I still can't remember everything that happened." *Just Tate. I remember him just fine.*

"That's because someone overdosed you with alprazolam. You might know it as Xanax. It's a short acting treatment for anxiety, but an overdose numbs you into submission. It can cause convulsions. That's why I asked."

Winslow honestly didn't know the names of the medications her mother had given her, so Xanax meant nothing. Dr. Keegan's scrutiny was too much. She couldn't bear to look at him, so she fingered the blanket instead. It was light gold with cotton-weave so loose she could've stuck the tip of her pinkie finger into one of the holes if she'd wanted to. Her mind was like that blanket—full of holes. From little on up, she'd never questioned what her mother had given her or done to her. Not once. She'd trusted Joyce Parrish with her life, only now...

She didn't know who Winslow Parrish was any more. Her entire life had been nothing but a game of shadows and her mother's lies.

"Mom likes to garden," she explained out of habit. "The arsenic could've been on her fingers, and she could've forgotten to wash her hands before she mixed my smoothie." She no longer believed that, but old habits were hard to break.

His brows angled over stern blue eyes. "No, Winslow. The level of arsenic in your system isn't extremely high, but the damage to your liver and heart are strong indicators this has been going on for some time. Arsenic poisoning explains all of your symptoms, your acute abdominal distress, your headaches, confusion, and drowsiness. Even your hair loss is a direct result of arsenic poisoning."

"No," she said firmly. "That's because of my cancer."

He cocked his elbow to the armrest and tapped his index finger to his bottom lip. "Who told you that you had cancer?"

"Mom." Winslow's stomach pitched acid just saying that name. *Mom, the liar.*

"Have you ever seen an oncologist? Has a doctor ever told you what kind of cancer you have?"

Winslow ducked her head into her shoulders. This line of questioning was getting intense. "Doctors always talk to Mom, not me." *Because Mom was crafty like that. Pushy and crafty.*

"Do you remember when you first came down with cancer?"

Winslow rolled her eyes. That story she'd heard enough to know by heart. "I was three and Mom was a single mother who didn't need one more sad thing in her life, but there I was. Sick and dying."

His brows furrowed. "Your mother honestly said that to you?"

"It's okay. She didn't mean anything by it. That's just how she talks." *Yeah, right.* Winslow found it difficult to shake the lies she'd been told out of her head. Why was she defending her mom?

"When did you lose your hair?"

Winslow smoothed a hand over the beanie Tate had given her. "Months ago."

Dr. Keegan leaned forward, his palms on his knees. "How many? Exactly."

She swallowed hard, counting on her fingers because he was making her nervous and she couldn't think. "Umm, it started falling out in April, so that would be..." *Three. Four. Five.* "Six months ago."

"What else happened in April? Did you and your mother have an argument or a fight? Did she do anything different? Get a new job? Buy a new car? Meet a guy?"

There were too many temper tantrums to remember them all, and with Joyce, it was a continual round of one drama after another. But Winslow couldn't bear to betray her mother anymore. "You have to understand, Mom's high strung..." *Or so she said*. "...and she likes to be the center of attention..." *All the time*. "...b-but she tries to be a good mom...." *I just can't remember when the last time was*. "Why do you want to know?"

The questioning had to stop. Winslow was trapped between her old life and her new life, like a woman with one foot in two different boats, both headed in opposite directions. This cross examination was tearing her apart.

He crossed his arms, trapping the clipboard to his chest. "Tell me when you first noticed the freckles on the back of your hands."

She splayed her fingers on the blanket over her lap. "Mom said they were just a side-effect of my chemo drugs." *More Mommy Dearest lies?*

"But when did they first appear? What month? What year? You haven't always had them, have you?"

She shook her head. "No, May, I think. Maybe June. They just popped up one day." *I think*. "Why?" *What now?!*

"Because those spots are an obvious indicator of chronic arsenic poisoning." He pursed his lips like he was thinking. "And because I think something set your mother off in April, and that's when the poisoning began in earnest. That's seven months ago."

Winslow didn't know what to say. Tremors rattled up her spine, making her head bob from nerves. "Umm, would you mind waiting for Tate to come back?' she asked. *Please? I can't take this anymore.* "He, umm—"

Dr. Keegan's knee bounced. Just once. "You don't need Agent Higgins here, Winslow." *Oh yes, I do.* "You're an intelligent woman and I'm sure you're stronger than you think. What if I told you that you don't have cancer?"

"I what?" She blinked at that astounding piece of fiction, overwhelmed and sinking between those two boats. "Ha. I'd wonder what you had to drink for lunch." She meant to sound facetious and more confident than she felt, but he didn't crack the barest hint of a smile. "You're... you're kidding, right?" *Mom said I had cancer. All my life she'd told me I had cancer. It can't be another lie.*

Again, his brows collided. "No, Winslow. I don't kid about cancer. After I saw the results of the blood work I ordered last night, I'm more convinced. Yes, I'll need to do more thorough testing to eliminate all the false positives we see when we're screening for cancer, but in my honest opinion, you don't have it, and whoever told you that you did is nothing but a twisted menace to society. She should be locked up and the key thrown away."

You could've knocked Winslow over with one finger. A skinny, little pinkie finger.

"You need to go," she said, her voice trembling from too—too much!

He cocked his head. "Why? Have I upset you?"

"No, I just..." *Really need you to go.* "...I'm tired and..." *Where's Tate?* "...my head hurts..." *Because my freaking heart is breaking!*

Dr. Keegan jumped to his feet. "Very well. I'll check back with you later."

He'd no more than walked out when the dam burst. Winslow curled up into herself, wiping her tears. Living shouldn't feel this bad. "Tate," she whispered to the tan blanket that—just like her—had thousands of holes in it. "I'm scared."

Chapter Twenty-Six

It turned out Shawna Truborn had no idea Winslow was in the hospital. She'd come to do a follow-up on the three sets of twins born that week in maternity, but ended up on Winslow's floor instead. Relieved, Tate pushed back from the hospital cafeteria table where he'd downed one too many cups of coffee while speaking with Channel Thirteen's savvy reporter.

Miss Truborn uncrossed her very attractive long legs, slid her high-fashion heels beneath her chair, and leaned forward with her hands clasped on her lap. "It's been a pleasure talking with you, and trust me. I will make this happen."

He lifted to his feet, but leaned his fingertips back to the tabletop. "That's what I'm counting on. Lives depend on you. Please don't let me down, Miss Truborn."

She batted her lashes, and blushed the loveliest shade of coral when she extended her right hand. "For you Agent Higgins, anything."

That almost made him feel, what was the word? Debonair? *Yeah, right.* He touched the tip of his tongue to his dry lips and shook her hand. "It's been good talking with you."

Shawna gave him a one-shoulder shrug that belied her innocence. "Tell me when you're ready for this segment to run."

What a flirt.

"Copy that." He rapped his knuckles to the table as he left her sitting there. Tucker might have something to say about the plan Tate had just cooked up with Truborn, but he wasn't worried. In fact, he felt damned good for the second time today.

Strolling back to Winslow's room, he ran into Dr. Keegan in the hall. "Hey, Doc. Anything wrong?"

Keegan's brows lifted when he looked up from the clipboard in his hand. "What? Oh, Agent Higgins. Hi. No, everything is actually quite good. Miss Parrish is in dialysis. I know you want to see her, but give her a few hours."

Tate scrubbed a hand over his chin, not sure how far he could get with all that doctor/patient confidentiality Keegan was supposed to be shielding Winslow with. "How's she doing?"

"I understand you ignored my advice and stayed overnight with her?"

"I did." No sense in lying.

"She's much better today, but I'm afraid she's still defending her mother," Keegan warned.

"Sometimes the truth is best delivered in small doses."

Keegan nodded. "I'm afraid the news I delivered this morning packed more of a wallop than I intended. She's quite naïve to the ways of the world, isn't she? I wasn't expecting that in a woman her age."

Tate bristled. "What'd you tell her?"

The doctor stared at him for a full minute before he admitted, "That I'm almost positive she doesn't have cancer."

Tate's fist instinctively clenched. "She doesn't?" *I knew it. That bitch!*

Keegan clapped a hand to Tate's shoulder. "Take it easy, but, yeah. I'm not seeing any markers. I'll run more tests to be certain, but I think it's best if we slow the information download for now. Miss Parrish seems to be struggling with her new reality. When I left, she was near tears."

That hurt Tate's heart, but Keegan's dumping that thunderclap of truth on her should've been done in Tate's presence, not when Winslow was alone. "Would you mind inviting me the next time you talk with her? I mean, if it's okay with Winslow."

Keegan nodded. "Sure. She's one of the rarest women I've ever met. She's lived in a bubble all these years, but she's a fighter. Did you know she's pretty much home-schooled herself? That worthless mother of hers couldn't be bothered to enroll her. How many kids these days would've done that?"

That explained the stacks of books in Winslow's bedroom, but Tate didn't like that Keegan knew things he didn't. "She told you?" A prickly itch commenced under Tate's skin.

"Yes, we had quite a long talk. I feel bad dumping on her like I did." Keegan shook his head in a pensive way, staring at the wall as if his mind was somewhere else. "Yes, quite a remarkable woman."

Tate rolled his shoulder and swallowed hard, the urge to hit something creeping up on him. "So what do we do now?"

"Well..." Keegan paused. "I'd like to keep her a couple more days for testing and observation. Once I release her, she'll need to see a good nutritionist and begin building a life for herself. I'll call social services to see if—"

"No," Tate growled. "Winslow's not going into any system."

"But where will she go once she leaves the hospital?" Keegan peered intently into Tate's face. "I know people, professionals who do this kind of thing for a living. She needs adult interaction and a balanced education, not more of the same crap her mother dished out. What would you suggest?"

Tate's heart told him she could live with him, but his brain kicked into gear, and he knew he had to be smart for Winslow's sake. She needed her life back, not his idea of what that life should be. Intimacy was out. Maybe Keegan had a point. "Some kind of a halfway home? A group home?" *Some place where you won't be.*

Keegan nodded. "I know of a couple that are highly rated and would suit her situation perfectly. They're for young adults who've been rescued from abusive situations, and most of the staff is female, including the on-site counselor. I'll make a few calls, and see what I can come up with."

Tate had to swallow his pride. He had no business feeling predatory where Winslow was concerned. She wasn't his. "Okay."

Keegan nodded curtly as if he'd solved world hunger. "Your turn. What'd you find out about her mother?"

Tate leaned a shoulder to the wall. "We haven't caught up with Hattie yet, but her buddy, Dr. Bly, is behind bars down at the precinct. I'm headed there once I touch base with my boss."

Keegan's eyes lit up. "Agent Chase?"

"Yes, have you seen him today?"

"No, but last night he struck me as a damned good guy to have in your corner."

You have no idea. Tate glanced down the hall to the elevator planning his next move. "Where's the dialysis center?"

A smile curved Keegan's lips even as he sighed. "Fifth floor, second door to your right. You can't miss it."

Tate didn't intend to miss it. Tucker Chase could wait. Winslow couldn't.

She stared at the ceiling while strangers came and went around her. Most were nice and kind, but Winslow didn't know any of them. She was lost and tired and alone. Tate hadn't come back to see her before the male nurse wheeled her to dialysis. Her entire world had been jerked out from under her like a dirty rug.

Recrimination beat a steady drum roll in the back of her mind. So many lies! *How could you have been so stupid? Were you born yesterday? Why didn't you try to figure things out sooner?*

Because I was sick! She had no other answer, just guilt for being a lousy daughter, and, although it made no sense, for believing her mother. A good daughter would've believed her mother—wouldn't have any reason not to. Somehow, this was Winslow's fault. She knew it to her soul.

A sloppy tear broke loose from the corner of her eye. Quickly, Winslow staunched the flow with the back of her hand before more could get away, but damn. She no longer knew anything for certain. Her world was a joke, and she wanted Pepe and Tate. They were the only two that made sense.

But what did she get? Something called a laparoscopic surgery that ended with a catheter inserted in her abdomen, so the dialysis machine could clean her blood. It was all too much! If she hadn't needed one of those Xanax things before, she certainly needed one now!

The door to the eight-bed dialysis center cracked open, and her head swiveled automatically in hope, but two nurses entered. Not Tate. Another tear trickled down the side of her head. Winslow blinked it furiously away, but the pretty nurse came to Winslow's side. "How are we doing, hon?" she asked, her tone filled with compassion. "You look tired. Can I get you anything?"

Winslow shook her head, needing this day to be over with. Tested to her limit, she had nothing left to give.

The nurse brushed the back of her hand over Winslow's cheek. "My name is Jane. Don't worry, Winslow, we've done plenty of treatments before. It won't take much longer. You're one of the lucky ones, you know."

Winslow spared her a quiet, "I am?"

Jane nodded. "You bet. See that little girl over there? The one with the pigtails?" She pointed two beds down and across the room. "That's Portia Meta. Her family just arrived from Turkey. Portia has complete renal failure."

That was another thing. Winslow was tired of feeling ignorant every time she turned around. A copy of Merriam-Webster would've been nice. "What's renal failure?" she had to ask.

"Kidney failure. Portia's on the waiting list for a kidney transplant."

Winslow swallowed her pride, embarrassed that she'd acted badly when others were in worse straits. "How old is she?"

Jane tucked Winslow's blanket in around her shoulders. "Nine and a half. She's a cutie, isn't she?"

Portia was that and more. Long dark hair tied back in pigtails. Dark eyes. Olive skinned. She was the epitome of womanly beautiful, not little girl cute. She lay sedately on her pillow with her hands clasped together while a dark-haired woman, most likely her mother, sat in the rocker next to the bed reading to her.

"Is there a limit to how many times she can, umm, get this treatment?"

"You mean dialysis?" Jane patted Winslow's hand. "She's young and she's still fairly healthy, so she's got time. I imagine she can have as many treatments as she needs. Elderly patients have the most problems with dialysis. But I hear you're only in here for this one time?"

"Hey there," Tate said as he ducked around Jane.

She winked and stepped away, and Winslow couldn't latch onto his hand fast enough. "You came."

He stepped to her side and his fingers stroked her arm. "Of course I came. What's wrong?"

"Nothing," she lied, her heart pumping hard. "It's just been a long morning." *And how.*

He leaned over the side rail, a tender smile in his eyes. "Breathe, Winslow. You're safe. I'm here."

The weight of the world lifted up from her at those simple two words: *I'm here.* But he probably had better things to do. "Th-thanks for stopping by."

"There's no place else I'd rather be." His fingers drifted up to her head. "You like the beanie?"

"Yes," she breathed. "It keeps me warm."

A shadow darkened his brow. "Dr. Keegan told me you don't have cancer."

All she could do was close her eyes, nod, and fight back the incredible sense of betrayal.

"Don't cry, Winslow."

But how could she stop? The dam was breaking. There was no way one woman could hold back years of lies and tricks and... murder!

He tipped his forehead to hers. "Do you need me to hold you, baby?"

Yes! She looked at him then. "You'd... you'd do that for me?"

"In a heartbeat. Just say the word, and somehow, I'll wiggle my big butt inside all these wires and tubes and..." He scrunched his nose. "And I'll keep you warmer than you've ever been in your life."

He made her smile. There, in her pit of self-pity, Tate made her smile with that silly picture of him wiggling his butt to get into her bed. "It's not big."

Those delicious brows crinkled. "Have you been looking at my ass?"

Her smile turned into a genuine chuckle. "O-kaaaaaay..." She stalled, the tension uncurling from her shoulders. "I admit it. I sneaked a peek when we were making popcorn." *And I liked it.*

Tate winked. "If it makes you feel any better, I sneaked a peek at yours too."

Another giggle. "Mine's so skinny," she breathed, her cheeks heating right before his eyes.

He shook his head. "Looked just right to me."

"I'm serious, Tate. Thank you for coming. I was..." *Just about to meltdown when you showed up.* "...tired."

"I'm surprised they haven't given you anything to help you sleep."

"I don't want to take any drugs, not ever again." The truth poured out. "My mom lied, Tate. I don't have cancer. I never did! How could she do that to me? All those pills and powders, and the shots and..."

He nodded. "I wish I'd been there when Keegan told you. He should've waited."

She squeezed her eyes shut. "I want to go home, only I don't know where home is any more. I don't know where I belong." *I'm... I'm lost, Tate. I need Pepe. And you, but I don't want to scare you while all this—bullshit—is scaring me.*

He placed the softest kiss in the middle of her forehead. "I've got a home movie to show you."

"What am I going to do?" she whined, her panic on the rise. "I don't have a job and my mom's a criminal and... Tate. I don't even know what Xanax is! What am I going to do, huh?"

He blew a short puff of breath into her face to get her attention. "First, you're going to relax. Take a deep breath." He inhaled, his shoulder lifting as if he needed to show her how it was done.

She mimicked him, thankful for his warm hand over hers.

"Second," he said, "you're going to learn how to stand on your own two feet, and you're going to go to school and get an education. Isn't that what you've always wanted?"

"Well, umm... yes." She licked her lips, not sure what she wanted. As weak as she'd always been, it was easier to let her mother run her life. Not like Winslow had much choice, but now that she did? She ran her tongue over her dry lips. Life was moving frighteningly fast, and the bright light on her horizon she'd once wished for seemed to be a speeding train.

He leaned into her face just long enough to brush a kiss over her cheek. "You don't have to eat the whole elephant all at once, Winslow. I'm here to help. Trust me. Take a deep breath and breathe. In. Out. We'll figure things out together, and we'll do it day by day, one problem at a time. I know you, and there isn't a thing you can't do once you set your mind to it. All you need to do right now is rest and heal. Let me take care of the hard stuff for a while, then, when you're ready, it's all yours, okay?"

That almost sounded like he planned to stay. She nodded, her panic in check. "But you'll tell me what's going on, won't you? You won't hide anything from me? You won't, umm, take my, umm..." *Why did everything have to be so hard?* "...independence?"

He had the nerve to tease her with a sexy wink. "There's my girl. That's the Winslow I saw on the water tower two nights ago. And no, I won't take your independence. Wouldn't think of it. You get to make all your decisions from now on, deal?"

Damn. Could she handle that kind of responsibility when she hadn't known what renal failure was two minutes ago? What was she thinking? "Well, maybe you could be like my advisor or something?"

He tapped the end of her nose with his fingertip. "I'd rather be your friend."

Sucking in a deep breath, she exhaled and let the stress slide off her shoulders. "Thanks, Tate. I'm sorry I'm so wired. It's just that—"

"It's just that you've never done any of this before, and some adventures are scary, huh?"

Winslow nodded. "She drugged me when I was a kid. Maybe even when I was a baby. Who does that?"

"Your mother's a very sick woman, and we need to find her, but you..." He lifted his cell phone for her viewing pleasure. "...need to see Pepe first."

Ah, there he was, her Honey Munchkin starring in his own home movie. She latched onto the phone and

Tate's hands to see better. "Aw, look, he's playing with a sock."

"Wait for it..." Tate teased, his cheek next to hers.

Sure enough, a little boy came into view on the hardwood floor, then another. Then a big German Shepherd that looked like a skyscraper compared to her baby. Pepe rolled to his back and barked, but not like he was scared. More like he was feeling rowdy. When the big dog bumped noses with Pepe, the race was on. Pepe flipped onto his paws and dug in, running circles around the Shepherd's long legs while the little boy squealed, "Go get 'em!"

"Look at him. He's happy," Winslow murmured. "Oh, good. I was worried. Where was he?"

Tate growled. "Your mom gave him to Ike. Do you know him?"

Winslow shivered. "He's a creep. Did he hurt Pepe?"

"A little, but Pepe's fine now. My buddy Harley's taking care of him until you're better. Those are his dogs and boys playing with your baby dragon."

That made Winslow smile. *My baby dragon.*

"So here's the deal," Tate whispered. "Doc Keegan knows a halfway house for women in your situation. I Googled it and it looks like a nice place, but..." He dragged that word out.

She lifted her gaze from the antics on the cell phone to him. "But what?"

"But you can't have dogs there, and I think you'd feel better living somewhere safe and warm with your own little fire breathing dragon in bed with you at night, right?"

She nodded, daring to hope. "Can I stay with you?"

He winked. "Trust me, I've thought about that, but you need to explore the world before you make a big decision like that. In fact, I think you'd be happy living where Pepe's living. Harley and Judy would love the chance to get to know you. What would you say to moving in with them once you get out of here?"

"Are you sure?" *Were there people in the world who'd do that, take a stranger in?*

Tate's dark eyes gleamed. "Absolutely."

The kindness of strangers overwhelmed Winslow. "I hate this," she admitted, fighting back more tears.

"What?"

"I hate what Mom did to me. I'm helpless, and I'm stupid, and most of the time I don't know what anyone's talking about, and it's all my fault!"

His forehead wrinkled. "Shush, baby. Just shush. You, Winslow Parrish, are not stupid, and none of this is your fault. Don't ever say that again. You knew something's been wrong all these years, and now you're going to prove just how smart you are to the whole damned world."

"But how?" Here she was hooked to a machine, wearing a flimsy hospital gown, and homeless. She didn't even know where her clothes were.

Tate lowered one arm alongside her pillow, his nose nearly touching hers. "It's your time to fly,

Winslow. The only one holding you back now is you. Are you brave enough to let go of what was, and look forward to what can be?"

Now that he put it that way...

"Ah-huh," she whispered, all of her fears put to rest in the hopeful glimmer in his eyes

"Go on, say it," he teased, bumping his chin to her nose.

"Say what?"

"You know. Say that good luck word, the one you've been living to tell that she-troll who abused you for years."

Winslow caught the word he'd used. *Living* instead of *dying*. He'd made her believe in herself from the second he'd caught hold of her on that water tower. The tiniest smile curved the corners of her mouth. "You mean bullshit?"

Tate's face cracked with the most glorious smile. "That's the one. Let it fly, baby."

"Bull-shit," she said in two very distinct syllables. "It's my new favorite word."

"It's almost as good as mine" His eyes went dark and hazy, his voice low and rumbling.

She circled her fingers around the nape of his neck, urging him closer. "What would that be?"

He closed his eyes just as his mouth crushed hers with a whispered, "Winslow."

Chapter Twenty-Seven

"Risky plan," Tucker Chase muttered, his big right hand shading his eyes and making it hard for Tate to get a good read on him. Wasn't that an interesting turnabout, him trying to read Tucker's mind?

The Deuces Wild Team was holed up in one of the hospital's consultation rooms. Tate had run home to shower. He'd changed into a fairly new pair of jeans and a gray button-up shirt. Work boots. His usual shoulder holster and a light jacket to hide the loaded pistol.

Isaiah sat at Tucker's left at the head of the table, Tate and Ky at his right. Eden was home icing her ankle. The breakfast order Isaiah had brought back for Tate cooled at the other end of the table while Tate revealed his plan to bring Joyce Parrish to justice. It came to him over coffee with Shawna Truborn. Now he had to convince his boss.

"Risky, but sound," Isaiah offered nonchalantly, kicked back in his chair. "What do you need me to do, Tate?"

Exactly. Without Tate's psychic friends, none of this would work. He took a deep breath. "I'll need you to influence Joyce Parrish psychically if you can. Get her to need to see Winslow."

Isaiah rolled one shoulder. "Should be easy enough, provided I can get through to her. How desperate do you want her?"

"Frantic enough to throw caution to the wind?"

"Consider it done." Isaiah tapped a fingertip to his temple. "I'll check her out as soon as we're done here."

"And you intend to keep Winslow at Bly's clinic as bait while he's up at Johns Hopkins in Maryland?" Tucker asked. "You're really going to use her like that?"

"Not exactly." Tate rolled his shoulder, not comfortable using Ky's wife as bait either. "Eden volunteered to pose as Winslow at Bly's. Winslow stays here in the hospital under police protection."

The scam was simple. Channel Thirteen was set to hold a press conference with Dr. Bly at their studio in Crystal City, during which he would reveal his cure for cancer to the world. The cure? The cocktail of drugs that Hattie had been poisoning Winslow with. In the course of the press conference, Bly would declare he'd kept his lucky patient secluded at his clinic, pending further testing and research. He would

Tate blew out an equally deep breath—of aggravation. This wasn't rocket science. "Joyce needs to believe Bly is capitalizing on her prescription drug cocktail, that he's getting rich on her idea. He'll claim that he and he alone found the cure to cancer just to egg her on. Channel Thirteen's going out on a limb with this false story. They're willing to do all they can." *Why aren't you?*

"Joyce, sorry—Hattie will already be antsy," Isaiah added. "She'll want to get to Bly before he turns on her or gets away."

"Dr. Keegan offered to speak along with Bly at the real conference if Joyce doesn't break cover before then," Tate said. "He said he could add credence to Bly's story, make it sound more plausible."

"No," Tucker said. "No civilians. Only FBI and Channel Thirteen. There'll be no collateral damage. None. Do you hear me?"

"The hook will be Bly telling the world that he's getting rich," Ky repeated.

"Once Hattie hears he stands to make millions" — Isaiah snapped his fingers— "We've got her."

Tate nodded his appreciation for Ky and Isaiah's tag-teaming Tucker.

"And the news conference is set for tomorrow night? Monday?" Tucker let that question hang.

Tate hissed. How many times did he have to say this? "The sooner the better." The only one guarding Winslow at that moment was another FBI agent. Why didn't that make Tate feel good?

"But you can keep an eye, so to speak, on Hattie during this entire op?" Tucker's brow spiked at Isaiah. "I don't want Eden or Bly getting hurt either."

Isaiah tipped back in his chair. "If she's anything like most criminals, no problem."

Ky hissed. "You guys better take care of my wife."

Tate glared at his boots, his left foot suddenly tapping along with Tucker's finger. It didn't get any weirder—or more annoying—than being in sync with his boss.

Isaiah leaned forward, his elbows to the table and his eyes on Tate. "The human brain is fairly generic. I can read most people. Their needs are basic, their minds wide-open. But everyone once in a while, someone like you comes along."

Instantly, Tate shoved back at the psychic probe Isaiah had just launched. He might not understand how his mental muscle worked, it just did. Slam. Bam. Isaiah was out of there.

Isaiah's eyes lit up as if he recognized the shove.

Tate stuck his chin at the guy. *Yeah. Stop messing with me, Zaroyin. I'm onto you.*

He'd sensed his fellow agents psychic probing more than once in the past. Eden's touch was gentle, more like the brush of a butterfly wing. Tucker's mental forays felt clumsy and heavy handed, like he was guessing his way into territory he wasn't sure of. His were the easiest to block. But Isaiah's? His probes were more like the kiss of a honeybee in spring, a sweet, soft whisper that almost left a guy craving another touch. Yet Isaiah could still back that subtle contact up with the promise of a sting when push came to shove.

Tucker slapped both hands to the table, startling everyone. "Stop sandbagging me, guys. What's the catch?"

Tate dropped his gaze to the table, not sure if Tucker was communicating with Isaiah at that precise moment. The catch was that Tate now knew for certain he was psychic. He just hadn't disclosed how psychic he was to his boss. Affinity with animals, check. Psychic blocking, check. And just possibly the ability to read certain minds.

Once before, he'd felt Isaiah in his head prior to the op that saved Eden's life. Alex Stewart might've sent him to Sierra Leone ahead of Ky, but Alex had only done it because Tate pressed him into it, and all because of a vision Isaiah sent him.

Bright and early one morning. Tate was at his bathroom mirror shaving, about to wash the last of the lather off his face, when an image of Eden on a balcony overlooking the stormy Atlantic came to him—the Joker—the least likely savior of anyone, and yeah. That's how bizarre this whole psychic thing was, and how gentle the prompting from Isaiah had been. How he'd known where Eden was, Tate never asked, but not once had he doubted that the vision came straight from Isaiah.

There was plenty more to the story, but it all zeroed down to Isaiah—through Tate—giving Eden what she'd needed to hang on for one more day. It was a funny, intangible, lighter-than-air thing, but it was every bit as powerful as love. Coincidentally, it was the same thing she'd given Ky years earlier when he was at death's door, trapped in a torture cell in Afghanistan.

Hope.

Because of Tate's already established alliances in Sierra Leone, Mama Chappy's son was on that beach the day Eden would've been murdered. All he did was wave at her. All she did was wave back. But by sunset, the kidnapper and his soldiers were dead, and Eden was safe in the arms of the man she loved. Tate wiped a quick hand over his face, perplexed at how his mind kept circling around to love. Had to be because of Winslow.

There seemed a margin of privacy and freedom without Tucker knowing this information, but once he did...

Tucker cleared his throat, that damned finger tapping. Waiting.

This was where everything could hit the fan. Tate had to say something, so he opted for misdirection. "The catch is—"

"That there is no catch," Isaiah interrupted smoothly. "Why would you think otherwise, Boss?"

Tucker's gaze narrowed to the evil glint of an ex-Navy SEAL who knew damned well he was being played. "Cut the bullshit, Zaroyin. I've worked with both of you long enough to know something else is going on here. Now spill."

Yeah, he deserved to know, but wasn't it interesting. Isaiah was outright taunting the guy. He wasn't the suck up Tate thought he was. Not by a long shot.

"You're suspicious of everyone. That's all." Isaiah leaned his elbows on the table, his fingers interlocked. "This sort of operation is precisely what Tate does best, Boss. He goes with his gut, and he hunts. You wanted him on this team for the very reason you doubt him now. He's a tracker like none of the rest of us, and if we're smart, we'll give him his head and follow where he leads. Think of that moose carcass."

Tucker's lips bunched. His brows collided as his fingers flattened to the table. "What moose carcass?"

"The one you guys snacked on in Canada. Whose idea was that? Yours? Who shot it? You? Not hardly. I can't see you dragging a yearling moose into camp in the middle of a blizzard, but Tate did and he did it alone."

All ten of Tucker's fingers drummed the table now. "I'd ask how you knew about that moose if I didn't already know."

Tate had forgotten that part of the Canada op. Even for him, that yearling moose was a lucky find. It kept him, Ky, Tucker, and Sam Becker, another hotshot SEAL, alive, but damn. Isaiah had some balls to take Tucker on like he did.

Isaiah winked, his gaze shifting from Tucker to Tate as he mimicked the big guy, tapping an index finger to his temple. "I also know about the four Omni-9000s you lifted out of the FBI evidence locker. You lied to Director Strong when you took them to Sierra Leone to go get Eden back. You told him you needed practice time on the range with the new high-tech gear in the inventory."

Damned if Tucker's face didn't split wide with a grin. That was one thing he did easily, forgive and forget. "You're okay, Zaroyin, you know that?"

Isaiah rapped one knuckle to the tabletop. "I'd say the same about you, but the jury's still out."

Tucker kicked back in his chair. "Let's do this."

It's about damned time. Tate kept the smile off his face. He needed to explore this link with Isaiah before he admitted it to anyone else.

Chapter Twenty-Eight

Finally back in her room, Winslow fell into a deep sleep that took her through the night and into the following morning. She lay there in the silence of her private room staring at the ceiling and wondering if this was how other people felt when they first woke. Warm. Tired, yet rested at the same time. At peace with themselves and the world. Dare she think it? *I'm normal.*

All she'd missed in her life waited outside her door, but for now, she was content to just lie there and breathe. One of life's smallest pleasures, but one that few appreciated unless they'd been to the other side of Hell. Stretching, she let a quiet yawn ease out of her. Then another. A person could stay in bed all day if she wasn't careful. *Not me.*

Tugging her trusty beanie down to keep her ears covered, she lifted to her butt, swung her bare feet over the edge of her bed, and rang for the nurse. This was a day for living, not sleeping.

She looked down at her wiggling toes just to be sure they were hers. Of course they were, but they didn't ache. Or tingle. Even the catch in her left shoulder blade didn't protest. Neither did her spine, which usually ached twenty-four-seven.

Wasn't that interesting? Just for the fun of it, she stretched both hands high over her head and let every last vertebra know she was alive. *Wow. So this was what waking up should feel like.*

Her knees started jumping just thinking of all she could do with a body that didn't hurt. Run. Dance. Tate had said something about proving how smart she was. That meant school, and that meant talking to that Client Advisor person Dr. Keegan had mentioned, and that meant...

She burst out singing, "I'm alive, and I'm happy to be alive, and I'm—"

"Miss Parrish!"

Winslow ducked her head into her shoulders, caught by the nurse. "Umm, hi. I'm up."

Pretty and blonde, her hair carved in a sassy tapered cut that barely covered her earlobes, the young woman came to Winslow's bedside. "I see that. I'll bet you're hungry too."

Winslow's fingers fluttered over her stomach. "You know what? I am."

How extraordinary—not to be the least bit nauseous. Sweet!

The nurse laughed, one of those lovely, bells-chiming sounds you want to hear again. "Then let's get you ready to rock and roll, shall we? I'm Breeze, by the way. It looks like that one round of dialysis did wonders for you. Most patients are drained the day after they go through it, but look at you. All smiles. And singing too."

Warmth buzzed up Winslow's cheeks, probably over her entire head, she'd blushed so hard. "I sing best in my shower, speaking of which, I could use one," she said, but added, "Is that okay?" *Just in case, you know, there were hospital rules or something.*

Breeze's forehead wrinkled when she smiled. "You betcha. Right now, you're our star patient, so whatever you want, short of leaving the hospital, you get, girlfriend. I think Dr. Keegan wants to talk to you before you start wandering the halls though."

Girlfriend? Best day ever!

Stifling her enthusiasm so she didn't make too big of a fool of herself, she asked, "But I could if I wanted to?" Winslow had to know she was in control. "Walk the halls, I mean."

"I don't see why not." Breeze was good for her word and had the IV out of Winslow's left hand in no time. The catheter went next, and darn. Winslow wanted clothes and shoes, not a flimsy gown that made her pasty-white legs look skinny and frail. "How about I order a bacon and eggs breakfast while you shower? Do you need help or do you think you can go it alone?"

"I'd rather shower alone, but I need clothes. Real clothes."

"What you need is to open the gift bag behind you, young lady. Go on. I guess someone couldn't wait for you to wake up, so they left a present for you. Doesn't look like flowers to me."

Winslow twisted around to the counter by the door. A brown paper grocery bag rested there. No flowers. No ribbons. Who would've left her a present? Tate? A shiver of excitement wiggled up her spine when she planted both feet to the cool linoleum floor and shuffled over to the bag. "Is this from you?"

Breeze shook her head. "No, but I'm dying to know what's in it."

"Oh, look." A pair of dark gray sweat pants that were just her size, and a white T-shirt, extra small. It had to be from Tate. *Aw, how thoughtful?* She held them up for her nurse to admire.

"Looks like someone's got a secret admirer," Breeze said, winking.

Winslow ducked her head into her shoulders, feeling like a kid at Christmas. Only this time, she'd gotten real presents. That were new.

Digging deeper into the bag, she fingered the cotton bra and package of three, white cotton underwear beneath those surprises. She cringed at the thought of him selecting intimates for her. *How embarrassing!* Breeze didn't need to see them. Simple black tennis shoes and red crew socks completed the surprise. No card. No note. *Oh, that man.*

Breeze was on the phone ordering breakfast, so Winslow shuffled into the bathroom and closed the door behind her. She set her new clothes beside the sink. Shifting out of her gown, she hung it on the hook beside the shower before she turned the faucet to warm and the shower spray to gentle.

One glance in the mirror was enough to bring a tear to her eye. Tate was the kindest man she'd ever met, and he was right. She couldn't eat the entire elephant of her brand-new life in one sitting. It would take time, maybe years, but by darn, this was her life and she meant to live it.

Oh, look. A big cheesy grin hit the face of that woman staring back at her. Winslow leaned closer to her reflection and smiled wider than she had in a long time, her shoulders lifting. Laugh lines crinkled the corners of her eyes. How'd they get there?

She hadn't had much to laugh at for years, and she wasn't much to look at. She had no distinguishing beauty to lay claim to. No long flowing locks that dripped sexy curls to her skinny butt, just a fairly bald head. No perky little nose and no freckles—unless the ones on her hands counted for something other than diagnosing arsenic poisoning. Her eyes were pretty enough, but the shadows beneath them had to go.

But look at the sparkle in those big green eyes. And her lips were pink today, not gray. That was encouraging. She pinched them into a pout just to see what they'd look like when they were ready to kiss Tate. *Cute!*

If she turned to the side, her profile looked, well, skinny and boney. *Can't hide that.* No fat or flare on her body, as in anywhere. Not on her boobs, her butt, or her hips. Her ribs and hips jutted out like she'd stumbled out of a Russian gulag. Some women might want this look, but she'd be okay with a little more curve. Cleavage would be nice. A soft flare at her hips. Big enough boobs to fill out the wrinkles in her bra. Small things to make her look more like a woman than a boy.

What Tate saw in her, she didn't know. Had to be pity, but she didn't think so, not the way his gaze heated when his eyes met hers. Not the way his nostrils flared or the way his pupils dilated, swallowing the dark brown irises when he drew close. Or how his fingers lingered on her skin when they didn't have to. He seemed to like touching her.

Winslow leaned over the edge of the sink, peering into her happy depths, because that was what she saw in the mirror. Herself. Happy. Maybe a little ugly at the moment, definitely a cue ball on a wobbly neck, but for the first time in her life, she had a future. Yes, things were going to be crazy tough for a while, but she could do it. She, Winslow Arizona Parrish, would be okay.

Where have I heard that before?

Another bathroom flashed to mind. Mint green tiles. A stainless-steel commode. A drain in the floor.

A syringe coming at her like a bullet train. The cold hollow look in her mother's eyes.

Winslow touched her fingertips to her neck, fingering the spot where that wicked hypo had hit. A bruise marked it now like a target, the center dark, the outer-ring yellowish.

"My mother thought she could kill you, Winslow," she told her reflection firmly. Resolutely. Ready to face the world, her chin up. "What do you say about that?"

Pride swelled within when that identical twin in the mirror answered, "Bullshit."

Chapter Twenty-Nine

"No go. I can't locate her," Isaiah reported to the Deuces Wild Team through their Bluetooth earpieces.

It was early Monday morning as the Deuces Wild Team searched for Hattie Beauregard. They were back in their FBI uniforms of the day, black button-up shirts, matching black slacks, and black suit jackets. The day was chilly and the sun was barely up. Already Ky was in the air, winging west to handle the California op. Eden was preparing her team to stand ready at Bly's clinic.

Tate, Isaiah, and Tucker already had that all-important, give-it-up-or-die-trying talk with Dr. Bly down at the local precinct. Turned out he was more than willing to turn state's evidence in exchange for a get-out-of-jail-free card. The man was smart enough to volunteer, not only where he'd thought Hattie's current location was, but several other hangouts, all bars, that she was known to frequent when she was working at, what was it, her bogus spa job? After their fruitful interview, Tate and Isaiah split up and hit the road in two different vehicles.

"Copy that," Tucker replied from his vehicle with a terse sigh. "I'm not seeing her, either. Tate? Any luck?"

"I came up empty here too." Tate had taken the stretch between Maple and Land's End, looking for Hattie, Ike, or Janice. The rats seemed to have fled the ship. D.C. Metro hadn't spotted them, either.

"Let's head back," Isaiah said. "I want us all prepared. We've got some details to iron out before the interview tonight."

Like what? As far as Tate knew, the schedule was already set. Channel Thirteen would hold their bogus interview with Dr. Bly live on the six o'clock news. Shawna Truborn knew to ask all the leading questions. Bly had been given a script to follow. The AMA conference would kick-off early Tuesday morning at John Hopkins. Tate only hoped Hattie would fall for Bly's initial come-on. She needed to be behind bars by then.

"Has anyone checked on our favorite girl today?" Tucker asked. "How'd her dialysis go?"

"That was yesterday," Tate replied. There was no way he'd disclose that he had breakfast with his favorite girl in her room earlier. "I'm on my way to see her now."

"Once this thing goes down, I want a guard on her around the clock. That means you, Tate."

"Copy that," he acknowledged. There was nothing else he'd rather do.

Only he didn't get that far. He and Isaiah were on their way to Winslow's room when Isaiah steered Tate to the left and said, "Step into my office," at the Starbuck's kiosk around the hall from Winslow's room.

"Now?" Tate asked. This had to be one of the details Isaiah wanted to iron out. "You want to do your test here?" *Out in the open?*

"Sure. You can see her room from here. Besides, it's not like I'm going to be sticking electrodes into your skull." Isaiah dropped his gear bag beside one of the chairs, then grabbed a handful of paper napkins before he pulled out a chair from the nearest table. "Take a seat. It'll only take a few minutes. Want a cup?"

"Sure don't." Tate slouched into the molded plastic seat, then pushed back, balancing it on its rear legs. *Then let's get this over with.* "What's next? What do you want me to do?"

"Pretty much nothing. Just close your eyes and take a deep breath." Isaiah set the napkins between them. "Let your mind go where it wants. Take a break. Relax."

Tate crossed his arms over his chest, closed his eyes, and did as Isaiah requested. Instead of letting his mind go straight to Winslow, he focused on his boss. That ought to confuse Isaiah's psychic probing.

"There's something about the number twelve," he said softly.

Here we go. More psychic mumbo jumbo. More cosmic realignment of the universe BS.

"That's how old you were when your life fell apart, Tate. Tucker's son was twelve when his mother nearly got him killed. And I was twelve when I came home and found my mom on the floor and..." Tate's eyes flicked open. *Don't say it.* "...dying."

His chair fell to all four legs. Isaiah wasn't looking at him any longer, just staring at his long, slender fingers, now intertwined, squeezing together on the tabletop. "Tucker knows a lot about me, but he doesn't know this."

"What happened?" Tate dared ask, his palms flat to the table.

Isaiah shrugged. "I was twelve," he said that like it explained everything. "The world was a noisy place for a kid whose mind was suddenly hyper-aware of other people's thoughts and problems. And I'm not talking about just hearing the kids at school or my parents at home, more like the world. Try waking up to that every morning. Hell, try sleeping through it at night. I didn't know how to turn the volume down or how to set any filters. I couldn't block them, like you do."

Which is why you think I'm psychic.

Isaiah's gaze slanted as if he'd heard what Tate hadn't said out loud, damn him. "I sneaked out of my room that night for the first time in my life. I mean it. I didn't do crap like that. I was one of those nerdy kids who followed rules. I did my homework right after school and I did chores for Mom. I was never in trouble. I never thought of disappointing her."

Figures. You seem the type.

A slight chin nod was the only indication Isaiah was reading Tate. "But that night, I climbed out of my window to meet a friend for coffee, just to talk. When I got back, it was after two a.m. The house was dark and quiet." Another sigh. "Some guy broke in while I was gone. Mom ran to my room, maybe for help, maybe to protect me. I'll never know. She was on the floor between my bed and the window. In a pool of blood. Twelve times. He knifed her twelve times."

There was that number again...

"I got to hold her hand while she breathed her last." Isaiah swallowed so hard it seemed his Adam's apple stuck in his throat for a moment. "Of all the people screaming in my head to be heard, morning, noon, and night, I never heard... her. Dad was always gone, and I should've been there for her. She was alone."

"You didn't kill her." Tate heard his heart reaching out to his friend.

"I know that intellectually." Isaiah tugged one of those napkins off the stack. Folding it, he swiped his eyes, then buried it inside his clenched fist. "She was lying on her stomach right beneath my window. I almost stepped on her. Blood was everywhere. On my bedroom wall. The ceiling. She'd scrawled a heart in the puddle next to her face. Three letters in the center. M. Y. I. Do you know what she was trying to tell me when she died?"

"My Isaiah," Tate breathed.

"Yeah." Isaiah grunted, nodding. "She loved me with her dying breath, but where was I? Out being reckless for the first time in my life. Drinking coffee. Chatting. Letting her deal with a murderer all by herself."

'I should have been there' breathed between them like a living regret for the mothers they'd lost.

"You were just a kid," Tate offered. *Didn't that sound familiar?*

"True, that," Isaiah murmured, his gaze on the table. "But not a day goes by that my soul doesn't ache for one more day... one more chance... to have stayed home and saved her life."

Shit. I know what you mean. Exactly. What. You. Mean...

Now Tate needed a napkin. Just one. Real men didn't cry, they just got dust in their eyes. Must be something in the air. "Fucking number twelve," he growled.

Isaiah rapped the table with his knuckle. "Damnedest thing, huh. Life's good until all of a sudden, it's not."

"So this is your idea of a psychic test?"

"I didn't have one in mind," Isaiah murmured, meeting Tate's eyes. "I just wanted you to know that shit happens. Your dad walked away from his only kid instead of rebuilding his family, and that wasn't right. He cheated you when he did that, and mine cheated me when he decided to save the world instead of hanging around and helping his only child survive the worst tragedy of his life. It was just as poor a choice, but in the long run, it doesn't matter, Tate. We both lost everything the day we lost our moms, and that's just the way it is."

Truer words.

The elder Zaroyin's attempt at turning military men and women into science fiction type drones had killed hundreds of volunteers before it ended, and it nearly destroyed Isaiah in the process. By the time Abraham Zaroyin came to his senses, Isaiah and Eden were both in the hands of his psychotic partners in crime, both slated to die. But that operation ended months ago.

Tate drew in a deep breath. Never had he expected to find kinship with the diabolical Dr. Abraham Zaroyin's only son, but there they were. Not ready to hug and sing *Kumbaya,* but leaning on each other like—brothers. Another hard swallow.

Isaiah lifted his eyes. "So, teach me how to block Tucker and Eden. Some days they drive me crazy." *Isn't that the truth?*

"You know how to block the world, but you can't block Tucker?" Tate asked, puzzled. Isaiah was the rock star on the Deuces Wild Team.

"That's the problem. I can't block anyone." Isaiah crumpled the stack of napkins, his knuckles white. "I can read most people's minds, but I can't block shit. All I can do is filter the noise in my head a little bit, but not enough to turn the volume completely off. I need to know how you keep people like me out. What's the key?"

"So you've got migraines all the time." Tate made that a statement. The clamor of too many people screaming, speaking, and crying in a guy's head could drive him crazy. How long had Isaiah suffered with that racket. Fifteen years maybe? That was a damned long time to put up with everyone else's pain, on top of his own.

"You have no idea," Isaiah muttered.

"Actually, I do." Tate remembered back to his worst nightmares and migraines, attributing both to grief instead of what might have been his psychic ability pushing through, like a weed in the frozen tundra that his heart had become. He'd been full of rage then, mad at his dad for being emotionally absent, mad at the world for—revolving—like nothing had happened when a woman as exquisite as his mother died. That was when he'd first started hating people.

But one by one, he'd eliminated those voices, picturing the ghosts who made them—right before he lifted an imaginary fifty cal and blew them away. All of them. Figuratively.

"Think blanks. Don't project cozy images or mantras or all that BS. Make a pistol in your mind and shoot blanks at the voices. End them." That was the only way he could describe it.

"You kill them?"

Tate shrugged. "Why not? They're not real, and it's not like I'm using live ammo."

"Do they bleed when you shoot them?"

"Hell, no. I just want them to shut up. That's why the blanks. They're silence. I picture the voices. I line 'em up in my sights, and pop. I shoot them with silence and they turn to dust."

"Wow, I've heard silence was golden, but... really? It works?" Isaiah cocked his head, a curious sparkle in his eye. "Amazing. In effect, you reroute their psychic demands though..." *Yada, yada. Yeah. Whatever.* This was where Isaiah got borrrrrrring. He trailed off, his fingers tapping the tabletop. "Let me try. Project something at me. Go on, I know you can do it."

"It'd be damned nice if you'd shut up," Tate projected without batting an eye.

Isaiah grinned. "Well, did you?" His eyes lit up with glee. "You did! I did it!"

Tate grunted at that no-brainer.

"Yes, I blocked you!" Damned if Isaiah's shoulders didn't drop with relief while he blew out a deep sigh.

"I'm saved. You have no idea what this means to me. You've got to teach Eden and Ky how to do this."

"Not Tucker?" Tate lifted an eyebrow.

Isaiah's face split wide with a toothy grin. "Not today. Soon. Maybe."

Interesting yet again.

Isaiah leaned into the table, his black eyes intense. "I know you don't think you belong on this team, but you do. You're not a joke, Tate. You ever play cards?"

"Solitaire," Tate pushed at him psychically.

A wide smile split Isaiah's face. He shook his head, looking pleased with himself, then answered in kind. *"It figures. You ever play poker?"*

Why answer? He already knew Tate avoided games.

Isaiah interlocked his fingers, still smiling. "A joker's a wild card, Tate," he said out loud, "and that's what you are. He doesn't know it yet, but you're Tucker's secret weapon, not a joke. You can block other psychics, which makes you more valuable in any strategic power play. They'll never see you coming. What other psychic skills are you keeping from us?"

Did talking to animals count? "I'll let you know when they show up," Tate growled. One was enough.

Chapter Thirty

"Hi. I'm looking for Portia Meta," Winslow said by way of introduction at the open hospital room door. "I'm Winslow Parrish. I saw her up in dialysis yesterday, and I was wondering if I could talk with her."

After her shower and a light breakfast of scrambled eggs and one slice of crispy bacon, Winslow had ventured out into her new world in her new wardrobe, dragging an IV tree behind her with Breeze's help. Except for her bare head, she looked cute in a waifish, they-just-let-me-out-of-the-asylum kind of way.

She'd spotted Tate and another man at a table in the break area on her way out of the ward, but they seemed serious, so she hadn't interrupted. Besides, her two appointed police chaperones followed at a respectable distance. That ought to keep Tate happy.

"I'll let you two talk," Breeze said. "Call me when you're ready to walk back to your room."

The dark-haired woman sitting with Portia nodded for Winslow to join her. "Come, come," she said in perfect English, a kindly smile breaching her face as she lifted to her feet and offered her chair. "We would love to visit with you."

That was easy.

"Oh, no, I'm fine. Please sit. I need to stand anyway. I need the exercise."

Portia offered a one-handed wave from her bed. "Hi, Winslow. How are you today?"

"I'm fine, but is this your mother?" Winslow asked.

"Yes, I am her mother. Ester," the mother said, bobbing her head, but on her feet at the other side of Portia's bed as if she wouldn't think of sitting while Winslow stood. "Can I offer you something to eat or drink? If I were at home I would offer you baklava and chai, but here..."

Winslow waved her kindness off. "No thanks, I'm the one who should've brought a gift for you. How long have you been in America?"

"Since July. My husband works with your country's Central Intelligence Agency. We are very happy to be here."

"You're very brave," Winslow said to Portia.

Portia shrugged both shoulders and offered a quiet, "Meh."

"How long has she been sick?" Winslow needed to know.

Ester ducked her head into her shoulders. "All of her life, but now here in America, we finally have hope for a transplant. So we wait."

"And we get to feel like a pincushion every day," Portia added with a tired smile.

Winslow cocked her head to look at the slender girl. Maybe twelve or thirteen, Portia Meta had long, black hair with no luster to it. Pulled back into a tight ponytail, it made her look more like a little boy as thin as she was. "Can I tell you a secret?" she asked Portia.

The little girl tilted forward, listening without any joy in her tired eyes. "What?"

Winslow tugged the beanie off her head with a sly wink. "I know just how you feel, and believe me, you're the bravest person I've met in years, well, except for my friend, Tate. He's pretty brave too, but you're the bravest girl I know."

Surprise brightened Portia's eyes as they scrolled from the beanie to Winslow's bare head. It was a small thing to do for another person, this one suffering worse than she was, but Winslow had made up her mind. "May I?"

When Ester said, "Yes, please," Winslow tugged the beanie over Portia's head, careful not to bind up her ponytail and making sure the USMC was front and center. "There. Now look at you. All ready for your transplant."

Portia's face turned lovely with a genuine smile this time. "Thank you, Winslow. I will treasure it forever."

Esther dabbed at her eyes with her fingers. "Everyone here has been so kind. Thank you so much."

But Portia eyelids sagged, so Winslow said a quick goodbye and promised to come back as soon as she could. She'd just turned to leave when she spied Tate with his arms crossed, leaning his hip against the doorjamb, a smile on his handsome face.

Winslow gestured over her shoulder. "Oh, hi, I was just—"

"I saw," he said warmly, his hand outstretched for hers. "It looks like I need to bring you another beanie."

"I hope you don't mind. It was the only thing I had to give, and Portia needed something to keep her head warm. She's waiting for a kidney."

His gaze took her in, shifting quickly over her bare head and back to her eyes. "But what about you?"

Winslow dusted her fingers over the bare skin where her brows used to be. "It's just hair, Tate, and it's time I stopped worrying about what everyone else thinks. I can't change yesterday."

Out in the hall, he tugged her into his side, his arm draped casually over her shoulder. Winslow snuggled into him as they strolled back to her room. "You've got some color in your cheeks today."

"Bullshit," she whispered coyly. "I bet you tell all the girls that."

A chuckle bubbled out of him. "That dialysis worked, didn't it?"

"I think so, yes, but I had a good talk with myself this morning, and... you're right. I want to go to school, Tate. Can you help me figure out how?"

"Easy," he murmured, "but first..." He drew her into his arms. Slowly and deliberately, he pressed his lips to her forehead. "I'm so damned proud of you."

Winslow wanted more than a peck on her head. She snaked her arms around his neck, which put her puny breasts against his muscular chest, and the heat sizzling off him was... *Oh boy*. Her heart skipped a beat at her sudden attack of over-confidence. "Kiss me," she whispered before she lost her nerve.

No sooner asked than granted. He ducked his head down and his lips made warm, wet contact, and...

Her heart set to tap dancing up and down every rib in her ribcage like drumsticks on a xylophone, making beautiful music.

His hand cupped the back of her head, and she didn't even cringe that he was holding her bald head. Not once. Not until some guy 'ahemed' on his way past them in the hall.

"I'd take this into your room, but there's a bed in there," Tate growled into her mouth, which only made Winslow giggle.

"You've seen me in bed," she teased, easing back from his delectable lips to speak.

"That's the problem. I might be tempted."

"By me?" *Hardly.*

He dipped two fingers under her chin and tilted her gaze up to meet his eyes. "By you, Winslow. I'm waiting for the day I can get that champagne you've always wanted. Trust me, that will be just as hard for me."

"But w-why?" Gosh, he was so good looking this close up. Intense, he set her body to thrumming like a live wire.

"Because I..." A look she couldn't decipher passed over his face. Not angry for a change. More thoughtful. Serious. "Just because."

He seemed coy all of a sudden. Winslow cut him some slack. Dropping her eyes to her new shoes, she said, "It's only because of you that I was able to get up and do something besides lay around all day. Thanks for the clothes and, umm..." *The underwear.* "...everything!"

His brows cinched together. "What are you talking about? I didn't get you any clothes."

"Then who did?" Tucker barked yet another angry outburst, his arm raised high, his hand skimming over his head.

For now, Tate stood with Tucker out of hearing range of the nurses' station on Winslow's floor. She was back in bed, upset that her mother might've been in her room while she was sleeping last night. Worse, when she'd come back from visiting Portia, she found out that her room had been changed. She was in the same ward, just on the other side of the centrally located nurses' station.

"She doesn't know and neither do the nurses," Tate growled back at his boss. "The clothes were in a brown paper bag on her counter when she woke up. Obviously they came from someone who knows her. All the sizes fit, even the shoes."

"Could it have been her mother? Did the officers on guard see who did it?" Tucker growled.

"They'd just changed shifts. The two who were there when it happened are gone," Tate replied.

"It had to be Hattie." Tucker didn't like surprises.

Well, neither did Tate. "Isaiah's checking hospital surveillance, but it couldn't have been. How would she know where Winslow is? Admitting doesn't even know she's here." Thanks to Dr. Keegan, only the FBI and the officers standing watch knew which room Winslow was in.

This new development threatened to blow their planned interview out of the water.

"Shit," Tucker cussed. "From now on, you stay with Winslow. Let me and Isaiah handle any false leads. Damn that Bly. Maybe he's still working with Hattie."

Tate shook his head. "Before we get any more excited..." And cause trouble for Metro PD's finest. "...we need to know for sure who left those clothes."

"God damn," Tucker muttered.

"Hey, guys," Isaiah's calm voice came over their earpieces. Not that he had to speak to Tate like that anymore, but Tate appreciated the smokescreen.

"What you got?" Tucker barked, his finger in his ear and his gaze on the floor at his feet.

"A compassionate doctor on the loose," Isaiah answered. "Keegan dropped that bag of clothes off early this morning when he was on rounds. I verified with him, so we're still on track with Operation Sucker Punch."

"Son-of-a-bitch!" Agent Chase bellowed. "Keegan again? Did you ask why he didn't leave a card or a note? Jesus Christ, he needs to butt out of this op until it's settled. Then he can romance her all he wants."

"He's not romancing her," both Tate and Isaiah said at the same time. *Keep your voice down, Boss. She'll hear you.*

Tucker shot Tate that look. "I know. I just meant... forget it." He cocked his head. "Isaiah, contact Channel Thirteen. See if Truborn can interview Bly earlier, this afternoon would be nice. Then call the local precinct. Get Bly's ass over there and get this done. Camera, action, and all that shit."

Winslow could hear Tate's angry boss from her bed across the hall. She'd opted to stay in her new clothes instead of an ugly hospital gown with strings in the back. Ugh. Whoever thought of that design didn't know the first thing about privacy.

Her walk to visit Portia had done her in, but it sounded as if Tate was getting his butt chewed for not having ESP and knowing who'd dropped off the clothes. She couldn't make out his answer, but it must've been enough. Agent Chase finally stopped yelling.

So Dr. Keegan was her mystery admirer, huh? Her fingers drummed at the edge of her blanket. Tate didn't know it yet, but Dr. Keegan had also left a nice bouquet of twelve yellow roses, sprigs of leafy ferns, and a mist of baby's breath, her first flowers ever. *Awkward...*

A tap sounded at her partially closed door before Tate peered around it. "Are you decent?" he teased.

"Come in!" She was dying to get her hands on him. *Please don't look at the flowers.*

One brow spiked. He'd looked. "Let me guess. Keegan."

Winslow ducked her head into her shoulders, embarrassed. "Yes-s-s-s-s. He left a card this time though." Not like the note that said *'Hurry and get well, Beautiful'* helped with Tate's mood.

Just then another man peeked around the corner. Tall, dark, and lean, nearly as handsome as Tate, he waved one palm to her. "Hey, Winslow. I'm Special

Agent Isaiah Zaroyin. It's good to finally meet you. Hope you didn't hear all the ruckus our boss was making."

How could she not? "I think the whole floor heard it. Come on in, Agent Zaroyin. He's mad at Dr. Keegan, huh?"

"He'll get over it, but please, call me Isaiah." He stuck his chin at the roses. "Your girl's got an admirer, Tate."

"No, I don't." Winslow shook her head. "Dr. Keegan's just being—"

"Nice," Tate hissed. "He's out of line, Winslow." *Wasn't that the pot calling the kettle black?* "He had no business moving you without FBI permission, either. Don't worry about it. I'll take care of it."

Warmth flushed through Winslow. Tate hadn't denied what his friend said, that she was his girl. But she didn't need him fighting her battles. "Let me talk to him about the flowers. I'm sure you've got better things to do." *Like catching my mom.*

His eyes narrowed as he dragged the easy chair over to the right side of the bed—where he could reach her. "Good idea. Want to watch the early edition news?"

Agent Zaroyin was already flipping through channels, so Winslow said, "Sure!"

Chapter Thirty-One

Tucker showed up in Winslow's room just as Shawna Truborn eased into her script, her dazzling smile in place and her bright eyes romancing the camera. When Isaiah called her to move the interview up, she'd eagerly had Dr. Bly in his appointed place for the early edition at three p.m. with two police officers off camera.

"Good afternoon viewers!" She oozed enthusiasm. "I'm Shawna Truborn and my special guest this afternoon is Silver Spring's own Dr. Jorge Bly. Thank you for joining us."

Tate eyed his boss. Tucker looked damned tight, the cords in his neck taut as Bly glanced at the camera, his smile tentative and unsure. The slender, silver-haired, middle-aged man looked nervous. His fingers were clenched into fists on the desk he sat at as if this were his first time on camera. Which it was. The mug shots taken at the jail didn't count.

"You have some very exciting news to share with America, don't you?" Shawna prompted.

"Yes, and I am happy to be here," he offered quietly. "It's not often a simple physician stumbles across such an important discovery."

Tate sneaked his hand under Winslow's blanket, seeking her fingers while Tucker had his eyes on the news. She twined her fingers through Tate's, not looking away from the TV. Damn, but she was something else. Stronger than she knew, but so innocent. And brave. She needed a new beanie, but did she cringe when Isaiah or Tucker entered the room because they would see her lack of hair? Did she act like she was anything but pleased to meet them? Not once.

"You're too humble," Shawna gushed over the doctor. "This news isn't just important, it's unparalleled. You might even call it historic, right?"

He nodded, seeming to grow more nervous by the minute.

"Shit, just say it, Bly," Tucker groused from the door where he stood. "Get this over with."

"Well, go on, tell us," Shawna urged. "America's waiting."

The camera zoomed in for a close-up. "Ladies and gentlemen." Bly cleared his throat, adjusted his tie, and cleared his throat again. "It is, umm, it is my unique privilege to announce that, after much research, I believe I've discovered a cure for cancer."

"The more I see this guy, the more I think he really cares about people," Isaiah murmured. "Look at him. He's not bragging. I think he honestly wishes he was telling the truth."

"You would know," Tate pushed at him.

"He's a son-of-a-bitch is what he is, and he needs to act more animated," Tucker growled. "Get his act together, damn it. This has to work."

"Bly's afraid of Winslow's mother," Isaiah told Tate on their private link.

"I can believe that. She's a formidable woman," Tate answered back. The corners of his mouth twitched. It was satisfying to be able to talk behind the big dog's back for once. Adolescent maybe, but yeah. Satisfying.

The camera panned to Shawna, then quickly back to Bly. He licked his bottom lip. "Much more work still needs to be done as I am only one man, but I've been in touch with several world-renowned research laboratories and many pharmaceutical companies with my findings. They have assured me that my research is correct, and they've offered their considerable assets to help."

"To say the least," Shawna added. "Miraculous is more like it. If I understand correctly, you have already cured a young woman of terminal cancer with your treatment, haven't you?"

"He's talking about me, isn't he?" Winslow asked.

"Yes, but he won't name you," Tate said. *Or I'll kill him.*

"You won't have to. Tucker will," Isaiah added. *"By the way, I left a present for you in my gear bag. Use it."*

Tate lifted a brow, not sure what that meant, but sure he'd soon find out.

Bly's gaze hit the camera dead on. "Yes, that is true. I can't reveal her name, but she came to me in a terrible state. Someone had been pumping her full of the oddest mix of pain pills and other medications, some of them quite illegal. I'm sure that person was only trying to help, but at first it seemed that she..." He coughed, his fist lifted to his lips. "I mean, they, the drugs, were killing her."

"I think he tried to help me." Winslow looked to Tate. "I felt good at his clinic."

"This interview's a hoax," Tate explained. "He's reading lines." *Mostly.* "It's a scam to draw your mother back to his clinic or to another interview he's giving tomorrow at the real medical conference. Once she shows up, we'll arrest her."

Bly's gaze darted to the side as if he was watching for Hattie over his shoulder. "Y-yet when I analyzed this poor woman's blood, I saw a peculiar change to her cellular proteins. An astonishing change, which is why I contacted every lab I could to double check my findings. If those illegal drugs, combined like they were, truly cured cancer, I needed them to validate what I was seeing. I needed the world to know." He rolled his eyes. "Ladies and gentlemen, think of the people we can save now. The lives we can improve."

"Keep him talking, Blondie," Tucker muttered at Shawna, his arm bent over his head and his fingers drumming the doorjamb.

Shawna beamed. "If I'm right, you've also received quite a few, shall we say, *offers* from these same labs and pharmaceutical companies? You're on your way to being a millionaire, aren't you?"

He nodded. "Yes, everyone is excited about this breakthrough, but that isn't why I'm here. I just want to share my research. I want this terrible disease eradicated from the face of the planet."

Isaiah glanced over his shoulder at Tate. *"See? That wasn't on the script. What'd I tell you?"*

Tate shrugged. Isaiah saw things he didn't. To him, Bly was nothing more than Hattie's accomplice. Unwitting maybe, but up to his neck in what she'd done to her daughter for years.

"But you'll be rich, won't you?" Shawna pressed, keeping Bly on track and her head bobbing as if she needed to convince him to say yes. "I mean, you and you alone discovered this crazy concoction, didn't you? And you did all the research to prove it cured cancer, right?"

Another humble shrug. "There wasn't much research, but yes, that is true. I have been assured of great sums of money from many countries. It's the oddest mix of chemicals, though, most of them prescriptions drugs. One would never suspect they'd serve such a noble purpose when combined like they were. To be honest, I was concerned when I detected arsenic in my patient's blood work."

"Bingo," Tucker said. "Pour it on, Bly. Let her have it."

"Imagine my shock when that simple component served as a dynamic catalyst with the other drugs. One moment I thought my young patient was dying, but the next, she lifted her head and she smiled at me." He laid his hand over his heart, his eyes lifted to the ceiling. "Her green eyes seemed to come back to life right there in my clinic. It was the best moment of my life to know she was going to live."

"Where is she now?" Shawna asked. "This patient. Can you tell us her name?"

"No, no, but I will tell you she is staying at my clinic," Bly declared, "but I'll be forced to move her early tomorrow morning now that the news is out."

Winslow's hand went to her chest at the same time. "I thought I was dying," she whispered, "but he might be the guy who my mom was talking with about assisted suicide."

Tate tightened his grip on her fingers. No two ways about it. Bly would die for helping Hattie.

"Could you at least share those physical changes in your patient with us?" Shawna's brows arched encouragingly. "I'm sure the world would like to know."

"Tomorrow," Bly stated emphatically, his chin up.

"Here we go," Tucker hissed. "Chum the waters, doc. Reel her in."

"I'm happy to say…" The man couldn't look prouder. "I'll be speaking at the American Medical Association's annual conference at Johns Hopkins tomorrow morning. After that exposure, I hope to get the funding I need to continue my work and—"

"Oh, I have no doubt you'll get plenty of funding, Dr. Bly." Right on cue, the camera panned to Shawna. "I'll bet every doctor in America will be calling you, maybe a few talk shows too. You'll be a celebrity. Think of the fame. This is a huge discovery."

He smiled a tight little smile. "Yes, it is, isn't it?"

"Would you mind if I interview your patient at your clinic?"

Bly shrugged. "Only if you can do it tonight. Tomorrow, who knows where she'll be."

"Bingo," Tucker bit out, his cellphone out of his pocket and at his ear. "The trap is set, Eden. Climb in bed and sit tight."

"And you did this *all by yourself,* Dr. Bly." Shawna gushed. She sure knew how to spin this scam. "This discovery is nothing short of amazing. I'm so glad you came to me for this breaking news, Dr. Bly. Ladies and gentlemen, you heard it on Channel Thirteen first. Dr. Jorge Bly has discovered the cure for cancer. All. By. Himself!"

The interview had no more than ended when a call rang out over their earpieces. "What the hell?" Agent Chase growled at Tate and Winslow.

"What?" Winslow asked.

"Shots fired. Officers down at 212 Maple Drive," Tate explained since she had no earpiece. He and Isaiah were already on their feet. Agent Chase was half out the door.

"At my house," she whispered. "Mom?"

"It could be anything," Tate explained. "Don't panic until we know what's going on."

Tate's boss pointed at Agent Zaroyin. "You're with me. Tate, keep our girl safe." He and Isaiah flew out the door.

"What's she doing?" Winslow asked. *What now?*

Tate had his head cocked, listening to whatever was coming over his earpiece. "Two agents. One dead at the scene. The other..." He stilled, his index finger lifted for her to hold on. "There's an active shooter. Police are engaged."

Winslow waited. It couldn't be a coincidence, not with her mother out there and angry with her only child. Especially not right after the interview. But scary. Did she know Dr. Bly was going to betray her? But why shoot those poor FBI agents? Was Joyce Parrish out of her mind? *Stupid question.*

"Shit," Tate hissed. "Another man down."

"Who is it?"

He shook his head, his focus on the floor. Still listening. Still waiting. The minutes stretched. Breeze came in to take Winslow's vitals. Dr. Keegan stopped by, but he didn't stay once he saw Winslow had company.

Still Tate listened. At last he looked up from the floor. "They've got the shooter. Dead at the scene."

Winslow held her breath as she prepared for her world to crash around her. "Is it... was it... M-Mom?"

Tate shook his head, his brows angled together. "No. It was Ike."

Imagine that. Ike Pitt. Dead after ambushing two FBI agents at Hattie Beauregard's home in Silver Spring, Maryland, then killing a D.C. Metro police officer who'd arrived on the scene. Tate hadn't seen that one coming. Without thinking, his fingers sought the bandaged bullet wound on his bicep. Had Ike shot him? Tate might never know now.

Tears muted Winslow's green eyes, turning them to a soft sage color. "Hey," he soothed. "It wasn't your mom." *And damn it, I've got to tell her the truth, that Joyce is Hattie.*

"But she might have put Ike up to it," Winslow's lower lip quivered. "I know she did. H-he's c-creepy, b-but he's not mean."

"You never know what a guy will do for the woman he loves." *Wasn't that the truth?*

"You think Ike was in love with my mom?"

Tate read the disbelief on Winslow's face. Pulling the chair away from the bed, he doffed his shoes and climbed in beside her. There was a day he hadn't known how to hold a woman, but he didn't seem to have that problem with Winslow. He captured the nape of her neck in his left hand as he cupped her cheek with his other. "Shhhhh," he whispered, his lips on her forehead, needing her to know she was safe. "I'm here and there are two armed officers outside your room. Tucker and Isaiah will call soon. Then we'll know what happened."

Winslow turned into him, her soft breasts to his chest, and her breath at the hollow of his neck. Warming him in ways he hadn't realized he'd missed so sharply, nor needed so badly. Her fingertips captured his collarbone. "I'm scared, Tate."

"I know you are. Your mom's nothing to tangle with." An image of that silly stuffed bear flashed to mind.

"H-hold me," she commanded in her shivering innocence.

With those two words, she swept his resistance away. "Yes, ma'am," he agreed wholeheartedly, needing to make Winslow feel safe and protected. Easing one arm beneath her, he pulled her frail body firmly against his. This was just a man comforting a woman, he told himself. That wasn't a lie, not exactly. Winslow had no one. Neither did he. It was only natural they seek each other at a time like this.

His lips pressed another kiss to her forehead, then his mouth trailed easily down her nose to her cheek, tasting the softest hint of honey as he went. He needed her to know he'd never let her face her mother alone. His natural instinct to protect wandered to the sweet warmth of her neck, his tongue along with it. Just for comfort. Just because.

Winslow arched, stretching her neck to reveal tender skin that had never known a man's touch. The pebbled peaks of her nipples rubbed his chest that, even beneath his cotton shirt, had grown hyperaware of the feel of her. The tempting warmth.

His hand moved of its own accord, gentling her as his fingers slid down her arms to her ribs. To her hip. Thunder beat at his veins, pooling dangerously low, hardening his body in the ways of a lover.

There were standards he wouldn't cross in the line of duty, yet he couldn't think of any reason to hold back with her in his arms, not with her thighs pressed against his thighs, her belly to his belly, and her taste on his tongue. Ordnance. He was playing with the most volatile ordnance on the planet, and he couldn't stop.

"Kiss me," she whispered, her eyes closed and worry fading from her face.

Tate brushed his lips over hers, intending to break contact as soon as he satisfied this last request, but the warm rush of mint on his tongue melted his resolve. When her timid lips molded to his, a surge of sparks tiptoed up his spine.

He tasted her lips, urging her to open for him with the tip of his tongue, to take him into her mouth the way he wanted his cock inside her body. The moment she touched her tongue to his, he was addicted at some elemental level where soul mates lived and breathed and found each other in the vast universe. Where Winslow revolved like the fiery sun to the eternal orbit of his world. His life.

His nose filled with the seductive scent of her body blooming as it drifted up between them on waves of heat—for him. This was her gift, but he dared not take it. Not like this.

"Winslow," he meant to say, but groaned when she latched onto his jaw with questing fingers, working her mouth over his lips, sucking at his tongue, nipping his bottom lip, then the top, then kissing with the ferocity of a woman who'd been starved for love all of her life.

A part of him felt sadness at that fact, yet another thrummed with male pride. One of nature's purest virgins lay in his arms, untouched and unloved, wanting all that life and love had to offer her.

His fingertips drummed from Winslow's hipbone to her thigh. She was so thin. So very much a little girl. His lashes fluttered open, needing to see her for what she was, knowing he had to end this seduction before it became an open flame he couldn't put out. But the look on her face when he did. The rapture glowing there. The joy...

What man could resist her? Tate smoothed his wide palm to her ass, massaging her and wishing he could think of one reason he shouldn't want her. With a mind of its own, his cock pressed against her, seeking its way inside. All Tate had to do was smooth his hand between her sweatpants and her panties and...

She growled. Winslow—the woman who'd been lied to, cheated, and denied a full and happy life for most of her years—growled at him. Demandingly. She was finally coming out of her abuse-induced shell. There was a world of pleasure in hearing that feral feminine expression of determination.

Enough said. Tate tugged her pants down to her thighs, leaving her panties in place, wanting this to be about Winslow, not him. Needing to pleasure her until she knew some of what it was to be with a man who valued her above all else.

Apparently, that wasn't good enough. She wiggled out of her pants, on her knees now and about to...

Oh, yeah. She stretched one bare leg over his lap, growling again, throwing more gasoline on a fire that needed no help blistering his self-control.

Tate rolled to his back, his hands holding her ass in place, rocking her core over his zipper. Uncomfortable now, his cock ached for release from his clothes and weakening his hold on restraint. Yet her whimpers kept his fingers from letting go of her.

He was so wide and she was so narrow, a mere wisp of a woman straddling the workhorse he'd become over the years. Even holding her as gently as he was, she seemed like a child captured in the hands of a giant. He was too big, too thick for such a tender, delicate body. The tender flesh of her backside was softer than rose petals under his callused touch. Yet he kept massaging. Gentling.

Just one breath from her mouth on his skin, and he was as stiff as steel. Hot and hard, his defenses were breached and blown away.

"More," she urged softly, her voice breathy and needy. "Tate, I need more."

And he knew what he had to do.

Chapter Thirty-Two

One minute she was perched right where she wanted to be, the next Winslow was on her back, pressed flat to the mattress by the hulking body of the man she adored. Tate breathed in her face, his air warm and rich with aftershave, a hint of minty mouthwash and pine. His elbows were beside her head, his knees edged between her legs, his manhood hard and promising at her quivering belly. Not exactly where she wanted it to be, but close. *Oh, so close...*

She wiggled for a better angle.

"Winslow," he rasped, his voice a vibrating growl she felt all the way in her weeping core. This was what it felt like to want a man. To need him inside her body.

"Yes?" she asked as she lifted her palms to his cheeks, her thumbs caressing the five o'clock scruff on his chin. This man had the softest, most delicious lips. Edible, and she wanted to nibble at them for the rest of her life. They already glistened with her kisses, and Tate wasn't frowning now. Arching, she pushed her belly to his, loving the heat rolling off him. She stretched the tip of her tongue, reaching for his mouth.

He'd tapped an appetite she very much wanted to satisfy. She had the most incredible man in her hands and she wanted all of her firsts to be with him. He already owned her first kiss. Her first dance. Her first and only love.

"Winslow," he said once more, his tone softer. More in control.

No, no, no. Not yet. Not now. Later maybe, but not now when we're so close... "Kiss me again," she begged, wanting his clothes off so she could see and touch all of him. There had to be a way to command his desire, to make him want her as much as she wanted him.

Instead, he captured her wandering hands easily in one fist, and stretched her arms over her head, holding her still even as she writhed against him.

Winslow blinked wide-eyed at the wonder of two bodies producing so much heat. Hers seemed to have a will of its own, as if nature was in charge. Every touch of his, even his hand circling her wrists, incited another surge of what felt like sparks beneath her skin that only Tate could put out. Every atom in her soul demanded he come closer. As close as humanly possible.

"I want you, Tate," she murmured, licking her lips, letting her tongue catch his attention.

The blackest eyes trailed over her mouth. They hesitated for a fraction of a second before they scanned down her chin to her neck and from there to her aching breasts. Knowing he watched her like a big cat toying with its prey, heightened the tingling sensation in her nipples, already so hard they hurt as if they were going to burst. If only he'd—kiss them. They'd feel better then. She knew it. Just one lick of his tongue. One suckle and...

Blood roared a fiery path to her core, already dripping with need. He could eat her alive and she'd die happy. Just the thought of his mouth on her pushed her starving libido nearly to the stars.

"I need to tell you something and you need to listen," he whispered, his voice tight and hoarse as he planted a kiss on each of her eyelids, forcing her to close them, only to open them once more as fast as she could.

"What?" she asked, blinking up in wonder at the handsome beast poised for action above her. He wanted her, and she wanted him. What else was there?

"I love you, Winslow Parrish. I should've told you that before, and I'm sorry I didn't, but I'm saying it now. I know it's too soon, but I don't care. I loved you the second I saw you on that tower."

Wow. That was a lot of words all at one time, but not once had she heard no.

"I love you, Tate," she said, meaning it. Gosh, she loved saying his name and kissing him and holding him and... everything about him.

"There's a lot you don't yet know about life, and I'll be honest. I want to be the one who teaches you."

"Like?" she asked coyly, still working on besting his self-control, sure she could get her way if he'd only let go of her hands.

"Like protection and timing," he said quietly, hoarsely. "Like making babies out of love instead of out of lust, which is what's going on between us right now. We need to give ourselves to each other at the right time and in the right place. For the right reason."

Oh. That. She stilled, finally hearing him. Yes, she knew about the birds and the bees, about how it only took one time to get pregnant. Though she doubted she could get pregnant after all that her poor body had been through, Mother Nature was still in charge. It'd be a miracle, but it could happen. And here he was, protecting her from herself this time.

But if he had a condom in his pocket... Just one...

His thumbs stroked circles over the pulses at her wrists, still above her head, holding her where she couldn't touch or tempt him. "I've learned something today," he said earnestly, his gaze piercing her with its intensity, his brows pinched in their usual V, those three wrinkles shadowed, but not with anger.

He tracked her lips when, with another lick and a nibble, she asked, "What did you learn, Tate?"

"Just this," he said before he covered her mouth and French-kissed her until her toes curled. There was not one part of her mouth his tongue didn't caress, map, or taste. *This man!* Succumbing to his passion left her breathless. She moaned to touch him back. By the time he ended the kiss, she was caught in a floating-into-space kind of dizzy. Scrupulously, remarkably, and oh, so thoroughly kissed. *Wow.*

"I learned that it's never too early to fall in love, Winslow," he told her, his voice deep and husky. "And it's never too late. But you deserve more. I'm not going to take you here in this hospital room, where anyone can walk in on us."

Oh, yeah. About that... She'd gotten so enthralled with what she felt with Tate, that she'd lost track of, well, everything.

He bumped his magnificent forehead to hers. She nearly crossed her eyes looking up at him. "But the moment you're up for it, I'm going to kiss every square inch of your body. I'm going to lick you and eat you and leave raspberries all over your ass—and other places. I'm going to make love to you upside down and right side up, over and under and..." He delivered another scalding kiss, melting her until she hadn't the strength to squirm.

Easing back, he nipped her bottom lip, leaving a sting. "I'm never going to let you go, woman. So get healthy. I'm damned hungry."

He'd scattered her wits so thoroughly, Winslow simply breathed, "Umm, okay."

Tate tucked her under the covers, not ashamed for one heartbeat at what he'd nearly done with Winslow, but embarrassed, make that aghast, at his loss of control while on duty. Men got in trouble when their cocks did their thinking for them, and his couldn't seem to shut up.

"I'm going to step outside and check with the officers," he said as he placed a reverent kiss to her forehead. He needed space to cool off, and so did Winslow. "Be a good girl and get some rest while I'm gone."

She yawned, so damned adorable with those big green eyes, soft and alluring after their tumble beneath the covers. "I'm not a girl," she groused, teasing, exciting his body with just the sound of her voice.

That brought him back to her side. He dropped over the edge of the bed, one palm beside her sleepy head. "Oh, yes you are," he whispered, nose-to-nose with the girl he planned to build a life with. "I'm sure of it. Now go to sleep, so I can do my job instead of doing you."

That elicited a girly giggle, the perfect answer. "Well, okay," she breathed. "I am tired. Have you heard anything from your boss yet?"

"I'll let you know when I do." He pressed an index finger to her lips. "I promise to wake you, now shhhhh. Rest. You've had a big day."

"Almost had a hard day," she mumbled as she turned to her side, facing away from the door. The tease.

Winslow had no idea what she did to him. Tate wiped the grin off his face and left her to rest, snagging Isaiah's gear bag before he shut the door. He checked with the officers outside her door, but they hadn't heard any more on the shooting than he had. One of the nurses, Breeze, came by. She ducked into Winslow's room, took her vitals, and did whatever nurses did. Smiling at Tate when she left, Breeze continued down the hall.

She was a pretty enough woman. Shapely. Confident. She stopped for a second to chat with the cleaning woman with her cart and mop, then waved to some guy in green scrubs farther down the hall before she ducked into another patient's room. Breeze looked almost as gorgeous as Winslow.

Tate scanned the halls, searching for anything out of the ordinary. The cleaning woman looked busy at her work. Stout. Matronly. Her salt-and-pepper hair seemed out of place for a janitor, but what did he know? Sometimes older people had to work past their prime. Age discrimination laws and people's poor choices happened.

He scanned the other end of the hall. More of the same. The officers followed his every move, as he did theirs. One could never be too careful. Dropping to a vacant chair opposite the officers, he dug into Isaiah's bag to see what the guy had left for him.

Well, what do you know? The latest tactical vest out of McCormack Industries. Damn. Tate tugged it out of the bag. The vest was lightweight. Better yet, it had built-in pockets filled with... *Oh man, Isaiah thought of everything!* Excited now, Tate reached one arm over his shoulder and stripped out of his shirt right there in the hall. It raised a few eyebrows, but he donned the vest and quickly redressed before anyone but the surprised officers saw him.

"You never know," he told them. "You might need one of these. They're top of the line."

"You go ahead," the one on Tate's left replied. "We're not SWAT."

Tate would've argued, but that was a discussion better left for another day.

"Damn it!" The sharp clatter of a mop handle hitting the floor, drew his attention back to the poor cleaning woman. He caught sight of her backside disappearing into a patient's room, two doors down. A wisp of smoke curlicued out of the room to the ceiling, setting off the smoke alarm.

Lights flashed from overhead panels while the alarm blared. Tate righted his chair, the two officers on their feet by then, on their way to investigate. One took position between Tate and the smoking room, looking both ways while his partner entered the room, his hand on his pistol.

"Fire!" someone else screamed from the room three doors farther down. "To your stations!"

Whatever that meant. Nurses scurried down the halls like bees from a hive, speeding to the vacant wheelchairs and the row of walkers lined against the wall. Winslow's police protection was nowhere in sight.

The poor thing was out cold, her bare head tucked under her pillow, no doubt to keep warm. She hadn't changed back into her hospital gown to sleep though, just the clothes Keegan had bought her. *Probably a good thing if they needed to evacuate.*

Just then, Tucker bellowed in Tate's earpiece, his words choppy and incoherent through the blaring alarm. "Say again?" Tate ordered even as he bent to lift Winslow into his arms to take her to safety. More garble Tate couldn't make sense of.

"Mmm. What's wrong?" Winslow asked sleepily, her forehead wrinkled. "What's all the noise?"

"Fire drill," Tate assured her. "Don't worry. I've got you."

The lights went out, plunging the room into darkness until the dim, emergency lighting flickered on from the hall. By then, a shadow lurked at the door. "Put her down," Hattie Beauregard ordered.

Tate would've argued but for that Beretta pointed at him.

"Mom?" Despite what she now knew about her mother, seeing Joyce like this astonished Winslow to her soul. "What are you doing here?"

"Finishing what I started a long time ago," her mother bit out, jerking the gun in her hand at the bed. "I said put her down, Higgins. Back on the bed. Do it or I shoot her where you stand."

Tate had no choice. Winslow sank to the mattress, away from the warmth of his body.

"Why are you doing this?" She needed to know as she scrambled to her knees.

"Your gun, Higgins," Joyce bit out. "I know you've got one. Nice and easy."

He unholstered the pistol under his left arm and lifted it high, pinching its grip between his index finger and thumb. "Don't hurt her," he warned as he laid it flat on the mattress.

"Why can't you leave us alone?" Winslow cried.

Joyce cocked her head, her eyes still trained on Tate. "Oh, there's an *us* now. How pathetic. The bodyguard falls in love with the poor little girl, is that how this cliché ends, Agent Higgins? What were you two going to do, live happily ever after?"

He grunted, his legs pressed against the bed frame. "It's about time you told your daughter who you really are, Hattie."

Winslow jerked her eyes from Tate to her mother. "What does he mean?"

Raking her fingers through her longhaired disguise, Joyce tossed it aside as her gun spat a round, startling Winslow with the loud report.

"Bitch," hissed out of Tate as he slapped his right hand to his chest.

"Mom! Stop!" Winslow shrieked, holding onto his elbow to keep him upright.

"At least tell her before you kill us," he growled at her mother. "Be honest for once with your daughter."

Instead of answering, her mother's wrist flexed. Tate jerked Winslow into his arms, curving his body around her as another round boomed. Winslow felt the impact hit him in the back, nearly dropping him to his knees. She twisted to grab hold of him, to shift him onto the bed with her, but he took a knee.

"There's no way... you're leaving this hospital alive," he told her mom. "My men are on their way." Groaning, he leaned into the bed frame, bleeding from front and back.

"Stop it, Mom!" Winslow screamed, on the floor beside him now, clutching his belt to support him. "You're killing him!" Frantic now, she smoothed one palm over the chest wound, needing to block every drop of blood from leaving his body. But bright red blood soaked his back, too, and she only had two hands. *What do I do?*

"Shut up, Winslow! You had one thing to do, you little tramp, just be in your room where you should've been, but no." Joyce still aimed at Tate. "You ran away like the helpless little girl you always were and always will be. Well, I've had enough babysitting."

Winslow's eyes opened in shock. "W-what are you talking about?"

"She set you up," Tate growled, trembling so hard that the bed frame rattled. "She never intended for you to go to any prom, Winslow. She planned for Ike to kidnap you before the TV crew showed—"

The gun roared again, and Tate fell backward, his bloody fingers clutching for Winslow's arm as his head touched down.

"Mom!" Winslow screamed. "Stop, Mom! Please stop!"

His leg spasmed, blood gushing from the hole in his mid-thigh.

Winslow angled her body around his sweaty body, cocooning his head on her lap to protect him from the vicious woman she no longer recognized. "Don't die," she whimpered. "I love you. Please, hang on."

"Get on your feet. Now, Winslow," Hattie ordered, "or so help me—"

"Or what?" Winslow yelled, not bothering to turn around to face her. "You'll kill me, too? Like you've been doing all these years? Just do it already!" She squeezed her eyes shut and bowed her head to Tate's, prepared to die with him if that's what today came down to.

But the door opened behind her and, sure that Isaiah and Tucker were coming to Tate's rescue, her gaze jerked to it. But no. It was Dr. Bly's nurse who'd closed the door, her eyes darting all over the room. "You'd better make this quick, Sis. You're running out of time."

"S-sisters?" Winslow couldn't believe what she was hearing. "You're sisters?" No wonder she'd taken Tate's cell phone at Bly's clinic. She knew all along!

"Told you she was dumber than shit," Hattie growled out of the side of her mouth. "Now get up off your ass, Winslow. You and I have a road trip to take, and I'm not missing it."

"To Oregon? So you can kill me?" That made no sense. "Just leave me here." *So I can die with Tate.*

"No, you little witch, to Texas, so I can finally get what's coming to me!" Hattie shrieked.

Texas? "Bullshit! Who *are* you?"

That earned Winslow a murderous glare. "I'm the woman who's tired of living a lie for you! Now do what you're told!"

Winslow no longer cared what this maniac wanted. Tate hadn't made a sound since he'd passed out, but his blood was everywhere. On the linoleum beneath him. On her hands. It was sweeter smelling than she expected blood to be, but her hands and fingers were thick with it. "You killed him," she cried, her tears trickling over his cheek.

"Come on, baby," Dr. Bly's nurse said as she tugged Winslow's elbow. "We don't have a lot of time. Those four fires I set won't last much longer."

"Who are you?" Winslow jerked away from this liar.

The gray-haired woman nodded at Joyce. "I'm Sue Ellen, Hattie's older sister. Now scoot before the firemen get here."

Again with the clutching fingers! Winslow scraped this crazy woman's hand off her bicep, her eyes riveted to the other liar she'd once called Mom. "I'm not going anywhere with you."

To her sister, Hattie bit out, "You got the bin ready?"

Sue Ellen nodded. "It's in the hall. Don't worry, there's plenty of smoke if we get moving now."

"Get up," Hattie ordered Winslow. "There's one more thing I need you to do."

"Bullshit," Winslow shot back at her. "I'm staying here, so do your worst."

Hattie's arm stretched, the pistol now aimed directly at Winslow's face. "Don't think I won't, you damned crybaby."

"All these years. I trusted you. I loved you," Winslow told her.

"You don't know the meaning of the word!" flew out of Hattie's mouth like a dagger. "I've wasted my whole life waiting for this moment, well, now it's mine. On your feet, *baby girl,*" she sneered. "If I'd known what a sniveling coward you'd grow into, I'd have left you where I found you!"

"You... you found me?" Winslow asked, her voice as hollow as this conversation sounded. "I'm not your daughter? Then whose am I?"

Bly's nurse whined. "Jesus Christ, we've got to go now."

The gun in Hattie's hand clicked. "Get off the floor, Winslow, or I blow your boyfriend's head off. You wouldn't want that, would you?"

"No, don't." Winslow whimpered as she eased her body out from under Tate. Resting his head gently to the floor, she lifted to her feet. She couldn't take the chance on Hattie shooting him again. He might yet be alive. "I'll go with you if you promise you won't hurt him."

"Then do it!" Hattie hissed, jerking her head at the door. "There's a laundry bin in the hall. Climb in and shut your mouth."

Winslow took one last look at Tate. His lips moved. Risking all, she sank to her knees at his side, her ear to his lips, daring to hope. "I'm here, Tate. What?" she asked, tearfully.

One word whispered out of him. "T-take."

Not understanding, she clutched his bloody hand to her breast, her heart breaking. "Take what?"

He squeezed her fingers, pushing something into her palm as he breathed out, "My... heart."

"Enough of this!" Hattie bitched, the butt of her weapon lifted over Winslow's head.

Being pistol-whipped hurt.

Chapter Thirty-Three

Tate dragged himself to his feet, sucking in a long, pain-filled breath that didn't come close to filling his lungs, not with that bullet snagged in his vest. Kevlar might keep him alive, but damn. It took a toll on what had to be a broken rib. The fake blood bags were a nice, deceitful touch. Still hurt like a mother though.

His thigh was another matter, but he didn't have time to waste on it. Hattie was gone, Winslow with her. Planting his palms to the bedrail, he shook his head to clear the buzz. Another one of those details, and the only one he'd insisted on, was still in play. Isaiah could track Winslow psychically, while FBI Central tracked the self-sticking GPS chip Tate had stealthily smoothed between her shoulder blades.

Winslow wouldn't get far.

Recovering his pistol, he holstered it and headed into the hall. Stumbling, he cleared the door, still dizzy. Smoke filled the halls, stinging his eyes and nose. Orange security lights flashed overhead while yellow emergency lighting lent the scene a surreal horror-movie quality. No doctors or nurses in sight. That much was good. They'd gotten out. They were safe.

The two police officers were missing, not a good sign. Which way to go?

This attack had been well-planned coming on the heels of Bly's first interview like it did. Tate didn't know how Hattie knew where her daughter was, only that she now had Winslow. He tapped his earpiece. An update from Tucker would be damned good. Even a psychic one.

"On our way back to you," Isaiah answered as if he'd read Tate's mind. *Duh.*

"She's got Winslow!" Tate was pissed, disoriented, but thankful for his psychic ability. *"Check parking. Ground level. Don't let her get away."*

"Are you injured?"

"I'm good."

"Liar," Eden hissed. *"He's been shot three times, Boss, chest, back, and thigh, and if you don't stop that bleed in your thigh right now, Agent Higgins, you're going to die. Paramedics will be on your floor in ten."*

Yeah, yeah, yeah. The problem with not blocking psychics? *Everyone's got an opinion.*

Turning left toward the direction of the freight elevator, he palmed the wall, fighting the demanding tilt of vertigo combined with blood loss. Eden was right. The round in his thigh might end his plan to rescue Winslow before he got to it.

Stopping just long enough to pull his holster off, he yanked his shirt over his head, then tore it in half. Using one piece to tourniquet his thigh, he cinched it extra tight, knotting it while he walked, his holster swinging against his calf. The Kevlar vest remained in place. The holster went back on. He bunched the rest of the shirt over his mouth to keep from breathing the fumes.

He hoped Hattie was headed for the ground-level parking garage like he'd thought, but his ears stayed tuned for the thwack-thwack-thwack of rotor slap just in case she had more help.

Hulking shadows loomed through the smoke. Firemen? "Boss!" Tate called out. "Here!"

Tucker emerged from the hazy gloom like the prow of a pissed off Navy destroyer, tall, wide, and bristling with armament. He had two pistols drawn and the butt stock of a rifle looming over his shoulder. Another pistol was strapped to his thigh. Penetrating dark eyes took immediate assessment of Tate's ragged condition, but not once did Tucker hint at leaving him behind. "Which way'd she go?"

"To the parking garage. She's got Winslow," Tate repeated. "I'm going down. Now."

Worry lined Isaiah's forehead. "You look like shit, man."

"I feel like it," Tucker pushed back at him. *"But that won't stop me."*

Back in the elevator they went. Tucker leading the charge, Tate limping along and Isaiah on his six.

"What'd she say?" Tucker asked as he hit the button to ground level. "Hattie."

"Bang. Bang. You're dead," Tate grunted. *Isn't that obvious?* "You don't think she's got a helicopter on stand-by, do you?" He didn't think she had that kind of resources, but this op had been one surprise after another.

"Wouldn't matter if she did. The chopper pad's over at the main complex," Tucker informed. "I've got men watching it."

"So she wasn't aiming at Winslow when she fired?" Isaiah couldn't seem to let it go.

Tate deflected. "She's taking her to Texas." *Over my dead body, which might not be the best comeback at the moment.*

"Did she know who her mother was before this?" Isaiah again. Damn, the man was a worrier.

"She does now."

"What's so great about Texas?" Tucker bit out.

Tate couldn't stand there and wait one more second for the slow-as-shit elevator to engage. "Jesus H. Christ! Do I look like fucking CNN?" With that, he one-eightied out of the metal compartment that wasn't taking him anywhere, and he left Tucker and Isaiah behind. He charged the stairwell door, not wasting time Winslow didn't have. Wounded didn't mean shit, but losing her did.

Slamming the door open, he vaulted the stairwell banister and dropped to a slammed crouch on the landing one level down. He took the next flight the same hard way—without steps or caution. Without one lick of common sense, either. His thigh seized up at the third iteration, but he'd expected it would as bad as he'd been hit. Traumatized muscles did that when you played Superman. One more time, he free fell to ground level, jacked out of breath and limping like a zombie, but—*God, please*—not out of time.

Palming the final door open and sweating up a storm, he took a deep breath of cold, concrete air and assessed the way forward. The garage was well lit. Painted gray. Concrete columns stood guard every fifty feet or so. Overhead lighting. Not many shadows. Physician parking along the nearest wall to his right. Red exit signs to his left. No sign of movement. No Hattie.

Despite his injury, the hunter in Tate roared to life. Mama Bear was out there laying for him and killing for sport. A man-eater was by far the most dangerous predator on the planet. Who cared? He'd hunted bigger and badder bears than Hattie before.

Gritting his teeth against the throbbing pain sending shockwaves up his thigh, he scanned the parked audience of cars, blinking to see past the rising blur in his head. The garage walls seemed to heave in and out, expanding then collapsing like a living, breathing thing. Yeah. Blood loss would soon drop him where he stood. Things had to happen fast.

A mini-truck roared past him, but the thin-as-rails African American male in the driver's seat wasn't Hattie. Three stalls from the end of the opposing row, a red Mini Cooper's rear taillights beckoned that a reverse was in process. Not the kind of car he was looking for, but okay. Hattie drove a Chevy Spark. Maybe she'd swapped it for something just as economical.

When the vehicle's driver maneuvered a K-turn and headed for him, he recognized its driver, the cleaning woman. Coincidence? No way.

Tate blocked the only exit and ceased worrying about a chopper swooping in and saving Hattie's dumb ass. Stepping out in the open, he declared war, the barrel of his pistol pointed up—for now—to show he meant business, that she needed to stop. The gray-haired woman floored it instead, that sissy car lurching forward like it had a dog in this fight.

Tate put one through her left front tire to slow her, then another through the right tire instead of her eye. *Don't make me kill you.*

The car ground to a stop then, but didn't that beat all? She pointed a gun at him over the steering wheel. Mexican standoff, nothing. This was suicide by sniper. The old bag just didn't know it.

Tate called her bluff and put one through the windshield, aiming next to her head, crackling the safety glass to oblivion. No one needed to die today. Least of all an old woman in a toy car.

That shot should've scared her, but she got one off through the glass anyway, the round whizzing by his ear like a supersonic hornet. Enough was enough. He charged the car, bellowing profanities, his gun on target but not wanting to end her.

Just like a crazed bear would do when its prey unexpectedly fought back, the woman hesitated long enough for Tate to elbow her window. The glass shattered to cubed crystals, and he dragged her out that same window by her scruffy gray hair. Damn her. She wanted to play rough, he could do that.

For an old woman, she didn't come easily, but pitched to her hands and knees on the concrete, scratching and kicking, shrieking, "Rape! Rape!"

No way in hell. By then, his thigh was on fire, and he knew he'd been duped. She was alone in the car and the walls were closing in fast. *Son-of-a-bitch.*

"Isaiah!" he bellowed mentally. *"You got her?"*

"Yes, I'm tracking her," Isaiah said smoothly as he and Tucker came up behind Tate. "Winslow I can read just fine."

Tucker pointed a key fob at his Challenger. "Isaiah, lock this situation down. Tate, you're with me."

Bullshit! This is not happening to me! Not again!

Winslow came to in the dark beneath mounds of smelly sheets and damp towels. Shoving her way through the disgusting hospital laundry, she lifted to her feet, swaying as the van she found herself in made a sharp left turn. With one hand to the ceiling overhead, the other gripping the edge of the bin, she lifted a leg over, then fell on her butt to the floor when everything shifted sideways again.

She had to get out of this van. Now. Before Hattie stepped on the gas and got any farther away from Tate. He needed her. On her feet once more, Winslow sniffed gasoline fumes, not what she'd expected. The source? That ten-gallon, black-capped can by the back doors.

Jesus, Mom, umm, Hattie. What are you doing?

That was the question of the year, wasn't it? Winslow knew then this was a fight to the death, and she wasn't the one going to die today. Just then the van lurched to a stop, and she fell backward, her bare feet in the air. Every loose thing in the back of the van shifted too. The bin rolled alongside her, but the gas can ended up at her ankles before she trapped it there between her bare feet.

When the driver's door opened and slammed, Winslow scrambled to her feet. It was too late to jump back in that bin and hide, and she didn't want to anyway. Those days were done. She was stronger now. Tate's last word made sense now. *Take.* He'd given her something in that last caress. His knife. That was what he'd meant. Well, she'd taken enough.

Tugging the folded knife out of her jeans pocket, she prepared to fight back with all she had. She lifted her fingers to her nose, her eyes instantly filled with tears. Her hands were sticky with Tate's blood, but why was it still so red? It smelled sweet like—syrup. This wasn't real blood. It was fake. *He's still alive!*

One of the rear doors jerked open, and there she was. Mom, Joyce, Hattie—*Whoever.*

"You killed him!" Winslow shrieked despite what she was pretty sure she now knew. The bulletproof vest would've protected his back and chest. But that bullet hole in his thigh...

"I did not," Hattie shot back at her. "I simply winged him."

"Three times! You shot him three times!" Lowering her head, Winslow spread her bare feet. Tate's open knife rested in the palm of her right hand, but hidden behind her thigh.

"Well, if I did, he wasn't much of a bodyguard, was he? Don't worry. He's a big guy. He'll pull through. You'll see." Hattie sounded so sure of herself. Had she done this before? Shot people and walked away?

Winslow steeled her nerve. Those new tennis shoes Dr. Keegan bought would've come in handy, but they were back in her room. It didn't matter. She had what she needed to win this battle. A nearly toxic-free body. Memories of years of abuse to fuel her rage. Anger for a life wasted when it could've been lived. The knowledge that Tate was alive, and, oh yeah, his favorite word.

"Bullshit," she hissed at the psycho with the hypo. "Real funny, *Mommy*. Another hypo for old time's sake? What'd you do, buy them in bulk?"

Hattie grabbed hold of the rear door grip and put one foot to the rear bumper, prepared to pull herself in. Laughable. That's what she was. A joke in her Halloween flip-flops with the dangling skeletons and orange pumpkins. Jack-O-Lantern fake nails. Enough studs in her ears to give snow tires a run for their money. You'd think she'd planned on shopping instead of killing her daughter.

Argh! That word. All this time, Winslow hadn't been a daughter. She'd been nothing. For years! How stupid was she? How blind! Soul sucking grief reached up from her gut for the lies she'd been fed, the evil medicine she'd swallowed like a good girl. For everything she'd missed and longed for and could never, ever get back again. For Tate!

"I hate you!" Winslow spat at her worst nightmare. She'd been prepared to die, had even embraced the possibility of it until Tate came along. If this was the day, she meant to take Hattie with her.

"I'm not going to kill you, baby girl," Hattie soothed, one palm forward as she hefted her ass into the van. "Settle down. Let me explain."

Winslow kept her right hand behind her back. "So talk."

"You were the cutest baby," Hattie said, both flip-flops flat to the floor by then. "Honest, you were every mother's dream. Chubby cheeks and chocolate spirals all over your noggin."

"You're not my mother!" Winslow demanded. "Just tell me who you really are." *And who I am.*

"I've had a couple names, Winslow, and yes, I've lied a little over the years, but only to keep you safe. Trust me, I—"

"Stop with the trust-me bullshit, *Mom*," Bitterness twisted that final word. "Tell me the truth for once in your life." *For once in mine.*

"Now, Winslow—"

"Tell me! Who are my parents? Where are they, and how'd you get me?" The thought that her real mom might be out there, sick and sad and searching for her lost little girl, nearly bowled Winslow over. *And a father. I might have a real father. A dad.*

Suddenly there wasn't enough air in the van. The muscles in her throat constricted. She might have truly been loved—before Hattie came along. How did anyone recover from loss like that?

Hattie shrugged her shoulders. "Trust me, I saved you from them, Winslow. Your real parents were a couple potheads from Amarillo, and you were their twelfth kid." She stuck her neck forward as if Winslow hadn't heard. "Can you imagine that? Twelve kids in one run down house, and all of 'em barefoot and playing in the dirty street. Screaming like a bunch of cotton-picking trailer trash was what they were. They had no grass, Winslow, not one blade in their dried-up yard, and some of them snot-nosed kids were sick. Why, it was mercy that brought me into your life and—"

"Mercy nothing." Winslow drew in a deep breath. "It's sick and degrading to steal another woman's child. What are their names? Tell me. Do you even know who you stole me from?"

An odd smile quirked Hattie's lips. She lowered the hand with the hypo in it. "Sure. I'll tell you. Once we're back in Amarillo."

"No. Now. I'm not going to Texas with you, so tell me, then get out of my way."

"That's not how it works." Hattie's head canted to her right, her thumb on the plunger at her side. "We've got five days of hard driving ahead of us, and I can't be late. So we can do this the easy way or you can fight, but it don't matter. Either way, I'm going to win, and we're going to Amarillo."

"Why?" Winslow bit out, tears threatening. "Why should I go anywhere with you?" The thought of meeting loving parents tempted. Twelve kids? That meant she had brothers and sisters. She'd always wanted a sibling. Maybe cousins. Yes, Hattie might be lying, but—what if she wasn't?

She almost looked sincere when she said, "Because your father owns one of the biggest ranches in the state, and he finally got off his fat ass and offered a reward to the person who brings you home. You're going to help me get it."

Chapter Thirty-Four

The problem with tracking a vehicle on the road that left ahead of you was the gap. No matter how fast Tucker made that Challenger go, he couldn't seem to close the distance between him and Hattie.

After a quick stop at the Emergency Room, which Tate finally admitted he might need, they lost more time when Tucker stopped once more for clean clothes, snacks, and water. "These are for you," he'd barked. "Now sit back and shut up."

Finally on the road, Tate snagged a bottle of water and reclined the passenger seat as far back as it'd go. Tucker had a point. Hydration was key to snapping out of the ozone layer a visit to the ER always left him in. His thigh was still numb from the anesthetic when Tucker hooked onto I-66 out of the District of Columbia and drove until it junctioned with I-81, headed west. Through Roanoke and onto Sugar

Grove, Tate slept. When he woke, he felt better and they were speeding past Knoxville, Tennessee.

In Nashville, they grabbed the I-40, still on Hattie's trail and still behind. Not even with Isaiah and Eden advising where Hattie pulled in for fuel or food could Tucker catch up. Alerting the authorities from truck stop to truck stop made no difference. Hattie had gone into stealth mode.

Throughout the chase, Tucker popped more energy drinks than anyone Tate had had the misfortune to work with before. Not that the caffeine made him chatty, but the man cursed traffic and drivers alike. F-this. F-that. Tucker was an arrogant brute at the wheel. Wild as a bull that had been cattle prodded one too many times and wouldn't be tamed. Driven to catch up if not get ahead.

It was the cramped space that drove Tate to rely on those two steady voices in his head. Isaiah and Eden. They kept him sane and informed. Even hopeful. Eden had a steady bead on Winslow's emotions. Isaiah focused on her impressions of Hattie, but couldn't put a pin in their final destination. Texas was a big state.

Tate cast a sideways glance at Tucker. Talking psychically wasn't difficult, not once a guy accepted that he was fairly decent at it, that he could control the flow and slam the door when he needed a time out. But Tucker was no dummy. There'd be hell to pay once he realized his team was talking behind his back.

Eden popped up with a psychic *"Holy Shit!"* all the way from D.C. *"I know where Hattie's going,"* she hissed into Tate's mind.

"Where?" he sent back to her.

"Tate!" Eden squealed again. Her mental squeal was every bit as loud as her verbal ones. Tate was certain his mental eardrums hurt. *"Amarillo, Texas. Hattie's taking Winslow to Amarillo. I'm sure of it."*

"Why?"

"You won't believe this!"

"We will if you ever get around to telling us." Isaiah's calm drawl balanced Eden's adrenaline rush.

The crinkle of papers shuffling whispered in the background just as if they were on a conference call until Eden said, *"Winslow isn't Hattie's biological daughter."*

Tate lurched forward, his back straight, his shoulders squared, and his palm on the dash. *"Say what?"*

"You need a break?" Tucker eyed him, his left hand on the wheel, his right on the stick shift, ready to pass the semi in the fast lane at the slightest provocation. His normal MO.

Tate slumped into the comfy leather seat, his blood pumping. "No, I'm good. I'm good." *And pissed.* He knew Hattie had a string of aliases, but this was despicable. *Winslow isn't her kid? Then what's that witch doing with her?*

Eden again. *"I'm still sorting through the last of what we pulled out of Winslow's house, boxes of newspaper clippings. I wish you could see this."*

"Yeah, well, I can't, so..." Jesus-Freaking-Christ! Tate stiffened and his pulse pounded up into his throat. There in front of him, so close it seemed he could reach out and touch it, a fragment of newspaper print materialized in the space between him and the dash, it's edges torn and blurry. He tilted forward, looking at an obituary for a Mr. Felix Lockette. The words were clear, but there was no indication which newspaper it came from. The accompanying photo depicted an older male, not bad looking, smiling into the camera.

"Who's this guy?" he asked, still avoiding alerting Tucker.

"Excuse me? Can you see it?" Isaiah asked, his psychic voice pitched high with disbelief. *"You're looking at the clipping, aren't you? You can see it."*

"Affirmative," Tate replied, his tone not as strong as he liked. He cocked his neck, cracking it. Was it normal for psychics to see things floating in the air like this? Not like psychics were normal, but—

"Ha!" Great. Now Isaiah was as pumped as Eden. *"I knew it! Your talents are growing. What'd I tell you, Joker? Joker?"*

"Shut the fuck up." Tate didn't care what Isaiah thought he knew. This new development was just plain weird and a little spooky, but there the article was, and, well, okay. Might as well read it. He

squinted to read the small print without drawing Tucker's attention. *"What am I looking at?"* *That I can't believe I'm seeing.*

"Skip the first five paragraphs and look at the survived-by part down at the bottom," Eden insisted, as emphatic as ever. *"Do you see it?"*

With an exaggerated stretch and a yawn to throw Tucker off, Tate rolled his shoulder and narrowed in on the lower half of the obit. Preceded in death by wife and parents, blah-blah. Survived by son, Booker, and wife, Emma. Two grandsons, Rhett and Gunn. One granddaughter, our—*Oh. My. God.* Our angel Brooklyn, the baby girl stolen from us all those years ago.

Tate's heart stopped. Just plain stopped. He jerked his gaze back to Tucker even as he told Eden, *"Winslow's Brooklyn."*

Another mind-piercing squeal hit his psychic nerve endings. *"Yessssss! You feel it too, don't you? You know!"*

"Shit, I..." Really hate to say this, but... *"I do. This guy was Winslow's paternal grandfather."* And she missed knowing him. Being kissed by him. Held. Loved. The cancer scam was bad enough, but this sin was unforgiveable. *I knew she had a good reason.*

"That's why she went willingly, guys. Hattie's taking Winslow back to her family. There must be a reward."

Another *"Yessssss!"* rocked Tate's psychic ears, and Eden needed to tone it down. Her enthusiasm was deafening.

"Holy shit," Tate hissed at his reflection in the window.

"What'd you say?" Tucker cranked his neck, his Oakley's high on his head, and his gaze stone-cold sniper sharp.

Tate could only stare back at his boss, dumbfounded. *Did I say that out loud?*

Eden kept going. *"As soon as I touched this obit, Tate, I saw a younger man. Sage green eyes. Handsome, you know, like Liam Hemsworth handsome, only with black hair. Maybe in his late twenties or early thirties. He was sitting near a Christmas tree with a pretty woman and two little boys."* A younger version of the guy in the picture. *"She had tons of long black curls over her shoulders and down her back, and she was holding a little baby wrapped in a pink receiving blanket. Those people were her parents, and that baby girl is..."*

Tate's mouth went dry. "Winslow." Out loud again. He couldn't seem to control his big mouth, but damn. Tucker needed to know.

"Yes, it's Winslow. This is Winslow's grandfather's obituary from three years ago."

"What's wrong, Tate? You need a break?" Tucker asked. "You look like you're coming down with something. You carsick?"

Wasn't that the truth? Heartsick. Love sick. Just damned sick at the pain Hattie had caused Winslow and her parents, her grandparents. She'd ruined their lives. This was a real-life story straight out of one of Grimm's grimmest fairytales.

Tucker's forehead crinkled in that fatherly way that annoyed Tate. He didn't want to like this guy. Had fought it since Tucker assisted with Eden's rescue out of Canada, but now...

But now...

Tate swallowed hard, his throat muscles rebelling at the effort, his mouth as dry as the autumn prairie outside his window. *I've got to tell him.*

Eden rattled on, her passion out of this world. *"I checked with our field office in Dallas, and it all lines up. The Lockette case is an unsolved kidnapping that got worldwide attention nearly twenty years ago. I don't remember it, because I was just a kid, but the profile fits Winslow, Tate. Brooklyn was five-months-old when her nanny stole her out of her bassinette and disappeared without a trace."*

"And get this," Isaiah chimed in. *"The Lockettes own a huge ranch outside Amarillo—"*

"Isn't this great? Winslow's got a dad!" Eden again, damn her. Tate jumped as if she'd screeched in his ear.

"Who is Booker Lockette, Inc., and—" Isaiah was much easier on a guy's nerves.

"Just this week, he renewed his offer of a three-million-dollar reward to the person who brings Brooklyn home!"

"It'd sure be nice if I could finish my own sentences," Isaiah groused at his partner who was still pinging so hard that her joy vibrated all the way from D.C.

Tate glanced sideways at his boss. *It's time for true confessions.*

"What confessions?" Tucker put his foot in it, and the Challenger growled its compliance, its tachometer pinging as much as Eden was. For some reason, Tate caught an image of an enraged bull let loose from its chute, only—

"Boss," Tate said, swallowing hard, facing the bull in question. "I know where in Texas we need to go. Hattie's taking Winslow to Amarillo."

"You know?" Tucker muttered, the cords in his neck tight. That vein in his forehead too. "How do you know? Jesus Christ, you are psychic, aren't you? Either that or you're talking with Isaiah."

"Eden," Tate qualified, but then nodded, "and yeah, okay. Isaiah too. But mostly Eden." *Because she keeps screaming in my head.*

"I am not. I'm just... squealing. It's different."

"How long have you been talking to them?" Tucker asked as one brow spiked, "and why aren't they talking to me?"

Tate shrugged, not admitting to more, not with Eden giggling like a little girl somewhere in D.C.

Damned if Isaiah didn't come through like a good boy scout though. *"He's a natural blocker, boss. Want to learn a new skill?"*

Damned if Tucker didn't tip that big chin of his to the ceiling and roar. "You son-of-a-bitch, you're just like the rest of us. I knew it! Hell yeah, I want to learn. Teach me, Tate."

Didn't that make a guy want to get his head examined.

"See?" Isaiah murmured inside Tate's head. Privately. *"That wasn't so bad."*

Every mile farther away from Tate stretched at Winslow's heart like a rubber band pulled too far, too hard. Frayed and ready to break, she stayed to her side of their latest stolen car, her heart broken at her deceit. After all he'd done to help her, even risked his life, she'd betrayed him. Tate had taken three bullets for her, yet off she'd gone into the sunset with her lying—*driver.* Not her mother. Not even a friend. Winslow didn't trust a thing that came out of Hattie's mouth, but oddly...

She was beginning to understand the crazy woman at the wheel, enough that she'd felt safe enough and she'd hidden Tate's knife under the seat. Winslow hadn't seen any sign of the hypo since they'd left Virginia, either. There was no need to defend herself from Hattie. The more states they sped through, the more she came to realize that the family of twelve snot-nosed kids was Hattie's. Not Winslow's. Which meant her parents probably weren't potheads either. She still hadn't gotten their names out of Hattie yet.

Hattie wasn't entirely mean. She wasn't completely insane, either. But she was emotionally starved for affection, maybe even warped by the complete lack of it in her childhood. And she was calculating.

"Your mother beat you?" Winslow asked, not certain she'd heard right.

Hattie nodded, her eyes on the road. "Oh, yeah, sure. You had it easy, trust me. Me and my sisters got beat on a regular basis. Mostly we deserved it, but mostly we didn't. I hated that self-righteous bitch. So'd the rest of us girls. 'Specially little Bet."

Generations of hard-taught and well-learned physical abuse defined Hattie and, by the sounds of it, her mother before her, like the wind and freezing rain defined the Grand Canyon. Like erosion ate into sand and stone until the design overcame the raw material, and all that was left was—scars.

For the moment, Hattie seemed content to share. She'd been born in the swamps of Alabama to the most bizarre family Winslow had ever heard of, one where the boys ate at the dinner table while the girls waited on them and ate their scraps when they were done. Talk about ignorant backwoods parents. Dysfunctional didn't begin to describe the woman who'd physically whipped, beaten, and even caged her daughters while her sons ran free and reckless. Stole cars. Ran drugs and moonshine. And worse.

Or else Hattie was lying.

"Ma liked her boys, didn't have much use for us girls though."

"Why'd she have so many kids then?"

"'Cuz she was a God-fearing woman, that's why." The farther from D.C. she drove, the more Hattie's words took on a southern inflection, not so much a drawl as a twang.

"Sounds more like the witch in Hansel and Gretel to me."

Hattie shot Winslow a sideways glare. "Might be right."

"So why'd you steal me?" *An innocent baby? Then tell me I had cancer and try to kill me?*

"'Cuz I wanted you, and I knew I couldn't have a baby as cute as you 'cuz…" Hattie raked a hand over her head, upsetting the spikes she'd moussed to perfection earlier that morning at the motel. "'Cuz I couldn't have children any more."

"Why not?"

Her jaw clenched as if that subject was closed, but then she said, "'Cuz of the abortions."

Winslow's breath caught. "A-abortions? You had abortions?" *As in more than one of those awful things?*

Hattie's face twisted into a devilish smile. "Like I said, Ma liked her boys best."

Winslow blinked at that sideways answer? Was Hattie implying incest? Did her mother encourage incest? How much worse could this story get? "H-how many?"

Hattie grunted, one hand batting the air beside her head. "It doesn't matter. One's all it takes when it's done wrong. The first chance I got, I ran away from home, and I never looked back. I wasn't having another one of them. I found a good job in Texas working as a nanny. The day I saw you laying there in your bassinette, all pink and pretty, I decided I could finally have what I wanted for once in my life."

She shrugged as if she'd merely shoplifted something she'd coveted, like a pair of sunglasses or candy instead of a living child. "So I sneaked out of there with you. Then I called Sue Ellen. Wish I could've called Bet too. That was a mistake."

There was longing in that voice. Somewhere deep inside, Hattie had wanted a family enough to steal a baby. Twisted longing, yes, but it was hard to hate someone who'd survived a nightmarish childhood, then sought comfort from an infant.

Winslow shifted the subject. "Did you live in town or on a farm?" *Were you one of those cotton-picking trailer trash kids you said I was?*

"On the river. No grass, just mud and dirt most of the year until the saw grass took over when the weather got hot. Alligators. Snakes. Possums and coons. It wasn't all bad. Every once in a while, one of the boys would find a dog or a cat." It was interesting how Hattie never called her brothers by name. Just boys. "They'd tie it out by the gator slide, you know, the muddy riverbank where the gators slip into the water without making a sound when they're hunting."

Winslow ran her fingers over her brow, shocked at how forthcoming Hattie was, but worried where this *wasn't-all-bad-story* was headed.

"Then they'd start tormenting whatever they'd caught. They'd take potshots at it, or set its tail on fire. Us girls would hang around and watch the fun. Old Henry was the biggest gator on our stretch of the Mobile River. He was usually first to show 'cuz he was the granddaddy of all the rest."

Oh, my God. "W-why?"

"'Cuz he liked white meat, what'd you think?"

Winslow shut her eyes, bile climbing up the back of her throat. White meat, as in cats and dogs, as in someone else's sweet little Honey Munchkin. She was afraid to ask. "T-tell me about Bet, M-m..." She snapped her mouth shut. She'd almost called Hattie, Mom. That had to stop. "Was she older or younger than you?"

"Younger. Prettier." A sigh escaped Hattie. "Smarter, but not fast enough."

"Why didn't she move in with you or Sue Ellen then?" *Why didn't you ever tell me any of this?*

Hattie turned to the side window. "'Cuz she got out of her cage one day, and Ma accidentally beat her too hard when she caught her. Now shut up. Once we get through Oklahoma, we'll almost be there."

"She k-killed her?" Just when Winslow thought the Beauregard story couldn't get any worse—it did.

Hattie grunted. "I don't wanna talk 'bout it no more."

Winslow faced the side window again. It made sense in a creepy way what Hattie had done to her. Hattie was her mother's daughter, just doing what had been done to her. That was all she knew. Lesson learned.

Winslow wanted to ask more about Bet, why she was in a cage if she was smarter. Heavens, why she was in a cage at all. At least Hattie hadn't done that to her. Only she had. In a way. All those drugs and poisons were an invisible cage, and don't forget the years of mental torment. The years of not being allowed to make friends. No school. *All those lies.*

It was better to shut up then and look out the window, but all Winslow could see was a younger, gentler version of Hattie trapped in a wire cage. Crying for someone to help, while the person who should have loved her the most—killed her.

Chapter Thirty-Five

After long-term parking the Challenger at Adams Field, the airport in Little Rock, Tate and his boss hopped a private jet in their race to get a jump on Hattie. They landed in Amarillo, grabbed a rental, then checked into a pricey motel off the airport to catch some much needed shut-eye.

"Amarillo by morning." The George Strait song almost sounded romantic until you got into Amarillo in the wee, I'm-so-tired-I-couldn't-give-a-shit-less hours of zero-dark-thirty. They ordered breakfast, showered and ate, not necessarily in that order. By noon, Tate was flat on his back on the cool sheets of queen-size-bliss. The anesthetic in his thigh had worn off and he'd popped enough ibuprofen to slow the pain. The only way the drive could've ended better would have been if Winslow was in that room with him instead of Tucker.

Their wake-up call rang at five p.m., then dinner. Tate was hammered, but ready to roll. The sky was full of stars when they headed out. Isaiah's voice came through the moment Tate sank into the passenger seat of their bright red rental, a Chrysler 300. Leave it to Tucker to rent a nondescript car to get from Point A: Amarillo, to Point B: the Lockette Ranch.

"More intel, guys," Isaiah murmured from D.C.

"Go ahead," Tucker ordered as he maneuvered out of hotel parking and into Texas traffic, which was mostly pick-ups, and, well, more pick-ups. An occasional Mercedes or a limo rolled past the Chrysler 300, but yeah. Texans liked their trucks. Go figure.

The entire Deuces Wild Team was tuned psychically to each other now. Chagrinned, Tate realized he'd been the only reason they'd used earpieces. Not anymore.

"Ike Pitt's real name was Beauregard."

"You're shitting me," Tucker hissed. *"Hattie's brother?"*

"And Janice, Hattie's friend from Land's End?" Tate asked. *"Is she related to Hattie, too?"*

"Not sure, but I don't like what we're finding on the Beauregard family."

"Really creepy," Eden added. *"Like you-can't-believe, American-Horror-Story creepy. Most of the children ended up in jail or dead."*

"I can believe that," Tate said.

"*And?*" Tucker again.

"*And one of the girls disappeared when she was eight, Boss. There's a birth certificate on file with the County Health Department, but I can't find where she ever attended school. Her name was Betsy.*"

"*Any missing person report filed?*" Tate asked.

"*Any follow up from son-of-a-bitchin' Family Services?*" Tucker bit out.

Whoa, that came out of nowhere. Tate cast a sideways glance at his boss, wondering when he'd clashed with Family Services. Over his son Deuce, maybe?

"*Nothing that I can find, but this family's had more accidental deaths than you can believe,*" Eden breathed, "*and no one's challenged them. Not one teacher, priest, or relative, least not that I can find. I've got a call into Alabama's governor for an assist. Someone needs to do something to help these people.*"

"*At least to help their kids,*" Isaiah added.

"*One more thing.*" Eden once more. "*Hattie's got an ex. Bubba Ackerman from Florida.*"

"*Let me guess,*" Tucker drawled. "*He died from an accidental death?*"

"*I'm not sure how accidental it was, but he fell out of his hovercraft while hunting alligators. At least that's what Hattie told the sheriff.*"

"*You want to bet she killed him?*" Tate asked.

"*You two be careful,*" Isaiah warned. "*Hattie's not stupid. I wouldn't be surprised if she's persuaded some of her family to join her in Amarillo. Watch your backs."*

"How's Winslow?" Tate needed to know.

"She's fearful, but she's holding her own. Mostly she thinks she let you down, that she deserted you," Eden replied. *"The good thing is that now she knows about the fake blood. She knows you're alive."*

That was good to know. *"But she's okay? Hattie's not hurting her?"*

"No, Winslow went voluntarily on this road trip. You know that."

I do, but I wish I could talk to her, Tate thought to himself, but he pushed, *"Copy that. Let us know what else you find."*

"Will do," Eden answered.

They drove in silence until Tucker turned the Chrysler onto an asphalt road that looked like it went on forever over the Texas prairie. A rustic crossbeam supported by two rough-hewn logs marked the way to the Lockette ranch.

"Will you look at that," Tucker exclaimed. "They named their driveway after her."

"You call this road with no end in sight a driveway?" Tate peered up through the windshield. *Lost Angel Drive* had been carved between two Texas stars on the overhead beam. It was a blatant, heartrending declaration of love and loss for the world to see. In a matter of hours, Winslow would pass along this same road. She'd see that sign, and if she knew all that Tate now knew, it would break her heart. He ached to be with her.

"You still think we should let Hattie go through with this?" he asked. The plan was simply to arrive at the Lockette ranch before Hattie, let her spring her news, demand the reward, then arrest her once she had the cash in her hands.

For now, Booker and Emma Lockette had no idea what was coming their way, but Isaiah had assured Tate and Tucker what kind of people they were. Hard working. Driven. The salt of the earth kind of people who just wanted their baby back.

"Look around. This is a natural trap. Long drive in. Long drive out. Don't worry. We'll have Ms. Beauregard by midnight. Besides we've got time."

"If you say so."

Tucker bumped a fist to Tate's shoulder. "You worry too much."

Not exactly. Tate knew how ferociously a grizzly sow would fight for her cub. He didn't want Winslow anywhere near Hattie when everything went down. He hunkered into his seat to think. To use the talent he'd suppressed for years. It was time to open the floodgate and be all he could be. He rolled his window down and let Texas in.

"*Winslow,*" he projected, knowing she might not be able to hear him, but sending her what he could. Strength. Hope.

He pictured her smiling, her head out the car window and the sun in her face. He pictured her smiling in her real mother's arms, at peace. Content. Home. He summoned his rarely used imagination and pictured Winslow as a happy baby girl, her green eyes bright with wonder and a loving family around her. She had brothers. They must've loved their baby sister. He willed her to be that happy child again. Somewhere deep inside of her, that little girl still existed. Tate knew it did.

Slowing his breathing—*I can't believe I'm doing this*—he stilled the ache in his mind. Tate had always found great power in silence. What sniper didn't know that? Internal silence centered a man's soul, but it also zeroed the universe down on him. It shut people and the noise they seemed to thrive on—out. It magnified simple things like the desert wind sifting over his brow, the silvery light of a dim moon in winter, and the shadows that came with it. The breath of an opposing sniper. The heartbeat...

"Winslow," he reached into the universe. *"You're not alone, baby. I'm coming for you. Breathe. Just breathe. Pretty soon this will all be over."*

It came to him like a shadow from a great distance that grew clearer and more distinct the nearer it drew. Hattie. All alone. Her teeth clenched. A weapon in her right hand. A revolver. Smith and Wesson. Her arm extended. Where was Winslow?

"It's all up to you, *son.*"

Wait, what? Someone else had just spoken. Had to be Tucker, only it didn't sound right. The inflection was wrong. Not brash and bossy, but...

"Dad?" Tate's pulse slowed to a standstill as the vision continued. It was a scene from his past. One he remembered well. He'd been on a mountain in Alaska, surrounded by green, and high above the clouds of mosquitoes and no-see-ums. He and his father had waited out an injured grizzly, one shot by sport hunters who couldn't be bothered to track what they'd missed.

"Let her come to you, *son,*" Shane Higgins had said quietly. There was that word again, the one that opened a world of pain to the man deserted by his father. It meant so much to hear it again. "Have faith in your God-given talent, *son.*"

Three times, his father called him son as if he needed to reinforce the tie between them. *Three times.* The vision cleared and Tate knew exactly what he had to do.

"Look at that?" Hattie exclaimed, pointing at the heavy wooden sign over the entrance to what Winslow now knew was her grandfather's ranch. The morning's sunrise had tinted everything a warm shade of rose gold. Even the carved letters above her head were bathed in it.

Lost Angel Drive. That's me, Winslow thought, a pang ripping into her heart like the blade of a well-honed knife. *How sad. I'm that lost angel.*

This trip couldn't end soon enough. The last leg of the mother/daughter road trip had ended up being more of a game of trivial pursuit with a bipolar woman who seriously needed to take her meds. On schedule.

One moment Hattie seemed willing to chat and share everything; the next she turned petty and argumentative, calling names and dragging up every humiliating thing Winslow had ever done. Who needed that when you were trapped with a crazy person in yet another stolen car, this one a Ford Taurus out of Oklahoma City.

Winslow only hoped her parents would believe what Hattie planned to tell them, that maybe, they'd recognize her, even though she had no hair and no looks. That maybe they'd want her.

"Ha. That can't be right." Hattie slowed the Taurus to a crawl as she passed a collection of empty buildings, a boarded-up ranch house and a gray, weathered barn.

"Do you recognize this place?"

Hattie's nose wrinkled as she stretched her neck to peer past Winslow. "Yeah. That's where they lived when I found you."

Found as in kidnapped, you mean. "What are their names?" Winslow asked, staring at the lifeless wooden corpses, scared she'd come all this way for nothing.

"Lockette, emphasis on the *Lock*."

Whatever that meant. "My last name was Lockette? What'd you call them?" *Just tell me their first names. Give me something to hold onto.*

"Booker and Emma, now shut up and let me think." Braking to a dead stop, Hattie's fingernails set to drumming on the steering wheel. "See that road?" She stuck her index finger over the dash. "That wasn't here twenty years ago. Nothing was but miles and miles of prairie."

Winslow had no idea what to say. Would her parents have moved after the loss of their baby? It seemed reasonable. Could grief have driven them elsewhere? She knew they were still looking for her, or there wouldn't have been a reward, but where were they now, and why didn't Hattie know where to look? She knew about the three million dollars. Why not the exact address to get that money?

"No, no, no," Hattie huffed, her eyes gone dark and her lids slanted. "This was supposed to..." A growl rumbled up from her throat and she looked at the houses then the road yet to be traveled. "Goddamn her. I'll bet she put him up to this. Your mother's a real bitch, Winslow. You know that, don't you?"

How would I know anything about my real Mom? It stung to hear Hattie cuss the woman Winslow had yet to meet. Fingering the black bandana Hattie had bought at one of the many truck stops along the way, Winslow braced her palm to her forehead, weary of the soap opera that was her life.

Right on cue, the obnoxious woman at her left grunted. "Want to bet Booker thinks he's smarter than me?"

Well, duh. He isn't here and you are. "You could, umm, Google him if you're lost."

"I'm not lost." Hattie turned a mean glare at Winslow. "I've got a better idea. Let's keep driving up Stupid Angel Drive and see where it ends, why don't we? If he thinks he's gonna beat me out of that three mil, the ass has another thing coming."

God, help me, Winslow prayed. *Please don't let her hurt anyone today. Keep my real parents safe. Tate and Pepe too.*

She turned her face to the sun and for that one moment, the warmth of it bathed her face like a gentle kiss. Her heart fluttered. Tate's smiling dark eyes reached out to her and Winslow took a deep breath, then let it slowly hiss out between pursed lips. *Hang on,* she told herself what Tate had said. *There is always hope.*

Hattie stepped on the gas, kicked up a cloud of dust, and onward they went. The Lockette ranch was Texas big. The road into it tracked over gentle hills lined with barbed-wire fences and miles of green fields with stubby black cattle. Then horses. Lots of them. Buckskins and Palominos. Dainty dappled grays with white faces. Bays and sorrels the likes Winslow had never seen before. The little girl inside of her reached out to them. *What would it be like to live here? To learn to ride a horse. A small horse.*

"Wow," Winslow gulped as the car from Oklahoma rolled over the crest of yet another Texas-sized hill. They had to be a good ten miles inside the Lockette ranch by now, and maybe that was what irked Hattie the most. She'd wanted a quick getaway, but that wasn't going to happen.

Winslow's pulse picked up. Booker Lockette had deliberately relocated his ranch deep into his property. He meant for the snake who'd stolen his child to have to work for that reward. *My dad is smarter than Hattie.*

Spread out below was a magnificent stone and log home the size of a small hotel. A large porch surrounded the front and ran along the entire side that Winslow could see. Barns, stables, and other out buildings stretched nearby, but the kicker? *Lost Angel Drive* led straight up to that wide wooden porch and the front door.

"Stop the car," she breathed, her heart pumping, make that banging in her chest at this once in a lifetime moment.

"Oh, no, you don't," Hattie hissed. "You're going through with this or I'll... I'll..."

"You'll what?" Winslow asked, her fingers squeezing the door handle and her calves bunched to propel her away from this nightmare. "Kill me on my parents' property? Give it a rest."

"You think I won't?"

"Please, I just want to take this slow." Winslow shook her head, not wanting to fight. If what Hattie had told her was true—*God, please let it be true*—then this was her moment. Her homecoming. She wanted to savor every last step in this journey, every mind numbing first sight of the life that had been stolen from her.

A slender woman stood at the top step of that front porch as if already waiting for someone. *For me.* Okay, that was—Winslow gulped—weird. How could this woman know that today her daughter was coming home? But she seemed to. She held one hand to her mouth, the other waving slowly as if...

She recognizes me, and she's still looking for me, and she looks like me—if I had hair. Doesn't she? It's her. I know it's her.

"Mom," breathed out of Winslow's heart.

"What?" Hattie snapped.

"N-not you." Winslow pointed through the windshield. "H-her." Goosebumps prickled up her bare arms and over her shoulders. "That's my real mom. I know it's her. Stop the car. I have to get out." *Now!*

But Hattie kept driving, so Winslow cranked her door open. Her heart beat like a hammer in her chest. She could barely breathe much less sit in that car any longer, not with her mother nearly in reach. *I have to go...*

Hattie had to slow down then, or risk revealing what a nut job she was in view of the family she intended to cheat. Compelled by a force she couldn't refuse, Winslow's heart zeroed in on that woman walking down the porch steps, the one in a white blouse and jeans with her head up and long black hair streaming behind her. The one who'd just started running toward Winslow.

"Mom?" she asked, her feet flying. *Oh God, Oh God, it's you! I know it's you!*

They crashed together, all arms and tears, gentle fingers and...

"My sweet baby girl," this strange, familiar person cried. "My precious baby. I never thought I'd see you again." She choked even as her hands slid over Winslow's bare head, sweeping the bandana away as her beautiful brown eyes brimmed. "I never gave up on you, Brooklyn, not for one day. Let me look at you." She eased back, then pulled Winslow's forehead to hers. "It's you. It's really you. Oh, baby," she cried as she crushed Winslow to her heart, her body trembling and her arms the best things ever.

"I know you. I don't know how but I know you," Winslow cried, burrowing her nose into her mother's neck, pulling in the scent of lilacs and vanilla. So familiar. Voices swirled around her where she stood, but this—*this!*—is home. *This warm place right here. This is real. This is my mom. MY mom.*

She could barely contain her sobbing until a screen door slammed and a mean, male voice barked, "Get away from her, Emma. That's not your damned daughter!"

The tormented rage in that terse masculine voice brought Winslow's head up. *Daddy?*

"Yes, she is, Booker. She's Brooklyn," her mother said, still smoothing her hands over Winslow's bare head. So much love washed over Winslow at that gentle touch, like a baptism of saving grace, that she simply closed her eyes and let it rain. Nothing had ever felt sweeter or more right. "This is our baby girl. I'd recognize her anywhere. She's got your eyes. Come look at her. Come see."

"I don't need to see anyone's eyes to recognize a couple liars. Bullshit!" the man spat.

The single word—Tate's word—struck a comforting chord in Winslow's heart even though it was spoken against her. She looked at her father then, certain that this man she didn't know was truly her father, and that he didn't mean what he was saying. Without a doubt, she knew he still loved her and he wanted her back.

Still on the porch, he stood there with his shoulders square, his jaw set, and his feet spread. A holstered pistol rested on his hip, beneath the curve of a callused right hand with long, thick fingers. Bristly black hair capped his head. He looked as mean and as angry as Tate could, but he couldn't take his eyes off her. Pride swelled in Winslow's ragged heart. Just like Tate, this man would fight the world for her.

"I'm not lying," Hattie said as she strolled nonchalantly from the now parked Taurus, a manila envelope in her hand. She'd spent extra time on her make-up and hair this morning, had even dressed in nice slacks and a silky, peach colored blouse. Insisting on making a good impression, she'd stopped at Wal-Mart the night before to buy a change of clothes for Winslow, nice of her after four hard days on the road.

But Winslow didn't care that her jeans were name brand for the first time ever, or that her red shirt was stiff out of the bag. She had hold of her mother. Her real mother. And judging by the way this woman held onto her, she knew it too. Her dark brown eyes brimmed.

"I can prove it's Brooklyn, Booker Lockette," Hattie said, the envelope raised high over her head. "Emphasis on the lock."

He stalked down the stairs, wary, one step at a time, his lips thin and his eyes as hard as diamonds. Soft green diamonds that seemed familiar.

Winslow cocked her head at him. *I know you.* "Dad?" she dared ask, timid but certain. "Is that my dad?" she asked her mother.

The lady nodded, but his gaze raked over her like claws. "You're not fooling me. Get off my land. Both of you!"

"I'll have you know we drove four days to get here," Hattie argued, "and we're not—"

"Take off!" he roared, his left index finger stabbed at the road behind the Taurus, his other still on the grip of that pistol. "I knew the second I re-posted that reward every scurvy snake and rat in the world would come pounding on my door. You think I don't know what you two are up to? Get out before I run you out!"

Hattie slapped the envelope to her thigh. "You're still as pigheaded as ever."

Booker stopped in his tracks then. "Do I know you?"

"No," audacious Hattie spit out, confident now, "but you knew my sister. She was your nanny for a couple weeks about twenty years ago." *Another untruth. You're going to blame Sue Ellen for your crime.*

"I watched her for years, ever since she showed up with a baby and no husband in sight. It took me all this time to put the pieces together, but," Hattie jerked her head in Winslow's direction. "God knows she ain't much to look at. She's puny and she's been sick most of her life..." *Because you poisoned me.* "...but this here kid's your flesh and blood, and I can prove it."

That merited a chin nod from Booker. "Then prove it."

Hattie strolled up to him, her hips swaying. She slapped the envelope to his chest with a, "Read it and weep, big guy. This little gal is your long-lost daughter, and like it or not, you owe me three million."

It took Booker Lockette seconds to scan whatever Hattie gave him. At last he looked up, his gaze on the woman holding Winslow. He blinked. "It's true, Emma. That young lady you're holding is... she's our lost angel," he said, his voice turned tight and thin, his chin quivering. His Adam's apple bobbed once, like it was a hard truth to swallow, or else he was near tears.

Shivers danced up Winslow's neck at that tender paternal acknowledgement. She whined, needing to be in two places at the same time, in his arms as well as in Emma's.

Crass to the bitter end, Hattie stuck her open palm under his nose, her fingers waggling. "Hand it over, cowboy, and I'll be out of your hair forever. Three mil and you get to keep the girl. Sounds like a fair trade to me."

Nice of you, Winslow thought as she held her breath. *After all these years, you hand me over like you're returning a jacket that doesn't fit. Like you can get a deposit for me.*

"I never thought I'd be doing this, but..." Her father swiped the back of his hand over his eyes before he reached into his back pocket and tugged a wallet out. Opening it, he produced a folded check. "I wrote this the day I posted the reward, just didn't know then whose name I'd be paying to the order of. Here, take it. Put your name on the line, and thank you, ma'am. I owe you more than that paltry amount for bringing Brooklyn home."

Hattie took the check, not even politely. She turned, scanned the ranch, and tapped her finger to her bottom lip. "Huh. If I were smart, I'd demand more than just three mil, but this..." She lifted the check to her lips and kissed it. "...is all I ever wanted."

Winslow nearly choked. *Wasn't that the cold, hard truth? That and a road trip to help me commit suicide was all you wanted.*

"My poor baby," Emma murmured at the side of her head, her arms still wrapped protectively around Winslow's shoulders. "That awful woman's had you all these years? I'm so sorry."

"Me too." Winslow nodded, her eyes fixed on the beautiful, crazy woman walking out of her life for the last time. There'd be time to explain everything to her real parents later, maybe. Some things were better left unspoken. Right then all she could do was stare at the monster who, even through the worst of times, Winslow had loved with all of her now breaking heart. She hadn't expected to feel anything when Hattie left—but she did.

"So we're done here," Booker stated, his hand extended, his green eyes sharp and as calculating as Hattie's.

She stuffed the check into the front of her blouse before she took hold of his hand. "I've got what I came for. I'll be seeing y'all."

He offered one short nod as he released her, his hand back on the pistol grip. "Count on it."

Winslow watched Hattie go without a glance in her direction. Without one word. No 'take care of yourself, Winslow'. No 'I'll miss you'. Not even a final 'goodbye'.

"Mom," came unbidden to Winslow's lips even as her real mother squeezed her a little tighter. Held her a little closer.

"Let her go, Brooklyn," Emma whispered into her cheek. "She's the worst kind of woman there is."

I know and I will let her go. I want to, but... A part of Winslow was crushed at being left behind like a piece of trash.

Hattie looked at her then, her eyes sharp. Questioning. "What?" she snapped. Like so many times before.

"I... I..." The words stuck in Winslow's throat. *I don't know what I want.*

Hattie scratched her neck below her right ear as if annoyed. "It's not like I came all this way just to turn around and take you back home with me, now is it?"

Winslow shook her head. No. Of course not. She'd never go back with Hattie, but the little girl in her was desperate to run to the only mother she'd ever known. To hold onto—something—before it was gone forever. This was goodbye. She'd never see Hattie—or Joyce—again. She'd never make excuses for her bad behavior, talk her out of her mood swings, or listen to her bitch about everything. She'd never need to rationalize Hattie's lies to make her seem better and kinder than she was. Somehow, that space in Winslow's heart where Hattie still lived, ached as if someone was tearing out a very long vine that stretched all the way to her toes.

"Winslow! Spit it out." Tap, tap, tap went those pricey heels that Hattie had charged on the credit card she'd found tucked into the visor pocket of the Audi she'd stolen in Nashville.

"I just... I just want you to know that... I still love you," Winslow said like a foolish, needy child. *I always will.*

"Well, goodie, goodie for you." Hattie shot a look of triumph over her shoulder at Booker, as if she'd won, when Winslow felt like she was losing everything. She could barely breathe. This was goodbye. Forever...

Hattie turned her back on Winslow then, her long legs eating up the distance to the Taurus like a super model on some runway in New York City. As if she couldn't get away from Winslow fast enough. "Buh-bye, losers," she said airily.

"Not so fast," another familiar voice barked.

Winslow's neck snapped to the man who'd just come around the shaded side of the porch, his pistol drawn, his eyes as black as coal. "Tate?"

Chapter Thirty-Six

Tate stepped off the porch, the red dot of his laser sight set dead center on Hattie's forehead, ready to take her down if she so much as blinked wrong. Yeah, she'd seen him. Her head came up. Her nostrils flared, and Mama Bear was pissed. Too bad, so sad.

"You," she spat, those ugly Halloween fingernails hooked over the top of her car door like claws.

Tate had seen the police reports on Hattie's car thefts, courtesy of his new psychic vision. She'd stolen more vehicles than Bonnie and Clyde had robbed banks in her mad dash across the country. It was no wonder he and Tucker hadn't been able to catch up with her.

"FBI Special Agent Tate Higgins to you," he shot back at her, edging closer and not taking his eyes off his quarry for one second. *I'm the wild card you never saw coming.*

"You go, Tate," Isaiah hissed from a couple thousand miles away. It felt good having the Deuces Wild team on his side.

"I don't have to tell you this, but Winslow's heart rate picked up the moment she saw you," Eden murmured.

Tate nodded, though Eden couldn't see him. He knew Winslow's eyes were on him, that he was the last person she'd expected to see here at her parents' ranch. But predators were unpredictable. Man-eaters more so. He didn't dare break eye contact with the woman in his sights to acknowledge the woman he loved.

Right on cue, Hattie's right hand dropped below the window, no doubt going for the weapon she'd hidden in the side pocket.

"Hands up," he bellowed, ready to shoot through that car door if that's what it came down to. She had a bullet coming. He owed her one for the one they'd dug out of his thigh. The hollow tips in his chamber would go through that flimsy car door as easy as a hot knife through butter. "Get them up. Now."

Did she comply? Did she ever do anything smart? Her hand came up, but just like that foolish old woman in the Mini Cooper had done, she brandished the gun he'd seen in his vision. A revolver. Smith and Wesson.

"She will kill you," Tucker stated the obvious from where he'd just broken cover.

"You don't want to do this," Tate told Hattie, his elbows lifted away from his body, his nerves as steady as the game hunter he was born to be. She needed to keep her focus on him, not what was happening behind her. "Drop it and I'll let you live." *Or keep it and die. It's all the same to me.*

She cleared the door, her feet spread, and her heels planted, pointing that revolver at Tate through the car window. "I don't think so, Agent Higgins. You're going to pretend you never saw me. Trust me. You will let me go."

Showdown.

"Think about what you're doing to that little girl you raised," he bit out. "She's watching you now like she's watched you all of her life. Is this how you want Winslow to remember you?"

Hattie's chin came up. "I could say the same to you. Do you want the bitch you've been fucking to dream about the day I turned your fat head to red crap?"

Tate winced at the language. God, she had her nerve to accuse a woman as pure as Winslow of something like that in front of her parents. "You know that's not going to happen."

He and Tucker had already searched the ranch and questioned the help. Hattie was outnumbered and on her own. Her family, if she'd contacted them and asked for their help, wasn't even in Texas, which was sad in a weird, pathetic way. Tate didn't know why that image of Hattie alone against the world bothered him, but it did.

This was, after all, the only mother Winslow had known, and Winslow was the only decent thing Hattie had ever had, and probably loved—in her way. Yes, Hattie was a twisted piece of work, but she was alone in the world. Even as a kid growing up, she had no idea what a decent home and family life was. Tate lost his parents and still carried that hurt with him, but they were both good people. They'd loved him. Not a day went by that he didn't know he'd been wanted.

But Hattie? He could appreciate the desperation that drove people to choose poorly. It was simple math. Wrecked people made wrecked choices. They drove people away or they left them behind. They blocked them out of their lives. *Ring a bell?*

"Let me tell you what's going to happen," Hattie barked. Quick as the snake she was, she flicked the end of her gun at Winslow, still standing in the arms of her mother at the front of the car. "How about we make it a twofer? You let me go, I'll let Brooklyn and her mommy live."

But Hattie had gotten over-confident, and Tate could see what she could not.

"Works for me, Ms. *Beau-re-gard*," Tucker bit out her name, the business end of his pistol now snug at the bottom of her skull, and his fingers securely trapping her pistol. "It's over, Hattie. Drop your weapon and let's call it a day."

God, the man was a—well—a godsend. Tate drew in a breath, relieved that Tucker had gotten the drop on Hattie as planned. What could have been damned ugly was—

"No!" Hattie shrieked as she nailed Tucker's family jewels with one well-aimed kick of her pointy heel, and down he went with a hiss and a "Son-of-a-bitch!"

Fumbling, she retrieved her weapon, aimed it at Winslow, and—

BLAM! Tate dropped her where she stood. In the dirt.

"Mom! No!" Winslow screamed as she let go of Emma and rounded the Taurus at a dead run. *Shit.* Tate holstered his weapon and intercepted her before she could see her mother, ah, Hattie, like that.

"You killed my mom!" she shrieked, elbowing him, hell-bent on getting to Hattie. "Let me go! I have to help her!"

"No, baby. You don't." Barricading her inside his arms, Tate dragged her kicking and screaming to the porch, away from the scene while Tucker stumbled to his feet. Tate never would have unholstered his weapon if he hadn't meant to use deadly force to stop this child predator. Hattie was where she belonged now. Where she'd never hurt Winslow again.

Booker took over then. Several of his ranch hands appeared out of nowhere with a tarp. Poor Emma stood watching, her shoulders set, her mouth set in a grim line as they covered the body, and Tate knew she was giving him time to make amends with Winslow.

"She's not your mother," he crooned. "She never was. She would have killed you and your mother."

"You think I don't know that?" Winslow cried, tearing at her bare head with her fingernails, leaving long red scratches over her scalp. "But she was my mom, Tate. For years. She took care of me, and yes, she was cruel, but she was all I had. I hate you! You killed her!"

Cupping her poor sunburned head, he pressed her under his chin, knowing this was shock and grief talking. He wished there'd been another way. "I'm sorry you had to see that, but you can't ask me not to protect you. I'm not made that way. I will always strike first. I will always be here for you."

A strangled scream choked out of her. "I know," she sobbed hoarsely, hiccupping she was crying so hard, "but this. I didn't want her to die."

Shifting his feet, Tate wrapped his body around her, swaying to comfort her even though he knew there was none to be given. Death sucked, and self-defense didn't mean shit when someone you cared for died as a result. That was Winslow through and through. She cared about others even when they didn't deserve it.

At last she melted against him. "I don't hate you, Tate. You had to do it, and I... I understand," she said, shivering from the adrenaline rush. "I do, and I'm glad you didn't let her kill my real mom and dad."

Or you. "Me too," he said as he pressed his lips to the top of her head. "Hattie lived a damned hard life, baby." *So did Ike and Sue Ellen and all the other Beauregard children. In a way, none of them got a decent break in the world.* "She's been headed down this road since the day she was born."

"It's just that she never had a... a chance." Winslow wept, her face in his shirt—right over his heart.

"Yes, she did," he whispered into the top of her head. "She had you for twenty years, Winslow. The second she stole you from your parents, she had everything. The sun. The moon. Every last one of the stars. She could've lived happily-ever-after from that moment on, and you never would've known she wasn't your real mother. She could've loved you and spoiled you rotten, but she chose to poison you instead. When that didn't work out like she wanted, she sold you back to your real mom and dad for three million pieces of silver."

How Winslow could feel compassion for Hattie Beauregard after all she'd endured amazed Tate. She should be damned mad at this despicable betrayal, but she wasn't Hattie, was she? Hattie was damaged goods from the get-go, but Tate had a hunch that Winslow was more like Booker Lockette, if those soft green eyes staring at him from across the yard meant anything. The man was poised like a snake to strike. He wanted his daughter back, and that clenched fist told Tate he meant to fight for her if he had to wait much longer.

An odd sad whine climbed out of Winslow's throat. "She stole me then she sold me, Tate. Like I meant nothing to her. How messed up is that?"

"She's the loser, not you," he murmured against her scalp, giving Winslow time to remember who was who, and what was what in this crazy mixed up life she'd been forced into. What else could he tell her, but "I love you, Brooklyn Lockette. So do your mom and dad. Look at them waiting to get their hands on you. They want you in their lives. Give them a chance."

It must've worked. He barely had time to close his eyes before her mouth crashed onto his, and there, under the bright Amarillo sky, he tasted the salty, tear-flavored kisses of the woman he would soon have to let go.

Brooklyn, aka Winslow, patted her Stetson, a lovely chamois colored cowboy hat with a pink and black bandana underneath it to protect her ears and scalp from the sun. Texas was hot. Tate was hotter. He'd stayed on at the Booker Lockette Ranch to make sure she settled in where she'd never been before. Or so he said.

As it turned out, Booker's display of righteous outrage when Winslow had first arrived at the ranch was an act. It had nearly broken his heart to deny the woman he'd known damned well was his child, but he'd had to do it. Pride and authenticity demanded he give that woman—he still couldn't speak Hattie's name without a long list of expletives—a small taste of what she'd given him and Emma. Besides, the ruse gave Tate and Tucker time to get into position.

Tate. Hmmm. Because of his courage, she now went by Brooklyn Winslow Lockette. Emphasis on the *Lock.* Sometimes...

Winslow wanted to move forward, but the one-eighty degree turn in her life was *humongous.* Make that *phantasmagorical.* Mind boggling too.

Some days she didn't know who she was. Booker called her his Little Bit, an endearment he'd blessed her with twenty years ago, but one she didn't remember. Without fail, Emma—*still working on calling her Mom*—called her Brooklyn, her given name. But Tate called her Bdub, short for BW, her initials. 'Course he usually said it with a sly wink.

Winslow still wasn't sure which name she wanted to go by. Both Winslow and Brooklyn betrayed someone she loved now or had loved in the past. Tate's solution seemed the best, but she wasn't Bdub when she'd met him, so yeah. *Lots of adjustments.*

The truth was she'd never felt better. Her eyes were clear. She hadn't thrown up in weeks, not since that last day when everything went crazy, *umm, crazier.* She smiled more and she'd put on a little weight, probably because homemade potato salad,

Texas-style barbecued beef ribs, and her father's baked beans were to-die-for good. Emma and Booker couldn't seem to feed her enough.

Her body had done some kind of system-reboot now that the poison was out of her system, and she was eating properly. Her hair was making a tentative appearance, still short but coming in as dark as before, and a little curly too. She could run her fingers through it and spike it if she wanted to, but that reminded her of Joyce, umm, Hattie. *Damn. I'm never going to get that right in my head.*

Every day the air smelled a little sweeter, the sky looked bluer, and wow. It was good to be alive. Autumn was different in Texas, but the nights were still cool. Thanksgiving was a week away, and Christmas was fast on its heels, but none of that mattered because her heart was on the verge of breaking again. Tomorrow morning, Tate was leaving Amarillo. He had a job to get back to and she had a family to reconnect with.

Winslow shoved the thought out of her mind. Life was what she'd wanted, but one without Tate in it? Not so much. She hadn't had any time alone with him, not between his boss calling him and her dad putting him to work. Every time she tried to get him to herself, either Emma came looking for her or something came up. Like family albums and clothes shopping. A visit with the Lockette family doctor or a drive around the ranch. Old Curly, one of Booker's ranch hands cried when she was reintroduced to him.

He'd been there the day Hattie stole her, and he'd blamed himself as much as Booker blamed himself. So yeah. Winslow had lots of family and friends now, and she was beginning to love them all.

Tate never complained, but Winslow did. Her days were filled, but empty at the same time. Her nights were spent thrashing, tangled in sheets and thinking about him. Wanting his arms around her. Needing the smell of his skin in her nose and the taste of his mouth on her tongue. She missed him with a craving so deep that she ached day in and day out for his touch or one of his infrequent smiles. *Damn, I've got it bad.*

Which was why she was where she was today, watching the calf branding in the dusty corral. With one boot hooked over the bottom rung of the rail and Pepe snuggled in the cradle of her arm where he belonged, Winslow kept a hungry eye on her cowboy.

Pepe came to Texas courtesy of FBI Special Agents Ky and Eden Winchester. Along with their baby boy, Kyler, they'd made a special trip just to bring Pepe home. How amazing was that, strangers traveling all this way just to deliver a shivering, big-eyed little dog to his mistress? By the time they'd left two days later, Kyler sported little cowboy boots and two front teeth. He wasn't walking yet, but he was the cutest thing ever.

Ky and Eden also brought an unexpected surprise, her handwritten journals. Eden thought she should use them to write a book, an autobiography of her experiences as a kidnapped child. Ky offered to help since the Department of Defense was vetting his book, *Surviving Life, A USMC Story of Hope,* before it could be published. Ky had a good agent who was primed to jump on Winslow's story too, but telling that life story meant betraying the woman she'd known as Mom again. Winslow couldn't do it.

For now, the journals rested under her bed in a colorful cardboard box that Eden had bought for her. Call it stupid or call it wrong, Winslow still loved that crazy, mean lady, Hattie Beauregard, so she went with her heart and let the chance to make millions pass her by. Life in Amarillo was enough of a treasure, and truth be known, this was all she'd ever wanted. A home and a family. Maybe a baby boy in her future, a sweetheart with dark shaggy hair and a frown that only she or his daddy could love away. *If only...*

But man, that cowboy on the back of that buckskin sure could ride. Winslow shook her head and schooled her runaway thoughts. She focused on what she had today. Tate was a natural at herding the pesky red calves around the corral and into the holding chute. He was on Romeo, the one her father called a damned good cow horse. When the calf dodged right, Tate and Romeo cut it off before it could get away.

Tate followed up with a quick as lightning feint to the left to keep the calf off-balance and moving forward. With a slap of his dusty black cowboy hat to this thigh, and a sharp, "Hey!" Tate startled the balking critter into the chute. The other ranch hands took over from there, herding the little guy to vaccinations, branding, and other stuff.

Her dad's registered brand consisted of two overlaid letters in a circle: **B** and **L** for Booker Lockette. Both letters shared the same bold vertical and bottom strokes. The two curves of the **B** were lighter, leaving no doubt there was a definite **L** to be reckoned with. Booker said a brand was the same as a man's word. Just as telling. Just as good. And the Booker Lockette Ranch had a name above reproach, which was why he always emphasized the *lock*.

Booker was a good horseman and a respected rancher, but Winslow's abduction had destroyed him as much as it had Emma. He'd blamed himself so bitterly for losing his only daughter that he'd built another ranch house, the one Brooklyn—aka Winslow—lived in today, as far from the highway and civilization as he could, nearly in the heart of his thousand-acre ranch. The home itself was stone and timber, unlike the deserted one Hattie had driven by at the start of the long drive in. Behind the rustic exterior, an extensive security system monitored every road, walkway, and door on the ranch. Booker had known the precise moment that Hattie entered his territory.

He'd offered the same reward back then, but apparently Hattie hadn't seen it. Was it wrong to believe that maybe—just maybe—she had, but that she wanted to be an honest-to-goodness mother so much that she'd chosen her new, albeit stolen, daughter over her greed? Winslow liked to think so, but she kept that thought to herself. Emma and Booker had been through enough. They didn't need to hear her defending the woman they despised.

"That's quite a decent young man you've set your sights on."

Winslow jumped, startled Emma was suddenly at her elbow. "Tate's a good friend." *To say the least.*

"You love him," Emma said, her eyes on Tate's broad back as he roped an escapee on the other side of the corral. She hooked her boot over the bottom rung of the corral just like Winslow.

"I do. He saved me. I owe him everything." *And I'll never be able to repay him.*

Emma crossed her arms on the top rail, watching the impromptu rodeo. "That doesn't mean you have to marry him, Brooklyn."

Winslow winced, not yet feeling like a Brooklyn. "True," she agreed with a sigh. *But look at him go.*

The man was cut out of granite, the dense kind that didn't crumble or flake under pressure. Didn't chip or buckle either. His wide shoulders were made for carrying heavy loads. For work. His chest was thick and powerful. His heart as hard as flint, yet as tender as a little boy. Even wounded when he'd arrived on the ranch, he'd never asked for help, not once, just stepped up and gave back at every opportunity to serve.

He might be a tough FBI agent, but he had a way with dogs, little boys too. Winslow had seen the way Pepe and Kyler gravitated to Tate, but then so did she. There was something about the man...

"Is he still leaving tomorrow morning?" Emma was worried he'd take her long-lost daughter with him when he left. That was what this conversation was about.

The sad truth was, "Yes. His flight to Reagan leaves at six-fifty-five." *Which means he'll be gone by five because he has an important job to do, and he's committed to serving America. That's what men like him do. They leave their loved ones behind and they die in the line of duty.*

"What will you do once he's gone, Brooklyn?"

"I don't know," she replied, but she thought, *'I'm seducing that man tonight if it's the last thing I do.'*

Chapter Thirty-Seven

As was his custom, Tate came into the Lockette home through the side door like the servants did, which put him in the mudroom. Doffing his boots to keep the dirt from the corrals and stables out of the house, he stripped out of his socks and stuffed them into his boots, just to be on the safe side. He might be a guest, but these fine people deserved respect for the way they'd taken Winslow, ahem, *Bdub,* back into their hearts and their home.

Like it or not, he was on the first flight out of Amarillo come morning. Damn, that hurt just thinking about it, but it was time he let Winslow— *Bdub*—get on with her life. He'd heard Booker talking to her about tutors and school, college even. Emma had already taken her shopping and filled her bedroom closet with more new clothes and shoes than Winslow had owned in her entire life. Booker had even given her a horse. Her brothers, Rhett and Gunn were due home for the holidays, so yeah. It was time Tate got out of their way and let Bdub become part of her family.

Interestingly, his guest bedroom was on ground level at the rear of the house while Winslow's was upstairs next to her parents' bedroom. That made sense. Booker Lockette apparently knew horses and men. Smart man.

Barefoot, sweaty, and smelling of horses, Tate padded silently down the hall and past the kitchen. His nose twitched at the luscious aromas in the air. Marietta, the cook, was at it once more, whipping up another zesty Southwestern meal. He hadn't eaten this good in years, nor eaten so much beef or so many jalapeños. He was going to miss her cooking.

She had her back to him, working at the sink, so he kept walking. There was no sense in disturbing a genius at her work. Once in his room, he closed his door before he stripped off his holster. Gun apparel was commonplace on this ranch. Not only did Booker and his wife carry, so did most of their hands. Nice.

His weapon went flat to the dresser where he could easily reach it if needed, his dirty clothes near the spare duffle bag Booker had given him. Tate hadn't much to put in it, just a change of clothes and some toiletries he'd purchased en route to Amarillo. Some ammo. The barest essentials.

The guest room was done in subtle earth tones with an occasional turquoise accent. Southwestern they called it. The furniture, a bed, chair, and dresser, was constructed of polished logs. Three red clay pots of fake miniature cacti—the kind without the deadly spiny thorns—graced the dresser. A lamp made up of horseshoes welded together topped the nightstand. A thick Mexican blanket, woven of more earth tones with a stripe of turquoise, topped the carved wooden chest at the foot of the bed.

Double-paned windows opened to a western vista of wide-open prairie, now purpling with the last of a sunset at the end of a hard day's work. Tate closed the curtains. He didn't need to be reminded what he was leaving behind. Or who.

The bathroom décor was an extension of the bedroom's, with a twist. A leather harness framed the mirror over a turquoise porcelain sink that matched the commode. The shower curtain, a damned good imitation of burlap, had been craftily hung from a wide wooden oxen yoke in lieu of a shower rod. More repurposed horseshoes served as hooks for clothes and towels. More cacti. A red clay, tiled shower stall.

Tate cranked the water to as hot as he could stand it. With his forearm to the wall beneath the spray, he leaned his head to his wrist and let the hot water work its magic over his back and down his thighs. The bullet hole was healing nicely. He'd removed the bandage days ago, but riding a horse worked muscles he hadn't known he had. Arching his stiff back, he rolled his shoulders and stretched, letting the heat seep in and loosen the kinks. Letting his mind wander.

Funny thing. It never wandered much farther than the courageous woman he'd met on a water tower one night in Maryland. Knowing he'd done all he could for Winslow should've made Tate happy, but he was pensive this late afternoon. In less than a month, she'd come to mean everything to him. It was going to be damned hard leaving her behind. But this was Texas and she couldn't be safer. Booker and Emma would make sure of that.

Tate soaped shampoo through his hair, rinsed, content to let the gentle spray wash his face and most of his cares away. Even now, the FBI's Deuces Wild team was in southern Alabama, dissecting the criminal offshoot of all that *good* Beauregard parenting.

According to Winslow, on the mad dash to Amarillo, Hattie hadn't once mentioned her brothers by name. For good reason. Except for Ike, the youngest of the bunch, her six living brothers were straight up gangsters. Also known as the notorious BBs—as in Beauregard Brothers—they were a lawless motorcycle gang out of backwater Creola, Alabama. All six were wanted by the FBI for pushing everything from drugs and stolen goods to moonshine—and their luck.

If Hattie had contacted them for back up in her attempt to swindle Booker, no one would've ever known where they were. That they didn't show in

Amarillo to support their sister illustrated one thing clearly. The BBs only rode for jobs that paid. They didn't much care for things like loyalty, honor, or family. 'Course, neither did Hattie.

In between scrubbing his chest and back with the coarse sponge and the manly shower gel that came with the room, Tate decided the wiser thing to do was to leave in the middle of the night. It would hurt Winslow's feelings, but his not drawing things out would spare her too. She might even be mad enough to forget he'd ever existed. Getting on with her life would be easier without him in the picture.

Yeah, that was the right thing to do. Cut the ties. Let her loose. Then he'd do what he did best. Stay out of sight while he kept her in his sight. Protect her while she grew into the woman she should have been. Love her from a distance that was safe—for her. Yeah. That's what he'd do.

The slight shift in the steamy sauna atmosphere alerted Tate that his bedroom door had been opened, most likely by Booker. He'd stopped by a time or two with a cigar or a good book, maybe a beer, just being friendly. Tate liked the guy. Booker and Emma were God-fearing people who'd worked hard to build their family and ranch. They considered the folks they employed more friends than just employees. The world needed more good folks like the Lockettes.

"Be right out, sir," Tate called. He blew out a deep breath, already counting the lasts. Last shower before he left Winslow. Last sunset he wouldn't get to share with her. Last dinner he'd eat with her sitting across the table from him. Last night sleeping in the same house—not in the same bed—with her. Last damned everything. The least he could do was make certain there'd be no last goodbye.

He swallowed hard, slapped the tap to off, and grabbed a towel from the handy horseshoe hook outside the shower. Only it wasn't Booker standing there with a good book and a smoke. It was Winslow. And she wasn't wearing a thing.

The black in Tate's eyes swallowed the brown as he wrapped his towel around his hips, covering himself. "You shouldn't be in here," he said, his voice ten octaves lower. Deeper. Rougher.

"Yes, I should," Winslow said, her head up and fully aware of her decision. Nervous or not, this was the perfect place to be. And this was the perfect man, dripping wet and with steam lifting off his massive tanned shoulders. This man was a god, and this was her now-or-never. "I'm not letting you break your promise to me." Honest, she didn't mean for her voice to come out as breathy as it did.

His brows lifted. "My what?" If he didn't remember, his body certainly did. That fluffy turquoise towel couldn't hide his reaction to her any more than she could hold back her pounding heart. Surely he heard it.

She took a step to him, his eyes big and wide, his gaze slipping over her breasts and down her belly like the last rays of golden sun when it kissed the prairie goodbye. "You promised you'd make love to me, and a man always keeps his word. You taught me that." She had him there. It was a childish ruse, but given her lack of sexy, curly hair and a full figure, it was all she had to fight with.

He rolled his eyes, breathing hard. Trapped and aroused was a good look on Tate. It made her feel—utterly feminine. Kind of powerful. She took another bold step into his comfort zone, her insides quivering like *Jello* at her audacity. Were all women scared to death their first time with a man or was it only her?

"Winslow," he ground out, his free hand raking over his hair. "I mean Bdub, I mean..."

"Winslow," she breathed, reaching her hands to his chest, needing to touch him after all these weeks of not being able to. "I've always been Winslow."

And she was in his arms and that amazing muscle under his towel twitched against her belly. "Kiss me," she ordered, not asked. Asking might make him think he had a choice when he didn't. Not tonight. She might be as timid as a mouse, but she knew what she wanted.

He hissed, his throat muscles taut. The man was perplexed, flummoxed, and enthralled, maybe a little angry, too, but he was also thinking. She could almost hear the wheels grinding behind that hard forehead and those dark brows. So this was what it felt like to tame the mighty grizzly. Exhilarating and scary and—wow.

Tate towered over her like a mountain. Broad and bold, the sheer size and bulk of his body should've frightened her, but she knew he'd never hurt her. Not this gentle giant. "Kiss me," she ordered again, her fingertips fluttering over his nipples, her voice hoarse with the fire in her blood.

A rumbling growl brought his head to her level. He canted it to the side, his warm breath coming in heated bursts over her bare neck. "There will be consequences," he breathed, "for both of us."

Being surrounded by him like this took the air out of her lungs. "I know," she whispered as she lifted to her toes and curled her arms around his muscular neck. The tantalizing scent of his clean, wet skin, and the lingering fragrance of manly soap nearly combusted her on the spot, but when he pressed his mouth to hers? Her heart erupted with a throaty growl.

Gasoline on burning coals, that's what they were. One sweeping taste of her mouth with his tongue, and he lifted her off her feet, cradling her against his belly and chest as he took her to his bed.

"I locked your door," she assured him between nips and licks, still hard at work stroking and tasting each other.

Carefully, he tossed back the blankets and set her head to the pillow. "This is crazy," he mumbled, his warm wet tongue licking its way to her neck. Slathering as he went. Savoring.

"Crazy in love," she whispered back, lost in the sensation of this rough male body blanketing hers. Mysteries unlocked at every touch of her greedy fingertips. The brush of crisp hairs that dusted his chest. The latent power in those rock-hard abs. The jut and angle of manly ribs and hips and...

Oh my. The smoothest velvet skin over the hardest steel. A thunderous, vibrating groan came with it.

"We shouldn't do this," he said between hot wet licks down her neck that told her he didn't believe what he was saying any more than she did.

"It's my choice," she reminded him, arching upward to align her body with his. That towel had to go.

"Your father's going to have my balls for this, and I can't blame him."

"Then you'd better hurry, Tate, because I know what I want, and I want you. Now. Here." Way to go. Sound like a spoiled brat. If that wasn't a turn off—

Rippppppp. His towel was gone, and they were skin to skin and heat on heat. Banked coals on flaming embers. It didn't get any hotter than this.

Chapter Thirty-Eight

He knew it then. All that noble BS about leaving town before sun-up? Kick that to the field with all the other horse shit. He wasn't leaving Winslow. He couldn't. Not tonight and not tomorrow morning. He'd have to cancel his flight, and Tucker'd be pissed, but he'd get over it. There was no denying Winslow. A stronger man might, but Tate was not that guy. This little woman beneath him owned him lock, stock, and barrel. As Booker would say, emphasis on the *Lock*.

There was manly satisfaction in knowing this was the ultimate of firsts for her, and in a way, for Tate Higgins too. He was no man-whore by even the weakest definition. He'd only been with one female, that back in Alaska when he was drunk and so was she—whoever she was. The sordid affair began and ended in an alley behind a bar he couldn't remember the name of. It left him feeling dirty and used, unsatisfied and disillusioned. It was just one of those stupid things horny teenage guys did.

But if this was to be his first time with Winslow, it wouldn't be their last.

"You're going to marry me," Tate told her. Not asked. She might as well get that straight right out of the chute. No do-overs, no doubts. No take-backs and no lies.

"Me? You want to marry me?" she asked, her eyes wide with incredulity, her lack of self-esteem showing around the edges of her tough girl façade, the one she didn't do very well.

"Yes, you, my future bride," he growled, loving the way goosebumps shivered up her belly and over her breasts at those words. It even made her nipples peak enough to...

Ah, what the hell. He dropped his head and captured that delightful rosebud, savoring the peaches and cream taste of her, and loving what it did to his manhood. The ache that had held him uncomfortably erect for days, now invaded his body like a tide with no ebb. The only thing that could break this hold Winslow had on him was if she said—

"Yessssss," she hissed, her body turning to the best kind of liquid heat beneath him. "I'll marry you, Tate Higgins. Tomorrow."

A grin that actually hurt a little split his normally stoic face as he mumbled around her breast. "You ought to talk to your parents first. Then give me your answer." Lick. Lick.

"Should I, umm, is that what I should do?" Ah, she was as innocent as a newborn bear cub in spring. She wanted to please everyone.

"Yes, ma'am. Respect them, which is what we should be doing now instead of..." He eased back enough to take in the seductive view of her naked body, her knees bent at the sides of his legs, her sex glistening and ready. Yeah, if he were a gentleman, he'd be putting her parents' wishes first, but this was Winslow. She'd already had a lifetime of putting others first and of coming in last. Never again.

Tonight she was first and only. *Look at the stars in her soft green eyes.* No one had ever looked at him like that. You'd think he was Prince Charming or one of those fairytale guys. That look. Sheer adoration. So damned humbling.

Booker and Emma would have to get over it, too, because Tate was in the best kind of love, and this thing with Winslow would happen right here and now. Then he would spend the rest of his life loving, protecting, and romancing this audacious woman.

"You like what you see?" she asked, so damned timid even as she tried to act sexy.

"You have no idea what you do to me," he muttered, his body on fire for this hot babe in his arms, and his soul reaching out for every last particle of hers, expanding to encompass her. It'd been a long time since he'd been this close to heaven.

She'd probably see herself as deficient for the rest of her days. That was what happened when life ran you down, backed up, and ran over you again. When it ground you so far into the dirt that you couldn't see a way out. But every time she might belittle herself in the years to come, Tate intended to lick her up one side and down the other with encouragement of the best kind.

Starting now. "I like you better than raspberry ice cream," he growled in the crook of her neck, tickling her as he suckled raspberries up the column of her shivering neck and down her shoulder, ending at the soft as silk mound of her breast.

The sweetest mewl purred out of her.

He drew her nipple into the cauldron of his mouth and growled, "Better than a lemon drop."

Her body flexed from head to toe, undulating against him. Inciting him. If she kept that up—up being the key word—he wouldn't last long.

Going for broke, he worshipped at her other nipple to the heady scent of her blossoming and the frantic moaning in her throat. "Tate, oh Tate, oh..." Hip bump. "Do that again."

Her fingernails dug into his biceps as he shifted his body to where it wanted to go while that heavenly sheath wept for him. Just the thought of what his mouth wanted to do nearly did him in, but that was another adventure for another day. Not eating the entire elephant here. Nor Winslow.

His back stiffened at the tender banquet sprawled beneath him, but this first—this once in a lifetime forever-after-first—was about her, not him. He took special care to make certain she was ready, then—ever so slowly—he eased to his haunches for two reasons. One, to drag his wallet out of his jeans. Nothing was happening without that condom. Two, to look at the woman he'd taken into his heart just weeks ago.

The sight took his breath away. She was bare and dripping. Writhing for him, her toes and fingers clenching the sheets. Her eyes, always too big for her face, were wide and black. Wanton. Needing him to fill her as much as he needed to be inside of her.

Gloving himself, he leaned over her, his elbows at the tops of her shoulders, his big hands cupping her head. Just like last time, the rest of the world fell away, and Winslow became everything.

"Tell me if I'm hurting you," he whispered into her lips as he began his assault on her virginity. His heart swelled at the thought of this one time gift.

She grumbled something he couldn't make out, but the fingertips digging into his shoulders and the thumbnails in his collarbones weren't telling him no. He slid forward, deeper, taking it slow and easy, giving her time to acclimate to his length and thickness. She was so damned tight. He didn't want to break her, but the slick warm fire was just a heartbeat away. Just another inch or two.

He froze. There at the cusp of forever, Tate held his breath, not going to take what he wasn't sure he deserved. Not certain that he was good enough for the innocent woman who lay so warm and tempting within his reach. A better man. Winslow deserved not just a better man, but a richer, smarter man.

She shifted then, her knees bent and her heels drawn up to his ass, spurring him on. "Don't you dare stop."

"Are you sure?" he had to ask. "I don't want to hurt you." *Not now. Not ever.*

Ten fingernails scraped over his chest, inciting him as never before. "I'm only sure I'll love you until the day I die, Tate," she whispered between angel kisses up his neck and over his chin to his lips. "I'm tired of waiting to live. I'm standing up for myself, and I'm fighting to be with the man I love. Love me. All the way. Now."

How could he not? Tate eased forward and broke the seal of her virginity, then held still to watch while she adjusted to this most intimate invasion. Winslow's eyes were closed, but the sweetest smile graced her kiss-swollen lips. She arched her lower back. "More. Do it again."

He took slow deliberate strokes, alert for any signs of discomfort. This first time was important. He had to make it good for Winslow. Yet with every slow stroke, she lifted her hips and met him halfway. "So good," she breathed. "You feel so good in there."

Nature took over then, moving them in sync in slow, steady thrusts until she stiffened and cried, "Tate. Tate. Oh, Tate!"

Tears pricked his eyes. He'd never seen such a glorious sight, such a glow. She put the aurora borealis to shame as she shattered, writhing against his hips for every last second of her pleasure. This was rarest display of love, her opening her body and her heart to him. This was belonging on an elemental level where hearts locked together. Where souls joined. Where a man and a woman had the power to make their own world. Their own time.

Tate dipped his head and planted a kiss in the center of Winslow's forehead.

Home. He was finally home.

This is what heaven feels like, Winslow thought as she lay sweaty and panting in Tate's arms. Heaven was a lot like flying—make that soaring—to unimaginable heights. Upward into the stars like a crazy rocket. Or fireworks, the kinds that spiral up and out of sight before they blossom into dazzling, scorching fireballs that clenching him with aftershocks as if her body didn't want him to leave. That's what coming with Tate was. Fireworks, flying, and falling all at the same time. *What a rush.*

She opened her eyes to find the handsome-as-sin face an inch from her nose. Hazy brown eyes gleamed down at her. With a soft thud, he bumped foreheads. "I love you Winslow/Brooklyn/*Bdub* Lockette, soon to be Winslow/Brooklyn/*Bdub* Higgins."

Ah, he made her giggle. Imagine all those names on their marriage license.

"I think I love you more," she murmured, loving his minty breath in her face, and the way his freshly shaved chin abraded hers. "Kiss me," she urged. *Again and again and again. Never let me go.*

He obliged, locking his mouth over hers. If this was heaven, she was never leaving. He kissed her thoroughly, nipping at her lips, then suckling as if he was still hungry.

She was. With her fingers threaded in his thick hair, she gave as good as she got, her energy level off the charts.

"Shower?" he asked as he ended the kiss, his voice guttural and so damned sexy. "We're late for dinner."

"I've got what I'm hungry for," she told him, "but okay. I guess you're right."

After another heart stopping kiss, he untangled from her arms and legs. She knew he was being gentlemanly and disposing of the condom, but what a sight, his tanned shoulders so wide at the top, his back bunched with coiled musculature that ended at the most glorious backside. Taut and solid, not an ounce of jiggle. His cheeks hollowed at every step, but the best part of that butt? *It's all mine.*

The shower was quick, and Tate was efficient, spending extra time on his knees in front of her as if he couldn't look at her bare body enough. He gazed up, his eyes big and black, water streaming over his face and through his hair. "You're perfect," he murmured, tipping forward to plant one kiss on her— *there.*

Her body clenched at the daring contact. Did lovers kiss each other—*there? Oh my.*

His rugged face shone, his lips wet and crystal drops clinging to his brows and eyelashes. "Just you wait."

Her heart pounded at that tantalizing promise. How did he do that? Turn her legs to jelly with just three words? She knew how the biology worked, but practice. She wanted more practice!

Tate straightened. Melting against his chest, Winslow linked her arms around his waist, and let the warm shower drizzle on their joined bodies. Her bear of a man was a good armful. Her fingers barely came together at the small of his back. She smiled, so happy that tears stung. What had begun as a burdensome blind date was ending perfectly.

She thought back to that day on the water tower when she'd been so depressed, she'd been tempted to step off the edge, to quit. The only thing that stopped her was the love of the little dog waiting for her to come home, the same little dragon now snuggled in her bedroom, probably on her pillow.

Tate was right. *Even at the worst of times, there was still hope.*

Chapter Thirty-Nine

Tate took a deep breath, scratched his left brow, then took that all important step around the corner and into the Lockette family dining room with Winslow tucked under his arm. Where she belonged, damn it. Ready to face the music.

Cue the evil eye. Make that eyes. Emma looked up, but her lips didn't crack the barest hint of a smile. *Oh, shit...*

Booker shot him a sharp green bullet. "Took you long enough. Dinner's cold."

Double shit. It was suddenly hard to swallow. Black operator or not, Tate felt as unprepared as he'd ever been. This was Winslow's father, and Booker had every right to knock Tate on his ass for what he'd just been doing to his daughter—in his home no less. Tate met those offended greens head-on. Winslow was worth fighting for. *Here it comes. Let it rain.*

Emma made a funny sound, not so much a cough as a twitter, right before she burst out grinning. "You two. You should see the looks on your faces." She waved them to the table, smiling now. "Quick. Come eat before Marietta takes the platters away."

Tate waited to seat Winslow, and didn't his heart flush with male pride when she took the seat next to his designated chair, putting herself in the sizzling line of fire between him and Booker. When Tate sank to her side, she grabbed his hand and rested them on the table between their place settings, her fingers intertwined with his.

Booker scraped his chair back, a toothpick in his mouth, his expression shrewd and grim. "You got something to say to me, son?"

Tate nodded, but damn. This was a different kind of bear trap than what he was used to. "Sir." He tipped his head to Emma. "Ma'am. I'd like permission to marry your daughter."

Emma's fingers fluttered to her lips with a soft, "Oh." Were those tears glimmering in her eyes?

Winslow shoved her chair closer to Tate's as if staking her claim. He risked a sideways glance. Here she was, still fighting for her man.

Booker snapped his fingers, fire in his eyes. "You come in here pretending to be a friend, then you sneak around behind my back to take my daughter?" His words hit Tate's heart as deadly as the calm before the storm. "I just got her back, damn it. Who do you think you are?"

"Dad, I—"

Tate cut Winslow off, not going to fight her father. "That's okay. He's right. Let him speak."

She huffed, but Tate could feel her holding her breath. And her temper. Who knew?

Booker slouched back in his chair, the fight gone. "Like I said. Took you long enough."

"Excuse me, sir, umm, err—" *What the hell just happened?*

Emma giggled. "Tate, don't look so surprised. We're not blind. It's easy to see you have strong feelings for each other. Your dad and I know we can't keep you from living, Winslow. You're not a little girl anymore. You're my lost angel, but you have a right to choose your way forward and who you want to stand by your side."

Emma had just called her daughter *Winslow.* Another telling word. Emma Lockette was just as smart as Booker.

Winslow seemed not to have heard it though. She lifted Tate's clasped hand with hers. "Him. This man right here. I chose him on the water tower the first night we met, and I choose him now."

Emma's eyes widened. "A water tower? I can't wait to hear that story."

"Now wait just a guldurned minute." Booker again, still a man to be reckoned with.

This meal was fast turning into a tennis match. Tate's gaze scrolled back to the father of the bride.

Booker's gaze flicked to Winslow. "Do you know that's the first time you called me Dad, young lady?"

Just that fast, she dropped Tate's hand and barreled into her father's arms. "I love him," she cried, "but I love you and Mom too, and I'm not leaving you, Dad. Not yet. Not really."

Booker's mean-as-sin eyes brimmed with his baby girl in his arms. "It's all right," he mumbled against her head, his voice raw and his fingers threaded in the short locks at the back of her head. "Your mom and I'll be okay. We'll be here when you decide to come home. Just don't forget us."

An anguished "Daddy" ripped out of Winslow, and Tate dropped his gaze to his plate, his heart pounding. This had to stop. "Sir. If I may."

Winslow twisted in her father's arms to look at Tate even as her father situated her on his lap and wrapped his arms around her waist like he meant to keep her. The sight of her tears spilling onto her cheeks wrecked Tate's heart. She'd pressed that cheek to Booker's, and wasn't that a picture? Rhett and Gunn, her brothers, were brown-eyed like their mother, but father and daughter were matching bookends, one's eyes as green as the other's. Their chins stuck forward at precisely the same angle. Their lips were as full. All Winslow needed was a little more hair, weight, and height, and she'd be Booker all over again. It did Tate's heart good to know she was her daddy's girl.

"I'd like to propose a solution if it's agreeable to you. To both of you." Tate looked into Winslow's eyes, needing her agreement more than her father's. This was her life now. He wouldn't take her independence away, not even for Booker or Emma. "I travel extensively on my job, at least, the one I have now. It's up to Winslow, but it'd be better if she stayed here with you while I'm gone—" He had to get this out fast. "—where I know she'd be safe and where she could go to school and learn to ride that mare you gave her, and—"

Winslow's eyes flashed. Her back stiffened. "You're leaving me?"

"No, Bdub, I'm asking for your father's permission to marry you *and to* live here with you afterward. For a while." Asking something like this went against every male bone in his independent body, but this was Winslow's family. This was where she needed to be, not stuck in some apartment all by herself back East, while he was who-knew-where in the world. What kind of man would give her back to her parents only to rip her out of their lives two weeks later? He couldn't do that to her. Or them.

"I'm strong, sir," he heard his dumb mouth say. "I can commute, and I'll work for my keep. Whatever you need done, I can do while I'm here between missions."

Emma breathed an audible sigh, her fingers drumming the table. "Well..."

Booker's eyes slanted, piercing Tate to his soul. To be honest, it'd been a long time since he'd been a part of any family other than the Deuces Wild Team at work. At the end of the day, that didn't count for much, not when a guy went home alone to four bare walls and the ghosts of his past, while his teammates went home to wives and husbands. Children.

It happened slowly, the sly smile that crept over Booker's face. He turned to his baby girl and cupped her chin, turning her to face him. "Are you sure you like this guy? I mean look at him. He's strong as an ox but he never smiles."

Another precious sight, the glow in her eyes as she smiled at Tate through her tears, her head bobbing as she told Booker, "I love him, Dad. I think somehow I always have."

There was that word again. *Dad.* Winslow might not know it, but she was the best secret weapon in Tate's arsenal. Hmmm. Maybe they were a pair of jokers.

Emma spoke up. "I was four years younger than you are right now when I married your father, Winslow. We had nothing when we started out, nothing but love."

"You were sixteen?"

Emma nodded at her daughter, her gaze shifting to Tate. "We were head-over-heels in love, and yes, we thought we knew it all back then. At least you two are older, more mature, though I doubt it." She zeroed in on Tate. "There's nothing in the world like young love, young man. Be good to my daughter. Give me a grandchild?"

What could he say? There was every possibility he'd already fulfilled that order. That condom he'd used *was* older than dirt. "Yes, ma'am," he said obediently.

Booker tipped his head back and laughed, his arm still around Winslow. "I guess this means I need to get on the horn and get this party started."

Emma's chair nearly toppled to the floor when she jumped to her feet. "I'll order wedding invitations."

"The mayor will want to be here," Booker added. "Don't forget Ross and Howie or the rest of the guys down at the feed store."

"And flowers. Marietta!" Emma was on her feet, ticking off things to do on her fingers. "The priest. A caterer. Music. And chairs, I'll need several hundred more chairs. We can clear the barn for the dance, and, Marietta! We need to plan a wedding buffet!" Off she went, talking to herself all the way.

Booker lifted to his feet and released Winslow. "I'd better make sure she remembers which beer to order and how much. Can't have a decent wedding without inviting the best spirits along for the ride." He pressed his lips to the top of Winslow's head before he let her go. "Yes, you can keep him, darlin'," he said on his way to the kitchen. "Don't you go making any decisions without me, woman!"

Winslow sank onto Tate's lap, her fingers threading through his hair and her lips to his ear. "Dance with me again?"

Oh, how they danced...

Epilogue

Three months later...

The Boeing 747 dropped out of the west at dusk and cut a wide slow circle over the Potomac, coming into Reagan International from an eastern approach. Washington D.C.'s monuments stood majestic and proud in the golden afterglow of another hard day. Tate liked Jefferson's memorial best. Late evenings like today, its Danbury marble dome and columns glowed like beacons in the dark. Its reflection in the Tidal basin was legendary. In a few hours, the bright spotlights surrounding the memorial would make it look like ivory. Jefferson certainly knew how to roll out the welcome mat.

But Tate was tired. After two back-to-back trips to assist Ky Winchester in California, and another scheduled for the south of Florida come morning,

Tate regretted leaving Winslow at the Lockette Ranch. His place in Occoquan, North Virginia, was too damned far from Amarillo, Texas. He missed coming home to her. He missed Pepe too.

The airport was crowded, and it took forever for Ky and Tate to get their luggage. Once he grabbed his duffle off the carousel, Ky fast-tracked for the door. He slapped Tate's shoulder on his way out. "See you later."

"Yeah. Later," Tate shot at his friend's broad back. Ky was in a hurry. Eden and Kyler were waiting for him in airport parking. The only one waiting for Tate was his Jeep.

Disgruntled, he slung his duffel over one shoulder and headed for long-term parking. The drive home and away from the city used to be a good time to decompress. He'd used the half-hour drive to put distance between him and his job, but now each mile was just another nail in his coffin. As much as he enjoyed working with Ky, Eden, Isaiah, and yes, even Tucker, working out of the D.C. office while Winslow attended school in Amarillo was killing him.

Like always, the lonely ride home ended at his assigned parking stall, and didn't that just suck? Tate dreaded walking into his empty loft. This shit had gotten old old. Long distance relationships were for somebody else, not him. He stayed in his Jeep, remembering the day he'd married Winslow. It seemed a long time ago.

By the end of that special day, he'd met more cowboys and ranchers, Lockette family relatives and friends, than he could've imagined. The wedding was Texas-style big. Once Booker opened his barn, Emma and her troupe of wedding planners decorated it. There wasn't one rafter not bedazzled with twinkling lights, nor one board on the wide wooden floor not covered in a clean layer of boot-stomping straw. Ribbons and lace decked the stalls.

A local DJ stood ready to play all western and country favorites until the last steer came home or until every last cowboy was too drunk to walk a straight line. Didn't matter which came first as long as everyone had a good time.

Booker had two barrel-sized smokers going, one for beef, the other for pork. Texans loved a good barbeque as much as they loved their trucks and their guns. By all reports on the society page, the wedding was the talk of the entire state.

But the look on Booker's face when he gave his one and only baby girl away? Heartstoppingly priceless.

Booker didn't just hand her over to Tate at the altar. No, that would've been easy. Instead, he hooked a callused hand to the back of Winslow's neck, another to the back of Tate's. He pulled them together for a good talking to. If that didn't make Tate feel like a schoolboy about to get taught a lesson, nothing did.

The audience, all five hundred and twenty-one of them, stilled. You could've heard Tate's heart pounding, it was that kind of quiet in the barn and the surrounding yard full of chairs and onlookers. But Booker's words weren't meant for the people, only for Tate and Winslow.

"Kids," he said, his whispered voice gruff and unusually tight. "Marriage is guldurned hard. It's a twisting bronco, is what it is. It's a stiff Texas wind that blows out of nowhere, and it can strip the meat off your bones faster than a mama javelina when you mess with her piglets. Trust me, I know. It's a job, not some romantic love story full of lingering gazes and all that bullshit you see in the movies. It's work, plain and simple. Git that through your hard heads right now before you lie and say 'I do', because I'm here to tell you, you kids don't."

This was not exactly the time or the place to argue, but Tate shifted his boots, willing to listen to the only fatherly advice he'd get that day. Winslow ducked her neck into her bare shoulders, at least as much as she could. Booker had a good hold on her, but she sent Tate a smile that made listening to this sage advice bearable. For her, he could do anything.

Booker tilted his forehead to hers first. "Here's the thing, darlin'. If you put that man of yours first every single day, you and Tate are gonna make it. I can promise you that. Mark my words."

His neck twisted as he turned a baleful eye on Tate then. "And you..." Tate did a little more boot shifting. "Love her tomorrow like you love her today, Mr. Higgins. Spoil my baby girl. Kiss her every chance you get, because a man never knows how much time he's got left in this world. Don't do anything without telling her about it first, you hear? Don't go anywhere and don't backtalk her, neither. She's the only one who counts, and what she says goes."

Tate nodded even as he told Booker, "Yes, sir." Winslow already was his moon, stars, and every last rainbow. She already owned his soul.

Booker's voice dropped a pitch lower, his eyes on the floor. "Besides your mother, Winslow, you kids are all I've got in this world, you two, Rhett, and Gunn." When he lifted his head, those steely green lasers pinned Tate to the barn door. "I count you as my son now, Tate, not just a son-in-law, so stop trying so damned hard to fit in. Relax. I'm not going to whup your ass, though I could."

A smile curved Tate's lips then. He took a deep breath and let air flow into his lungs, surprised he'd been standing as stiff as he'd been. He didn't want to be one of those grooms who passed out because they locked their knees during their wedding ceremony.

"Yes, sir," Tate said as he grinned past his father-in-law to Winslow's pretty face.

"Make each other happy every single day," Booker said, "and you'll do just fine."

The tough old guy tipped Winslow's forehead to his mouth and kissed her, then released their necks *and stuck his hand at Tate. Instead of a handshake, Tate got pulled against the guy for one last word. "You're alright, son, you know that? You're alright."*

What a lie. Tate wasn't alright, not by any definition of the word. Winslow was pretty that day in her pearl-studded gown, her shoulders bare and her green eyes glowing like emeralds as if someone had lit a fire inside of her. Since Tate left, she'd grown lovelier and more confident every day. He could hear it in her voice when they talked at night. She'd always been strong, but now she was coming into her own, and he wanted to be a part of the new Winslow. Every day. Damn it. A man shouldn't have to visit his wife.

Sitting there in his Jeep under the glow of the parking lights, Tate rubbed that hollow ache his chest, the one that never went away in between visits. "I love you," he told Winslow, though she wasn't there. "And I miss you, baby. I miss us."

He'd pledged allegiance to the flag when he'd signed onto the Deuces Wild team, but something had to change. He needed Winslow more than he needed his next breath.

His phone vibrated in his jacket pocket. Didn't it figure? The last person Tate wanted to talk to after a long flight and a hard week. Tucker Chase.

"Higgins," Tate answered, staring across the quiet parking lot to the stairs that led to his empty loft.

"You tired?"

Dumb question. "No more than usual. What's up?"

"The op in Florida's been cancelled. Why don't you take a couple weeks off? Lay low. Mohammed Ur's trial started yesterday, and I'll need you as an expert witness. You'll have to stay in town. Might take a couple months. Maybe longer."

Mohammed Ur, the latest homegrown terrorist. Tate had singlehandedly disarmed the guy during a *peaceful* protest on the National Mall. Ur claimed FBI harassment. Must've been because of the brick of C4 in his backpack.

But a couple months sounded like too damned much down time. "You couldn't have mentioned that before I boarded in California?" *I could be in Amarillo with Winslow now instead of here by myself.*

"I just got word, so why don't you fly out first thing tomorrow to see Winslow? Want me to make the reservations?"

Tate shook his head. A good night's rest would do him some good, but he'd rather spend it with Winslow. "I'll take care of it."

"Goodnight, Tate."

"Night, Boss." There was a time Tate hadn't considered Tucker much of a man, much less a boss worthy of respect, but that had changed. The Deuces Wild team was a good fit for both of them. Tucker seemed to know how to build a team, then how to hone it until it was one of the best in the Bureau. Tate knew he'd take a bullet for any one of his team members. Even Tucker.

Sure would've been nice if Tucker had called before Tate flew across country, though. A flight this late to Amarillo would be another five to six hour flight. Might as well book the first one in the morning.

The trek up to his loft seemed extra long tonight. The shadows seemed darker. Unlocking his door, Tate stopped at the threshold and took a deep breath, for the first time in his life tired of being alone. He couldn't bear to turn on the lights, just stood there in the dark. Why confirm what he already knew? That he was a very stupid man?

"What the hell am I doing here?" he asked the empty apartment.

"I was kind of hoping you'd want to take me to bed," a sweet voice murmured from the other side of the room.

"Winslow?"

She was grinning when she turned on the lamp. "Hi, honey. I'm home."

Tate couldn't get to her fast enough. The duffle hit the floor as he gathered her into his arms, his heart pounding. He took her mouth ferociously, and as usual, Winslow gave back with vigor. They growled together, their hands mapping each other's bodies like they couldn't get enough of each other.

This was precisely what he needed. This woman. Her mouth. Her soul. Tears pricked his eyes. He captured her face between his palms. "I can't do this anymore," he told her. "I'm leaving the Bureau. I'll find work in Texas." It was a big enough state. There ought to be something he could do there.

She mumbled something, but he swallowed her words in his hunger. Their teeth clashed and their tongues tangled, but a starving man lacked finesse, and he was that man, too hungry to go gentle. Threading his fingers into her short-cropped hair, he cupped her head to the side for better access to that delicious mouth. She came willingly, still mumbling. Still kissing. Still smiling.

As last he came up for air, embarrassed he'd mugged her on sight.

"You didn't hear what I said," she told him slyly, licking her lips.

"What, baby?" he asked, his body thrumming to get her out of that button-up shirt and to unzip those jeans. To toss her cowboy boots to the corner. She had a head full of brown curls now, and her cheeks were plump. Her green eyes sparkled. He adored every last curve her body had blossomed into and every last ounce of her round, sassy hips. God, she was a sight for his sore eyes.

She laced her fingers around his ears, but a frown creased her brow. "Why so sad?"

Tate shook his head, but said, "Just missed you, girl. What did you say I was too in love to hear?"

A sultry glimmer shifted in her eyes. "I said I'm home, Tate."

He nodded. He got that. Yeah she was home—for now—but she'd be leaving too soon, and he just plain didn't want to live like this anymore. He needed her in his life, not waiting on the peripheral while he chased around the country for the FBI. This wasn't living. His fingers strayed to her collarbone on their way to the soft, plump weight of her breast. The burden he'd brought with him fell away.

She smoothed her palms over his chest, her fingers splayed and capturing him in their gentle warmth once more. "Home, Tate. I'm home. Here. To stay."

He cocked his head, not sure he'd heard right. "As in you're not going back to Texas?"

That brought her ear against his chest. "Yes. This is where I belong. I start school on Monday. That gives us the weekend to do whatever we want to each other."

All he heard was *that gives us the weekend*. He bent to curl an arm under her knees and carried her into his bedroom. In seconds she was naked. What a sight, his woman in his bed. He stripped while she watched, then climbed up and over her, intent on tasting every inch of her skin. Making her scream his name. Loving her while he had the chance.

Nose to nose, he could see that the fire burned both ways. Winslow had changed into a woman of strength. She knew what she wanted and she had no problem letting him know. "More," she ground out as her fingernails dug into the cheeks of his bare ass. "I'm not going to break. Give it to me."

A more obedient man had never lived. Tate gave her every last inch, lick, and kiss until she climaxed, calling his name as he tipped her over the edge and into pleasure. Thunder rolled up his spine, squeezing off a live round of utter male satisfaction as he came within seconds of Winslow.

Breathing hard, he bowed his face into the crook of her neck, sweating and tired, but at peace. This was where he belonged, wrapped up tight inside her body. The problems he'd brought home with him faded in the delightful glow of her feminine fire. Taking a deep breath, Tate rolled off Winslow but took her with him.

She nestled under his arm, her head on his shoulder and her fingers languid on his chest. "Do you feel better now?"

He nodded, his eyes closed and his heart content. Being with her blocked the rest of the world, exactly what hc needed. More of Winslow. Less of everyone else. "You're really moving away from home to be with me?"

Her fingers fluttered over his left nipple. "It was Dad's idea and Mom agrees. A wife should be with her husband and besides, this is my home now. With you."

"I thought I could make this arrangement work," Tate told her, "but the job's been demanding lately and... Wait a minute. You start school on Monday?"

The tip of her tongue slid over her bottom lip, hardening him on sight. "Ah-huh. I'll be a student at

Washington Alternative High while I finish my GED. Then, I'm going to college. Journalism, Tate. I want to try my hand at investigative reporting. I've already got a job offer and an interview next week if I'm interested."

"Let me guess. Shawna Truborn."

Winslow climbed up his body then, straddling his hips, her hands splayed for balance on his pecs. The sparkle in her eyes morphed into fire. "Can you believe it? She wants me to join her staff. I won't be doing much more than copy editing at first, but isn't it great?"

Winslow glowed when she was happy, and there it was, her light, filling his empty room and his heart along with it. But there was more to the story. "Who? How...?" He didn't know what to ask, and this sexy naked lady riding him like a horse wasn't helping the blood supply in his brain. Tate cupped her jiggling breasts, his cock aroused and ready to play again.

"Who helped me get into Washington Alternative? Oh, that was your boss. Mr. Chase can be quite persuasive, can't he?" Why that irked Tate at this precise moment, he didn't know.

Winslow rattled on. "I wrote my story, Tate. Shawna said it was good. She wants to interview me for a follow-up piece, and from there..." Winslow lifted her arms, her palms to the ceiling and her lovely body on display. "Look out world. Here I come."

"You asked for it, babe. You are most definitely coming." Tate cupped her hips and slid inside of her.

With a jostle and a jiggle, he was home again and speechless. His woman and his heart were in the same place at the same time. With him. Like they should've been all along.

She giggled, but gave him a solid hip thrust that seated her just right. He reached one hand to the nape of her neck and tugged her flush with his body. When the tips of her nipples kissed his pecs, he knew. He, Tate Higgins, the lonely man who'd been fighting the world for too long, had finally found his place. It wasn't in this apartment or at the Lockette's sprawling ranch in dusty Amarillo. It wasn't in the J. Edgar Hoover Building on Pennsylvania Avenue and Ninth Street either. No, it was here inside this woman. In her body. In her heart.

He'd think about Tucker's assisting Winslow later. He might even thank his boss for reaching out to her—later. But for now... "I love you, baby," Tate told her from the depths of his warrior's soul. "I always will."

She cupped jaw in both hands, her thumbs on his chin. "I am going to make love to you, Tate," she promised. "All. Night. Long."

Tate settled his palms to the flare of her waist and let her rock his world.

Over and over again.

The End

Excerpt From *ALEX*

In The Company of Snipers,
Book 1

©2013 by Irish Winters

The weathered porch creaked under his cautious step. Alex froze.

What the—?

There stood Whisper on the porch with his lips pulled back, his canines bared, and standing protectively over the splayed legs of a—what? A department store mannequin? A dead body? He couldn't believe what he saw. Those outstretched legs belonged to a young woman sprawled against his cabin door, her head bowed to her chest, her hands limp at her side, palms up. Covered with blackened patches of blood and bruises, she looked dead.

Whisper growled, for an instant threatening both master and his canine companion, Smoke.

"Knock it off." Alex brushed the dog out of his way, annoyed that the mutt thought he could get away with that kind of behavior. There was no contest. This was no fresh kill, and Whisper wouldn't have won if it were. The dog whined once and backed away, relinquishing the porch to Alex, his tail tucked between his back legs.

Alex knelt beside the woman, feeling her neck for a pulse. It took a few seconds to locate, but a weak beat stuttered beneath his fingertips. Lifting the tangled mass of hair away from her face, he ducked closer to get a better look. Her eyes popped open.

"Don't hurt me," she moaned, shielding her face with her arm. "Please—"

"Who are you?" Instantly, he was angry she would say something like that, but she didn't answer. Her head lolled to her shoulder. He knelt closer, peering into her bloodied face. *Did she just die?*

"No," he ground out between clenched teeth. "You started this. You'd better not die on me now."

Whisper whined, crowding Alex while he eased the woman to her back. "Back off." He elbowed the dog. "Get out of here."

Whisper only stepped back two feet, turned a full circle, and came right back.

Alex pressed his ear to the woman's chest, holding his breath while he listened for a heartbeat. It was there and fairly steady considering how bad she looked and smelled. Sweat and dirt was not the welcome he had expected at his cabin. Neither was she. A ragged groan sounded deep in her throat. Okay. That was a good sign. Maybe she heard him. Maybe she actually listened and decided not to die.

He sat back on his legs and blew a deep breath, his heart pounding at this abrupt about-face to what had been a relaxing afternoon walk. Glancing at the immediate forest around his cabin, he searched for a reason this mess of a woman would be here on his porch. There was nothing. No one. Just her.

He ruffled Whisper's thick black mane. "Sorry, tough guy, but you've got to give me some room to work, okay?"

Still trying to calm down, he checked her pulse again and smoothed his hands over her shoulders, down her arms, hips and thighs. It didn't look like she had anything major wrong with her, no broken legs or arms, but there was plenty of what looked like road-rash across her extremities and dried blood in her hair. As bad as she looked, he was afraid of a gunshot, but he found nothing. A concussion was a possibility, but it's not like he was a doctor. He'd had some medical training in the Corps. A man didn't survive warfare without knowing how to tourniquet a bloody limb or plug a sucking chest wound, but this was different. This was a woman.

Damn. What do I do now?

Whisper nestled his big black snout over Alex's shoulder like he was offering free advice with his whine.

"I know." Alex scratched the dog's nose. "You found her. Now what do we do with her? You got any bright ideas?"

Whisper slapped the porch once with his moose-sized paw.

"No. You can't keep her. She's not a toy," Alex muttered as he came to grips with this new development. Talking to his dog helped normalize the shock he had just received, but he also found Whisper's reaction odd. Smoke had taken up residence at the bottom of the porch steps, but Whisper acted like he knew this woman. *Dogs. Go figure. They're as hard to figure out as women.*

"Well, let's get you off the porch and out of the weather, shall we?" Alex said to the woman. There weren't a lot of choices. The option to hike back to the road had expired with the fading afternoon sun. Besides, he wasn't convinced she was stable. She might die while he went for help. His cell phone wasn't any good either. No bars out this far in the sticks, not like it mattered until now. Like it or not, she was all his.

It took a minute to unlock the cabin door, and another to scoop her up and off the porch. She didn't resist, her head limp and her arms dangling while he angled her through the door and set her on the cot inside. She was barely an armful, light as a feather and cold to the touch. Grabbing a blanket from the back room where he stored his supplies, Alex covered her gently. She was a pitiful sight, her cheek bruised, one eye swollen and bloodied. Even now a bloody tear trailed over her cheek. He patted her cheek in an attempt to rouse her.

"Hey there. Can you hear me? Can you talk?"
Groaning, she rolled away.
"Guess not."

ALEX is free!

To start reading, click **HERE**.

https://www.amazon.com/Alex-Company-Snipers-Book-1-ebook/dp/B00H4J4KOC

Thank you for reading Joker Joker!

If you enjoyed Tate and Winslow's story, you might want to check out Tucker and Melissa's story and find out how the Deuces Wild team got its start in:

King of Hearts, Deuces Wild Series, Book 1

Book 3 is Isaiah's story, *One-Eyed Jack*. It's already in the works, so stay tuned!

Also, pay a visit to the sexy ex-military snipers in the 15 book series,

In the Company of Snipers.

Coming soon in 2017 - Jake, Book 16

Other Irish Winters' books

Smoke, Hearts and Ashes Series, #1
Ash, Hearts and Ashes Series, #2

The best way to keep up with my new releases, giveaways, and actionable intel is to sign up for my spam-free newsletter at IrishWinters.com.

YOU ARE THE KEY TO THIS BOOK'S SUCCESS!

Please tell other readers why you liked Tate and Winslow's story by leaving an honest review at the retail site where you purchased it.

Recommend it to your friends.

Lend it.

Most of all, enjoy it!

About the Author

Irish Winters is an award winning, Amazon best-selling author who, when she isn't writing, dabbles in poetry, grandchildren, and rarely (as in extremely rarely) the kitchen. More prone to be outdoors than in, she grew up the quintessential tomboy on a dairy farm in rural Wisconsin, spent her teenage years in the Pacific Northwest, but calls the Wasatch Mountains of Northern Utah, home. For now.

She believes in making every day count for something, and follows the wise admonition of her mother to, "Look out the window and see something!"

Connect with Irish online:

On Facebook
https://www.facebook.com/IrishWintersAuthor/

On Twitter
https://twitter.com/irishwinters1

www. IrishWinters.com

www.ingramcontent.com/pod-product-compliance
Lightning Source LLC
Chambersburg PA
CBHW060939190726
48286CB00005B/1341